From Denis to Dorothy
with love,
Happy Christmas

Janet K L S

The King's Chalice

An East Dorset Town in Saxon Times

Janet K L Seal

For Harold, whose support and encouragement is so much appreciated.

www.BretwaldaBooks.com
@Bretwaldabooks
bretwaldabooks.blogspot.co.uk/
Bretwalda Books on Facebook

While most of the events and characters are based on historical incidents and figures, this novel is entirely a work of fiction.

Front cover phot: Krzysztof Mizera
Back cover photo: Jean-Pol GRANDMONT

First Published 2013

Bretwalda Books
Unit 8, Fir Tree Close, Epsom,
Surrey KT17 3LD
info@BretwaldaBooks.com
www.BretwaldaBooks.com
ISBN 978-1-909698-19-2

Printed and bound in Great Britain by
Marston Book Services Limited, Oxfordshire

Contents

Prologue
The Clearing

The old man muttered and shifted in his sleep, his age mottled hands plucking at the fur rug. Waking suddenly, he wiped his sweaty forehead, brushing the wispy grey hair behind his ears impatiently.

In the gloomy interior of the house, lit only by the dying embers in the hearth, Udda's breathing sounded harsh and laboured. An ox sighed deeply in its stall outside then was still, chewing contentedly in the darkness. Suddenly aware that he needed to use the midden, Udda reluctantly swung his legs to the floor.

His daughter in law walked quietly across the crushed bracken to the fire and added a few small twigs. Her shadow fell across Udda as he struggled to stand upright then pull the rug over his shoulders. Wincing with pain as he drew on a pair of sandals, he followed her slowly out into the night. His stick made little sound on the leaf-mould but somewhere close a bird squawked in alarm.

When he returned to the clearing Edith was placing logs on the fire. The turfs which had damped it down were drawn to one side, smoldering with deep red curls of ancient fibre. Now in the last month of her pregnancy she stood, arching her back against the ache of the heavy child within her.

"Your grandchild is kicking lustily. I could not lie still and would only disturb Udric if I had stayed in bed. Shall I heat a drink?"

Without waiting for a reply she set an earthenware pot of water among the embers and pulled two stones from the centre of the fire towards her. Gripping them in green wood tongs, she skillfully dropped them into the water which hissed and spat before steam rose to mingle with the wood smoke.

Udda tried to make himself comfortable on one of the low stools and pulled the fur higher to shield his body from the cold night wind. It no longer seemed to go round his aged bones but to delight in entering the very heart of his being. Crossly he shifted his weight once again and was grateful when the old dog rose wearily from its shelter to join him by the fireside. Sitting close to his legs, Udda ruffled its coarse grey fur affectionately while the dog appreciated the mutual warmth which came from contact with its adored master. It yawned widely, showing a mouth full of yellowing teeth.

Edith passed him a small mug of herbal tea before sitting down awkwardly to sip her own drink.

"I built most of this house with my own hands, felling the trees to make this clearing. I had to burn the base of each to get them down. The only blade was my small knife you see and I could not risk breaking it... Hidden for so long, it was my only weapon..." Udda's voice tailed off as he remembered his first days so many years before at Uddings.

"Should have told Udric long before now", he mumbled dreamily. "He ought to know how his mother and I came by this land. Perhaps I should tell him the story of Uddings. Yes, it is time."

He ignored the rich loamy smell of the woods around the clearing, stretching his legs towards the fire. The old dog sighed, then adjusted his own body to fit beside Udda's thin, scarred legs, one ear cocked to listen to the night sounds around them.

CHAPTER ONE

Turning the beaker thoughtfully in his painful fingers, Udda smiled and took another sip of warm honey-ale. The day's work was done, the meal finished, a time to stretch tired muscles and relax.

"Years ago I drank from a jewelled cup. A work of art it was, with red, blue and green gems all round the base."

His audience of family and fieldworkers looked up with interest. Sitting round the fire as the evening sky faded to orange with streaks of turquoise through the trees, conversation was usually of a more domestic nature. Often it was of nothing more important than the chores to be done the following day, or short comments about the work that had been accomplished since the cool of the dawn that morning.

"It belonged to my master, Prince Aethelwold. He was killed you know by the king's forces. I was there when he came down to Wymburne just after King Alfred died. I remember ..."

"Hold on father, what do you mean he was 'your master'? You make it sound as if you worked for him. I mean,' master' usually implies a bond servant at the very least."

Udric had been unable to stop himself from interrupting, puzzled by the initial phrase. He ran one hand through his thick brown hair dislodging a burr which he threw in the fire.

"Oh son, there is much about my life that you do not know. Let me start at the beginning. My father's farm was at Woodcutts, just outside Sexpenna Hanlega and leased direct from the King. We had a hut, not like this one with timber, but built of flint, bracken and clay. It was snug enough and seldom damp inside for my father kept the drain clear in all but the worst weather. My mother and sister worked around it while father and I spent our time in the field. Mother was always busy, she always had her spindle in a bag even when she and my little sister went down to the lane to forage or pick the wool from the thorns.

"I built this house with my own hands from the woods around us. Like me, it has witnessed happy times and sadness too. Before I found

Uddings… well, that's almost another life." Udda nodded thoughtfully, his sparse hair once again falling across his eyes. Brushing it aside, he gestured at the dark trees just visible by the light of the flames.

"My father's steading was thriving, the barley almost ripe. Then he was accused of murder and we were turned out of the farm." He paused, the bitter memories causing an overwhelming storm of emotion that tightened his throat painfully. Brusquely he wiped his eyes of the hot tears which threatened to fall.

Edith tentatively put her arm round Udda while he drew deep breaths, holding him closely, comforting him like a child.

Udda straightened his back abruptly, shrugging off the rug. He kicked a log back into the fire so that sparks flew up and flames lit the clearing briefly, the huge trees rising like posts out of the darkness. Moths which had been fluttering in the glow rose hastily out of harms way.

Everyone had waited impatiently until the day's work was done, the meal eaten, and the children asleep. The dogs settled down beside the fire as Edith poured ale for the men before taking her own seat a little distance from them. She pulled a rug around her shoulders as she eased her swollen body into a comfortable position against a pile of logs. Udda cleared his throat and spat accurately into the fire. He glanced at his son and saw the man he loved; the child created out of love, the boy who chance had moulded.

"I have often spoken to you of grandfather Udric for whom you were named. You briefly knew him, a bitter man, old before his time. We all did what we could to ease his passing but the jealousy and greed of others reduced my father to a shadow of his former self. Of course I was only a young man, a boy really, when he was accused of murder.

Guthrum was our neighbour and had the fields next to ours. He had a rather surly nature, unwilling to share when harvesting was done. Although I do remember that he was eager enough to attend the feasting! Many thought that he and his son gloated as my father was led away at the end of a rope behind the sheriff's horse." Udda paused to scratch a flea bite on his thigh and took a deep draught of ale before continuing.

"Throughout my father's trial, the fact that I was not of age was emphasised so that I could not swear for my father, and he could not prove his innocence having no other witnesses. Guthrum was the accuser so he was not going to say a word in my father's defence. The King's sheriff, standing there in all his fine clothes, demanded the whereabouts of each man the day of the murder. I remember his sword flashing in the sunshine as it swung from his jewelled belt. The sheriff's clerk took notes, his pen scratching on the tautly stretched skin. Since then the sound has always reminded me of that scene." Udda paused to shift his weight on the stool. The darkness was now complete, the woods silent. Only the firelight illuminated the faces of his audience.

"Leaving my father that night was one of the hardest things I have ever done. He was shackled to a pole outside the sheriff's tent. It was the way a man was held in those days. Some villagers glanced at him sympathetically as they returned to their homes, but nobody spoke to him. No doubt they were resentful about missing more working time the following day but not one gave a thought to favours he had done for them. No-one spared a kind word. I had to go back to the farm and tell my poor mother that her man was in the custody of the king's law man. I can still see her now, rubbing her hands on her kirtle and weeping. My little sister did not understand so she cried too. I was nearly unmanned myself but perhaps the trial and the injustice of it all meant that anger was uppermost in my mind.

For generations my father's kin had owned that land direct from the King, perhaps a cause of some jealousy among the villagers who rented their land from the church. Even the sheriff had known of my father's standing and seemed puzzled by the accusations against him when he would have so much to lose.

I remember mother lighting the small mutton fat dips. It was as if their feeble light would banish the misery and gloom which hung over the house. The oily smoke rose sluggishly to the roof vent, the spider's webs wafting in the rising heat. My guts were so knotted that I visited the midden twice during the hours of darkness. That's another thing; I have never smelt that odour since without remembering that night.

The cow had to be milked before returning to father in the morning for he would need my support even though I could not speak on his behalf. I remember cutting grass and throwing it in a heap beside the beast but did little more than that.

The second day of the trial was even worse. The village elders were indeed grieved that they had been forced to spend more time away from their own affairs. Many were clearly called from the fields, their leggings already thick with mud. I tried again to support my father's sworn statement that he had only attacked the king's messenger because he had dishonoured his daughter but the men who formed the jury said I was only a boy. The death of a King's man carried a huge penalty but my father did not kill him, nor did he steal a purse.

It was Guthrum who had first shouted out that I was not yet twelve years old, and therefore could not be heard; he and that lazy, snivelling son of his. They spoke louder than the honest priest Bata, who had christened me and my father too for that matter. Bata could not read but told stories of the saints and comforted those who were injured or near death."

Udda wiped away the hot tears which pricked beneath his eyelids and stretched his legs. The dog shuffled closer, laying its huge head on Udda's lap. Absentmindedly, he stroked it, gathering his strength to continue.

Udric carefully added more fuel to the fire anxious not to disturb his father's train of thought. His face was ruggedly handsome in the firelight, the dark hair neatly cut beneath his headband. Across the fire he exchanged a quick, affectionate glance with his wife as the older man continued.

"Shocked by the guilty verdict, I went to father. Those who had previously supported him quickly distanced themselves from a friend who was now a convicted felon as if his guilt might be contagious." Udda laughed bitterly at the memory. Udric smiled at his father's attempt at humour and passed him an oatcake which he dipped in the ale. An owl hooted overhead then launched itself silently into the darkness. Someone pointed at it as it disappeared through the trees to the fields beyond.

"The sheriff had gone to his tent. I can remember my father's words as if they were spoken yesterday. He was never a talkative man you know, but he knew that he would be taken away. He told me to care for mother and guard Jenna, for some take advantage of a simple mind. I was to look after the stock and pay the king his dues. 'Trust Bata to advise you well, he has been an elder of this village for longer than any other man and will help you keep the farm safe until my return. Believe me, he said, this new way of judgement before twelve men will not be accepted as the old system was. I would be happy to hold the hot iron to prove my innocence.' Those were his exact words, I remember them clearly. Since then though, I have seen mens' hands, misshapen like claws, no longer able to hold their own children or indeed a weapon, but at least they had cleared their names which my father never had the chance to do.

Our few moments together were rudely shattered by the return of the sheriff, his clerk almost running to keep up. I held my father's arm as if that would have saved him from being taken away. The words of condemnation, the sentence, the enormous fine of one hundred shillings for killing a King's messenger, all passed in a blur. The King would have the final decision on the punishment since my father had little money. Even selling the cow, the sheep and the fowl would not have raised enough.

I almost shed tears in front of my father's accuser. Even Guthrum hid his face as if he were too appalled to watch. More likely he felt remorseful even then, for the villagers shunned him from that time on. It was only Bata's gently restraining hand on my shoulder which had prevented me from throwing myself bodily at Guthrum's son who made so little effort to hide his delight, almost grinning at his neighbour's discomfort."

Udda shivered as his sweat dried coldly in the night air. He scratched at a new flea bite and rose stiffly. Everyone got up silently, some hastily visiting the midden. Not one of those who lived and worked at Uddings knew anything of their lord's past. There was much to consider as the men and women stood around the dying fire. The distant screech of the owl echoed in the clearing as he finished his ale. People rearranged rugs or pulled shawls around chilled shoulders whispering of the revelations they had just heard. A jug of ale was passed from hand to hand, many nodding their gratitude to Emma for she supplied her father in law with much of her best brew.

Even a small effort now exhausted him but the need to tell Udric his life-story had given him new strength that evening. Despite her own weariness, Edith helped her father in law to wrap up warmly and set the biscuits and the ale jug near him. The dogs eyed these delicacies with speculation and lay down beside the fire. In the warmth the aroma of the honey used to sweeten the wafers laid heavily on the air, mixed with the perfume of seasoned wood.

To help his father, Udric reminded him of the trial and his grandfather's disgrace leaving the village. "What happened to him? Did Guthrum get your father's land?"

"Not him no, but it was given to another almost immediately. But that's another story. When the sheriff's soldiers were out of sight, my father tied with a rope behind them, I went home to tell mother the bad news. Since that day she hardly spoke. She became grey-haired overnight.

I carried on with the daily chores and the sheep were sheared with the village animals. The sheepward sold the fleeces at Wymburne for us and bought salt, honey, fish and a new knife with some of the money. It was the nearest market to Sexpenna in those days you see.

As now, we could not graze the sheep on the common land until they were marked so I herded the sheep into the fold. Some had cuts, which had to be painted before flies infected the wounds. We made our tar from soot, boiled until it became a sticky black glue.

In those days, dye was made each summer from soaking the yellow flowers of the woad plant that grew wild along the edges of the fields. The water became blue. Mother used it to dye woollen fabric as well as marking the sheep each year.

So easy with two people, it was nigh on impossible on my own! Many times the pot was overturned so that the grass was blue and only a few sheep marked in the correct place. My legs were splashed with dye. Despite using the strongest soapwort, the stains remained stubbornly dotted all over my legs for ages. When Bata, the priest, visited as he had promised, I remember him laughing as he recommended using leggings for the task in future!

The day of my twelfth birthday came and went. Apart from a freshly killed fowl in addition to the usual bread, cheese and pottage, the day passed in an endless round of essential farm work. Now of the age to be a man and admitted to my father's fyrd, no-one mentioned the ceremony which would formally introduce me. Nor had the annual demand from the King's treasurer for the fleeces or fowl been made even though they had already been selected.

When I saw the soldiers approaching the farm some days later, I presumed their arrival had something to do with the overdue tax and waited for them, leaning on my stave until they entered the yard. The leader, a stout, bearded man whose tabard was brightly decorated with the red dragon, stepped forward flourishing a sealed scroll. It was at this point I realised that something was wrong because there was no baggage cart for the fleece and no cages for the fowl.

The Captain obviously didn't like carrying out evictions or sequestrations as they were called. He may have had some sympathy for me but he just read out his orders, glancing at me occasionally.

"Your father has been found guilty of homicide, of killing the King's body servant. The King commands that all Udric's possessions are forfeit."

The Captain studied his feet for a moment before explaining in a far less brusque manner that his orders were to escort us all to Winchester. We were not allowed to take possessions with us and had to leave immediately.

I was so shocked it must have been obvious to the soldiers and they were embarrassed for me. I needed time to recover my senses. When asked if my mother and sister really had to leave as neither of them was strong enough for a long journey the Officer just repeated his orders saying that they were quite clear. Mother and Jenna were crouched in the doorway, so I told them to put on winter cloaks and wrap food for the journey. A soldier, who attempted to prevent them going inside, was ordered to stand aside by the Captain but that was as far as the leniency went.

Ordered to wait with the soldiers until they reappeared with a bundle of provisions and cloaks, I struggled into my own sheepskin jerkin. Not because of the cold you understand, but because I was scared to the pit of my stomach, sweating with fear for us all. There was no way to escape from the soldiers, and foolish to even try. The sheer helplessness of the situation was not easy to cope with when trying to appear brave in front of armed men. My smile was more a grimace, so tightly were my teeth clamped together!

Another man had come with the soldiers but this was the first time I had seen him. No doubt I was biased but when I tell you that he had a narrow, ugly face with a receding chin and sharp malicious eyes with the cruel expression of an experienced bully, I am being fairly kind. Nature had not been generous in her favours to him. He wore no colours but just walked into my father's house as if he owned it. I remember being astonished, angry even, that a complete stranger could be left at Woodcutts.

They tied my hands, but the women were left unbound while they walked beside the Captain's horse. He let them hold onto the saddle for support. By the end of the day, as dusk fell, we were glad to sit beside the road. The steady rhythm of the horse's hooves was almost hypnotic but walking with tied wrists was difficult. We slept now and then, despite the cold drizzle during the hours of darkness, but at dawn, when the land was still shrouded in mist, we were once more on the way to the king's prison. They fed us bread and weak ale but my stomach was rumbling in protest before the sun had any heat in it. My throat felt so tight that I could not even comfort my mother. She walked as if she was in a dream, eyes glazed and unfocused. Even when my sister cried it had no effect.

I overheard one of the soldiers remarking that he had done the same journey very recently. He had accompanied the Sheriff of Dorsetshire and a prisoner who was being taken for sentence by King Alfred because he couldn't pay the fine. The spearman casually said that the man had got short shrift, banished, and everything forfeit to the King.

Of course, when I heard him say that the man had murdered a royal body-servant it was obvious they were talking about my own father. My blood boiled with anger at the casualness of their chatter and I hoped mother had not heard them. She had enough to do getting herself and Jenna along the track safely.

The soldier strode on, hoisting his spear to the other shoulder without breaking his stride so that it was impossible to ask what he meant by 'short shrift' although I was well aware of the effect of forfeiture, having just been marched away from my own home! I remember hoping that the stranger would milk the cow before she got uncomfortable. She and the other animals did not deserve to suffer. A cynical thought I know, having concern over the pain an animal might endure, but neither should we have been punished, but the king had made the laws and there was no changing them." Udda sipped the ale thoughtfully and sucked at a biscuit, praising Edith's cooking absent mindedly as the mashed oats and honey slipped easily between his almost toothless gums. He let a crumb fall, smiling when the dog put out a large pink tongue to retrieve it.

"By the time we entered the huge gates of the King's capital," Udda continued, "we were exhausted. Mother and Jenna, who still sobbed, were taken to the women's quarters. I barely had time to glance in their direction before being roughly pulled along by the guards. There had been no warning that we would be split up, I never had time to say good-bye or to tell them to be brave. My hands were freed after the guards pushed me through the iron-studded gates of a large stockade.

Inside, several men were already gathered beside the huge timber walls which rose to at least two or three times the height of a man. Eventually I forced my way to peer through a crack between two bars. An identical formidable wall was situated some distance away beyond a sandy platform studded with upright wooden posts. That, they told me, was the punishment place. My father had been shackled to a similar post in the village. I backed away from the walls feeling ill, sick with fear and dread.

Sinking shakily to my knees reminded me of the knife still hidden in my leggings. The one from my belt had been taken away by the soldiers, but no one had searched for other weapons. It felt as though the bulge became more and more obvious. I still had my belt but could hardly put that round my waist under the tunic for that might have raised suspicions. It stayed lashed inside my leggings for days and thank God it did!

Guards handed out manchets of bread and a water barrel was brought in with an earthenware cup tied to the rim. Each man could take turns to gulp as much as he could before another snatched the mug from him. There was nothing orderly about the rations. I witnessed men fighting over a crust.

Later the following day, I saw soldiers light the brazier and fix leather straps to the upright posts dotted around the square between the two prisons. Branding irons were being pulled from the fire by a guard who spat on the glowing metal. Despite my fear, I couldn't stop myself staring at the scene. We were all watching through the small gaps in the walls."

Udda caught his breath suddenly; the horror of what he had seen causing him to shiver violently, the details recalled so vividly despite the years. Instantly Edith was beside him patting his bony shoulders as Udda rocked back and forwards in the grip of his memories. Udric brought a fresh pot of ale and plunged an iron rod into the liquid causing steam to spit. He passed it to his father who drank gratefully, a rime of froth clinging to his upper lip. The night was now dark with a light, chill wind causing the leaves to rustle. Occasionally small eyes reflected the glow of the fire before a scuttling in the leaf mould signalled a hasty retreat.

"It was a scream from beyond the walls that brought us all to our feet. Through the squint we saw a man spread-eagled on a wooden frame. He had been neutered then blinded, now just a bloody wreck of a fellow soul. Some men were actually sick but someone commented dryly that minters of false money, who cheated the King, and fornicators, were treated like that. Then they came for me, two burly, heavily armed men. The gate slammed shut behind us. My terror nearly unmanned me. If they had not held me so tightly I swear even a full grown man might have grown faint.

I tell you that the sight which met my eyes was worse than the hell that Bata, our village priest, had ever described on Sundays. Men sat clutching their heads, moaning with pain, or simply lay on the ground as if dead. Blood was everywhere, the smell a pervading stench. I must then have fainted with sheer horror when I saw the fire, the glowing branding iron and the blood bespattered soldiers. Even the leather masks they wore to protect them from the heat of the braziers added to the awfulness of that moment. Then I saw my sister weeping. Mother's face was ashen except for the livid letter A on her forehead, the skin blackened by the branding iron. The scar would identify her as the lowest form of life, a serf, owned by a master, at his beck and call day and night.

They tied me to a post but just as the hot iron was being brought towards me my mother started screaming that I was still a child. From somewhere behind me a voice stopped the soldier's hand, only a moment before the brand would have burnt its deep furrow on my own forehead. I shall never forget that moment, the smell of sweat and fear, of blood and my own soiling.

I opened my eyes to see the Sheriff. At this moment he appeared as a saviour, contrary to my previous opinion which had not been so Christian." Udda laughed dryly.

Edith and Udric hardly dared move for fear of missing his next revelation. The fieldworkers had tactfully left their lord and his family alone, sure that they would be told the story another time. Easing tired muscles they put more wood on the fire and waited for the old man to continue, only glancing at each other briefly as Udda spoke again.

"You must remember that all my deep rooted belief in justice had been dashed when father was found guilty. My mother had just lied to the Sheriff, but I was quickly released and marched to a barn. I saw him striding off, his familiar sword swinging in time with his step.

Inside the barn we were forced to place a leg on a small anvil where an iron shackle was fitted and hammered shut by a surly blacksmith and his assistant. The door was barred leaving us prisoners in the dim light among piles of filthy straw. I learned later that those who survived branding would eventually be sold, the money going to the King's treasury but in the meantime we would work in or around his court, returning to the prison each night. The whole place smelt of sweat and dirt. There was no midden just a large bucket for our use. Men were praying while others cursed or ranted at their misfortune. Most were branded on the cheek or forehead, livid scars of puckered flesh, some oozing evil smelling liquid.

One day could be spent in the kitchen, another in the stables or mews cleaning the perches of the royal falcons. The smell there was so pungent that it made one gag with revulsion. I've never forgotten the eye watering effect of the droppings or my time in the dye shop mixing materials to make the rich colours preferred by the nobles. The only recognisable one was woad, the same dye used to mark the sheep, and my own legs." he added light-heartedly.

"Furze flowers and madder roots were kept in baskets stacked high against the wall, while more valuable imported ingredients were guarded jealously by the master dyer so that prying eyes could not steal his trade. Many of the colours were mixed with stale urine, the cloth being steeped in the liquid for days while other powders were mixed with oil or fats to apply to shields and banners. I made brushes from badger hair, horse hair or even human hair bound tightly in a split stick. If there was a moment to spare during daylight hours there was the endless filling of water casks using leather bags slung from a pole carried over the shoulder like the yoke the oxen used to plough the outlying fields. We boys waded into the fast running river to fill the bags and if the guard was not alert, I used wash myself to get rid of the soil of both man and beast.

Each day was filled with work from first light when the slave masters shouted and kicked us into wakefulness. I chopped oak tiles for the palace roof with an older boy for a time. He once called my father a murderer to my face; we were both been beaten for fighting!

I was also sent to work in the King's kitchen where the only relief from heat of the fires, was behind a screen of wet straw. Sometimes a scrap was thrown but more usually it was a cuff round the ear if the meat singed. When I complained that my tasks were all smelly the slave master told me to be grateful that he had not yet sent me to clean the royal midden!

Rumours of the King's deathly sickness spread through the town and court quickly so that even we slaves were aware of the tension mounting as thegns and nobles from all parts of the country arrived at court demanding service from us at any time of day or night. Often, when we had only just lain down to sleep after working all day, the King's housecarl would rouse someone to attend to newly arrived guests or horses.

Early on I learnt that three days each month used to be set aside for King Alfred to preside over his high court, listening to cases already heard by his Sheriffs and passing down his final judgement. It would have been on one of these days that my father's case was dealt with, I suppose.

While the King had a reputation for fairness, matters were dealt with speedily so that those who sought a favour or had come to reaffirm their loyalty were not inconvenienced by long delays.

There was always a constant stream of visiting nobles with their armed soldiers after grants of land, positions of power and rewards. Many brought their own servants who in turn made the slaves' lives a misery. The difference between a freeman and the bondsman or slave at court was vast. I was beaten severely for daring to raise my eyes to one man's bodyservant.

The palace and every courtyard surrounding it filled with men who were sure of their own importance, raising their tents alongside the extra horse lines. All had to be fed, requiring daily food wagons to be unloaded, by slaves of course. The atmosphere of the court became secretive; even the King's own body servants were subdued when it was known that he was close to death. King Alfred had apparently suffered illness before but had always recovered, the Court moving around Wessex then returning to Winchester to deliver judgements or deal with the finances of the Kingdom much as I suppose it does today. This time it was different. There was now a double guard on the treasury provided by armed housecarls. As the moment of death approached, soldiers in Prince Aethelwold's service hovered around the compound forming a separate guard, confident that as the son of the king's elder brother, their master would take the throne.

I watched these men in their leather jerkins, armed with short spears, knives and coloured shields by pretending to adjust my leggings. My knife still remained in its secret hiding place, but I sometimes dawdled too long and got kicked for idleness.

Suddenly the atmosphere of the town changed. The King was dead! The law maker, Alfred, King of Wessex, had died in the night. Some slaves talked in the early light of dawn of returning home, of freedom. This was the first time I had heard of manumission, the freeing of a dead man's slaves.

It gave me hope, that even if I was not to be freed immediately, it could happen in the future.

Watching the funeral from a high wall we saw the whole ceremony. The king's body, attended by servants, liveried retainers, nobles and his sons, who looked genuinely grieved, was taken into the church. The King's horse had gone from the stable and the hounds whined in their kennels. They killed the horse and many of the hounds were also destroyed, being the personal property of the late King. I was upset over the deaths of beasts not killed for meat but because of custom. We were all desperately tired but there was so much work during the next few days that there was no time for me to fret about the dogs, or about my mother and Jenna for that matter.

Messengers were sent out to Bishops and other councillors to attend a great assembly, a 'Witan Moot', to vote on the succession. Prince Aethelwold strode around the palace surrounded by his guards, greeting the nobles as if he was already king. He was such a confident figure, tall and fair-haired like all the King's family. I had served him on several occasions being cleaner than many of the others. The Prince had a habit of bathing!

Refreshments were required day and night while noisy debate over the rights and wrongs of the succession could be heard well into the early hours. We snatched a few hours sleep where we could because no one shut us in the barn but it took two days of noisy argument before Edward, Alfred's eldest son, was eventually confirmed as King.

The new King swaggered round the town with a retinue of his own soldiers and retainers. Lord Aethelwold, his cousin, I suppose, walked beside him stony-faced. All of them were dressed in colours I had only imagined, with furs and gold braid on every garment. We slaves were now made to prostrate ourselves on the ground whenever the procession passed. It was undignified but protests were useless with guards or slave-masters standing close by.

Life returned to normal a few weeks after the crowning, the guards relaxing a little. King Edward apparently ordered the sale of surplus slaves. Most brands had now healed leaving permanent raised scars but other sores still wept and festered. My own leg was sore where the shackle rubbed even though I stuffed the cleanest straw in the gap. Potential buyers walked amongst us with their slave masters who selected men to carry out particular duties then took them away, manacled together. I waited with two or three other men until we were led away to buildings on the south side. It was thatched like my father's house except that there was no fire. A smith added the owner's mark to the shackle before we were sent to work in a kitchen, the largest stone building.

It was not until I saw our slave master talking to the tall noble who had walked beside the new king, that I realised I had been bought by Lord Aethelwold. His bright blue mantle and tunic were even more richly embroidered than the sheriff's if that was possible! I was washing in the yard when the Prince walked past. Really I should have fallen to my knees but was in the act of pulling on my tunic. He ordered me to fetch his cloak from the hall. You never saw anyone dress so quickly, especially as I still had the knife hidden in my leggings.

I fetched the cloak and bowed to the Prince like the housecarls did. It made him laugh and he asked me where I came from so I told him Sexpenna Hanlega, to the west and that my father was a freeman and had owned his own farm outside the village. He frowned when I mentioned that King Alfred had been his lord. You see, his hopes of becoming the next king had been dashed, despite the fact that he was older than Edward and his own father had been king before Alfred. He flung the cloak carelessly round his shoulders and strode off, calling irritably for his horse.

I managed to be near the stable when he returned with the sweating beast. He flung the reins to a slave boy and gave me his cloak to take back to the hall. It was worth a thrashing for leaving the meat to burn for lack of turning. From then on though, I worked without pause, our meal consisting of left-over gravy-soaked manchets of bread from the high table. I was so tired next day that I fell asleep in the great hall, a grave offence punishable by a beating if caught. Luckily no one had missed me. The lighting wood stacked up by the fire irons in the middle of the vast room was where it had been left but the shackle on my ankle had chafed the skin again.

There was some argument between the slave master and the Prince but his voice had the arrogance of someone accustomed to unquestioning obedience, after all, he was a King's son.

My master's voice startled me ordering me to collect food, giving me his head band as his authority. I dashed off to the kitchens to get the rations. He had held up three fingers and I did the same in the kitchen. It was not time for a meal to be served and the cooks were reluctant, especially as little remained from the previous evening meal. Waste food was firstly considered the perks of being a cook, second rate pieces were given to the slaves and lastly the pigs were fattened with the scraps. I had to thrust the Prince's head band under the cook's nose and hold up three fingers to indicate the portions the Prince required.

Eventually I got meats, bread and ale in a large leather flask and was taking it back to the Prince when the slave master caught me. He twisted my ear as he marched me back to the hall but let me go and bowed himself out when the Prince told me to put my load down. Then he ordered me to stay while he talked to some men. They stood in the half light beyond the door. I was stacking the wasted roof tiles by the fire trying to look inconspicuous when I saw a magnificently dressed fair haired noble surrounded by three or four finely dressed men some distance away. Men, slaves and labourers regardless of their rank made obeisance immediately. I was quite sure it was the king even though I could not see his face.

Prince Aethelwold swore and told me to throw his cloak over the food then light the fire. I already knew that the Prince and the King were not the best of friends so I picked up some coarse rushes from the floor and stuffed them under the pile of kindling. I couldn't get the flint to strike for shaking but was more surprised to be cuffed and berated loudly for laziness. The King seemed quite pleasant when he finally came into the hall, his fair hair neatly cropped below the gold circlet. Prince Aethelwold bowed politely, asking if the King's hunting had been rewarding. We all knew King Edward had inherited his father's royal gerfalcon, a bird of long ancestry. Its hunting skills were often spoken of with awe and no doubt some exaggeration. They discussed the days' hunting while I watched the smoke begin to curl upwards towards the hole in the ceiling some ten to twelve feet above. Prince Aethelwold's steward ordered me to wait at the far side of the hall. I forgot to bow and had my ears boxed. It was only because the King raised his voice that I could hear him ordering his cousin to attend to a matter of business on his behalf and to be ready to ride in one hour.

He swept out of the hall followed by his armed housecarls, his cloak swirling round his shoulders so that the smoke billowed all over the place.

Striking one clenched fist into the palm of the other, Aethelwold's smiling face changed instantly to a frown, muttering that the king was treating him like an underling, a henchman. He went on about being as royal as he was. He was furious to have been ordered on an errand, muttering that a messenger could have done just as well. Prince Aethelwold was working himself into a rage until his companion gently coughed and touched him on the shoulder, reminding him that he was not alone in the hall.

Eventually he calmed down and told Osric, his steward, to order the horses. I was to ride a baggage horse as being country bred I could presumably ride. Me, ride a horse! In fact the only time I had ridden was with other children we had stolen a few rides on the Reeve's horse in the village, hardly enough to qualify as a proficient horse rider.

Anyway, I went with Osric to the stables where the Prince's horse, a huge grey stallion eyed me from a great height. Grooms put saddles and bridles on the animals under the steward's watchful eyes. He turned down a smallish pack pony and chose a sway backed horse of doubtful origin instead. Honestly I was appalled by the size of it! Osric fitted leather bags to each side of the saddle and fastened a fold of leather over the opening to keep its contents dry. The Prince went to the King taking a moment to retie his headband, and fasten the cloak with its bronze brooch. He always demanded that his cloak was brushed clean. It made him look royal you see. I got my sheepskin while they were both gone. It was a risk but not so much as secretly carrying a knife. It still astonished me that even when the smith had riveted the shackle round my ankle, no one had queried the slight bulge under my leggings.

The Prince returned, muttering 'Puppy-dog' and usurper' in his barely concealed fury. Apparently we were to ride to Dorsetshire. The horses tossed their heads stamping impatiently. I stood by the brown gelding packing the food into the bags when my master suddenly strode off to the kitchen to demand food for the King's business. The Prince came out bearing a similar quantity of flat bread manchets, meat, some small sour apples and another skin of ale. I was as puzzled as the cook must have been but not so wise and was told sharply to mind my own business and to speak only when spoken to.

Chapter Two

"My master and Osric were mounting their horses. I had to watch what they did as I had never tightened a girth strap. I managed to copy them and was amazed that my horse was so patient. It trotted after the other two who were by now some little way ahead in the half light. All I could do was to hold on tightly to the front of the saddle. I laugh at it now!

We left the busy streets by the Western gate and set off toward the county boundary. Out of sight of the city however the Prince drew rein by some tall trees where a rider wearing his colours was waiting. The scroll of parchment wrapped in leather was passed to him and he galloped off westward, the beat of the hooves fading into the distance. While this was going on I took the opportunity to alter the straps of the saddlebags which had already pinched the inside of my calves. Osric noticed my adjustments. I think he guessed that I had not ridden before.

We also rode the same road as the messenger but stopped at the outskirts of Romsey on the edge of a wood. The sky darkened quickly as I watered the horses in the nearby stream before letting them graze. My legs were sore but I had to hold the reins of all three horses. I remember patting mine, silently thanking Osric for his wise choice. The swaybacked brown gelding was in fact ideal, teaching me balance and rhythm. He followed the horses in front so I did not have to use the reins. Leather hobbles were put on the unsaddled riding horses which immediately shook and rolled on the grass, their feet waving ecstatically in the air. I undid the girth of my saddle-pad which knocked me to the ground as it fell off!

Meanwhile having eaten, the Prince had wrapped his fur-lined cloak round him and lain down to sleep. His steward ordered me to keep watch.

A bark from the forest made all the horses nervous and it was followed by howls that made the hair on the back of my neck stand up. I led the horses closer to the sleeping men, but even so the night was long, cold and frightening. At one point I would have sworn that wolves padded close by.

Dawn came slowly when the two men stirred, glanced at me, and ate their breakfast without a word of thanks or encouragement. I was cold, hungry and desperately tired. I remember feeling rather bitter. Being a slave meant that one could be worked all day and apparently all night. Osric generously relieved me of the horses while I ate a portion of flat bread with meat. There was no time to savour the luxury of cooked fowl. The nearest I usually got to meat was the gravy from it soaked into the left-overs.

I must have fallen asleep on the horse for the next thing I knew was my master prodding me with the point of his sword and threatening to make me run alongside. I wriggled to find a more comfortable position but had no idea how long I'd been asleep. The sun was well up in the sky, our shadows short on the ground.

For quite some distance the track across the heathland had only been marked by white stones. The turf had been grazed almost smooth on the higher slopes but the Prince chose a valley that must once have been inhabited but which was now deserted and overgrown. We approached Cranburne across the common, scattering the grazing sheep, past small strip fields belonging to the church tenants.

The orderly pattern of agricultural life brought back memories of the farm. Believe me, there was no way I could escape. My horse was not a fast stallion like the Prince's. Besides which, I doubt if I could have persuaded mine to leave the others.

Eventually, shortly before dusk, we arrived at a farm run by a small group of monks. The Prince and Osric were invited into their house by the Abbott who told them he was there to inspect the work and welfare of those who belonged to his Tewkesbury church. The horses could sense the comfort of a stable and were impatient. I spent that night in a barn chained to the central post by the shackle ring and slept soundly until dawn when I was woken by the sound of a small bell. An elderly man released the shackle and put me to work in the yard. Anyone can order a slave around you know, especially to do the dirty work." Udda's laugh broke into a cough, soothed by a few sips of ale.

"When I was a boy there were no actual slaves in Sexpenna Hanlega. The farm Reeve was in charge of everyone who lived and worked on the church-owned land, but their duties involved farming. Besides, most of the work was in return for their homes and their own small plot of land. I was starving hungry by now so went to the stable where the saddle bags hung on the wall and helped myself. I was just pulling a piece of meat apart when my shoulder was suddenly seized by a man dressed in dark robes, a deep hood obscuring his face. He hauled me to the barn and roughly secured the shackle to the post. The priest, for that's what I thought he was, then drew out a whip and started to lash out at me. I barely had time to notice the man's ugly face with its broken nose, before curling up as tightly as possible. Thank god Osric entered the barn just then. The man told him that I was a thief and that he had taught me a lesson. When I managed to tell them that I was hungry and had only taken a little food from the saddle bag, Osric laughed! From my own point of view there was nothing funny at all. The welts of the whip lash stung abominably. Fortunately the sheepskin of my jerkin had softened some of the blows. He said that Lord Aethelwold had more important things to think about than feeding slaves and that I was his property and was to be released. The priest deliberately jerked the chain through the ring catching the raw skin as he unchained my leg.

Inside I seethed with anger, having been forgotten by the Prince, beaten without cause, and life generally seemed to be unjust.

Osric turned to lead the way out of the barn but we could both feel the man in his dark robes glaring at our backs, his eyes resentful, starkly focused with rage. The Prince's companion clapped me on the back in defiance of the usual distance between master and slave. I remember wincing with the pain even though it was the first show of affection I had experienced for months.

The Prince greeted Osric who promptly related the incident to him. The Prince was furious, standing up abruptly. He was fully dressed in royal regalia and looked magnificent. His sword swung from a jewelled belt beneath the ver-lined cloak which was thrown over both shoulders. Even the diadem around his brow had a deep red stone fastened to it, emphasising his height and slim build. Looking round the almost deserted courtyard he announced loudly that no-one should touch what was his and that we were leaving for Wymburne immediately. He proceeded with the formal leave taking, offering thanks for the hospitality. For myself I left the manor farm gratefully. I was even glad to be back in the saddle despite the pain in my thigh muscles. As we passed through the stout wooden gateway I saw the priest watching us. Even though he had pulled his cowl halfway over his face I knew he was frowning darkly.

It did not occur to me that the man had entered the barn for his own purposes but had perhaps been prevented from searching the saddle bags by my urgent need to eat. As far as I know the Prince never gave it another thought. He pushed the stallion to a canter in the morning sunshine chatting to Osric beside him. I would much rather have looked about for familiar landmarks, but forgot all about that with the exhilaration of speed. I had never travelled so fast or indeed in such style. Had the circumstances been different I might have enjoyed myself!

We rode briskly past tumuli, then a few moments later an ancient stone circle. My father had always taught me to respect a burial ground but these boulders had an aura of mysticism, standing starkly black against the frosted turf. It's not a place to get left behind, among the grassy hillocks marking the resting places of the dead.

At noon the food was more equally shared. The horses grazed on the scanty grass close by. Two or three small huts belonging to turf cutters blended into the heath, the houses being made of turf slabs, the roofs thickly thatched with furze, reedy grass stems or scrubby twigs. It was the first time I had seen a house where the turf still grew on the walls. There were several small grassed over hummocks nearby, obviously from turf houses which had collapsed. I remember commenting out loud that these houses were not as long lasting as my father's. It was built from flints, clay, chalk and stones, you see. After the meal the Prince mounted up before cantering off towards the wood on his own. Osric appealed to him not to go alone, but the Prince became haughty, stressing his royal appearance would give him immunity from robbers.

He returned later in the afternoon, appearing pleased and told us to mount up quickly, and follow him closely to the woods. Once there we could not see the sky and some trees with their twisted boughs seemed to form terrifying shapes. On some, small pieces of cloth and white bones hung from the lower branches. A white skull was pinned to one trunk. I remember taking my hands off the reins long enough to cross myself.

Suddenly we entered a clearing where a crowd of men, some

wearing long white robes with hoods over their faces milled round the horses. The Prince addressed the leaders as 'priest' or 'father', telling them that he would take what was his by right, and that there would be little resistance from the townspeople for they had much fondness for his father.

I hastily adjusted the baggage straps so that my leg would be more comfortable. The Prince's army seemed to consist of the Old Ones, followers of the old religion who supported the idea that as Ethelred was King before King Alfred, by right Prince Aethelwold, as son of the older brother, should have been his heir. It was Osric who told me that we were travelling to Twyneham and Wymburne to take the towns from the King. Treasonable to even think of doing such a thing but acted upon and caught, punishable by death. All of a sudden the woods were very cold.

Hailing Prince Aethelwold as King, the men followed the prancing stallion. I had to follow because Osric kept his eye on me, but I remember wanting to turn round and go back, even if it meant going back past the ghoulish relics. We followed the river bank watched by a few labourers. The Prince called a halt and addressed his forces from the top of the burial mound at Barrow Pool. It is still called that now but the chalk shows through in places. I have always wondered why someone of rank was buried so close to a river. All the other burial mounds were on high ground. Anyway, we were ordered to cross the ford north of the town. He announced that those who wished could attend Mass the following day after which Osric would lead a party on to Twyneham as soon as Wymburne had submitted. He said there would be no fighting unless challenged, because he was known and would be welcomed by the people. High walls rose from the flood plain which we followed to the centre of the town.

I dropped back to the rear feeling totally confused at the turn of events, tired of riding, with an aching leg, too exhausted to be interested in the neatly farmed fields or the quality of the beasts. Osric edged his horse alongside to tell me that Wymburne was built on the land between two rivers; the Wym, not much more than a stream, which we followed down from the woods near Chalberie and the Stour, a much bigger river rising a long way east of the town. As you know, the two meet to form one big river on which boats can go down to Twyneham.

Behind my master's banner, we entered the town just before dusk causing the people to flee. Prince Aethelwold purposefully made directly for the Church calling for the priest. A thin man with tufts of ill-cut hair appeared. He was obviously startled to see such a large force and kept wringing his hands, even as he welcomed the Prince, his voice squeaky with nerves!

When he was told that King Edward was no longer their Lord the priest had to conceal his surprise by hastily bowing. Osric posted guards on all the high points and at the stones above the fords. Two men guarded the centre from the Church tower.

I followed the Prince to the priest's lodgings but on the way banged my leg on a wall, opening the sores to produce a sickening smell. Suddenly I was sitting on the ground clutching my leg and trying to hide my knife. The Prince sent for the smith but when he arrived with his tools, he started talking about the time he had met the Prince's father and King Alfred some years ago. Osric interrupted, reminding him that Prince Aethelwold was now Lord of Wymburne and had instructed him to take off my shackle.

When the Prince returned to hear the smith complaining that his standing within the town's three hundred population would be lowered by attending to a mere slave, money appeared to be an immediate sop to his injured pride. He was told not to injure me, a threat which the Prince made abundantly clear. Harm me and the penalty for so doing would be awful. It was widely known that there had been a streak of cruelty in King Alfred's brother, Aethelred, doubtless inherited by his son.

It was an agonising walk to the forge. The smith was breathing heavily as he flung the hammer and anvil down on the beaten earth with a thud. As he applied a large chisel to the bolt I must have fainted, coming round when cold water washed the sore. He called his wife in a dialect I had heard in the fields outside the town and she applied an ointment to my wound. Another customer was waiting impatiently so I left to find the priest's lodgings on my own, reminded that any delay in doing so might reflect on the smith's own safety. Looking back, should I have made a bid for freedom? But to where?

It was then that the second attack occurred. I recognised the voice of the priest from Cranburne. He was shouting that I was a runaway slave as he hit me. I remember twisting from his grip and kicking him sharply before running for my life, keen on this occasion anyway, to report back to my master.

Mass was attended by the Prince, shoulder to shoulder in the church with the local townsfolk and his soldiers. The elderly and infirm sat on the stone shelving round the sides where they could hear the service. Of course they could see nothing for the packed throng standing between them and the priest. I looked for my attacker but the man was not there.

I remember the Prince inspecting his father's tomb beside the altar during the service. His steward later told me that the Prince had been a small boy when Aethelred had been killed, the battered body having been buried almost before it was cold. Alfred had been elected King immediately and had not permitted lengthy mourning for his elder brother, which was another thing which contributed to my master's bitterness towards King Edward. Too young then to succeed his father, when Alfred had died in the October of eight hundred and ninety nine, he had been fully prepared, and indeed expected, to take on the responsibility. It was the Bishops who had stood in his way, persuading the council to elect Alfred's son. It was not altogether surprising that he felt entitled to take possession of at least some of the royal manors. Osric was ever loyal to the Prince… but I wander."

Udda rubbed his ankle thoughtfully. Even now there was a thickening of the skin where the shackle had rubbed. Edith was winding her hair round her fingers, something she always did when nervous or excited. Even the unborn child had remained quiet as her husband's father told them of his early life. She could see that Udric too was fascinated by the unfolding story. Neither of them moved, waiting patiently for Udda to continue.

"After the priest had blessed everyone the Prince quickly knelt to touch the tomb of Saint Cuthberga on the other side of the altar before he faced the townspeople to tell them that he had returned to his father's lands again. He said he intended to hold them while he was alive and die among them, but in the meantime the people should know their lord. There was only the briefest hesitation before the momentarily stunned congregation shouted their approval.

After the service, people picked up their weapons from the boundary ditch of the church, where the fence is now. He spoke to the leaders about the attacks on me, his personal property. The men nodded their understanding and agreement of the fact that a man's property, including bonded men and slaves, was his to treat as he pleased. He swore he would not allow another the same licence without his permission. Aethelwold told his soldiers of my attacker's broken nose and dark robes, ordering a search for him. He pointed out that the guards on the outskirts had not reported any requests to leave Wymburne, but bearing in mind that an ox was to be roasted in the shambles, that was not surprising. Indeed my own mouth watered at the prospect!

By now the Prince was mounted, his cloak spread over the beast's haunches. He rode off back the way we had come, the winter sunshine glinting on his gold circlet. Townspeople on their way to the feast stepped hastily aside as we passed through the narrow street to the high walls surrounding the nunnery. At the door he rapped sharply at the grille but was apparently refused entry and became very angry. That oak door, studded with iron, had probably been put in when the nunnery was founded by Cuthberga and her sister, daughters of King Ine of Wessex nearly two hundred years before. To everyone's astonishment he ordered the soldiers to break it down. I led his horse out of the way. Under a barrage of axe blows the door broke, and the Prince and several soldiers pushed their way in. I could see very little beyond the tall candles illuminating the pictures and wall coverings, similar to those at Court in Winchester. The Prince came out pulling a nun by one arm. She may have been scared but when he lifted her onto the stallion's back she arranged her habit as if it had been a costly dress." A sharp intake of breath interrupted the tale. Udric had been listening in silence until now but he could not contain his shock at this revelation that Prince Aethelwold had actually kidnapped a nun. His eyes were wide in sheer disbelief that anyone, let alone a Prince could invade a religious house.

"Oh yes, he took her away, leaving the Abbess surveying the damage and calling down curses on the ungodly. She called him a violator of women! Mind you she was beside herself with rage at the invasion of her domain, the loss of dignity in front of mere men!

With a final threat of God's punishment falling on those who blasphemed or transgressed His laws, the Abbess gathered her nuns about her and led the way back to the confines of the nunnery. It was by pure chance that I caught sight of the man with the broken nose so

I followed him back to the centre of town where he knocked on a door and went in. A few minutes later the man left from the rear, riding a dark bay horse. I ran back to the prince's lodging to report but was told brusquely to stay with the horses in the stable. I saw the nun sitting at a table with the Prince, her wimple discarded, blonde hair spilling over the shoulders of her white habit. She was not frightened; indeed they both looked exceedingly happy, with a flagon of wine set between them.

In the stable I discovered that only the stallion remained, already unbridled, eating his way through a pile of hay in one corner. The dark bay gelding had gone. I was furious. That horse had carried me further in two days than many travelled in a lifetime. There was no-one else around to tell and Osric had already gone to the coast.

The two of them stayed in the private quarters, apparently ignoring the priest's fury over the break-in at the nunnery. No-one demanded work from me so I walked with the priest to his church. He had no suggestions as to how to find out where my family had gone or how to appeal a sentence passed by the late King. He kept telling me to trust in the Lord as he showed me the watch tower. The roasted ox had been reduced to a bloody carcase but I still found enough meat to satisfy my hunger.

It was late afternoon before my master summoned me. He enquired about the health of his horse and the state of the townspeople. I could see that his thoughts were far more involved with his lady friend than the unwelcome news of the theft of the brown gelding. He dismissed me quite curtly, ordering me to saddle the stallion immediately, a task more easily performed by a much taller person! Prince Aethelwold lifted his lady on to its back, smiling broadly as he thanked the priest for his hospitality. The churchman too, looked happy, but I am sure that was because he would no longer have to provide for his expensive royal visitor.

As you know it is not far to the King's manor, the Cynings Tun. Even in the fading light, the fields appeared well tended and the road clean. The palace gates were just closing as my master demanded admittance. The royal guards hastily drew the stout wooden doors back on their iron hinges. They then escorted the Prince, his arm around the nun, up the bank and through the inner gates to the main hall. Although it was much smaller than the palace at Winchester, it had many comforts for housing its royal owner. Colourful tapestries hung from the walls, and the windows were mainly shuttered or covered with skin membranes, while a roaring fire warmed the room. A great deal of food and ale were consumed by the men who crowded the space below the royal table. Some of them must have been town elders from Wymburne. I tasted fresh fish for the first time and sampled sweets. Two minstrels played, singing to the assembled company after the meal. The names of Lord Alfred and King Ine occurred many times, but I could not understand the saga that was being sung. Soldiers and servants fell asleep on the floor of the hall when the Prince and the nun retired behind a screen for the night.

For two days my master walked round the manor, admiring the defences, store rooms and workshops when he was not closeted with his lady. Satisfactory reports had apparently come in from Twyneham where Osric had taken charge of the royal manor there.

It was not until news came in that King Edward was extremely angry at the invasion of crown possessions and was intending to surround the town at dawn that the Prince reacted furiously. Having publicly declared on his arrival that he would remain at Wymburne, alive or dead, he had made no further preparations apart from closing the gates across the old Roman road which passed through the manor and posting look-outs as night fell. However when a guard arrived with the information that the King's forces were already camped only a short distance away, orders were given to saddle the horses immediately. I must say that there was a certain amount of reluctance because the evening meal was about to be served. The savoury smells coming from the kitchen had excited everyone's appetite. Suddenly the Prince roughly grabbed the stallion's bridle from the stableman. It sidestepped nervously while the Prince shouted orders to a soldier holding a torch. Men who had been resting rushed out fastening buckles as they ran. The fact that King Edward's forces were camped at Badberie, less than an hour's march away was shouted from tent to tent, followed by commands to double the guard and warn the townsfolk. The prince was in the middle of giving me instructions to collect his possessions from his chamber when I had to step back to avoid the flying hooves as the stallion reared and pranced in excitement. The nun was lifted up onto the saddle before him where she held on nervously, trying to straighten her cloak with one hand.

He told the soldiers that they should follow him in a north-easterly direction as quickly as possible, bringing food, ale and warm clothes with them. By the time I was halfway to the hall the Prince had gone, galloping off past the barns and workshops, shouting for the gate to be opened.

In the chamber I collected his jewelled drinking cup and the thick, fur-lined cloak with its brooch and pin fastener. Securing the cup inside before fastening the bundle with the gilt clasp, I backed out after snatching a leg of cold fowl, drawing the curtain quietly. The place was dark and deserted except for the manor servants. Putting the bundle on my shoulder I set off after the Prince, through the unguarded gate. A soldier, escorting the nun back to the hall passed me. She looked dishevelled, having obviously fallen off the stallion, but no-one challenged me as I walked back to the town and out through the northern road. One thing I did do was to put the knife in the loop of my belt, hidden most of the time by the jerkin. Even a slave would be pardoned for arming himself in the circumstances.

A loud wolf howl close by encouraged me to leave the wood, clutching the cloak as I ran. It was then that I was challenged by two soldiers. They were drunk and could not have been members of Prince Aethelwold's regular bodyguard. I did not trust them. What if they had discovered that I was carrying princely plate and jewellery?

Initially one of them held my shoulder in a vice-like grip, forcing me to walk between them, but I stopped frequently to adjust a sandal so that gradually the two soldiers, who continued to drink deeply from a flagon, drew ahead.

I had to take the chance to escape, dodging between huge trees, scrambling down a bank. They shouted as they tried to find me, at one point their heavy footsteps so close to my hiding place that my bladder released itself in pure terror. I was sure they would smell my fear. It seemed an age before the two ruffians finally lurched away with their ale, arms linked to support each other. Only when the night silence was complete did I relax and sleep fitfully, miserably chilled. Then dawn was breaking through the trees so that the trunks looked massive against the pale light. Finding water was not difficult so I washed; splashing in the icy cold stream, then drank slowly. When the sun came up fully there was no heat in it. Thank God for my sheepskin jerkin.

In my mind I listed all that belonged to me. Still, after all these years I can remember - the knife, a leather belt, six thongs of leather, my amulet bag on another short cord containing two flints and a hazel tally stick. I still had my master's fur lined cloak, drinking cup and brooch which had to be guarded at all times. A straight pole cut from the nearest copse, trimmed with the knife became another weapon.

I have never felt hunger like that before. Even the hazel nuts had been stripped from the nearby bushes as I headed towards a small rise in the ground. To the east there were thick trees but a fairly well used track went south-east towards the edge of the forest. Round the edge of this, the heathy land sloped gently upwards towards some more trees. There was no sign of dwellings, only a few well worn animal tracks. The land appeared to be unoccupied and there was plenty of firewood already on the ground. That was how I found 'Uddings'.

Chapter Three

Under the trees the light was dappled and shadowy. I hid the bundle in a bole of a huge oak tree before gathering firewood then lashed my precious knife to the end of the stave to make a spear and eventually killed a small fowl. By the time it was cooked I tell you my mouth was watering.

It took many days to find my way around the woods, sleeping up trees to escape from the animals that rooted about during the hours of darkness. I found a pond used by the animals when following some tracks one day and took a lump of the potting-clay lining back to the clearing where my den was taking shape.

Every day I made a mark on a broadleaved sapling, the tree over there which has the scored trunk." Udda pointed at a tall tree which stood at the edge of the courtyard, where during the day the fowl busily pecked beneath its shady leaves searching for the fallen seeds. Its trunk showed scars rising high into the darkness.

"I remember one occasion when a curious wild boar shuffled past followed by three tiny piglets. The sow turned on me and I only escaped by climbing a tree." Laughing at the memory Udda stroked his legs, muttering that he had been much stronger and quite nimble in his youth. Edith refreshed the tankards and slipped quietly away from the fire. Udric raised his eyebrow, concerned for her but turned back to his father when she waved reassuringly.

Udda was wiping spilt beer from his chin with the rug. He grinned at his son having seen the glances exchanged between the young people. "She needs to walk round, son. My grandson is weighing heavy on her now but she is well formed and will birth easily. I would hold him, God willing."

Udric was initially embarrassed at his father's frankness regarding Edith's ability to bear children but quickly realised that Udda had referred to the possibility of dying before the event took place.

He gripped his father's arm firmly, assuring him that he would be with them long after the birth of their first son and many after him!

Udda shook his head doubtfully but did not contradict Udric's optimism.

Edith returned with wheatcakes still warm from her skillet, honey oozing from the delicacies. The men grinned and accepted the treats with genuine appreciation. Licking his fingers, Udda continued with his tale.

"My first hut was built against the hollow oak tree using dried bracken packed tightly into the framework of saplings. I must admit to using Prince Aethelwold's cloak to cover the bed. It was only dried grass of course but much softer than the bough of a tree! Life was hard but at least I was free. I knew I had to remain free for one year and one day and then prove it to someone who would vouch for me. After all, unless I could return to Sexpenna Hanlega there was no way to establish my father's innocence.

Prince Aethelwold's sudden departure from Wymburne the day after Christmas, the year of our lord eight hundred and ninety nine, would be well known to the priest at the church there, of that there was no doubt in my mind. All that was needed was to stay free until the next Christmas. Hence my record of the days was so important."

Udric nodded slowly, the significance of the scarred tree and its importance in his father's early life now explained. Such wisdom and foresight in the circumstances was surprising but he said nothing and brought his attention back to the events Udda was describing.

"It was some time in the summer when I was paddling in the stream when I caught my first eel. I hacked off its head with the knife and threw the beheaded creature on the bank where it continued to wriggle. It was delicious and a change from fowl. They smoked well, staying edible for some time. Pieces of meat stored in stinging nettle leaves baked in clay kept well too. My emergency store hung above the bed out of reach of inquisitive animals. It was about this time that I saw the piglets again. I had already trapped and eaten a young deer then guiltily swept all traces of it into a pit. I dared not even keep the hide. Now I fancied pork for dinner!

Some days I explored the heathland to the North, leaving just after sunrise. It was more or less flat, covered in short turf, heather, or low furze bushes, just as it is now. The occasional whynberry bush bore a few black berries which I tried for the first time and got my fingers stained. It was then that the idea of using the juice to stain my pots came to mind. That's when I first saw Gerhard digging turf, stacking the blocks to dry. He said he was from Holt village, and used to take peat to the monastery and burgh of Wymburne regularly. He knew that the King's cousin had attempted to steal the royal lands. He also knew that the nun who had been abducted by the aetheling had to do penance in the church before her whole community.

It was at that point that I confessed to leaving Wymburne the day after Christmas, shortly after Prince Aethelwold had departed in such undignified haste. He seemed unconcerned and carried on building up his pile of fuel. If he was going to claim a reward for returning me to the Prince's household then that was his opportunity. Not that it was discussed that my status was that of a slave you understand, after all I had no shackle to announce it to all and sundry but I'm sure he guessed.

It was then that I saw Galena. She was bringing her father food while he worked. She was so beautiful, a dark haired girl whose womanhood was just showing through the brown knee length tunic she wore. She smiled shyly at me through a veil of hair which fell forward despite the twist of hide which tied it back.

We ate my pieces of smoked eel and her bread. It was delicious. Remember, I had not eaten bread for ages. I spent two days with Gerhard and his family in a turf hut before reluctantly returning to Uddings. Before I left, Gerhard assured me that he was not interested in making money in return for a man's life and we trusted each other from then on.

To ward off the increased loneliness I had to keep busy. Many hours were spent gathering hazel nuts and tangy roots to store. By this time I had built a clay-lined cache in the hollow of the big oak tree, and found a bees' nest in another partly rotted tree. Having made a lidded pot, after many attempts, I took some honey as a gift next time I looked for the turf cutter. Do not forget that I had few clothes but never wore the cloak, leaving it hidden inside the oak tree whenever I left the woods. It could not be found in my possession by someone curious as to who was living in the makeshift hut.

Gerhard suggested that my pots might sell in the market. It was at this point that I told him that until I could gain freedom officially, it was not possible to return to Wymburne without great risk. The most important thing to me at that time was clearing my father's name before returning to Woodcutts Farm. It had not occurred to me at this point that Woodcutts could not be reclaimed when justice was done.

When Galena and her mother came, I gave Galena the honey as a present. It was not right to have approached her directly like that. Youngsters used to have respect for their elders you know! It was not done for a girl to receive gifts without the father's permission. Your mother was their only child. Anyway, I was forgiven for my presumption! It was on my way back to Uddings that I decided to build a house, a proper house, not just a shelter propped up against the oak tree. You see, I had already decided that Galena would be my handfast wife.

I chose a site where the ground rises to the West with a good view past the edge of the wood down to the stream. Many weeks, no, months of work with my few tools and even less knowledge, went into building that first house. Meanwhile, avenging the injustice to my father would have to wait. Do you know I eventually had to resort to lighting a fire at the base of each tree, having scraped away as much earth as possible. Each felling took a week. I dug pits in the ground, saving the earth for mortar, and the stones for ramming. At dusk each day my arms and legs ached with tiredness.

Galena's mother had already joked that she would exchange clay pots for a new tunic so I took her the ver skins and the skin of a pig. It had been injured but despite its wound it had attacked me, the bite festering for many weeks. Some of the meat was smoked, hung in the old oak tree for the winter. The lard had filled many pots, while the rest of the meat was eaten in a succession of evening meals with berries, sorrel leaves, wild parsnips, mushrooms and a hot spicy root that almost burnt my tongue. Your mother cooked with all these things. Much better than I ever did!

That autumn the old oak lost a branch or two, but still hid the prince's brooch and the jewelled chalice above my larder. I used to take them out occasionally, just to marvel at the workmanship and the colours. I still did not know what to do with them. My main concern was to finish the house and have your mother as my bride. To do this I needed to be a freeman, to be a member of a tything and take my turn in fyrd-service.

Even if I had been sent to fight, repair fortifications or bridges at the King's command, my home and wife would be protected, our children guarded, and a complete tally kept of transactions during the my absence. As it is now, no-one cheats the man called for duty.

Gerhard suggested that the priest might advise me or even attest to my self imposed banishment from society, if no other way was possible. After all, I still could not travel alone, suggesting instead that we go to Wymburne together with his next load of turfs. It should at least be possible to establish if the same priest served the Church. I could pose as Gerhard's servant, better than a slave I suppose!

On the appointed day Gerhard brought his ox wagon to the fork in the track. I was scared, not just of travelling openly but in case the priest was no longer there. When we had unloaded the fuel he spoke to the Abbess when she paid him. She came out to the open shed with another nun. You can imagine my surprise. I stared at the woman attending the Abbess, wisps of blond hair escaping from her wimple. She was the lady who had been abducted by Prince Aethelwold!

Gerhard explained that I had been a slave of the Prince and since my master's hasty departure had lived a solitary life some distance away. I now wished to be granted freedom in order to attend mass. This last reason was inspired. He said it just came to him in a flash!

The Abbess questioned me as to my full name, age and parentage, all of which would be needed to establish my identity. She also had me relate the details of the raid on her nunnery. That way she knew I was telling the truth. Gerhard swore to the fact that he knew I had lived as a freeman for more than one year. In the meantime she had ordered refreshments to be brought to us but I was so nervous that I could not eat a thing. It wasn't until she said that she would issue a temporary deed of manumission that my appetite returned. The bread and meat were the finest I had ever tasted. You see she had no love for the prince and certainly did not want to return me to his evil influence!

Clearing her throat discreetly, the Abbess read the document. I can still quote it now.

'I, UDDA, formerly of Woodcutts Farm, Sexpenna, of the manor of Sexpenna Hanlega, only son of UDRIC of Woodcutts Farm, do solemnly swear that having been free since Christmastide, in the first year of the reign of King Edward and served no master since that date, do claim manumission by right of freedom from this date, the ninth day of September 902 and this is my mark.' I can still recall the exact words all these years later. She made me swear an oath that I had lived by my own deeds and taken neither service nor served another from that date.

There was a lengthy pause, no-one spoke a word, perhaps to give weight to the oath, or to give the Almighty time to carry out retribution if I had lied. She said that it should be read in church before the congregation as if the Bishop himself had written it.

Later we learned that Prince Aethelwold had put aside the Lady Elise, the kidnapped nun, for being barren, and that she had done penance since that night. Apparently the Prince rode day and night for Northumbria where he joined forces with a Danish army. The King and his army of mercenaries followed, leaving the town untouched except for demanding stores. The King later fought the Danes somewhere North of London.

I scratched my mark on the Deed then pressed my thumb onto the wax before the Abbess wrote her name with a quill pen alongside, dating it with a flourish. Even now I can see her in her woollen habit, the gold cross hanging from a chain. I still have the deed, although it has needed a new wrapper from time to time.

After leaving the Abbess we went along the same little lane, to the market. Sheep were bleating, stallholders shouting. Maybe I was still a bit dazed from my good fortune but there were so many people it made me quite scared. We looked round the stalls and Gerhard made his purchases before sharing a mug of ale with me.

There were pots for sale on one stall and mine were indeed as good or even finer. You see, I needed money to buy an ox and sheep and also to provide a bride gift for Gerhard, to pay for your mother, you understand.

It took me all the long winter months to clear a field and prepare suitable timber for the house. Gerhard helped raise the cross beams. The pulling power of his ox made the task so much easier and by the first signs of spring the walls were almost watertight.

I finally caught a wild piglet and kept it in a thorn edged field with a small shelter where he grew quickly. At market one day selling my pots, I saw a young female pig going cheaply because she had dark marks on her back. I hadn't sold enough pots by then but Galena and her mother looked after the stall for me for a time and sold many more. Everyone likes a pretty girl!

At the seed seller's stall I exchanged three of the best pots for a quantity of corn. That was the first bargain I had ever done.

Finally buying the piglet for two pennies she was put over my shoulders squealing her protests loudly, much to the amusement of the other traders. She wet my new jerkin in fright. I should have taken my gift for the Abbess before I bought the pig.

I had spent hours decorating the lid with fine clay shaped into leaves and acorns. This was some of the finest work I had ever done. She thanked me and then told me that Prince Aethelwold had been killed in battle.

It was Gerhard who explained that now the Prince was dead I was automatically free and that it would be possible perhaps to go back to Woodcutts Farm, if it was still mine. May be also, to find out what happened to my family. The Wymburne priest, who could write, might approach the right people for me." Udda paused and looked round at the expectant faces around the fire. No one moved, only the dogs turned over to toast the other side beside the fire which had been fed with fuel so discreetly that he had not noticed. He stretched, took a long draught of ale, and then continued his tale.

Chapter Four

"It was probably two years before the shadows here no longer terrified me. The shuffling of night animals was so normal that I would have missed them had there been complete silence during the dark hours. Complete silence might even have been interpreted as an approach of danger.

You know, I used to talk to myself in the darkness. It helped me sort out any problems. With help the chores could be done more quickly, but I worried whether Galena would agree to come if all I could offer her was a life of work and considerable hardship. We all know it is the man's job to provide food, shelter and protection for his woman. In return the woman cooks the food, gives comfort and bears children, God willing.

It was then that I knew I could not leave Uddings, not just because the pigs could not be left for long without attention. Unless Gerhard and his family could be persuaded to come here for a season, I would have to forget my father's banishment for ever and accept that my mother and sister were lost to me. The injustice could not be swept from my memory but my love for Galena burned strongly and seemed the most important thing in my life.

I swore an oath that one day my father would be avenged. There were no witnesses but the sky darkened suddenly, a cold wind sweeping across the hill. Icy rain lashed down as I shouted defiance at the world. My forefather's gods seemed more powerful and much more tangible than the church and its Saints. I have always understood the reluctance of some older people to give up their more natural beliefs. Anyway I crossed myself to be doubly sure.

Shortly after, I had my first visitors. The two men were on the King's business but one horse was slightly lame. I knew that a messenger carrying the King's staff or other sign of office had the right to claim food and shelter but my own hut would hardly be good enough for such visitors. Hesitantly I told them that Wymburne was less than two hours walk from here and that they would doubtless be welcomed and well entertained at the King's own palace. However they made it quite obvious that they had no intention of going any further so I had no option but to take the two men to the clearing. From their clothes I could see that they were thegns of some standing, their horses being quality beasts. The mare had cut her foot on a sharp stone. Her head was lowered, each step causing her obvious pain.

The two men introduced themselves as Waergan of Worcester, younger brother of the Bishop of Worcester and Algar of Winchester."

Once again Udric could not prevent himself interrupting, remarking that he had not known of this first meeting between his father and his Good-father. He hugged Edith who was kin of the late Algar in whose service he had learned so much and who had been responsible for much of his good fortune in life. He was still grinning widely as Udda continued, frowning as he tried to remember the sequence of events.

"They used the house, such as it was, for their shelter. I looked to the horse's foot then made a meal of a hare from my store.

It emerged that they were on their way to Wymburne to prepare the Cynings Tun for a visit by King Edward. Since the seizure of the town by Prince Aethelwold, the King had not been to his palace, preferring to send his court officials to oversee the accounts and collect the revenue of his farm. Now he was coming to hunt deer in the forests and parks of Cranburne and Badberie for a few weeks. There would be feasting and entertainment at the court they told me.

I did not sleep well that night. For more than two years I had occupied the land and had called it mine, but it was undoubtedly part of the King's land. If the forest keepers felt that the hunting of the deer had been damaged in any way, punishment would be meted out. Even dogs are prevented from chasing animals in some forests by having two toes cut off. I would lose more than my toes if it were known that I had caught and eaten one of the King's deer!

The two courtiers woke early and left after thanking me for my hospitality and healing the mare's leg. I remember being so relieved; after all they could have recognised me as having been in the service of Prince Aethelwold. They might have known that I was sent back for his cup, to say nothing of the brooch. Being freed on one's master's death is one thing but to steal from him is quite another, besides my only thoughts at the time were to feed them and see them safely away in the morning. May be I should have taken the opportunity of returning the Prince's possessions but there was too much to think about.

The ground was raked for my first crop of barley that winter, the piglets having devoured every weed. I suggested we try roasting one of them at Christmas having invited Gerhard and his family to feast with me.

Of course, I could make no proper approach to Gerhard for your mother until I had joined a tything group. Although free, the stigma of being the kin of an outlaw could deny me membership. The court regularly met at the Cowgrove moot as it still does, but the first step was to go to Wymburne church. I found the priest, a young, fervent believer, not the elderly man with the tufts of hair, and asked him for advice. He asked my father's name and his father's name before he took my request seriously. I told him that our priest had been Bata, of Hanlega as well as Sexpenna and that the two communities were as one under the Church of Salisbury. It was unlikely that Bata had told him of my father's trial and punishment so I had to tell him the story, from the trial to the arrival of the King's men at Woodcutts Farm to evict us. When I mentioned that I had been with Prince Aethelwold when he kidnapped a nun from the nunnery he went quite pale!

Having examined the parchment from the Abbess reinstating me as a freeman, the priest said he would do what he could. We stood near the back of the church to hear the service at the end of which the priest held up his hands to demand silence. He requested that several leading men meet him outside. I was called over to answer questions. I told them of the smith who had removed the shackle, and the attack on me by a lay brother from Cranburne. They sent for the smith who verified my tale, but I could tell they did not want me joining their close knit society. An outlaw, or kin to one, was a person to be shunned. They turned me down and said that only a pardon from the King would change their minds.

We came back here for our Christmas feast and forgot our worries for a while. It would need money to approach the King. Don't forget I had seen courtiers at Winchester demanding payment from those wishing to see their royal lord. Then I remembered the visit of the two King's thegns, Waergan of Worcester and Algar of Winchester. If they remembered their night at Uddings they might put a word in for me. We were all excited but to pass the time I taught Galena how to make pots. I used to keep yellow clay under a mat, breaking pieces off with a sharpened pole before grinding it up. It had to be cleaned of all impurities before being mixed with a small amount of water to make it workable again. Together we worked the coil round, adding water and smoothing the surface as it built up. When we had finished we were spattered with clay like a couple of children, then we went to the stream to catch eels. Apart from the townsmen's refusal to adopt me it was a wonderful Christmas.

That was the time that I got the first dog. It was starving, and had a savage wound on one shoulder. It had cornered the pigs in the pen. It was too weak to jump out of the fold and thought I was going to kill it. It took me months to heal its wound and get it back to health. All our dogs are descended from that first Lymer-cross. They still use them now to dislodge a boar from its hiding place. There were similar reddish dogs in Winchester where they were led about by the court huntsman. They belonged to Lady Eathswith, King Alfred's widow if I remember rightly. But I digress from the point."

Udda fondled the ears of the dog which had been leaning against his legs. It looked at him adoringly before sinking down again across his feet. He drank ale and nibbled a biscuit thoughtfully. Edith adjusted her woollen kirtle as the baby moved so that she was forced to walk round for a few moments and relieve herself. Hastily adjusting her clothes she hurried back to listen to Udda who had not been aware of her absence.

"In spring we found out that the King was coming to his manor with his new Queen, so we set off to find the earls and hoped that they remembered me. My last time at the palace, don't forget, I was a very lowly part of Prince Aethelwold's court.

Luckily Lord Algar was there and recalled staying at Uddings. After telling him my story I finished by adding that I wanted to marry a neighbour's daughter but could not join a tithing group, because my father was still banished. He promised to look into the matter on my behalf. On the point of leaving, having thanked the thegn for his trouble, King Edward himself arrived. Apart from his gold circlet he was dressed in fairly ordinary clothes. We both bowed and I would have withdrawn immediately but instead of dismissing me Lord Algar spoke to the King straight away. He ordered me to fetch Galena and her parents. I was astonished, as were the soldiers on the gates. None of us were well dressed and probably none too clean.

Algar told us that the King had commanded that we accompany him to the great hall. I can still remember the King speaking to us.

"I understand that you wish to be married and that you are of age to do so. Our priest will witness your vows if you are ready."

Gerhard and Galena's mother looked totally bemused but nodded their consent to the King's request. Mind you, no one had mentioned a bride price!

The smaller building next to the great hall served as the King's chapel. We were taken to the porch where a lady waited holding a length of fine lace which she placed over your mother's head.

She looked so beautiful, the veil around her face and smiling at all of us. You see, the King, Algar, and some of his companions came to witness our marriage. The king kissed your mother you know, in front of everyone! Then he announced that he had given consent for this marriage, and that the assembled company bore witness.

Queen Aeflaed, a small, blond haired lady with the brightest blue eyes I have ever seen, introduced us to the King's son Aethelstan, and the baby Editha, whose mother had died giving birth to her. The queen was expecting a child too I believe. Anyway she took the baby away leaving Aethelstan, then a sturdy ten year old, to play with the dog. No one noticed when he wandered off until we heard him scream. Everyone turned towards the line of tethered horses which were plunging and pulling on their head ropes. The prince was almost beneath the beasts. I ran over and snatched him away, but got kicked for my troubles. The nurse was screaming hysterically, the child sobbing. The noise alone was enough to frighten the horses.

Algar had already cuffed the woman, threatening her with dire punishment if the little aetheling had been harmed. Fortunately only the Prince's pride had been hurt. There wasn't a mark on the boy, but after dusting him down he was taken away. The king was very grateful. Not only had I healed Algar's horse now I had saved the life of the future King! I was embarrassed with all the fuss. All we wanted to do was go back home. It was then that the King spoke of Uddings. My heart sank as I told him where it was and admitted scraping an existence there for some time. He asked me for details and I could not lie because Algar knew the extent of the clearing and of the house. Then the King asked me to become his man and I gave my oath with people crowded round to witness yet another ceremony. He summoned his clerk and dictated the gift of Uddings to me!

'I Edward, son of Alfred, King of the English, do hereby grant the land known as 'Uddings' to Udda my loyal subject for the period of three lives.' Actually, he first said two, and then altered it to three lives.

The King was beaming, as was Lord Algar who of course must have told the King of his overnight visit to Uddings.

I was ordered to tell the clerk the main points of the boundaries to ensure there was sufficient land, wood and water to sustain my family. These details would be added to the King's gift.

Your mother was completely overwhelmed by the proceedings and held my hand tightly. Even the dog sensed the atmosphere, occasionally pressing its cold nose against my leg. We were going to leave when Algar pressed a coin in my hand for a wedding present and advised me to mark each corner of our land and put posts at every point along the boundary within sight of each other.

We came back here bemused by events. Now I was a freeman with my own land, married and there was no proper bed for your mother!

We sat by the fire that night admiring the stars and the full moon. The old scarred dog sighed deeply with its head on its paw watching us. That was the night darkness spread over the moon until it had been completely blotted out. Galena was a Christian but the moon covering its face was something she had never seen before. Of course I comforted her as best I could."

Giggling at the memory of their first close embrace, Udda recalled the smell of her hair, the leaves on their clothes which told their own story to her parents when the light returned.

"We killed a pig for our wedding feast the next day. I still remember the taste now."

Smiling with the memory of the event he took a deep draught of the weak ale and continued to speak unemotionally now that his recollection was clear. The dog, a descendant of the old one, watched them curiously, its head on one side, puzzled by his master's inactivity. It scratched in a leisurely fashion as he continued and then lay down again.

"There was no furniture in the house except the hastily built bed in its log frame in one corner. A hole in the roof allowed the smoke out, but apart from the narrow doorway which let in very little light, there was only a small unglazed window at one end. Gerhard suggested tying sheaves to the wall at that end, out of reach of rodents, and storing the baskets of threshed grain on a raised platform beneath them. There was also room for a water jar, the precious store of fat and cooking pots. We put a screen between the bed and the doorway to cut down the draught and for privacy.

That year we caught another wild piglet. Well, actually Gerhard caught it but the dog kept the mother busy while he ran to the pen. At first the sow attempted to rescue her protesting offspring but she eventually backed off followed by her three remaining piglets."

The dog sat up wagging its tail, waiting to be praised. It had heard its name, even though Udda was referring to a long dead ancestor. Udda rubbed its ears thoughtfully and it lay down again content in his love. The rug had slipped from his shoulders but he seemed unaware of the cool wind rustling in the trees around them. Udric replenished the firewood while Edith fetched another ale jar. The moon was now sinking in the sky while small clouds scudded in the distance.

"We worked together to cut the first harvest of barley while the women collected autumn berries, roots and edible plants. We made a shelter for Gerhard's ox in the lea of the house and added the store room. By the end of each day everyone was tired but the improvements were essential. Your mother's parents stayed on here. In return, I helped my father in law cut and stack turf blocks on the heath, returning most nights to the comforts of Uddings. I thoroughly enjoyed his companionship. He was far more talkative than my own father had been, with no subject too sensitive to be discussed. While my family had been farmers at Woodcutts for generations, the land there was on a chalk slope with few trees. Uddings was mostly trees or scrub; hence clearing some grazing land had been an early priority. The ox pulled the trees out by the roots, instead of taking weeks to fell a single trunk by burning the base. I have shown you the blackened scars on the corner posts.

It was that winter when a burst of light across the night sky had startled everyone. Both women crossed themselves in fear before running into the house. This was the second strange happening in the night sky within a few months but apart from these events, life continued smoothly. We went to Christmas mass and chatted to the townsfolk afterwards. One or two people mentioned the shooting star but as no catastrophe appears to have befallen the town, it was soon forgotten. Our marriage at the Cynings Tun in front of the King had apparently caused more of a stir. Few realised it was me, the young man who had been refused admission to their tithe group.

Galena and I asked her parents to consider staying at Uddings on a more permanent basis. Gerhard had already given thought to a more settled life. He still had the ox cart which had come to him on his father's death when Lord Cenwulf, thegn of Dorsetshire at that time, had claimed the best beast. The one he inherited was but a young, weak animal, but with care and good feed it had improved. He had to deliver four cart loads of fuel to the royal manor each year but any more he could cut were his to sell or trade. The monastery paid immediately in coin, but most of his other customers rendered services or provided food in return.

As you know, he had no son to follow as turf cutter. Your grandmother's inability to have another child was inexplicable and she felt the lack keenly, but to my knowledge, Gerhard had never reproached her or put her aside to take a more fertile woman. They left the village of Holt and moved to Uddings permanently.

It was by common consent that meals were cooked and eaten round the one hearth in the same way that each person worked for the good of all. The ox grew fat through lack of exercise while the pigs flourished, working the ground enthusiastically in each new plot. The old dog guarded us, his russet fur re-grown over the wounds.

Galena shared the housewifely duties with her mother, and when the freeze gripped the ground and the wind blew cold enough to chill through to the bone, there was time to spin the small bits of fleece collected from the sheep drovers track to Wymburne. We had no sheep then you see but a loom stood in the light opposite the door.

It was shortly after your mother first realised she was expecting you that I went to my first Moot, now that I was a recognised land owner. We all went to Wymburne, the women to the market and Gerhard took turfs to sell. The few pots raised enough money for them to buy salt, nails and furs.

Work had already started on an extension to the house, a room for Gerhard and his wife, with a proper stall for the ox. Its warmth indoors was a valuable contribution to everyone's comfort and it lost less condition.

The final touches were put to the building as spring arrived with a day of weak sunshine. The whole building was now roofed with reeds. It was just after we had done this the sound of a horn warned us of approaching strangers. Galena and her mother had also heard it. They came out of the house with spindles still in their hands, wool spilling out of the bags slung round their shoulders. They were preparing woollen thread to make swaddling clothes for the baby.

It was three men on horses and two people on foot. One was a messenger from the King and he brought a written roll for me. It was the gift the King gave us on our marriage, the gift which restored my standing and my faith in my father's lifelong belief that his lord was just.

'In the year of our Lord 905, I King Edward, son of Alfred, by Gods grace King of Wessex, command that the land known as Uddings, lived on by my faithful servant Udda, formerly of Woodcutts Farm, Sexpenna, shall be his for three lives in return for favours and service which shall be requested of him from time to time. The land extends to one hide bounded by a stream on the South side, the edge of the woods to the East and North, while the West shall extend to the boundary road from North of Holt forest proceeding to Colhill and Wymburne.

Signed, Edward at Wymburne.'

Of course the man had to read it to me but the King had made this land mine in law. The deed is still kept in the clay pipe for safety. It is yours and your son's and who knows after that." Udda added looking directly at Udric whilst hitching the rug more comfortably round his shoulders.

"I was also commanded to take the two slaves as a gift into my household, and to meet with my Lord King on St.Cuthberts Day at Wymburne. The two slaves as you know were Owen and my little sister Jenna, of blessed memory. She was pregnant too but sadly, neither of them survived. It was a weakness since her birth you understand. Anyway, I must not be distracted by her tragedy.

The King's messenger was Brihtric, son of Algar, the King's server. He travelled with my Lord King wherever he stayed to hold court or to attend to business around the Kingdom. Lord Algar had apparently wanted to bring the deed himself but was too busy. I was so excited at seeing my sister again that it was a good thing he reminded me about the meeting with the king for it had already become of little importance compared to greeting my own kin after all those years.

Apparently, she and mother had been sent far away to work for a noble thegn on his manor farm. Mother had died some time the previous year of a wasting disease and since then she had shared quarters with Owen who had been very kind to her. A visiting noble had required an extra slave and had bought Owen for a good price. He had then examined her before buying her too, even though she was heavily pregnant. They had been taken first to Winchester and then made to walk all the way here. I was supposed to keep them securely but how could I do that to my own sister and her man? Owen could not speak much English – mind you I think he chose not to, so many people thought he too, was simple. At first they used my old shelter under the oak and told us their story during the coming days. The next morning, I explained to Owen that although they had been ordered to work for me there was no intention of keeping them shackled as slaves. Obviously I hoped he would stay willingly, not least because he was strong looking. He was dark haired then, and heavily branded on his forehead, but if he was my sister's mate and had cared for her in the past then he was welcome at Uddings. Your mother and my sister grew larger until both the births were imminent.

The main difficulty was that Owen refused to speak English. Gerhard and I showed him the land and stock while Galena and her mother tried to interest my sister in her new surroundings. But I digress ….

The two babies were due at almost the same time and we needed more room for Owen's new family. I also wanted his child to be born free. You remember my meeting with the King on St. Cuthbert's day. Well it was my intention, on the same day, to find a clerk who would write a deed to free Owen and my sister immediately. Who would have thought that I would ever have become someone's Lord?

I left the dog to guard the womenfolk at Uddings and went to Wymburne with Gerhard. It was a market day and he was going to sell my pots so that we could buy salt and utensils for the house. I can still smell the stench of the dye shop and the butcher's stall as I walked through. It brought back the memories of my time in Winchester.

Eventually I got past the sentries at both gates of the King's palace and reached the inner courtyard where your mother and I were married. There was time to look around, to take in the covered windows of the palace. My clothes were drab compared to the rich robes of the nobles who strutted around trying not to appear curious about me. The King's room was guarded by yet more soldiers but I was led through into the presence of my Lord Edward and seated on a bench next to Wilbert, a thegn of some standing. I tell you now, it was like a dream. Ale was poured out from a jug, which has since been copied many times, and I was questioned closely about my journey in front of all the men present. Apparently the King had received word from his sister Aethelflaed of Mercia to the effect that Ealdorman Aedwulf in the next county had been approached by the Danes who intended to invade Wessex. Rumour had it that their fleet was to land at Twyneham. Their army was to join forces with men from Northumbria and to invade from the North. The thegn had met secretly with the King's sister and told her of the plan even though the Danes had already taken his son as hostage. Danish spies were apparently already in Wessex and the King urgently needed his own local informants. Lord Algar was to stay at Wymburne so that messages could be sent to him at any time. If we suspected someone of being richer than they ought to be, or saw any activity that was unusual it was to be reported. In other words I was recruited as a spy for the King!

I remember being so surprised that I put more wood on the fire to hide my astonishment. No one else thought to do it. No doubt they thought I was a real country bumpkin. The door was guarded and no servants were allowed anywhere near the room. He gave us tokens so that Algar would know the messages were genuine. I still have mine, kept safe with the Deed of Uddings. It is jewelled, a copy of his own father's cloak stud. I kept it in my amulet bag for years but told no-one – men have killed for less than the value of such a gold piece.

We were dismissed after each of us had sworn an oath of loyalty and secrecy. Lord Algar beckoned me to follow him. Quite frankly I needed time to think before returning to Gerhard but I owed a debt of gratitude to the King's friend. It was bitterly cold after the heat of the King's room and I was glad to enter his tent. He had such luxury in there with tapestries on the floor as well as glass beakers for the ale we were served. A brazier glowed in the centre.

Spies could be crossing to Wessex disguised as traders, Algar told me. What we were to do was listen to gossip in the market place and at the quarterly moot where all the free men met, just as we do today.

The king had also told Algar that the special duty mentioned on my Deed involved caring for the royal horses when they were injured during the hunt. He produced another Deed then, for the extra hide of land. That's where we grow the best barley Udric. That area west of the woods, right up to the road which passes over Colhill and eastwards following the course of the stream to the ford as far as the road from Ringwood to Hortune. It was mostly heathland but the soil was good after the pigs had spent time on it.

Two surprises in one day – I nearly choked on my ale, and it was strong ale too!

Of course there was a catch to it. The king wanted me to note if I heard of horses being prepared for long distances. I had to bring two perfectly healthy horses back here to Uddings that day and return one if there was any news for Lord Algar. I then took any injured or lame horse back with me. I wore a headband to show that I worked for the king.

My head was whirling so much that I almost forgot to try and get a deed of manumission for Owen and my sister. When there was an opportunity to bring the subject up Algar smiled secretively. He admitted that it was he who had found my sister and arranged to send her, together with Owen to me at Uddings. He was putting forward a case to have my father pardoned. He said that the Sheriff had been unconvinced of my father's guilt right from the start but King Alfred's sentence could not be queried. Of course, it was thought he died shortly after and anyway, by that time I was a slave myself and could do nothing to bring the case to anyone's attention.

A clerk was summoned to write two documents. In case they were not legally married, Algar advised that the child would be free if my sister was freed first. I could then judge when the time was right for Owen to receive his freedom if he proved to be trustworthy.

By the time I left with the two horses, one in foal to Algar's own stallion, Gerhard had already returned to Uddings with the ox cart. Not being the best of riders I walked all the way back home leading the two horses. Neither of them was as good natured as that elderly brown gelding which first brought me to Wymburne. Imagine their surprise when I led them here, into the clearing! Apart from the fact that I did not possess a horn, there was no way to let go of the lead-ropes and wave. Gerhard and Owen had already armed themselves with staves until they recognised me. There were no stables then. We had to put them behind the house in the old ox stall for the night. Naturally I told everyone of the extra land which was for the keep of horses but only Galena knew of the jewelled stud I carried.

It was shortly after Owen and Gerhard had finished posting the new boundaries that Galena gave birth to you, Udric. In those days women went apart from the household into a small shelter. No sooner had she returned than my sister gave birth there to a puny girl child. I had given her the document by then. She was free and her child was born free. We kept it safe for her because she had no understanding and was confused with her pains.

When her child died the last vestiges of reason departed with it. She would not sleep with Owen again and we buried the child quietly in the woods up there."

Udda waved his arm vaguely in the direction of the trees behind and wiped his face on his sleeve. He took a sip of ale and ate a little pottage which Edith had discreetly heated for them all. In the East the first glimmer of the dawn light showed as a paleness against which the trees stood starkly against the increasing day. Refreshed Udda spoke again, his voice trembling with emotion at the memories he was recalling.

'We had to go to the moot after church a few weeks later. The earth was cold as we hunkered down to listen to the usual reminders of our responsibilities from the king's man. We were supposed to practice arms each week but few actually did this. Now we were told that defaulters would be sent to serve an extra term in the army. Obviously the king was taking the threat of invasion seriously and this was his way of ensuring that each man had his own arms ready for use. Some man was sentenced to be whipped for short weight loaves and there were a few complaints about missing stock and boundary quarrels. As usual we were also reminded about repairing the roads and taking our corn to the king's mill for grinding, something that all housewives hated doing if they owned a hand-mill of their own.

I needed to see Lord Algar on a personal matter not something to discuss with the King's servant. He was a small pompous man, puffed up with his own importance, and he was most put out when I met him later at the palace and my lord Algar welcomed me to his tent, shutting the curtain in his face. As there was no news to report there was no need to take one of the mares with me. You see, Lord Algar agreed to my request to act as your sponsor Udric.

Returning to Uddings there was pandemonium. My sister had gone missing. I found her much later with the help of the dog. He followed her scent. She had lost blood, all her blood, and just died deep under the trees. We stayed all night beside her in the darkness. The woods were shady enough in broad daylight but on a moonless night I tell you they are nightmare blackness. I could not move her on a night like that but made a sledge at first light and brought her body back here. Owen wanted her cremated and this was done. We put the little babe with her to give her comfort. Galena put her own bangle on my sister's limp arm. We found it many years later when the plough brought it to the surface."

This time when Udda wiped his face it was quite clear that he was wiping tears from his eyes. Edith held his hand suggesting that he was undoubtedly tired and should leave the rest for another time. Smiling, grateful for her concern, Udda sniffed loudly and cleared his throat rather noisily, spitting accurately into the fire.

"Owen did not leave after his woman's death but the morning of your christening I took him aside and offered him his freedom and a position of trust here if he would pledge fealty to me as his lord. So Owen became my first bonds-man. I took him to St Mary's church with us to watch Lord Algar hold you as you were given my father's name before all the townsfolk. To further astonish them, I granted Owen his freedom in front of them as witnesses. He made his oath before the altar of saint Cuthberga, to me as his lord and to King Edward as his monarch."

Udda chuckled to himself, his self control restored, as he recalled the people's astonishment, not only at Lord Algar acting as sponsor for his baby, but at a landowner freeing a slave. "And I didn't even pay for him in the first place, that's what was even better. I laughed with Owen all the way home!

It was after dark that night that a bright light moved across the sky as if in celebration of the special events of the day. This time we were not terrified at all but knew it was a good omen for all of us. The Danes did invade the north-east and made it their land but Dorset remained at peace. Horses came to us for healing and we taught ourselves to ride, even you as a small child had no fear of the biggest of them, Udric.

We all worked hard on the new fields during the day and made pots by the light of the fire at night. You tottered and fell, got picked up and dusted down by anyone close by. Even Lord Algar stayed overnight and brought toys for your amusement. He was still trying to find my poor father and persuaded me to accompany him to Winchester, using one of the King's horses. It was not only the banishment that irked me but the false accusation levelled against him by a neighbour. Apart from the use of the water on the boundary there had never been disputes between Guthrum and my father. I know the man was a poor farmer, not being keen on putting heart back into his land each autumn but that does not seem a good enough reason to accuse a man of such a heinous crime as murder. My father thrashed the messenger for raping Jenna but he did not kill him. Neither did he steal the purse. It always baffled me why our neighbour was so jealous of my father.

I wore the king's diadem on my forehead after having my hair cut for it had grown long and needed to be neater for the journey to Lord King Edward's capital. It's still a painful experience but was worse then with only our working knives to use!

We rode steadily talking about the old village where I grew up. The horses were rested at Cranburne where we had wine with the Abbot. Needless to say I did not remind him of the short time I had been secured in his stables or the beating at the hands of one of his lay-brethren.

Mentioning Sexpenna, the Abbot recalled that Bata, the village priest, had died shortly after the murder and my father's lands had been awarded to a distant relative on a high rent. The man had actually called at Cranburne and stayed with them having ridden in on an exhausted horse. The Abbot actually described the man – heavy browed, with dark hair. The one that beat me, then attacked me in Wymburne? Tell me does he sound like a relative of mine? No one in our family is heavy browed or very dark haired for that matter. We may even have Norse blood in the family somewhere. My hair was like straw when I was a lad. The Abbot was still annoyed because this man stole a horse from their stable when he left, leaving his own blown animal in its place.

We left as soon as we could without offence and I reminded Algar that no kin had stood by my father at his trial. As far as I knew there had been only a distant relation, being the younger son of his great grandfather, and I understood that he had been killed in King Alfred's wars.

In the village itself the reeve's house was in disrepair but we met the woodcutter who told me that the relative using my father's land was a younger son of man who had died in the wars. Called Garth, he had arrived only a few days after my father had been taken away. The same man who had come with the soldiers. The priest too, knew little of this man and less of my father's trial. He mentioned in passing that Bata had died at about the same time. It was difficult to be civil to him when it was quite obvious that he enjoyed his ale more than tending to his flock as Bata had done.

So that we could pass the farm without causing alarm we took the road to Shaftesbury planning to stop and pick a fictitious stone from the stallion's hoof on the track above the fields. We saw the man running towards us so Algar, who had recommended we both take the precaution of removing our headbands, remounted quickly and waved casually as we rode on, preventing him from getting close enough to recognize either of us. There was no doubt in my mind; it was definitely the man who had attempted to murder me. I remember sweating as I told Algar of the attacks in Cranburne and Wymburne. The original idea was to ride straight for Winchester but then Algar decided that his presence so near Shaftesbury might have been noted and that he could not be discourteous to the Abbess who was, after all, the late King's sister. Greeted enthusiastically by the lady Abbess and taken to her own quarters for refreshments we had to stay the night, sharing a luxurious guest chamber and could only leave after attending mass and breaking our fast the following morning. My thoughts were confused to say the least. I may have been somewhat impatient and short with my thanks, but to see that man on my father's land angered me beyond reason. We rode almost in silence for the rest of the journey.

Winchester appeared huge and daunting but at least this time I was not walking into it bound as a felon. As we passed the stockade I said a silent prayer for those within before following Algar into the royal hall where he demanded immediate admittance to the king.

The young Aethelstan came into the hall, obviously bored with his siblings so I spoke to him of his father's horses and he remembered being hauled unceremoniously from beneath the feet of the stallion. Quite unselfconsciously he took me outside to show me his own pony, a tough little beast that would have no trouble carrying the small weight of the prince. He stroked the glossy neck and buried his face in its fur. The pony clearly adored its little master, blowing down its black nostrils into the boy's jerkin.

The king's messenger summoned me to Lord Edward. His great table was covered with documents, some rolling to the floor while a young man frantically tried to keep them in order. Finally the clerk found the grant of Woodcutts farm and gave it to the King. The deed was for two lives only. It was made out in favour of Garth, younger son of Uder, once of Woodcutts, whose death was noted as being on the same day as King Aethelred. We calculated that my great, great grandfather had died in the year of our Lord eight hundred and sixty six, I think it was.

I knew that my father's father had been called Udric and that the name had been used in one form or another since. Bata would have known the family names as well as we did. It turned out that Garth had begged a favour from the king only days after my father had been banished.

Algar explained to me afterwards that King Edward was newly crowned and had needed to secure the revenue as soon as possible. Of course what I wanted to know was how Garth had known so quickly that the farm was vacant, but it was hardly the sort of question to ask one's King. We ate in the hall, where beside the fire a pile of kindling consisted entirely of broken roof tiles. Obviously I had not been the only slave who could not cut them properly!

After the meal Algar told me that the King had given permission for my father to be brought back to Wessex even though he could not repossess Woodcutts. I was now in a fever of haste to return to Uddings, not only was Galena pregnant again and I was anxious to be there for the birth, but the need to share my news with her was overwhelming.

Delayed by a messenger asking me to look at a sick hound dog, I was about to leave the kennels when the king sent word that he wanted me to take two slaves with me to help with his horses and other work at Uddings. To save time I chose Dai, the red haired boy who had once taunted me and then befriended me, and a sturdy companion of his.

I had to travel more slowly than I would have liked but passed the time telling Dai what had occurred since we last met. I told him the truth knowing my tale could be repeated to others, as these things are, only leaving out any mention of Prince Aethelwold's drinking cup and the jewelled brooch which remain secret to us.

Owen took the two slaves, who were both of his country as I had suspected, and fed them before accommodating them in the old oak shelter. Not that there is much left of it now but at one time it was snug and secure."

Udric nodded his agreement glancing quickly towards the oak tree which had now lost many of its once magnificent branches and much of its pitted bark. Edith filled the mugs from the jug, stretching her hips to try and remove the sharp pain which lanced down the back of her leg. She rubbed her thigh, massaging the muscles before resuming her place by the fire. Udda ran his gnarled hand over the domed head of the dog which sighed ecstatically, sliding down his leg to lie belly up. He rubbed its fur absent mindedly; his thoughts already back on the two slaves who had accompanied him from Winchester.

"They worked hard, those two, even after they discovered that there were no whips or punishment posts at Uddings, and were sorry when they were recalled to the King's court.

Meanwhile, Galena's mother sickened of joint ill and died. Only the crushed seeds of a flower gave her some relief at the end but she lived long enough to see your sister born. We named her Aelflaed, in honour of the king's wife who lent your mother the veil at our wedding.

We had the fowl by then of course, and had replaced the old forest boar. Oh, and a new cow had joined the ox in the pasture. There was now too much work for your mother. That's the disadvantage of a small community. She cooked for us all, so reluctantly we had been forced to send our grain to the king's mill for grinding and Galena made bread daily. She much preferred to use her mother's stone you see, but with two children to see to and all the other work I took the grain to the mill and went to the market while it was ground. Had a mug of ale while I was there too!" chuckled Udda mischievously, spilled his drink and hastily mopped it up with the back of his hand, embarrassed by his clumsiness.

"The king stayed at the palace and celebrated the New Year there that year but he had gone by the time the great snows came. The old dog was weak by this time and I took a pup from the palace kennels which would have been destroyed because it was of mixed breeding.

In fact from the mixed roan colour of it I am quite sure that our old dog sired it! He used to go missing sometimes and come back exhausted. Strangely, the old dog was not too put out by the youngster, just pushing it further away from the fire when it forgot who the senior was.

I buried him, beneath a tree. He had served me well and been my companion for many years and deserved decent burial. The children would have been upset had I just thrown its body on the midden heap.

Of course, you made a pet of the young dog Udric, but you did teach it to follow a scent as well as herd the stock."

Udric nodded, remembering how he had been upset when the pup had been whipped for killing a fowl.

"Mother tried to explain why the pup had been punished but I bawled my eyes out when I was out of her hearing." Udric admitted, rubbing the back of his neck. He glanced at Edith fondly, loving the fullness of her body and the firelight shining on her dark hair. She felt his eyes on her and smiled shyly, raising her mug and taking a sip of ale.

Udda cleared his throat noisily and continued his tale.

"As I said, we had to return Dai and his friend to the palace after half a year, taking two mares back at the same time. That was when I heard of the invasions. The king now demanded more men for his army, each village being obliged to send every available man which was not popular because it was almost harvest time. At the moot I heard my name had been listed but the King's clerk was later instructed to forbid me to go because I healed and tended the King's precious horses. Owen had to go in my place which was a sore blow to us. But even this calamity was entirely overshadowed when Lord Algar sent word that my father had been found in mid-France. He was sick, not just in the body, and still bitter after all the years. God forgive me, I did not recognise my own father. We had to bring him back to Uddings on a cart.

Gerhard moved his own bed so that your grandfather could lie closest to the fire. He said that it would take time to heal his mind but I think the hurt was too deep. I often talked to my father of Woodcutts farm, of Garth and the events before his banishment but he was too confused to really understand and frequently called us by the wrong names. Your grandfather spent hours staring at the fire or stroking the dog. Galena fed him the choicest morsels but gradually it was like having two babies to care for. He never really recovered although he helped outside on fine days.

When the Danes invaded Mercia the king's main forces were off the shores of Kent so it was our men who fought them off and became rich with the rings and brooches they took. Owen brought back a sword and tales of terrible deeds of cruelty he had witnessed. It's not for nothing that we say the prayer 'A furore Normanorum libera me Domine', from the coming of the Danes, Lord deliver us. I have said it with great fervour ever since.

The king's sister kept control of her country even after her husband Aethelred was killed, and those who owed forty days fyrd service provided the labour to build fortresses along the borders. Much of the land that the Danes had occupied was now under the king again but many thought that our southern towns were providing more than their fair share of soldiers. The Queen had brought the children with her and taken refuge at Wymburne so that many people became wealthier by supplying woollen cloth and meats for her household. Udric played with the young prince and his half brothers and sisters every time I took horses to or from the palace stables. Thegn Algar was already quite old by then but he was the one who was so much in favour of you joining the young Prince at his lessons."

Udda chuckled at the memory of his son's face on being told he was to be taught his letters by the Prince's tutors. So much of the family's good fortune had come from those lessons, even if Udric had been the butt of cruel pranks and childish attempts at bullying before the present friendship had developed.

"Your grandfather died peacefully and was buried by the church in Wymburne. I know that his sickness had been caused by treachery back in the days of King Alfred but my Lord Edward was generous to me and my family so it would have been ungrateful to pursue the matter of his banishment after his death.

Now my children I am old and cantankerous and would rest these old bones. Sleep will be easier now. I shall dream of your mother, my beloved Galena."

Udric and Edith glanced quickly at each other, smiling secretly. They had intended to only stay one night and were both exhausted, having stayed up to listen to Udda's saga. Sometimes the tale had been rambling, parts repeated but essentially they had heard the story of the founding of Uddings.

Chapter Five

Pounding the dough energetically, Galena made it plain that she was loath to part with her only son at such a young age even though there could only be benefits from such an unusual opportunity. She frowned as flour dropped from the board, her lips pursed with concentration. Although her hair was well covered with a white cloth, wisps of brown curls escaped and had obviously been pushed to one side with a floured hand.

"Udric is half-way to being a man and well grown for his age, dear wife, let the boy leave here with your blessing. Learning his letters is more than enough reason for him to go. We may see him from time to time when the princes are at their father's palace here." Udda said persuasively.

He could of course have insisted that the boy went, with or without her consent, but most decisions were made after they had talked quietly together, sometimes long after everyone else was asleep.

Comforted by this thought Galena hastily set the loaves to rise and brushed the flour from her hands. The baking was late because earlier she busied herself cleaning her son's best tunic. She had sewn a new leather belt to hitch the fine woollen fabric around his slender waist so that he would no longer resemble a newly dressed toddler. The soft green fabric, the colour of newly unfurled beech leaves, had been woven in Wymburne. Bands of darker hues just above hem added style to the simple garment.

Reminded for the last of many times to remember all that he had been taught by his parents, Udric kissed his mother a fond farewell. "Of course I shall behave. When do I not?"

Galena laughed and aimed a slap at his bottom now accentuated by the new belt which he had pulled as tight as possible. He avoided the blow easily, giggling as she once again pretended to chastise him. He did not see her tears as she watched him walk away down the track with his father. She did not notice the sunlight penetrating the young leaves on the trees, nor the fowl busily pecking in the leaf-mould. Turning reluctantly to resume her bread-making, her daughter dragging at her hand, Galena's steps were heavy as she returned to the kitchen. Her thoughts were all on Udric, her firstborn and his journey to the far side of Wymburne where her precious son would doubtless grow away from her and the household who loved him.

Udda had heard that young lordlings went to the household of another at a similar age. It was supposed to prevent a male child clinging to his mother, but in his class of people this exchange of boys was not normal. For a child of his to learn to read, was well beyond the expectations of a farmer. "Even my father could only write his name. I wonder if Udric will learn Latin for that is the language of the court, the church and lord Algar, for I have heard him talk in that language. Even my own speech had a different sound to his. The boy will learn to speak nicely, even if it is only by listening to those around him."

"At first, father, I did not look forward to lessons but it will be fun to learn with the Prince. Will I go to the capital do you think?"

"There you go again, more questions! At first it may be better to listen to your elders. Perhaps there will be other boys sharing the Prince's tutors. Lord Algar arranged this opportunity for you so make sure he does not regret it. Quite honestly son, your mother and I are just as nervous as you probably are. I did Lord Algar a favour many years ago but never dreamed that a son of mine would be taking lessons with princes. Do your best and learn all you can. There may be times in the future when reading and writing will be useful," stated Udda straightening his tunic and trying to keep his face innocent of the wonder that was deeply affecting both he and his beloved Galena.

Udric had been so excited to be going on this new adventure. All the time there were so many questions, almost always starting with 'Why?' and most of which neither she nor Udda could answer to his satisfaction. The great day had arrived, the day on which he would really grow up and Galena had dreaded it. So far she had hidden the ever ready tears so that she would not upset him or Aeflaed who was too young to understand that her adored brother was going away.

The summer sun had not yet warmed the earth enough to dispel the chill of the night when they set out. While they made their way down the sunken lane Udric was happy to hold his father's work-calloused hands, but as soon as the town was in sight he strode out, calling out in his treble voice for Udda to make more speed. It would not be long before the child's voice took on the deeper tones of a man but first would come that interim period when the timbre could not be relied on, a cause of embarrassment to many. No doubt Prince Aethelstan already spoke in a manly way.

Accompanied to the huge gates by Udda, the boy entered the King's court with only the briefest nervous glance at his father. The guards had stopped them at the entrance but let them pass when it was explained that Udric here by invitation of the aetheling Aethelstan and two of the younger princes. Asked to wait beside the guardhouse the boy had time to look at the courtyard where men at arms were practicing. Covered in armour of hardened leather the two men were giving no quarter, their weapons flashing in the sunlight. When one man slipped Udric gasped in dismay fearing that blood would be shed. His attention was brought back to his father when he coughed lightly. A bodyguard had been summoned and it was he, magnificently dressed with a red and yellow tabard showing the King's lion, who led the way through the hall to the royal apartments.

"Your father may return home now Udric if you would like to say goodbye. The Princes have been told of your arrival and are eager to meet you so let's not keep them waiting." The bodyguard spoke unemotionally but hinted that the leave-taking should be a short one. There was an enigmatic smile on his face as he watched father and son embrace. Many years ago he too had been left with strangers and remembered the wrench from all that was familiar.

"God keep you son." Udda had intended to be strong, fatherly, and unemotional at this parting but his blessing hid inner feelings which were in turmoil. A quick hug, reciprocated by the young boy, and Udda turned away to walk alone, back the way they had come only an hour before. He did not notice the singing of the birds or the clear blue sky being only aware of the loss of his son who only moments before had chatted and giggled beside him.

A great sense of loneliness descended on him. The hill was unaccountably steeper, the leafy trees plunging the lane into deepest shade which matched his mood. Speaking aloud to the Almighty he voiced his sadness, his feeling of bereavement before asked God for forgiveness for his selfish thoughts. When he strode out into the brightness of the sunlight blessing the heathland with valuable warmth it was as if his prayer had been answered for Udda was suddenly conscious of feeling calmer, of accepting this wonderful opportunity for his son for what it was, a chance to rise in the world, to prosper beyond Udda's wildest dreams.

Udric marvelled at the colourful hangings and the carved chairs set about the hearth, staring at the patterned shields propped against the corner posts. The hearth-thegn encouraged him to keep up by putting a large hand on the boy's shoulder. Udric felt oddly comforted by the warmth of his grip through the fabric of his best tunic as he was ushered into the room where the princes studied. There were tiles on the floor and a brazier to provide warmth. Light was provided by the open window and by beeswax candles fixed on sconces nailed to the posts in the wall. A pile of books lay carelessly on the trestle table. Stools had been positioned neatly along one side, all suddenly, and no doubt gratefully vacated when the heavy leather curtain was pulled back.

The King's guard attempted to make formal introductions to each of the princes in turn. Good manners momentarily forgotten, the young boys stared at their visitor. Udric bowed uncertainly but was completely taken aback when Prince Aethelstan bounded across the room, ignoring the tutor's annoyance at the interruption.

"Come on, I've had enough lessons for today." Pulling Udric out of the room, the two young lads dashed into the room where they all slept. It was little more than a rectangle of stout screens off the hall but afforded a little privacy for those within. "This is your bed, next to mine" announced the prince proudly, pulling out a large paillasse, a linen mattress stuffed with straw and covered with many furs and rugs. "We can talk when the others are asleep. Now come and see the puppies."

Completely under the older boy's influence, Udric was infected by the excitement of the moment. Charging down the outside staircase to the courtyard, servants stopped to gape as the boys ran into the barn, laughing as they raced each other to touch the log posts. Inside the familiar smell of hay, barley, root crops and animals reminded Udric momentarily of home and he paused, a lump in his throat preventing speech. Aethelstan strode confidently to a corner where a hunting dog had whelped, the tiny puppies lying in a row, like peas in a pod, beside her swollen belly.

"This one is to be mine" announced the prince picking up the largest dog puppy. "Do you want one?"

Udric knelt beside the bitch and stroked her head, whispering endearments. She stretched to encourage him but did not disturb her suckling brood. The glossy fur was smooth beneath his hand. Tentatively he stroked a puppy. "You mean that? Would you have to ask permission, of your father I mean?"

"Oh probably, they belong to my lord father, but if I ask him he will let you have one. You have a dog at home though don't you?"

They talked for a while of the brindle dog at Uddings then moved on to watch the smith working.

Sparks were flying from his anvil, falling on the beaten earth where they died. The air was filled with the peculiar smell of hot iron and steam. The underlying body odour of the smith was ignored as the boys watched the horse-shoe take shape before it was plunged into the trough of water. Spluttering and bubbling, the droplets reflected the red glow of the furnace built against a stone wall. Udric's eyes widened in admiration, noting the huge muscles of the smith's forearms, the breadth of the man's chest. He sucked in his breath to expand his own small chest to its maximum but let the air out with a rush when the smith looked up smiling, showing the many gaps in his teeth.

"I am hungry. Let's go to the kitchens and see if the cook has any treats." Aethelstan confidently pushed aside the leather curtain and entered the gloom. "Come on, you are hungry too."

Udric followed the prince and was unable to prevent his mouth falling open in sheer surprise at the size of the kitchen. Shining pans hung along one wall reflecting the light from the huge fire which had been allowed to die down to a deep red glow. Baskets of firewood were ready to bring it back to life when needed. A massive trestle table was being used by an army of minions under the direction of the fattest man Udric had ever seen. His forearms, above the crease which marked his wrist, were covered with coarse black hairs which made him appear dark-skinned but his face was split by a huge grin when he noticed the two boys.

"Young master, welcome to my domain! I rather thought you might visit when hunger's pangs visited! There might be a little something, if I can remember where they have been hidden."

Making great play of searching high and low for the missing treats and surreptitiously watching as Prince Aethelstan's face looked more crestfallen by the second as he failed to find anything, the cook produced a basket of tiny bread rolls containing melted curd cheese, as if by magic or sleight of hand. The gasp of surprise from his two visitors was sufficient thanks! This game was obviously played frequently; the Prince enjoying the cook's little pretence. It was not long before every one had been demolished and followed by mugs of light ale. Clearly it was not unusual for the Prince to eat between the more formal meals and the heartfelt thanks mumbled through a mouthful of crumbs and a badly disguised belch were all the praise required by the cook. Standing arms akimbo in the doorway of his kitchen, his vast stomach emphasised by the white linen apron, he beamed from ear to ear when the Prince and Udric muttered their thanks and bade him goodbye.

Apprehensive at first in such awesome surroundings Udric soon came to enjoy the lessons in repetition, calculus, Latin and French under the priest's watchful eye. Although he was starting well behind all three princes, a natural curiosity and keenness helped him to make quick progress with the letters and numbers that would be required for more advanced studies. His wax page and stylus were rapidly covered in the forms and shapes required by his tutor. Under his guidance, in the light of real wax candles, the young boy soon advanced to words of more letters and syllables. There were one or two squabbles when a younger prince outshone Aethelstan, much to the exasperation of the harassed teacher. Udric quickly found that it was not wise to outdo his friend, tending to make less of his achievements than the tutor did. After all, he would have less need of Latin and writing skills than the prince in the future so Udric stored the learning in secret parts of his mind. He learned of other countries and cultures; that salt water seas surrounded the land of England. Never having seen a wider expanse of water than the width of the river Stour at Wymburne it was hard to imagine a great ocean.

King Alfred's retired bodyservant, a man of great dignity and age according the princes, taught them etiquette, both for general manners and the rules of the hunt. Having been injured in the northern battles, he now limped. When he was younger, he explained to the princes, he had taught their father, the lord Edward, so he knew exactly what standard they must reach. He showed them how to clean their hands and nails, taught them table manners and how trophies of the hunt should be distributed.

Yet another man, a grizzled soldier of some experience, taught the boys to handle arms in mock battle and ride the ponies. This was Udric's favourite lesson. He was far and away the best of the boys, both at balance and tricks. He did not mind what the weather was like when they went out to practice on the nearby meadow. The younger princes grumbled if they got wet or cold but were brusquely told that battles did not wait for the weather to be pleasant.

"It's all right for him with his cloak, helmet and long boots. We have to ride in just our tunics and braes. I'm frozen to the marrow. My fingers are so cold, how does he expect us to grip a lance?" grumbled Aethelstan putting one hand under his armpit to try and restore some circulation.

Indeed, when the princes returned to their chamber and warmed their fingers at the brazier the two younger boys hopped up and down in agony when the warm blood returned.

"I suppose it would be too girlish to ask the cook for goose grease? My chilblains are throbbing!" complained Udric clenching his fists. "My mother would have used it by now," he thought, trying to hide the pain of the swellings.

At the end of each day the boys took turns to serve as a page at the high table holding clean napkins and a bowl of water for hand washing. Mistakes were punished quickly and severely, even the elder aetheling not being exempt from his tutor's cane. After he had received a blow for splashing some water on a visitor to the royal palace Aethelstan was particularly critical of the treatment he had received.

"By God's Blood, Udric, one day I will snatch that stick of his and break it across his own arse! When I am king,…"

"Sh.. he'll hear you," reminded Udric who could not help sympathising with his friend. "But I swear you did it on purpose. You are not such a numbskull usually. Were you looking at that girl?"

"I may have been, but next time you can serve Lord Walter. He is one of those men who demand instant obedience and tells tales to my lord father. He's a prig of the first order and his sons copy him. My servants do what I ask because they love me not because I am royal and could punish them for disobedience. My brothers do not understand that one needs friends, people who can be trusted like you."

Udric blushed at the unexpected compliment, thrilled to be considered the friend and trusted confidante of a Prince. He was about to reply with fulsome gratitude but some inner caution prevented the words from being spoken. He nodded instead before distracting his friend with a suggestion that they once again check on the progress of the puppies because they would be ready to leave their dam any day now.

Udda saw his son occasionally; never ceasing to marvel at the transformation, for the boy was far more richly dressed than he had ever been, while reports of Udric's aptitude for both learning and sports were glowing. Although he confined his visits to the stables, talking to the horsemaster and his assistants, they passed on to him the gossip and news picked up at dinner in the hall. The stalls were roomy with mangers and feed bowls built against the far wall. Udda had little fear of the large beasts, ducking under the bar to feel suspect legs or stifles. Hoping for tidbits most of the horses nosed his jerkin or blew gently into his face, their whiskers only an inch from his cheek.

On occasional visits home to Uddings the growing boy related stories of court life, sometimes imitating his monkish tutor. He also told them of the aetheling's prowess in armed combat, his voice full of admiration for the older boy.

"It would have been selfish if we had denied him this chance do you not think lass?" suggested Udda one night after the household had retired. "Mind you, he talks of things I have never heard of, never needed to know I suppose."

"One of my fears was that he might get too wrapped up with his royal friends and not want to come home. He must surely consider this house to be rather humble. I pray every day that he stays safe, that he continues to love us. Fine clothes and learning might turn his head but it's a risk we took and I for one do not regret it." finished Galena proudly. She too had admired Udric's new clothes which he had told her hung on pegs on the wall above the bed. He now wore boots with soft leather around his ankles. They had been made for him by the cordwainer in Wymburne who had been called to the palace to make a form of his foot to ensure a good fit. 'Funnily enough,' thought Galena as she drifted off to sleep, 'I never asked who paid for these things? And did I imagine it or does he speak slightly differently?'

Returning a rested horse to the royal stables some months later Udda saw his son riding, a merlin perched on his gloved wrist. The master of the mews was checking the small leather straps which were attached to its legs. Concentration was complete; the boy was totally unaware that he was being observed, least of all by his father. Udda himself was so engrossed that he started when Algar spoke to him.

"I hear you have volunteered again for the army."

"Forgive me my lord, I was watching Udric and did not hear you approach. I feel guilty that I am exempted from serving. Some men at the moot and on Sundays too, mutter that it is nothing short of favouritism. After all, the king has given me land and now my son lives like a lord and grows more noble-looking every time I see him." Udda waved his hand towards the departing riders now passing out of the great wooden gates. Although a competent rider now, Udda could not have risked using only one hand for the reins, never mind holding a bird steady on the other wrist. He smiled at the mere thought of it.

"Indeed my godson is nearly a man now and he will undoubtedly bear arms for the king in due course. In the meantime you serve the King best by keeping his beloved horses well. Several births have been difficult but you have increased his stables considerably. He is tired of constant travelling and fighting. Soon he will come to rest and hunt again. He is grateful indeed for loyal servants and friends who do not constantly seek reward or favours. His silversmiths and jewellers are kept busy making rings and tokens with which to reward services but now that his territory is larger he seeks people he can trust to oversee the burghs on his behalf. Come to him here with your wife. He had fond memories of the day he helped to get the two of you married. Leave your serfs to look after Uddings for a day or two."

They reminisced for a few moments longer before Algar remembered his duties. He sent his best wishes to Galena then returned slowly to the hall, his clerk following a few paces behind. Age was now evident in the way Algar walked although he did not yet rely on a stick. Once a fine, broad-shouldered man, his frame seemed to have shrunk so that his elaborately embroidered tunic creased into folds where his sword belt hung above his hips.

'I did not like to remind him that there are no slaves at Uddings' mused Udda smiling to himself as he turned for home. The refusal to let him serve in the fyrd would no doubt cause problems again. 'They say that being a new-made man, I will become the worst kind of snob, one who looks down on others. Many have inherited land from their fathers worked with sweat and tears whereas mine was given to me without any apparent effort on my part. Well, they do not know the facts and they will not hear them from me! Why do people make judgements so quickly? I would rather take a man at face value than suspect him of ulterior motives. Maybe that is a bit naïve, simplistic, but God knows, life is too short to foster suspicion or jealousy.'

Relating his conversation with Lord Algar to Galena she agreed that he appeared to be growing older very rapidly.

"It is good of him to be interested in Udric; for all that he is the boy's good-father. When they all went to the King's court, life around here became very quiet. The market is still busy but the trades-people have much less work and do not spend as much. When the princes come with all their servants and the men who teach them there is a constant flow of messengers along the track. I am getting to recognize one or two of them now. It must be Algar and his clerks who wave each time they pass. There are always men at arms with them. They of course, look neither right nor left at humble folk like me but my heart gladdens to know that Udric is back here at Wymburne. Not only are the princes well guarded here but our boy may have time to visit us."

CHAPTER SIX

Two years passed in relative peace due almost entirely to the fortification of the burghs. These formed a defensive ring on the boundary of the Kingdom. The coasts were also guarded to prevent seaborne invasions of Norsemen. Great wagon loads of stone were drawn all over King Edward's lands. There was a rash of complaints about the wheels of the heavy carts breaking the surface of roads. Officials shrugged, unconcerned that even the smallest property owner was responsible for the road outside his house or farm. Without constant repairs, the surface of the tracks became deeply mired in winter months. Deep ruts froze solid so that beasts could not pull the mighty loads of rock to the towns. Delays threatened the safety of the land; masons argued that they could not build in winter, but the King's officials seldom took much notice of those they considered to be their inferior.

Constant rains, flooding of rivers and grazing lands caused even stored grain to moulder. Each winter in turn seemed to be worst than the last. Everywhere the silver glints of standing water, puddles so vast that when they froze children skated on solid ice.

The king stayed a few nights at each town, praising or chiding the workmen, rewarding the leaders with rings, swords and jewels. Sometimes Aethelstan, accompanied by Udric, went with his father but as only three princes had survived childhood, his safety was considered paramount to the succession. In Wymburne, near the heart of Wessex, guarded by the King's loyal soldiers, the Princes were relatively safe.

When there had been rumours of unrest any stranger was suspect. In Wymburne an innocent pedlar had been given a hostile reception until a former customer from an outlying village had spoken up for the man. His pack had been tossed to the ground, many of the wares suffering in consequence. Appeals for compensation had fallen on deaf ears and all because the man had a cleft palate and had been unable to make himself understood to the town's constable. At the moot similar tales were told with relish, each man trying to outdo his neighbour recounting stories of eager watchfulness. Watching the naked glee in the expressions of those who had bragged of their own prowess, Udda was sickened by the mindless violence being done to travellers. On returning to Uddings he had immediately provided his field-workers in the outlying pasture with a horn in case of trouble. "I cannot afford to criticise others for their obvious enjoyment of the pain they inflicted and then not take adequate precautions on our own land," he stated to Galena embracing her gladly. "You would think there was a hob-goblin beneath every bush the way they were describing the increased state of tension in the land. One or two acted first and thought afterwards. A bruise or welt is nothing but somebody is going to cause a death before long."

"Oh love, that is exaggerating surely! I did hear of that poor pedlar though. The King fears invasion but foreign spies are not going to come to a small town like ours. Surely they would try to enter the ports?" she queried, the frown lines becoming pronounced on her normally smooth forehead.

Udda agreed between mouthfuls of hot potage. Although it was little after mid day the daylight was already fading, a uniform greyness of sky with no discernable clouds stretched from one horizon to the other. Few birds wasted effort on singing; only the buzzard overhead screamed defiance at the world at large. Udda added fuel to the fire to dispel the gloom, sparks rising sharply from the disturbed embers.

"I guard your back; see that you do not drink too much and that if you do, the King does not find out! It's father Benjamin who is more likely to sneak on us now that we have more or less grown too old for lessons. He hangs around muttering hell-fire and damnation should either of us eat before he has finished grace at mealtimes. He is so long winded and most of us are hungry. God love us, Aethelstan, does he have to ride with us all the time?"

Punching his friend lightly on one shoulder which was almost the same height as his own, Aethelstan responded light-heartedly. "What the eye does not see the heart will not grieve over. We can out-ride him anytime. Next time we hunt we can give him the run-around. Beat you to the river!"

Dashing off without warning Udric was left at a disadvantage. He ran faster, leaping over dogs and hens which seemed to conspire to get underfoot and hamper his attempt to catch Aethelstan before he got too far ahead. In the warm sunshine they played in the river, the local boys who were taking the same opportunity backing off to leave the Prince and Udric the best swimming spot. Willows edged the bank which shelved steeply into the fast flowing water. Sunlight danced off the ripples and the spray as they swam briskly before climbing out to dry themselves.

"We smell much fresher wouldn't you agree my fine lord!" joked Udric, "mind you, it looks as if it is time you shaved."

Aethelstan had been embarrassed when his voice had started to break, sometimes in the middle of a sentence leading him to flush with embarrassment. "Do you really think so? It's not much more than fluff really. Thought I might grow a beard, you know, make me look a bit older." He stroked his chin, imagining the fair beard which might be there in the near future. His face had character having already lost the chubby look of a child. Either side of a long straight nose his grey eyes revealed little of his thoughts and missed even less.

"It might," agreed Udric after some thought, pulling on his tunic and fastening the belt. He had been offered much grander belts but preferred to use the one his mother had made for him when he first left Uddings. It seemed like keeping faith with her and he knew she was touched to see him still wearing it.

They talked, as young men do, of girls. Neither of them had done more than fumble under the kirtle of a kitchen maid or stolen a few kisses and been chased by the cook for their trouble. Gone were the days when a platter of sweetmeats would be forthcoming when either of them dared to enter that man's domain. His temper was legendary, no man's rank protecting him from harsh words or invective that few gently born men had heard before. Udric had taken to other methods of satisfying their hunger between meals. If a dish of something tasty was close to him at a meal, it would be removed from the trestle after the older men had left and before the servants came to clear away. It had to be kept safe from prying eyes, especially those of Father Benjamin who would doubtless tell tales at the first opportunity. From there the illicit rations would be sneaked up to their room for consumption during the night, especially if Aethelstan had been unwell for he lost weight rapidly. Food had to be chewed slowly not gulped down in his haste to satisfy an immediate hunger, but even so, there had been many occasions when Udric had been obliged to hold his friend's head while he heaved the contents of his stomach out of the window.

Numerous times the King's physician had tried to treat the Prince with purges and even bleeding on several occasions. This had left him exhausted and very bad tempered so that it had been mutely agreed between him and Udric that little mention would be made of the bilious attacks. The night-time nibbling of delicacies purloined from the table continued in unspoken conspiracy. Udric still slept alongside the prince, further security for the safety of the King's heir. It also promoted the deep friendship which had formed between two young men, regardless of rank.

Trying to be the friend of all the princes had been a dismal failure. The younger boys now had their own tutor and shared another room after they had mocked Udric for his manner of speaking and cast doubt on the benefit any learning be to one of his background. The quarrel had involved all four boys in a no-holds barred fight. Fortunately none of them had been armed for the bitter ill-feeling against Udric by the two boys ran deeper than either he or Prince Aethelstan had imagined. They had been separated by irate tutors and guards, but even being man-handled by powerful adults had not stopped the hurtful name calling by Edwin, half brother of the older princes.

For weeks Udric felt as though he were tip-toeing around the royal court, wary of calling attention to himself, suspecting every friendly overture. Conversation stilled the moment he entered the chamber only re-commencing when he left the room. Inwardly hurt by the injustice of the taunts he became gaunt, the new tunic once again appearing several sizes too large. His eyes which had always been watchful now filled with apprehension and fear.

Often he heard men discussing him. Snippets of conversation lingered long after he had left the vicinity of the speakers. It seemed that men thought he was rising above his status, taking advantage of the King's good nature and worse, that he was yet another of the King's bastards. The last caused the final, major upset, occurring in the courtyard outside the hall. In full view of rooms occupied by Lord Algar or one of the other lords sent to prepare the King's Tun for the arrival of King, Edwin had taunted Udric beyond all endurance. Their tutor had impressed on them that honour was to be valued above all other traits. This and many other lessons in manners were totally forgotten when the young prince suggested that Udric return to the peasant whore who had birthed him.

While evenly matched in height and weight Udric was spurred on by the vulgar slur against his mother's standing in the community. On one occasion he pinned Edwin to the ground, kneeling on one arm while pressing his own thumbs into his protagonist's windpipe. With cold dispassion he watched as Edwin's face first went red, his eyes appearing to bulge from their sockets, then grey as the fight went out of him.

He felt strong hands pull him away but could not for a moment hear the man's voice for the beating of his own heart. It took some time for the fever of rage to calm, to be replaced with dread for what he had done.

Edwin's face was once again puce and his breathing ragged. He fingered his throat tenderly. Already two purple bruises were deepening in colour. Any threats he issued against Udric lost their impact because the boy had little but a hoarse croak in which to deliver them, his breathing sounding like broken bellows.

"I'll see you hung for this! You almost killed me, you lick spittle churl! Father will not forgive this insult. You and your kind will suffer and I will be glad. Get out of my sight."

Udric turned away from the malevolent gaze of the prince who continued to call on heaven to witness his injuries and his oath of revenge.

"Jesus Christ! He's right; the King will not forgive an attack on one of his precious sons. Father is not the only one who will be disappointed in me."

"Are you talking to yourself or can anyone join in?" laughed Prince Aethelstan. "You did no more than take revenge for his insults over many months. Father might not be too pleased as Edwin said but I know he will ask to hear both sides before giving any sort of judgement. We have all heard his taunts; he has been reminded many a time to treat others as he would like to be treated. That's Saint Benjamin's maxim by the way!

I cannot take his side even though he is my half brother. Insulting you with taunts and jibes is childish and we have been told to ignore that sort of behaviour, but when it comes to casting aspersions on ones' parents that is different.

The servants are moving his bed and that of Prince Aelfweard into another chamber. So we will have my room to ourselves; we can talk or bring wenches in without being watched by goggled eyed youngsters."

To hide the tears of relief that threatened to un-man him before his friend Udric bent down to re-fasten his boot. That the Prince would support him should the King hear of the thrashing he had given Edwin was a sign of the genuine friendship which completely disregarded their difference in status.

"I thank you for your support. As you say, taunts and name calling did not really bother me but when he called my mother a …. whore," he whispered the dread word, then everything went red. I wanted to kill him, really I did. It was like a fever through my head. The strength seemed to come from nowhere. All of a sudden he was on the ground, spitting fire and feathers so I silenced him. I felt a sort of jubilant triumph when he was silent. Thank God someone stopped me in time."

"Say no more for now. Some ale sounds like a good idea before we see what they've made of our room."

Edwin had sulked and cast smouldering looks of contempt at Udric whenever the two met. He lost no opportunity to make Udric's achievements look small or purely down to luck. When his father visited the King's Tun he immediately hurried to his private chamber to report the attack on him.

"Are you sure you gave the lad no provocation? He has always struck me as…. No do not interrupt me; Udric is usually a good tempered boy so I am loath to believe that you are guiltless in this. I want the truth now Edwin, for there were doubtless some witnesses if you say it was in the courtyard here. Tell me what you said to him." The King sighed; tired of unrest in his kingdom the last thing he needed was rebellious sons or quarrels among those he cared for.

Edwin tried to look his father in the eye but found that he could not hold the intended bold expression. Instead he concentrated on staring at the jewels on the King's fingers while trying to work out how he could still cast Udric in the worst possible light. "Well I did call him a few names, father, but we are always teasing each other. It was nothing really but suddenly he was throttling me, trying to kill me, a prince. He should not even have touched me let alone thrown me to the ground."

A clerk had seen the king beckoning to him and approached quietly. A short whispered conversation followed as Edwin's voice tailed off, puzzled by his father's inattention to his accusations.

Udric was summoned to the King's chamber, the messenger stressing that the King was in no mood to be kept waiting. His heart plummeted to the very soles of his boots. He felt he needed to visit the midden on his way to hear his punishment so great was the fear and dread.

"I am coming with you. That little whelp will have told so many lies to my father," stated Aethelstan forcefully, ignoring Udric's protests that he needed to put his own case to King Edward.

The two young men strode confidently across the courtyard where the offence had been committed. Udric's head was held high with a self assurance that was acting of the finest degree. They were admitted to the King's chamber by the huge bodyguard. For one fleeting moment Udric thought that the man did not seem as massive as he used to be, surely a figment of his over-active imagination.

"My Lord King," Udric bowed deeply then stood silent, unafraid to look the ruler of England in the eye. There was a moments silence when the only sound was the settling of twigs in the brazier. Edwin shuffled his feet, studying the rushes with uncommon intensity.

When the King spoke his voice reflected the tiredness of body and mind which were taking their toll on his health. "Well Udric, son of Udda, I am told you attacked my son Edwin, here in the courtyard and would have killed him had you not been prevented. Is this truly what happened? Prince Edwin tells me that the assault was entirely unprovoked, that you have insulted him on many occasions. How say you?"

Prince Aethelstan snorted, partly in disbelief at the story Edwin had told his father and partly because he could not contain the laughter which had almost erupted when he heard that Edwin claimed there had been no provocation. The King glared at him before turning back to regard Udric expectantly.

"My lord King, we have been taught that jibes and taunting are to be ignored unless they affect the honour of a man or that of his family. For several months Prince Edwin and I have grown apart though I do not think much of it was of my doing. He cast aspersions upon my mother's chastity which did affect the honour of my family. I appreciate that my family are not of noble birth but lessons here have taught me standards of behaviour which should be applicable to all, high or low-born. I ask your pardon but do not regret teaching Edwin to keep his opinions about my family to himself."

"That is boldly said, young man. Tell me what did my son say of your mother, the young woman who I saw wed to your father right here in my court?" The King's voice had developed a steely edge which should have warned Prince Edwin that matters were not going his way. When he attempted to interrupt, the King barked at him to hold his tongue.

Edwin reddened at the abrupt command from his normally mild tempered father. He fell silent but Aethelstan could see how difficult it appeared to be.

Udric was reluctant to admit to the king that the young prince had accused him of being a bastard, progeny of his mother and the King himself. He settled for merely mentioning that Prince Edwin had called his mother a 'peasant whore'.

"I have a feeling that that is not the whole truth, although God knows that is bad enough. Do you honestly think Edwin, that lord Algar would be Udric's good-father if there was even a hint of impropriety? You will apologise to Udric and mind your manners in future."

'If looks could kill', thought Udric, 'I would be dead right now.' Edwin's apology was accompanied by such a potent look of hatred that it was almost tangible. Prince Aethelstan stood impassively, his face giving nothing away as the pantomime was played out in front of King Edward. He left after bowing briefly to his father followed moments later by Edwin, sullen and subdued, already plotting his revenge. Udric bowed to the King who smiled and nodded approvingly.

Chapter Seven

When the King's wife died giving birth to a stillborn boy, Udda grieved for him and Galena recalled the kindness of her young daughter's namesake. "She was a gentle woman suddenly thrust into the King's bed. But she was not so high and mighty to lend a veil to the daughter of a turf cutter. I shall remember that time at the King's Tun to the end of my days. I am truly sorry that she has died. It is a woman's lot to give her lord children but ten is more than enough for any man surely?"

Aeflaed never tired of hearing the story of the marriage of her parents, frequently using it as a ploy to avoid or delay doing some domestic chore. Once again, when she should have been collecting the eggs, her mother was persuaded to describe the softness of the King's lady's voice and the narrow escape of the young prince amid the panicking horses.

Several years younger than Udric, Aeflaed yearned for more excitement in her life. Her light brown hair was disappointingly straight despite plaiting it every night. In the damp morning air the waves just melted away. She envied the girls on Sundays, curls escaping enticingly from small head scarves. Her eyes were slate grey, turning to a startling blue when her temper rose. Galena frequently criticised this un-feminine trait, saying that no man would want a wife with such a bad humour.

It was while the mood in Wessex was still sombre, for the king's lady had been much admired for her gentleness and piety that news of a rebellion far to the north near Northampton was brought to Wymburne. Once again the king called loyal subjects to arms and two of the young princes were among those who obeyed, Udric acting as their bodyservant. Aethelstan was glad of his support but Edwin once again caused an atmosphere of tension in their tent, forbidding Udric to grease his weapons or touch his armour.

A short skirmish was sufficient to put down the insurrection, the losses being almost all from the ill-equipped rebel force. The leaders were executed and savage taxes imposed on the people before the King left with hostages to ensure future good behaviour. Once again the swift action of the Royal army directed by the king and his most successful leaders had brought peace back to the country. The hostages were heavily guarded as the cavalcade rode cheerfully southwards. Men at arms held pennants which fluttered in the southerly breeze, a number of ox carts lumbering at the rear so that their dust did not hide the lord king from his people who came out to watch him pass. The rebels had been ill-equipped, affording little booty to the soldiers who had not been allowed to ravage the town. The most men could look forward to was pay in coin of four silver pennies for each day, a small reward for putting ones' life in danger.

"So what usually happens?" asked Udric for whom this was the first experience of fighting. "The soldiers are grumbling that their pay is not sufficient, but most of them are from the fyrd of the southern shires."

"Well, my lord father feels that the people of Northamptonshire are his subjects, not enemies like the Scots or Danes are. Taking the wealth or beasts from English rebels would probably cause a great deal of resentment. Another spark, another leader and the population might rise against the King again. This way, having taken the town leaders or sons of the nobles insures that there will be no further trouble, from that region at least." He ended hopefully. "I think my father hoped to disarm the rebels rather than kill them. Personally hanging one or two might have ensured that no further risings take place for a very long time, but then it is not my decision, yet."

Udric digested Aethelstan's explanation quietly riding alongside his friend in the weak sunshine. He had noted the last word but hesitated to comment. Over the last few months as the Prince grew into manhood, Udric could not have failed to notice that he was developing a more regal poise. He copied his father's walk and studious mannerisms. When he talked to people he now gave them a direct look, seeming to examine their very souls which some found disconcerting. It was only in the privacy of their chamber that Aethelstan fully relaxed and felt able to voice his innermost thoughts. Even so, they often talked softly for neither of them trusted Edwin or his servants.

News of the death of the king's sister, Lady of Mercia, was brought by an exhausted messenger to the royal tent when camp had been set up one night. Despite his unkempt and dirty appearance the man was admitted to King Edward's tent where he fell on his knees before the brother of his Lady.

"My Lord, I have ridden through the heat and dust of the day and half the night to bring you the bad tidings. Lady Aethelflaed was shriven before she died, sending her loyal and fond greetings to you even as she expired. My lady leaves her child in your care until she is of age or wed as you see fit. That was my lady's true message to you my lord King."

"See to it that our loyal messenger is fed and rested." The King dismissed the young man whose eagerness to be first with the news would be rewarded. He backed out of the tent bowing several times.

It was too late to start out immediately. Although the air was still warm from the mid-summer sun, it had set many hours ago to be replaced by full dark, broken only by the first quarter of the moon. He and his commanders had been in the saddle all day so the horses would also be tired. The guards and soldiers had marched behind or alongside the King for many hours and needed the night hours to rest. Udric was not there to hear the tense discussions between King Edward and his army commanders but the following morning, before the sun had warmed the air, the King ordered the court and some of his soldiers to ride immediately to Tamworth to take possession of his sister's lands. Aethelstan too, was eager to see more of the realm he would one day rule, even if Mercia had been deemed a sovereign state in its own right under the King's sister and her ealdorman husband. It would have been a very foolish man who argued that the King did not have such rights and Udric had learnt to keep silent. He watched all that went on, fetched and carried if required, but voiced few opinions until Prince Aethelstan asked for them. It was as if Udric was a sounding board for the innermost thoughts of the King's heir. The level of trust that had developed between the royal prince and the son of a small Dorsetshire landowner was such that any criticism of the King or his advisors could be freely discussed but would go no further.

Those selected to ride with the King reached the Mercian capital in good time having pushed their horses and men to the limits. Riding behind Prince Aethelstan, Udric was able to admire the changing countryside. The sky was bleached blue-white, totally devoid of clouds. Men sweated uncomfortably in the heat but had been instructed to march in full armour, royal tabards forming a colourful cavalcade as the royal party arrived to find a scene of pandemonium. The courtyard was crowded, men and women in every vantage point, dogs barking and excited children running amok: All this despite the court being in mourning for their Lady.

Udric was not party to the King's discussions with his late sister's council and his young niece. He stayed with the guards in the great hall, having time to admire the comfortable furnishings, the twin thrones on the dais padded with deep red cushions. The central fire had been allowed to die right down as its heat was not required on such a warm day. He took a vacant stool while waiting for the Council to conclude its business. Occasionally a servant passed through carrying refreshments for the King and Mercian lords who were meeting in private in the Lady's private chambers. There was an overlying air of bewilderment among the Mercian guards. They feared to relax in case they should be charged with dereliction of duty but many appeared nervous, uncertain as to their future allegiance.

When the royal party returned to the hall, King Edward escorting a small girl whose tiny hand rested on his arm, the guards bowed in unison. Red eyed from weeping for her mother, the child made every effort to be dignified until she saw her nurse on the far side of the hall. Abandoning her uncle, Aelfwyn fled to the comfort and security of the woman's arms, enfolding her against her motherly bosom.

Even the sternest Counsellor could not prevent a smile at the scene before them. Compassion is the human attribute not given to animals; it creeps into the hearts of men and women regardless of birth.

There was a great deal of quiet discussion when the nurse had taken her charge away. By standing quietly at Prince Aethelstan's shoulder Udric learned that Lady Ethelfleda of Mercia's only daughter, Aelfwyn, had apparently ceded her estates to her uncle, King Edward.

"But it seems unduly hasty. After all her mother has not even been given a ceremonial burial as is surely her due," remarked Udric under his breath, careful to hardly move his lips in case his words could be identified by those with sharp eyes.

"Father is even now talking to the churchmen. It will be arranged with as much splendour as her court can manage. Come; let us get something to eat for I am starving, as usual. Do you know where we spend the night?"

The two young men made their way to the trestle tables which had been hastily erected along one wall. Cold meats of fowl and venison together with pasties had been laid out on white linen cloths. Several branched candlesticks had been lit for although it was still bright sunlight outside, the contrast inside the hall was cooler but dark. The King sat himself carefully in his sister's throne looking about the hall and those who crowded around the impromptu meal.

Men of the Mercian household whispered together. One approached the King, bowing gracefully.

"My lord King, now that the funeral of our Lady is to be on the morrow we shall arrange accommodation for you and your guards. The servants need but an hour if you could tell your people this. Your horses are already stabled but if there is anything else you require please ask. We need time to mourn our Lady. Indeed, the household is only just coming to terms with the loss."

Seeing that the man could not continue, his voice strained with emotion, the King dismissed him with kind words.

Calling for silence he announced that the Lady Ethelfleda would be buried on the morrow. Tonight would be spent in her capital, the servants preparing chambers and accommodation for everyone. Udric was glad that they would have one night in comfort before the committal. No doubt the return to Winchester would be shortly after.

Leading a procession of Mercian nobles and Council members with his niece beside him, King Edward entered the church for the service. The Princes stood behind their father, grim faced as befitted the moment.

A requiem mass was held before the wrapped body was lowered into the grave which was then surrounded by candles. Outside crowds pressed towards the church, weeping for their Lady. They called greetings to the King's niece as she stepped into the brilliant sunshine, pausing before waving to her mother's people. The nurse helped her into a covered litter drawn by two white horses led away to join the procession returning to the King's palace.

"She is little more than a child," reported Udric loftily to his parents during a visit to Uddings. "We escorted her back to Winchester with a few members of her household including her nurse. She could never have ruled in her mother's place. Too many would seek favours or influence. The king could not allow that."

This was the first visit when Udda had been sad to notice that his son was becoming less interested in developments at Uddings. Hardly surprising since he is rarely here. He is enjoying his life at court with the princes and sons of nobles.' thought Udda sadly. There had been no appreciation of the veritable feast of dishes put before him upon which his mother and other women had worked so hard. Even the new foals in the pasture had not provoked admiration. Udda was forced to admit, somewhat unwillingly that his son had grown away from the lowly background into which he had been born.

In the privacy of their own house Udda and Galena whispered about the king's moral right to deprive his niece of her inheritance.

"I dare say the King is right to take control,' murmured Galena, there's no saying who would have married the girl to win the territory. At least he will find her a worthy husband and keep her safe."

"Up to now though, Udric would have been on the side of the less fortunate. It was always he who defended those who were hurt or bullied. Now I fear he is taking the King's part without any hesitation."

"But he can do no less being housed and clothed totally at the King's expense" interrupted Galena sighing. "He will not want to come home now; he's better off trying to make something of himself. I knew that it would not stop at joining the princes' lessons. You yourself have seen him being trained with weapons. What would a farmer want with a hawk?"

"Well I still think it would have been kind if he had appreciated all the trouble you went to over the meal; it was a veritable feast, my love."

"He has always had a good appetite and enjoyed his food. He ate a bit from every plate. Yes, on reflection a word or two of praise would have been pleasing."

Galena fell silent realising that her outspoken remarks sounded as if she was accusing Udda of the change in their son's attitude. She picked up her spindle which was restful and watched him poke the small fire to raise a flame.

They were more or less untouched by the intrigues of court at Uddings, only hearing snippets of news from Udric or from gossip in the market. The priest had mentioned the death of the King's sister and said prayers for her soul during the Sunday service. Knowing of the following events, when, according to Udric, the little girl had more or less been disinherited, they said little of their inner thoughts regarding the justice of this when they socialised with friends and acquaintances outside.

The young men swaggered off to practice at the butts watched by maidens who for the sake of decorum had to stay beside the adult women. Aeflaed for once was wordless having for a fleeting moment caught the eye of a young man. The blush spread upwards from the very core of her being to colour her neck and face. When asked if she was feeling quite well she could only nod before resting against the buttress of the church.

Seasons passed and the crop yields rose as the land was rested, grazed and fertilised by dung from the horses. Firewood was gathered with the cart, the track through the wood becoming more accessible as hazel was coppiced for hurdles and poles cut for fencing the paddocks. The whole household gathered fallen branches for the winter fires. Acorns were harvested for the pigs which would later be let loose to do their own foraging. Late blackberries were eaten on the spot but a small sour apple tree which was revealed when a birch was felled was an extra bonus as far as the cooks were concerned.

There were now two young men from the town working for Udda. Their own families had been less than forgiving over their disabilities fearing that they would become a burden and gladly gave permission for them to live at Uddings. Despite the lameness of the one with a club foot and the partial blindness of the other who had lost his eye in the recent fighting, they were willing learners, silently admiring Aeflaed and grateful for Galena's care of them. She too now had help with the domestic chores in addition to that of her increasingly attractive daughter.

"There are moments daughter, when your thoughts are far from here! Tell me, have you met a young man, I mean a special young man?"

Aeflaed had little to tell and took refuge in shrugging her shoulders in a casual way. 'After all, who was he? Will he be there again?' She wanted to hug her secret to her for a little while longer. For now she would keep busy until the Sunday servicc; how slowly time passes when in reality she longed for the day to dawn and another glimpse of the young man who had thrown all her emotions into turmoil. Even recalling that one precious glimpse caused a heat between her thighs. In a moment of madness, taking advantage of her mother's absence, she danced away from the autumnal fruits that she had been checking and spun across the kitchen, the skirt of her kirtle swirling around as she sang in pure joy.

Only a few foods could be stored for any length of time but meat that could be salted and hung was kept high above the floor on hooks suspended from the stoutest roof supports. One of the young men had made useful baskets from hazel and willow which grew by the stream which formed the border of Uddings. Galena had smoked eels by trial and error until they too added to the winter diet.

Sitting outside in a moment of warm autumnal sunshine Udda and Galena chatted with the familiarity often found between fondly married couples. Her plaited hair reached right down her back fastened with an ornamental clip which Udda had bought for her from a passing pedlar. They shared secret smiles and memories of their love-making the previous night, precious moments when they had both been swept away on a tide of passion.

"When Prince Aethelstan spends more time with his father he may want to have a high born body servant. What will happen to Udric then? He gets paid now but he spends little because the Prince insists he is clothed at his expense. No doubt, like all young men, he goes to ale houses and such like. Of course he may end up wealthy enough to employ a reeve of his own to look after Uddings when I am gone," mused Udda quietly stroking his greying beard thoughtfully. "It is nevertheless time we thought seriously of a husband for Aeflaed. I saw her flirting with the young men last Sunday when they should have been at arms. You only have to take your eyes off her for a moment and she is either playing games with the other girls or watching the boys." Kissing Galena lightly he stood up, rested for the moment. He scratched a new flea bite thoughtfully as he walked slowly out to the fields leaving Galena even then wondering where her errant daughter was at that moment.

On the advice of his ministers King Edward had remarried. His new queen, Eadgifu, gave the king a son exactly nine months after their marriage and had almost immediately become pregnant again.

Once again Udric was staying at Uddings while Aethelstan was away on his father's business. On this occasion Udda and Galena were secretly pleased when their son admired the horses, appreciated the food and complemented Aeflaed on her maturity.

"Of course" Udric assured his parents, "even though the lady's father insists that the baby boy takes precedence over the other princes and will be the king's heir, I will remain loyal to my prince." He emphasised the last few words before continuing in a less indignant tone. "I mean, we fight sometimes and the servants rush in to separate us in case Aethelstan gets hurt. I am ten years younger but he moves much more slowly. His father is insisting he takes a wife soon. And something else I tell you, but it is sort of secret. We, that is, Prince Aethelstan, and his half-brother Prince Aelfweard were sent to the king's western towns. Aelfweard is jealous of his elder brother's status. He considers himself the true prince and heir because he is the eldest son of the legitimised marriage between his father and Aelflaed. Apparently the previous lady, Ecgwina, Aethelstan's mother, was not actually married to him, only his hand-fast woman. I have heard gossip saying that she was the daughter of a shepherd but that may not be true. Edwin also bears a grudge against the aetheling, but he is considered too young for anyone to take his spitefulness or opinions seriously. He is too young to travel with us.

I have often put Aelfweard to bed after he has drunk too much. He has always been subject to ills, the flux or exhaustion. He asked his father if he could enter the church but the king laughed and said it was only for women or misfits, not for princes of the blood who would eventually marry to continue the line. Frequently my role is peacemaker. Don't misunderstand me, most of the time they are the best of friends. Do you know, even now, Prince Aethelstan never saddles his own horse or goes into the stables on his own. He has never forgotten the stallion that kicked him as a child." Fearful that he may have sounded disloyal, Udric wiped an imaginary speck of dust from his sleeve.

He was now almost as tall as his father which was obvious when they stood together but the fit of his clothes emphasised his slim waist and broad shoulders making him seem taller to a casual observer. Never dressed in the vibrant colours favoured by the Princes, Udric preferred the russets and bronze colours of autumn leaves that favoured his colouring. Many admiring glances had come his way from ladies at court, a cause of teasing later in the Prince's quarters.

Udda covered his son's sudden silence by retelling the story of the rescue of the prince from the restless, stamping horses and how this had changed his own fortune and that of his family. Galena smiled fondly as Udric raised his eyes heavenwards. He had heard the tale so many times and was grateful when Galena pulled him gently away from the evil smelling pile of plaster that was being prepared for the exterior of the walls. Even though Udric had offered to help with the farm work on this visit to Uddings she had reminded him that he might spoil his fine clothes.

The house had been built from green timbers which moved as they dried out. Every few years the walls were re-plastered filling in the holes which had become wide enough to admit the rain in bad weather. It was a task everyone disliked so Udda had devised a rota system whereby each man took turns. Afterwards, when the whole surface was once again wind and waterproof, a bath could be taken. It had been created in a framework of poles covered with two layers of hide inside the ox stall. Galena made sure that her daughter was occupied indoors even though privacy of even the most basic functions was never been high on the list of anyone's priorities. She cut the men's hair and trimmed beards so that the whole business of such a dirty task was lessened by the thought of temporary cleanness.

CHAPTER EIGHT

When Udric had brought the king's heir to visit his home Udda had for the first time felt momentarily ashamed of his home and its lack of fashionable furnishings. The two young men often rode out to get away from the cramped accommodation at the King's Wymburne base. There was little privacy, for everyone slept in the hall, either rolled in thick cloaks or on straw pallets with rugs. Only the King and the princes had bed space behind screens, curtains of dyed leather reducing the draught. If King Edward wanted to hunt in Dorsetshire the court had little option but to accompany him for the month or as long as the stores lasted. All those who owed the king food rent instead of service were obliged to hasten to the palace with their proscribed quotas of grain, fowl, mutton, fish and other ingredients for the King's meals.

All day wagons rumbled through the town taking produce to the kitchens at the King's Tun. Imports from Hamtun were often guarded because of their value, the carts covered with waxed or oiled fabric to keep the precious cargo dry. Sheep and pigs were driven up Pamphill, often hampered by children whose attention was taken by anything unusual.

There were always horses to be attended to when the court came to Wymburne or Cranburne. Sore shoulders or torn tendons caused by riders who were over anxious to be close to the King's person when a kill was made or over-ambitious when jumping a fallen tree. Most were stallions, bad tempered and fractious even when fully fit. Some never recovered and had to be destroyed, a decision which Udda never took lightly. Indeed, Prince Aethelstan now rode one of the horses which had been in his care for over a year because its previous rider had ignored warnings about a boar they were hunting. Now Udda could barely feel the scar tissue under the belly beneath the prince's saddle as the two young men had waved their farewells.

"He's a thoroughly pleasant young man, prince or no. Not a word about the lack of servants or luxury which I am sure he is used to in his father's palaces. Did you hear Udric telling him about folding pigs on fallow land? The prince hardly knew what fallow land was and I'm certain he did not know about dunging the soil!"

"I frowned at Udric a couple of times when I saw Prince Aethelstan looking rather puzzled. Anyway, he has gone away wiser about farming and how ordinary people live. It will be a shame if he is not to follow his father."

"Hush love, our Lord King will choose wisely but Udric told us that there was uncertainty in this matter in confidence which we must not betray."

It had been an innocuous comment by the Prince which had given Udda the idea about enlarging his house. Now that the King was building stone palaces with rooms upstairs accessed from an outside staircase he had wondered how to build store-rooms on to the original framework of the building. The clearing in which it had been constructed was now much bigger although a ring of trees still sheltered the homestead from the worst of winter weather. In summer the green canopy spread to shade people when they rested, the dappled sunlight constantly forming new patterns in the slightest breeze. Many of the trees served other purposes having pegs driven into the trunk to hold bags of fruit or coils of rope off the floor. Between two smaller trunks a framework had been stretched to help with flensing of hide or skins. Close to another was the clay heap under a series of mats which could be worked when time allowed.

In autumn there was a harvest of beech mast, a useful addition to the pig's diet and it added flavour to many of the winter pottage dishes. These consisted of stock from a meat, vegetables and barley or other thickener. Fish or meat could be added when it was available although Galena often found it difficult to keep to the 'Fish' days that the church tried to enforce. Dried or salted herrings were often on sale in Wymburne market, as were the occasional river fish but most of the latter went to the King's palace or the nunnery on the far side of the church. Only eels came into the steam at Uddings but the occasional large fowl, a bustard was caught on the heath and was a welcome change to salted pork or mutton from the autumn slaughter.

Plans of Udda's new house were sketched onto stretched skins and had been refined and altered many times. Gradually Owen had shown an interest in the ideas being discussed around the fire. Sometimes a taciturn man, English had not come easily to him in the early years, preferring deeds to words. He had never married or even had a permanent relationship since the loss of Udda's sister and their child. He had proved loyal, acknowledging Udda as his immediate lord often expressing his wish to remain at Uddings for the rest of his days. For many years now he had supervised the farmworkers and servants with fairness and firmness. Most had small plots to support a few fowl or vegetables to supplement the bread and other produce provided by Galena. Many days, everyone ate together on the scrubbed trestle tables, the meal having been prepared communally by Galena and the farmworkers' wives.

Some visitors had even commented that there was no whipping post or other punishment quarters at Uddings. All the cottagers worked together for the common good. If a man did not do his share then he would be chivvied by his fellows using good-hearted persuasion rather than reporting the matter to Owen who supervised the work on Udda's fields and pasture. Owen rarely ordered others to do the most unpleasant jobs alone, even helping to move the sows to new pens on the waste ground which was gradually being turned into pasture for the horses. This made him popular among the field workers, for a man who shares the tasks and knows the land well can lead the work force willingly. Three furlong fields were now in use. Moving a sow to pastures new tried the patience of a saint. Tempers flared and everyone involved got covered in evil smelling mud. "It's useless trying to explain to a dumb and stubborn animal that a feast of bugs and earthworms awaits it if it would be so kind as to move along in the right direction!" shouted Udda who had also got involved. "Wait 'til Galena sees the state of me! Anyone coming down the stream with me when this beast decides to oblige? Oh for heavens sake! You great lumbering beast, the butcher will come and …."

The sow quickened her steps and without any further detours from the track, slipped easily into the new fold.

Everyone fell about laughing. The hurdle was fastened in place with difficulty because one of the boys had tears running down his face. It had been his job to move the sow. Now, half the afternoon later, most the workforce were splattered with mud. No one would be allowed in the lady Galena's hall unless they had washed.

As the sun started to fall in the sky and rooks sought roosts for the night there was a dash for the stream accompanied by much laughter. Children splashed and were admonished for their cheek in light hearted banter. It was a happy and much cleaner crowd that made its way back up the hill to Udda's hall. Turquoise and pink streaks promised fine weather for the following day, suddenly darkening in contrast to the newly lit oil lamps. Moths entered the un-shuttered window until Udda abruptly closed out the night sky.

What little spare money had been saved could be used for the new house although much of the material could be found within the boundaries of Uddings. If Owen would supervise the building instead of the farmworkers and crops for a short time, Udda's work would be less strenuous from now on.

"I cannot concentrate on the horses and oversee the building at the same time." Udda explained when Owen had scowled initially at the change in his responsibilities. "Already the king's horsemaster is advising which mares should be mated. You know most of the trees round here. It will be your task to select and check the timbers sawn for the building. The children can collect any waste for firewood. You are my senior man here and I trust you. No one else will look after my interests as you have always done." Udda smiled encouragingly at his erstwhile brother in law. He had no shyness now and spoke English with ease. Owen often thanked Udda for releasing him from bondage. Being on the losing side in a battle was often the fate of prisoners but he had never sought to return to the furthest western shires.

With his pride mollified, Owen stood more upright than he had for years and agreed that no one else was more qualified to oversee the task. Udda grinned and clasped the wrists of the man he considered would have been his brother by marriage, had Jenna lived. They discussed the positioning of store rooms and of a new kitchen area since the trestle upon which Galena and her helpers worked at present was now too small. The fire would need to be away from the sleeping quarters to reduce the risk of an accidental spark.

"It was alright when there were only four of us, the womenfolk managed in the house but Galena cannot be expected to bake for all of us with people milling around." explained Udda, pointing to the north end of the house. "If the fire sparks, we are all at risk in the house. Put the kitchen across a passage-way, with store rooms beside it. Also, we need to keep winter fodder for the horses in a dry shelter and stables alongside it. They will mostly be used for horses which need a lot of attention so they could go on the far side. I have several sticks here which the head stableman cut for me."

As neither man could read, the dimensions of the stables had been shown by marks on a stick. Twelve notches, each to represent the length of a man's foot, by twelve feet was the minimum size required for the King's horses.

"If you can make them bigger, even by the length of one foot Owen, then so much the better. Mark them out during the day then we can check that they are square before the holes for the corner posts are dug. Is there a bright boy who could help?"

"No problem, there are a couple of boys who can tally a little, but what about the barn?" Owen picked up a larger stick and counted off the notches. "Where does he think we can put a building this size? Is the King's horsemaster likely to come here and check on everything?"

"I suppose we could clear a bit more to the South. They are only birch so no good for building. They'll end up as fire wood unless you need poles for something else in the meantime. I must leave you to it as it's already late according to the sun. Look after everything. I should be back by nightfall or first light."

He had already said his farewells to Galena and should have left then but had been waylaid by Owen and the new ideas for enlarging the homestead.

He was relieved that Owen would not only be in charge of the building but would also be there to guard Uddings in his absence and left for Wymburne before anything else could delay him. There were things on his mind since a man had spoken out at the last moot not content that Udda had never taken his turn in the fyrd and seemed to be harbouring a grudge against him. The King's reeve had explained that Udda had been explicitly told he was not to leave the King's horses, but there was an underlying feeling of jealousy that made Udda nervous each time he left Uddings. His homestead was somewhat isolated from Wymburne. Not even the loudest blast on a horn would summon help which was one reason he had been eager to allow fieldhands to build their small houses on the outer edge of the cultivated areas of his land. Even if the men were working at the furthest point from the homestead the alarm could be sounded and would be heard in the house. The two single lads worked with the clay, leather and hazel, making hurdles which were always in need to form pens or shelter. Their skills with the bow were below average but their fierce loyalty to Udda and Galena would make them dangerous adversaries if a thief tried to take his stock or harm the beasts. He had often found them wrestling or pole-fighting for the pure pleasure of trying their strength against each other so he knew they were both strong. Having disabilities in one area of the body seemed to enhance the strength of another. The boy with the cast eye was not prepossessing to look at but he could hear the slightest movement in the leaf mould around the house. He had the lean wiry strength which endured rather than packed muscle and sinew. Many times he had lifted weights which were beyond bigger men, laughing off the praise and admiration which such feats produced.

The courtyard of the Cynings Tun was in utter chaos. It seemed as if the entire household was preparing for the arrival of the King. Freshly filled mattresses appeared to be transporting themselves on legs as a succession of servants crossed to the hall, the upper body entirely hidden by their burden. The smith was shouting at his apprentice to work the bellows harder, his voice only partly drowning out the sound of squealing pigs as the butcher skillfully wielded his sharpest knife.

"Hello there! Welcome to chaos and turmoil. The King is coming but has only sent his seneschal one day in advance. The cook is spitting fire and probably brimstone! Come inside, we'll get a bit of peace. Give me horses any day!" He stroked the large equine head which thrust forward for his attention. Udda grinned at the horse-master's description of the cook. He doubted if it was the same man who used to give his son and Prince Aethelstan the treats he had been told about. Even so, it was not difficult to picture a cook with an attitude problem, whose skill was so valued that men put up with monumental ego and a temper to match.

At the royal stables the two men discussed the advantages of various combinations of mares and stallions. The details took precedence over all other topics.

"The Prince Aethelstan, for instance, needs a heavier horse than his brother, or indeed Udric," suggested Udda, "but he still needs speed and agility for battle, not a sluggard."

"A stallion of course, mares are for ladies and servants. Why should we not mate a large mare of strong bone and good carriage to a Norman horse? That way we get stamina, a wide back, but power in the quarters when needed."

The stable-master was a small, wiry man with skin the colour of a walnut from his outdoor life. He wore leather trousers because he often rode a horse bareback. While he never failed to control a stallion he lacked the gentleness required to encourage healing and trust. His knowledge of the conformation of a horse however was outstanding and Udda never failed to learn from him when they met in Wymburne. A mutual admiration between the two of them had quickly developed when Udda had assisted at births when both the mare and foal were expected to die, bringing the event to a successful conclusion.

They continued to discuss the merits of individual beasts but the conversation was a little one-sided as Udda had his spare needle in his teeth as he gently sewed up a gash in a gelding's leg. He had recently been granted permission to take a deer from the king's woods because he was short of the fine sinews necessary for his work. Needless to say, some of the meat had made a handsome meal before the remainder had been smoked for winter, another welcome change from pork or fowl.

The two men inspected the King's horses as the sun sank behind pillows of cloud. The light had a pinkish hue which augured well for continued good weather in the days following when hopefully the new building at Uddings would be constructed. They sat and drank a companionable draught of ale in the shelter of the stables observed by the brown gelding which had been returned after resting for a few days.

"You'll be glad when things are calmer then?" suggested Udda finishing his ale.

"Even the horses get excited with everyone hurrying to get food, bedding, hounds, hawks, and all the other things done before our lord arrives. New rushes cut for the hall, new candles and torches and all for a few days hunting. Mind you, King Edward often comes to the stables himself. He likes to see the horses, particularly the mare in the end stall." The stablemaster indicated the dapple grey horse. Her belly was already huge but so far there was no sign of foaling. "We need to keep an eye on her. The King will have my hide if anything happens to his precious beast. On the basis that two pairs of hands are better than one, I may send a lad for you when her labour starts. Sorry, Udda, here's me telling you what needs to be done as if you worked here!"

"No matter, I'll be glad to help with the foaling. Is it her first?"

The two men carried on discussing horses until well into the night only interrupting their conversation to eat in the hall before returning to the tiny hut alongside the stables where the master had comfortable quarters.

The maelstrom of activity in the courtyard only ceased after dusk. Guards sharpened weapons and cleaned armour before the King was due to arrive the following day. Both the smithy and the butcher had stopped working allowing a temporary silence to envelop the palace. Throughout the hours of deepest dark the only sound was that of the guards on the night patrol, their footsteps often muted by leaf-mould from the nearby woods.

The new building at Uddings proceeded quickly during the dry weather under Owen's direction. Set close to the old house, little needed to be transferred before Galena moved her family to the new hearth. The thatch was supported by poles interlaced with alder withies. The heath had provided heather and bracken which tied tightly in bundles could be lashed to the spars. Small boys vied with each other to be allowed to climb the framework. Usually tree climbing was punished for time wasting or tearing clothes so to be licensed to show off their ability, lack of fear of heights and to their mothers watching the procedure, an apparent total disregard for their own safety, was a treat indeed.

Until the thatch had bedded in to form a complete cover there would be drips from the roof in the worst weather. Everyone harvested thatching material during the winter months when there was little else to do. The two single men would now have the space to work undercover in the winter months as a lean-to had been built to accommodate a hurdle stand, the poles and withies being stacked carefully against the original wall. Both of them had lodged with other cottagers for years. Now not only would they have their own accommodation but room for wives since neither wished to return to their families in Wymburne.

The visit by Thegn Algar, accompanied by his two housecarls on their return to Winchester after King Edward's visit to Wymburne caused a flurry of excitement. His hair was now liberally sprinkled with grey. Galena was shocked by his appearance. He looked so haggard, so bone weary and aged. Only his voice retained that tone of one expecting instant obedience, softened instantly when he embraced her and held her at arms length admiring the woman she had become. His guards were to use paillasses in the old house while the guest of honour would have the bed behind the screens in the new house.

Now an elderly statesman, somewhat shrunken in stature, his obvious approval of the new house was much appreciated by Udda and Galena. Udric too, had taken time away from attending to Prince Aethelstan when lord Algar had announced that he would call on his parents at Uddings.

At first the prince had sulked, questioning why his friend wanted to spend time which such an old man. The inference being that surely Udric would prefer to spend time with young men and in particular with Prince Aethelstan.

“Lord Algar is my good-father and a particular friend of my father. He grows old quickly; possibly he is ill but still serves your father. Many years ago he helped my father and of course he persuaded the King to have my parents wed here so he was a witness. If he is suffering from joint ill or worse, I would not have him think that he was not in my thoughts.”

“Well don’t expect me to wait for you,” responded the prince petulantly. He looked totally bewildered and puzzled by what he thought was akin to disloyalty on Udric’s part.

Sighing with exasperation Udric grinned impishly before suggesting “If you will miss me that much why do you not come to Uddings with me? That would really cause a stir! My father has just built a new house. Alternatively call in on your way north. Lord Algar is only staying one night; my mother is already in a spin with anxiety. She has cleaned everything that is fastened down and probably most of what is not, including bathing!”

That raised a laugh, the two young men giggling like children over the images of Galena and her broom.

"No my friend, I will not impose on your mother nor take away Lord Algar's limelight. I cannot think what made me behave that way, sulking like a spoilt toddler. Forgive me!"

Galena had indeed surpassed herself in the kitchen and provided all her best dishes. There were many compliments causing her to redden with emotion since she knew that they were honestly spoken. Hare cooked in weak ale with sour apples and honey produced tender meat with uniquely flavoured gravy. She was pleased to notice that her elderly guest ate plenty, wiping his wooden bowl with soft bread to relish the last of the sauce.

Talking later to Udda and Galena over a mug of small beer, while Udric balanced on a stool, Lord Algar told them of the King's latest hunt in Wymburne forest.

"Udric could of course have told you much of that. How many does, the number of stags taken and who gets which carcass; he can go into as much detail as you like. However, what I wanted to tell you, or rather suggest is that when Udric is ready to marry, my own grand-daughter would be a good choice."

There was a collective gasp of surprise; three open mouths, three sets of eyes round with astonishment. Galena felt the blood leave her face until she became quite faint and gripped Udda's hand for comfort and to steady her racing pulse.

Choosing to take no notice of his hosts astonished faces he continued without interruption. "She is a handsome girl and well dowered, although my son has heirs who will get his properties and manors. She will be fourteen summers old shortly and is skilled in all the duties of a housewife. She serves the new Queen at court," he added proudly. "I will introduce you when you next come to court. After all, your father looks to you for grandchildren soon…"

Saying that he needed to seek his bed, stifling a yawn politely behind one arthritic hand, Lord Algar left with dignity, leaving Udric wiping his jerkin clean of the ale which had spilt when his much admired sponsor had recommended his own kin for a wife.

The matter could not possibly be discussed with their guest in the chamber only feet away. Udda was thoughtful, his brow furrowed with concentration. Galena was flushed, nervous of what such a match might bring to her small household. The benefits could only be imagined and until such a match for her son was actually arranged she had difficulty believing it could ever happen.

Udric was still laughing as he mounted his horse, waving farewell to his parents. There would be an hour's hard riding if he was to catch up with Prince Aethelstan. Fortunately the moon was almost full casting enormous shadows across the track. All the cottages were in darkness, the shutters closed. A dog barked when he rode past the horses in the pasture field until he spoke to it. A man tumbled out of the hut clutching a wicked looking seax, the moonlight glinting on the sharp blade. Udric called a greeting which was acknowledged. The homestead was silent once more save for the soft hoof beats dying away in the distance. Only tiny creatures stirred in the grass beside the track, the stillness broken when an owl killed its supper, the tiny screams soon cut short in the night.

Everyone was going to the King's court for the festivities. Udric was all eagerness to accompany them, anxious to meet or at least see the girl Lord Algar had suggested. If she was as comely as he described, then it would not be long before she would be pursued by another young man. He knew of his own parents' courtship and was aware of their love for one another. To his knowledge his father had never even visited a brothel, let alone enjoyed a quick fumble in the dark corners of Wymburne with a woman of easy virtue. He had however, seen how other men treated their womenfolk, without love or friendship, and barely with respect in some cases. Men suggested unions of their offspring at the moot where all freemen were expected to gather but on the whole he knew that in Wymburne, the girl could express her wishes regarding a life partner. Among those who frequented court however, their marriages had for the most part been arranged for territorial gain or monetary advantage.

“‘ would like to marry for love” he said dreamily to no-one in particular as he helped the Princes carry saddle bags into their sparsely furnished chamber at Cranburne. Plain straw-filled mattresses lay side by side beneath a wooden cross on the whitewashed wall. One candle stuck in a bowl provided the only light apart from a high, un-shuttered window. Udric shivered in anticipation of a cold night. “If these are the guest quarters I dread to think what the monk's dormitories are like! If it rains there is nothing to prevent the nearest sleeper from getting wet unless the shutter is on the outside.”

There were no pegs for clothes, no coffer on which the saddle bags could be placed off the floor.

"By Our Lady, there is no heat at all. Does the abbot think our souls are in danger from too much luxury?" Aethelstan's voice held an edge, a warning to the unwary that his temper was rising.

He stalked through the dark cloisters towards the refectory, every step proclaiming his dissatisfaction with his chamber, the total lack of any comforts and as far as he was concerned, a complete lack of respect for his position as heir to the throne.

It came as no surprise to find that the hall where the monks ate and heard the day's reading was equally devoid of comfort. Only weak ale was served, the earthenware mugs being filled by a silent novice. The pottage too, was ladled onto a trencher with complete disregard for a man's status. Both the Princes were now offended by the ignorance of etiquette shown by the brothers. To avoid the matter coming to a head Udric said the first thing which came to mind.

"My father came here, many years ago. I don't suppose it has changed much. Perhaps it is run by an order sworn to poverty!" Neither of his companions replied being engrossed in cutting the tough meat. The whole meal was poor and the room draughty so there was no cause to linger. Pausing only to dip their fingers in a bowl of freezing water the travellers returned to their accommodation.

"God's Blood, but I'm freezing. The ale was a disgrace and the meat was what?" the younger Prince whined as lay down fully dressed, his thick cloak wrapped around so only the top of his head showed.

"Before you go to dreamland young lord, I suppose it would be bad for your soul to sample one of my mother's honey cakes?"

The small brown head instantly rose from its cocoon, eyes sparkling in anticipation of the treat. "You mean, all this time you have been secreting food? Oh yes, temptation or not, your mother's cooking is wonderful, especially tonight. My stomach is still complaining even now." The youngster reached out to take one of the cakes and bit into it with relish. A crumb fell but was quickly snatched up and popped into his mouth.

Udric and Aethelstan derived greater enjoyment from Galena's baking because of the air of conspiracy that developed. Eating what felt like forbidden sugary delicacies in the gloomy room lit by a single smoking candle, all three ate every morsel, licking honeyed lips to enjoy the last vestige of sweetness.

In the guesthouse the following morning, Aethelstan remarked cynically that the only reason the lodge-house was still open was to relieve weary travellers or pilgrims of their money before they reached the capital. Obliged to thank the Abbot for his hospitality the Prince was stiffly formal. Providing Udric with low value coins to put in the offertory box they were both surprised by the corpulence of the Abbot.

"T'is obvious that he eats better than most, and certainly more than we were served," complained Aethelstan once more astride his horse. Having broken their fast after a disturbed night his humour had not been restored. The midden had been in the open and while privacy was not thought to be important for natural functions the Prince had made his displeasure known to those around him.

There were so few people in the fields that it was obvious that Cranburne Abbey made little money from their farm lands. There was a general air of neglect. Even within the refectory there had been a surly attitude when serving the meal. Robes were obviously dirty, the serving mens' nails grimed with filth, a fact which made the meal even less appetising.

They entered Winchester through the West Gate in the old roman walls, the outer defence of the city. Cartloads of food heading to the royal store houses were blocking the road until a soldier cleared a path for the king's sons enabling them to reach the courtyard in the shadow of the Minster church.

The servants were busy preparing for the Christmas celebrations, some barely visible under armfuls of greenery. In the kitchens cooks sweated over their huge cooking fires while small boys turned spits or ran on other errands encouraged by threats. Udric grinned as a child dodged a red faced cook armed with a long handled pan who was in turn discomforted to notice the Princes watching, and grinning in the wide doorway. The small boy escaped, winking cheekily as he skipped out of reach.

Chapter Nine

As winter gripped the countryside there were opportunities to slide on stretches of ice which had formed in gulleys. Serving men cursed imaginatively when they accidentally stepped on surfaces honed to polished perfection by the stout leather soles of skaters. All over the land the icy conditions seeped into the most well insulated dwellings. Fires roared to combat the cold, men wore as many clothes as they possessed but still the old and sick died in their hundreds.

In Wymburne the river Stour froze in the floodplain. Children climbed the lonely barrow close to the ford and ran across the ice while adults held their breath in collective apprehension. At the monastery monks broke the ice on their fishpond carting it away to the cellar where it would be used to preserve food for many months to come. It was too penetratingly cold for the nuns to continue their laborious work of copying prayers or texts into beautifully illustrated books for the wealthy. Inks froze in the precious glass bottles, chilblains split in bloody sores that no amount of ointment could heal.

At Uddings the oxen rested comfortably in their stall, their grassy breath hanging on the air while they chewed the cud. Most of the horses were in the paddocks munching piles of summer hay, thick winter coats protecting them from the biting wind. Tall hurdles had been rammed into the northern edge of the field to divert the fiercest blasts. The hut where the keeper spent his nights could be moved on its runners to best advantage. Udda suggested that a small brazier was kept lit all day to warm both the man and beasts on the coldest days. Close by, mares nodded sleepily as their bellies swelled with the growing life within.

Wrapped up in a much despised cloak of wolf skin, Udda spoke quietly to each beast in his care. "It's lucky that you know me for a wolf pelt would, in normal circumstances have you racing off to the furthest reach of the pasture. Soon Spring will come and with it fresh grass."

Unaware that there was a man approaching, Udda continued to admire the growing herd.

"Do you often talk to the horses?" enquired the field-hand who often spent his night in the small hut. Beneath auburn hair his face was freckled even in winter, brown eyes straightforward and trusting. "Before I came here the only horses around were owned by thegns or the King's man. Never had anything to do with them but you have given me a chance to be close to them. My son wants to work with them too. Would you consider letting him spend time with me. He would still do his ordinary work of course."

"These are the King's horses as you know. Providing you do not allow your son to feed anything to them which you have not checked yourself, then he may of course watch over them. They are valuable and my lord Edward would be rightly enraged if anything happened to his precious mares."

The man's face lit up with gratitude, a flush spreading up from the woollen scarf to the roots of his hair. His thanks were interrupted when Udda laid a hand on his shoulder. "Feed the fire and get home to your hearth. The sky has been grey all day with not a glimpse of the sun. Hopefully there will be no further frost tonight. I will check the mares later, hopefully they will have colts!"

The younger princes' lessons would no doubt resume after the yuletide season and although Aethelstan felt he was too old for playing he was soon persuaded to join their games.

"You know father wants each shire to appoint a man to enquire into suspicious deaths, fires and finds at sea? I believe the law men call them 'crowners'."

"Surely the lord on whose land a death occurs does that already?" replied Udric who was warming his hands before the fire. "Mind you, I suppose he could be biased especially if he also punished the guilty man if murder has been done."

"Exactly, that's why father wants two knights, who have their own income and will supposedly be immune to bribes, to hear evidence. The local tithing will be responsible, as they are now, for making sure that anyone accused does not run off and attends the hearing, but the Crowner will most likely be from another area of the shire and should therefore be unbiased.

If he deems someone to be guilty then they will go for trial before qualified judges."

"Well, it sounds like a good system. The shire-reeve in Dorsetshire used to do something like that but he got paid a part of any fine. Surely, for a knight to do this at his own expense is not going to be popular."

Having exhausted the subject both men were thoughtful as they went to the prince's chamber.

They were no sooner settled into their large, tapestry lined room and unlaced their leggings than a bodyservant demanded their attendance on the King. A conspiratorial look passed between Aethelstan and his younger brother, hastily extinguished when Udric turned towards them having fetched Aethelstan's best tunic from its peg on the wall.

"What does father want? Why both of us? Have we offended someone or do you think the Abbot at Cranburne has complained that my contribution to his coffers was too small. Well, between you and me, that was all his accommodation was worth and I would have told him to his face. We were all glad to leave. I swear my mattress had fleas!" Aethelstan endeavoured to make his voice sound petulant, glancing at Aelfweard, silently asking for support.

"You know your brother agreed with you and for what my word is worth, I will support you if that is why your lord father has summoned us. We had better hurry or his anger might be worse." Udric had developed a sense of practicality. Having been involved in many escapades with the princes when they studied together, he now hesitated before acting, considering possible outcomes. Aethelstan sometimes accused him of being staid, less impulsive than a few years ago but many times his caution had prevented accidents or far reaching consequences.

Thongs were hastily retied and sleeves straightened as the princes prepared to meet their father. Encouraged to go with them, Udric followed at a respectful distance bowing deeply when they entered the King's presence. A soldier stood at ease at by the door at one end of the hall, his spear sunk into the deep rushes on the floor. Suddenly bright rays of sunlight entered through the un-shuttered windows, dust motes swirling in the light and warmth from a huge iron brazier. Since early morning a uniform greyness had enveloped the land. Only occasional breaks had allowed unheated shafts of sunlight to reach the earth, a small pool of brightness lasting only minutes. A small boy put more logs beside the fire and crept out almost unnoticed, his pinched looking face, with huge wide eyes easily betraying the fact that he was underfed. While he carried no shackle Udric wondered if he was perhaps the son of such a man and as such, born to servitude.

While Aethelstan and Aelfweard, the next eldest brother spoke to their father, Udric had time to look around him. It was not often that there was an opportunity to enter the King's private chamber since only family or special advisors and counsellors were normally admitted. He was absorbed, studying the elaborate painted figureheads carved on the massive beams when the king demanded he approach. The soldier coughed politely to draw Udric's attention to the immediate need to respond to the King. He blushed and bowed, noticing as he straightened the Princes' barely concealed grins at his momentary fall from grace.

The King was speaking to him, ignoring the by-play and Udric's embarrassment. "I am told that you have carried out your duties well yet have never been rewarded for this service." The princes' father was looking him straight in the eye, man to man.

Shaking his head slowly, ignoring the smiling faces of Aethelstan and his brother, Udric was puzzled by the conspiracy that seemed to be forming around him. "I have not looked for payment my lord. For years you have given me bed and board, clothes and arms. Indeed, my lord King, provided me with horses and falcons."

Re-iterating that he did not expected to receive further rewards for he had enjoyed the lessons alongside the princes, Udric was still expressing his gratitude when the king raised his hand interrupting him. He summoned the young servant standing stiffly behind his chair, sending him out of the hall. Udric glanced questioningly at Aethelstan but he shrugged, playing his part as an innocent to perfection. Aelfweard's face was also a picture of guilelessness, his gentle grey eyes beneath a thatch of unruly blonde hair giving no indication of what was to follow.

The boy returned some moments later with lord Algar, now forced to support himself with a stout stick. Dressed in long robes with decorated borders, the dark green wool fell into soft pleats. Udric noticed how thin his good-father appeared but a glance from the old man revealed that his sharp eyes still glowed with pride and satisfaction. A padded stool was placed adjacent to King Edward's lavishly upholstered chair. Invited to sit beside his lord, they held a whispered conversation giving Udric another opportunity to seek reassurance or information from the two princes. He had been left standing on his own in front of the King's chair and so far had not the slightest hint of what the King intended. Thoughts crowded through his head so fast that his breathing quickened in something akin to panic. He dare not move but brushed a speck of mud from the front of his tunic. Suddenly he had the greatest urge to use the midden. The longer he stood, and every second felt like a minute, every minute like an hour, the greater his need became.

The two princes continued to smile, but now it was in friendship rather than the mocking grin they had adopted before. He raised an eyebrow but still got no sign from either of them as to the meaning of this interview. They were whispering, their closeness only emphasising Udric's isolation, his exclusion from their kinship. He felt heat rising from his guts, spreading uncomfortably to all parts of his body where sweat first breaks out. The discomfort of both his body and mind increased beyond endurance forcing him to take a deep, steadying breath.

"Thegn Algar tells me that you are the son of my loyal horse-healer, Udda. Tell me Udric, why you have been so loyal and still choose to bear my sons company?"

Totally unprepared for the question Udric gasped in astonishment before collecting his wits. "My lord king, I honour my father and mother and love both them and my sister, but when my sponsor, the lord Algar offered me the chance of education with your sons, my family was grateful for the chance. I attended to my lessons and many years have passed since the tutors washed their hands of me. Since then I have served the princes in any capacity that was required, even travelling to the borders of your kingdom. I also acted as bodyservant to my sponsor when he led his forces into battle." he added proudly, "but all this is known to you lord. When the aethelings have no further need of my services I will return to Uddings, with your permission of course."

The reply was considered thoughtfully, King Edward scratching his now greying beard. Other people had now entered the chamber stopping to stare at the scene before them. There was complete silence until the Queen slipped through the private doorway with her youngest child in her arms. All heads turned and bowed to her as she approached her husband. The baby was unusually fair, wrapped tightly in traditional swaddling. Having shown it to the King, a nursemaid tiptoed in and took the infant gently as a servant hastily brought the queen a stool. Arranging her skirts neatly, the king's new wife acknowledged everyone with a slight nod of her head. Her wimple was of finest fabric, a gold band securing it to her plaited hair. Udric had not seen her so closely before, the two older princes having little need of mothering. He studied her pretty face with its well defined eyebrows and rose-tinted lips above a chin which indicated that she might have inherited a certain strength of character.

The king stood up to speak, normally a signal that others must also rise but on this occasion he indicated that they should remain seated.

"Udric, son of Udda, villein of Uddings, it is my desire that you have a reward for your loyalty to my sons, to keep for your lifetime and that of your own sons. There are manors in my new kingdom of Mercia which need a new master, or there is waste land north-east of your father's land. You may make a choice. The one is a ready made living of more than ten pounds a year and the other needs tilling and taming. Which will you choose?"

Glancing at Algar to see if he too was puzzled his eyes met those of his sponsor but he received no hint or help in his unexpected predicament. It was rare enough for a man to be given a choice in the matter of reward but it seemed that the entire court had now crept into the room to hear the king's offer.

"My lord, I am not worldly enough to know if you are teasing me. I may have lived well in the company of your sons, for which I thank you, but at heart I am a farmer's son and would choose the land near the homestead of my birth." Udric's mouth had suddenly gone dry. He had made his choice in front of witnesses; it was done and could not be undone.

Algar sighed loudly so that many turned to him. "My lord Algar sounds disappointed in my choice, but I will create a homestead and tend the land as my father has done. Two parcels of land next door to one another could offer more grazing or surplus grain harvests."

His mind in turmoil; there had been no time for consideration which went against all that he had learnt. Decisions should be thought through; judgements should not be made on impulse but after weighing up each side of the argument. Was he being dismissed from the Prince's service? He was relieved when the elderly man smiled fondly at him and asked him for assistance returning to his quarters.

If Udric had turned round as he left he would have seen the look of utter disbelief on Aethelstan's face. While the prince had only the briefest idea that his father intended to reward Udric by offering him a grant of land he had not realised that there was to be a choice. Had the repossessed and ready-made manor been chosen there is no doubt that Udric would soon have joined the ranks of thegns in due course. He left the chamber wondering if he should persuade his young friend to change his mind. 'Would father have already dictated the grant, only the name of the recipient awaiting completion?' He returned to his own room determined to point out the merits of his argument as soon as Udric returned.

Outside, the dusk was already beginning to close in although it was only mid-afternoon. Udric was surprised that it was not later. Torches were already being lit in the iron sconces which branched out, away from the oak tiled roof of the hall. They cast leaping shadows in the courtyard as servants dressed in decorated tabards bustled between buildings.

Udric and Thegn Algar wasted no time in responding to curious glances as they left the King's presence. Striding as quickly as his old bones would allow and much faster than many judged he could possibly move, they were already discussing the King's gift seated comfortably on cushions in the alcove of an upper room. One of the elderly man's personal servants had appeared with a jug of ale, two beakers and a plate of sweetmeats before retiring out of earshot but close enough to be summoned should his lord need anything. Algar applauded his godson's choice pointing out that he too had worked for all he now owned, both by battle and by service. "My father had little to pass to me, being a second son. Men know that my position is hard earned. My lord King trusts me to prepare for each visit of his court. The king will surely require service from you. In time you will no doubt be required to provide soldiers and arms. He may ask if you care for horses as Udda does. For now be content! You know the land well and there is land for sheep and a good house. Only one thing will be missing ….."

"A wife!" interrupted Udric, "You suggested … er.. When shall I meet your son's daughter?" Suddenly flushing nervously in case lord Algar thought he might be appearing presumptuous, Udric endeavoured to rescind his question but failed miserably.

Before Algar could answer, the horn sounded to announce the evening meal. Men, women, soldiers, servants and children all made their way quickly to the hall which had now been set for dinner, the trestle tables and benches arranged in rows below the high table. All the wall sconces had been lit adding to the warmth provided by the central hearth where dry logs burnt with clear flames and little smoke. Visitors to court, men from all the departments, some with ink-stained fingers, servants and guards all took places according to their standing, a muted rainbow of colours when compared to the brightly coloured tunics and robes worn by those at the high table.

Algar insisted that Udric sit beside him as the King and Queen entered, closely followed by their body-servants with washing bowls and cloths. Now too old to act a page to his sponsor, Udric nevertheless called a nervous young boy to him and offered the bowl to the old man. Once his hands were dried Algar patted the youngster on the head so that he would not be offended, a small gesture which was one of those small acts ensuring love and respect from so many of the court servants.

"You treat them well Udric. Many a young man becomes prideful when he has become a friend of a thegn, let alone a quiver full of princes!"

"My Lord, I but copy my betters! There is no example I would rather follow than yours. The manservant who brought ale and sweetmeats; he would give his life for you if need be. Did you not see the love and loyalty in his eyes? My own skill is but pale in comparison!"

"Flatterer!" exclaimed lord Algar picking out a soft piece of meat from the dish put between them. Having few teeth remaining he was careful to avoid food which might threaten the longevity of those which were still embedded in his jaw bone.

Busy cleaning his knife blade Udric failed to notice the Queen's ladies taking their seats opposite. When he looked up it was to see the young lady who had taken the child away earlier in the day. He blushed to the roots of his hair, stammering a greeting. The warmth quickly spread to those parts of the male anatomy that remain flaccid and unremarked until galvanised into action by a powerful emotion. Algar, unaware of Udric's inner conflict, made the formal introduction before returning his attention to the meats, sopping up the rich sauces with bread. It was impossible to talk comfortably across the table, especially as there was a noisy election of the Lord of Misrule for the twelve days of Christmas in the centre of the hall accompanied by loud laughter as the successful candidate was crowned with a richly patterned crown with holly and laurel interwoven around the brim.

There was no opportunity to arrange a meeting in a less crowded place. They could only smile shyly at each other, silently acknowledging the instant attraction, one for the other. Udric forced his attention from the delectable sight of clear skin, shining un-bound hair and the bluest eyes he had ever seen. He tried to be interested in his neighbour's conversation, mostly a diatribe about the recent increase in the tithe levied on his manor. He did not notice the young man further down the table whose eyes had narrowed until they were mere slits of rage which directed scorching darts of hatred in Udric's direction.

When most of the tables had been cleared for dancing lord Algar excused himself, bowing shallowly to the King. Balancing with his stick, he nodded at friends and acquaintances before withdrawing from the noisy throng.

"Tell me tomorrow how matters go between you. Did I not describe my grand-daughter perfectly? The noise confuses me and I am tired so will bid you a good night, and you my dearest child," he added when Edith had taken hold of his arm. Very gently he patted her hand and put it on Udric's arm. "Enjoy the dancing, but this old man is ready for his bed!"

Musicians had already started playing a rousing tune. Udric led Edith to the end of the nearest set where they joined the dance, moving in unison with those around them. He only had eyes for her, heard only her voice, raised sometimes to penetrate beyond the music and the noisy chatter.

He was loathe to let the tall and haughty young man who claimed Edith for another dance take her away from him. Good manners prevailed but by the narrowest of margins. While Edith was absent from his arms he took a beaker of ale and stood by the wall. Every nerve felt strained watching another man talking and laughing with his chosen woman. So dark was his demeanor that few even tried to open a conversation with him. The music was interminable; the dance continued as more people joined in.

"No partner? I thought you were with Lord Brithric's daughter. She is one of the Queen's ladies. Ah! Now I see why you are stood out here. She is dancing with Chester's young son, a lad known for breaking hearts. No forget I said that, but he has been known to show favour to one or two and then drop them when a new face appears." Aethelstan was not fond of dancing but had of necessity been taught to take part or appear priggish. Udric called his attention to a young lady hovering hopefully nearby, her eyes demurely lowered.

The music at last ended. The servants offered ale to thirsty revellers who made space before the high table when the tumblers entered with a flourish. Trying to see over the heads of the people who were now in front of him, Udric was unable to spot his erstwhile partner. Chester's head stood out clearly being exceptionally tall and red haired. They say that one can feel the impact of someone staring at you and it may well be true. Within seconds the young man turned to face Udric. With a face that might have been handsome with dark eyes, a strong nose and a forthright chin, it was spoilt by what can only be described at a supercilious sneer. His eyes swept up and down Udric's tunic which although of excellent quality was the shade of beech leaves in autumn and adorned with only a small garnet pin.

"And you are?" enquired a surprisingly deep voice. "My father is earl of Chester, an advisor to the King. He is there now, at the high table. The lady Edith and I have been friends for some time."

"My name is Udric, son of Udda of Wymburne in Dorsetshire. He is the King's horse-healer in that shire. I share a chamber with my lord Aethelstan."

To say the lordling of Chester was surprised by this revelation would be an understatement of huge proportions. His eyes widened in shock. It was well known that King Edward favoured his eldest son as heir to this throne.

They parted in a hostile atmosphere; Chester momentarily lost for words, but equally determined to pursue his courting of the lady Edith who so far had not succumbed to his charms.

Back in the princes' quarters Udric was teased about his encounter with the lovely Edith, but took it all in good part. His emotions were certainly aroused, not the least by his wish to tell his father of the newly acquired land adjacent to his beloved Uddings. They had often walked through the heath to the Cranburne road but had not paused to consider its' ownership.

Christmas days passed quickly at court with feasting, music, storytelling, games and church services. Although the slaves worked tirelessly, it did not take long for the middens to overflow so that he longed for the fresh air of Dorsetshire.

"Are you not going to court the lovely Edith?" asked Aethelstan as he lay on his trestle bed, his hands joined behind his head as he watched Udric packing his saddle bag.

"Not wishing to appear too eager or presume upon your father's generosity I would ask leave to inspect my new land. The courting bit will have to wait until there is something to offer the lady. Besides, she seems to spend time with Chester's son. Perhaps his rank is more attractive to her. I regret my boasting to him of our friendship but the way he looked at me reminded me of the way a market trader inspects a beast he is about to buy."

"Oh lord save us Udric! He always appears proud, especially on first acquaintance. Rumour has it that he needs an heiress, a woman with land of her own since his father is not likely to grant him much. Take no notice; you have land of your own now.

Come, we will go with you to the keeper of the rolls and see if the new grant has been written. Mind you, it is Christmas and the clerks may be too drunk to write clearly!" joked Aethelstan swinging his legs to the ground.

In the candle-lit corner of the chief clerk's curtained office Udric read the finished grant, occasionally uttering the odd word out loud. It was the extent of the grant which momentarily stunned him.

"Five hides, he's given me five hides! Of course very little of it is prime land, but, ah, I have to build a mill to provide flour on a regular basis to the King's manor of Wymburne and to the King's panterer for hunting parties visiting Cranburne woods and heaths. That must be the service Algar mentioned, and the track from Cranburne to Wymburne passing through my land, that is to be kept in good repair and free from vagabonds and thieves. Half the fines levied are to be sent to the treasury."

"Sounds like father" commented Aethelstan dryly. "When are you leaving to see this magnificent land of yours?"

Edwin was waiting for his brother outside the clerk's office. Without waiting for Udric's reply he rudely announced that Aethelstan was to attend the King. In one moment the atmosphere had changed from pleasant discovery and discussion about the land grant to one of hostility. Edwin's eyes seemed to bore into his chest. Udric could almost feel the power, like the scorching heat of the mid-day sun in the hottest months. Ever since the young prince had been reprimanded by his father for his rudeness to Udric, the young man had allowed his thoughts of revenge to fester and breed into implacable hatred.

The two princes turned to leave, Edwin placing his arm around Aethelstan's broad shoulders, a gesture calculated to exclude and divide.

Udric rolled the grant thoughtfully and placed it back in the clay pipe. Wishing the clerk a joyous Christmas he left the small writing room with its smell of skins and inks, drawing the heavy leather curtain behind him. He was still engrossed and almost collided with the lady Edith crossing the courtyard.

He addressed her quietly, still somewhat shaken by his encounter with Prince Edwin, enquiring if she was to spend further time at court.

Her reply, in calmly composed tones, further confirmed his good opinion of her. "I return to my father's house when the King goes north again, or sooner if need be. My mother is to be confined again shortly and she needs me to take care of the younger children. There are nursemaids of course, but the boys take advantage of my mother's absence to plague the life out of their tutor. They play pranks on the babies in the nursery." She giggled and then remembered her dignity, straightening her face with some difficulty. Today her long brown hair had been plaited, chestnut lights amid the darker tresses. When Udric encouraged her to tell him about her family, leading her by the arm to a sheltered corner in the hall, she told him that grand-father Algar had always been the dominant figure.

"His wife, my grandmother, died when I was but a child. He often brought little presents for all the children on his return from a journey. He bought me a puppy once, a darling little bitch with a black patch over one eye. It is with the other dogs at home now of course.

You have got your land grant I see. Is it true you could have had a manor house?"

"You should know that I come of simple farming stock. My father was granted land near Wymburne some years ago which he holds of the king. He is a healer of horses and cultivates land where he breeds them for the King. He also makes earthenware pots, ornamenting them with natural symbols like an impressed leaf. Your grandfather has several bowls and jugs which my father made for him. It was Lord Algar's suggestion, supported by the King, that I get an education with the princes when they were young. He is my sponsor and my father's friend you see. Father saved Prince Aethelstan's life when he was just a babe."

Encouraged by her obvious interest he went on to explain, "One day, the two parcels of land could be joined as I have no brothers, only a younger sister named for the late queen. This would make a reasonable estate to support a wife and family in the future," he added practically, not realising the effect which his words might have on a young girl, especially one who obviously found him attractive. They sat in a sheltered spot almost facing each other but in full view of anyone who crossed the courtyard. Not for one moment would Udric have anyone cast aspersions on the chastity or morals of the lady of his dreams. Still euphoric over the land grand and the even greater happiness engendered by meeting Edith, he had given no thought to the opinions of others when inviting her to sit and talk.

Their conversation was relaxed, punctuated with laughter, smiles and youthful giggling so that time passed more quickly than they realised. It was not until they heard the guards march past to close the gates of the town that Edith sprang up, nervous in case her long absence had been noticed. They parted reluctantly, both of them aware of their attraction to each other. Her face was slightly flushed, blue eyes sparkling with inner happiness. Udric asked if he could seek her out on his return from Uddings. Deep within he knew that this was what he wanted more than anything else. A chord had been struck and still vibrated. If this was love, not the lust one feels for a woman of easy virtue, then he would wallow in the strange emotion which now engulfed his whole being.

She smiled shyly, agreeing that she would look out for him and left with a small wave, her dark red cloak blowing out behind her as she hurried back to the queen's quarters.

Leaving a message of farewell with Algar's bodyservant shortly after dawn the following day, Udric saddled his horse while trying to recall his conversation with Edith. He sang loudly and somewhat coarsely after he had left the town gates behind, the deed to his new land secured in his tunic. Jumbled thoughts briefly surfaced - of his tutors' displeasure over the type of song he was now bawling to an audience of a few startled sheep, the Christmas festivities at court, his anticipated arrival at Uddings and mixed with these the delicious memories of holding Edith by the arm, if only briefly.

So wrapped up in his recollections, the distance passed without noticing familiar landmarks. He was reluctant to rest at noon but discovered a surprising hunger. As if sensing his mood the horse snatched at the lush bank-side grass before drinking from a small drainage ditch. Udric cupped his hands and quenched his own thirst murmuring that it was well known that horses will not drink fouled water. It tossed its head as if in agreement so that Udric laughed as he emptied his boot of a small stone. The light was already fading and he was anxious to reach Uddings before nightfall. He patted the small bulge formed by the charter under his tunic, admitting that he felt wonderful, almost triumphant.

"Although God knows, I never expected to have land of my very own! If I am surprised, mother and father will be nothing short of astonished. I long to see their faces when they hear what is written and addressed to me! They will not believe that the King himself has signed the grant."

He rode through the small hamlet of Hortune pausing only long enough to greet those he passed. Riding fast and wearing the King's colours may have given rise to speculation among the villagers but he gave little thought to the possibility that he might be the subject of gossip as he reached the division of the road. He slowed the horse to a walk to savour this moment, his eyes almost caressing the land he now owned. There was the rising ground mentioned by the clerk and from his vantage point, almost as far as he could see, was his land. Even the road upon which he now stood was in his charge. "It certainly does need some repairs," he commented to the horse which twitched its ears in response to this confidence making its way skillfully round a particularly deep pothole.

At Holt he paused, passing the last rapidly crumbling house in which his grandfather Gerhard had lived then pressed on at a gentle canter across the heath until he could see the boundary posts of Uddings. In his excitement it was difficult to withdraw the horn from its keep on his saddle. He blew three blasts before replacing it, urging the horse forward onto his father's estate, no more than one hour's ride from the high ground of his own land.

In the distance his parents emerged from the house, the dogs barking at their feet. Waving cheerfully, Udric trotted along the bank top between the barley fields to dismount, breathless with excitement. Even as they approached he could not help a final nervous check that the charter was still safe.

Aelflaed brought a cup of mead, formally offering it to her brother who thanked her with great courtesy, making her blush when he referred to her beauty and deportment. Udda gripped his son's wrist before pushing his wife forward so that she could embrace him as only mother's do.

"You are welcome my son, but let us put courtly manners aside and hear all your news." With an arm around his son's broad shoulders and the other round his wife's comfortably proportioned waist, Udda steered his family inside the house where the hearth glowed its own greeting to dispel the chill of the evening air.

On a bed beside the fire grandfather Udric lay quietly, watching as the dogs greeted his namesake before settling down beside him. Grandfather Gerhard rose from his stool stiffly.

Udric had learned sufficient manners as a young child, further reinforced by his time with Prince Aethelstan to address his grandfathers with respect and affection before enquiring after the prosperity of the homestead and the stock. With difficulty he also listened to his mother's news that his sister was being courted by the son of a retained Wessex man currently serving at the King's palace of Wymburne.

"Come Udric, I can see you are bursting with news", interrupted Udda laying his hand gently on his wife's arm as Galena prepared to launch into the virtues of her daughter's suitor. "Tell us of court and the king."

Grinning gratefully at his father, Udric slowly drew out the precious roll of parchment. He read the contents fluently, impressing his family not only with his skill but with the contents of the deed.

Quietly pulling the shutters over the window Galena could not hide her pride in her son. A wide smile would not be denied; it encompassed her entire face, crinkling the laughter lines around her mouth and eyes. She had an urge to tell the world, to shout the news to any who would listen. Her emotion was about to surface when Aeflaed touched her gently. She too was smiling broadly, happy that her parents were content with her choice of suitor and thrilled for the brother she had admired for many years. "Shall I fetch some honey cakes? We are celebrating now Udric has returned" she whispered, leaving the hall gracefully when her mother nodded wordlessly.

"This land is near Holt is it not?" queried Gerhard, his brow quite furrowed with concentration as he tried to place the gifted hideage in relation to his former village home. Now shrunken with age, his physical infirmities had in no way lessened his quick intelligence. "From memory, it is heathland with only a few open grass meads. It is a long time since I went that way."

"At least you will be occupying the land legally, unlike me all those years ago," Udda joked as ale was passed round by a servant. "We could ride out there tomorrow!"

Late into the night the men talked of the land to the North. They ate beside the fire, hardly noticing the extra ingredients which Galena had hastily added to the pottage. Udric's excitement was infectious and Udda admitted to being proud of his son's achievements, especially for one so young and of relatively humble birth.

He would not sour the atmosphere by mentioning the recent quarrel he had had with Thomas, a butcher from Wymburne whose jealousy had become deep-rooted and sour. There had already been small incidents involving rumours that Udda was bribing officials to let him off the service which all other healthy men had to give. For forty days each year a man had to work as the Shire-reeve directed and in times of war to serve in the King's army. The period most hated being away from their work or lands was when the harvest was due. One could send a replacement which Udda had done, but even this had not pacified the butcher. The man had developed an ability to stir up the crowd, turning the Folkmoot on the slopes of Badberie into a dangerous weapon which threatened to divide the normally friendly town of Wymburne into factions supporting the accuser and himself, the accused.

As the horses were readied shortly after the sky reddened with the dawn, the two men, dressed warmly in sheepskin jerkins against the cold, ate a hurried breakfast before leaving. Udric admitted that he had hardly slept for excitement. He still found it hard to believe that with one stroke of the clerk's pen, the King's gift of Didlington had become his. The deed would be his most precious possession, wrapped for the moment in a supple leather pouch, the strap around his neck and the roll of parchment tucked inside his jerkin.

A thick grey pillow of cloud divided the crepuscular rays of the sun so that they appeared above and below it. Where the shafts of light fell to earth ahead, it drew them onwards like a beacon with magnetic qualities. The men rode quietly into the sunshine each man inwardly in awe of the Creator's work. Gorse flowers were more brilliantly yellow; a lone brimstone moth fluttered purposefully, its lime-green wings contrasting with the dark prickly foliage of the bushes.

No sooner were the riders out of sight than Galena ordered the servants to freshen the house by laying new straw on the floor while she selected stores from which to make a feast to mark the occasion.

"There may be fruit and nuts there. I hope they remember to note such things."

"I doubt Udric will notice the plants at all," retorted Aethelflaed petulantly as she pounded a particularly stubborn spicy root in the bowl. "Now if I had gone with them, I could have looked for herbs too." She sighed melodramatically, knowing that it was not her place to go riding all over the countryside but inwardly longing for her young man to seek out her father, a sign that he might be asking to marry her. At least then she would have her own household and would cover her hair before she left the house. Aelflaed ran her hands through her long unbound hair imagining the embraces and intimacy of marriage. Her dreaming was interrupted by an overwhelming need to wipe her eyes, the stringent vapour from the root causing her to wrinkle her nose unattractively.

Knowing a little of her daughter's longings, Galena praised her cooking skills, sniffing the aroma rising from the large iron pot appreciatively. The barley would absorb the gravy and mellow the spicy flavour of the root which had grown stronger the more it dried in the store room. When beaten to shreds the aroma rising from the small wooden bowl had been eye-watering. Horseradish grew wild but needed bland food to lessen its sharp tang on the tongue. Aeflaed sampled her potage frequently and was pleased with the result. At least at Uddings meals were eaten hot, in temperature, not necessarily in flavour. Udric had mentioned many a time how the food at court was barely warm by the time servants had brought it from the kitchens beyond the hall.

The atmosphere on the whole estate was one of curiousity, word of Udric's good fortune having spread from the house servants to the stableboy and the swineherd within moments of the news breaking. Owen too, still in overall charge of the fieldhands, could not avoid feeling the excitement and waited impatiently for the return of his master and Udric. Everyone was cheerful. Good news was rare enough but for further good fortune to bless their household was indeed wonderful. Many laughed or sang as they worked, eager to pick the weeds or cut grass for animals. Fir cones which should have been added to the kindling pile became missiles in the children's games as they danced around ignoring calls to quieten. Even the birds united in joy, singing from the tops of trees in the unseasonable dry weather.

As dusk fell, the two men at last returned to Uddings to find almost the entire household in the courtyard. The day's work was done and the meal was ready, appetites sharpened by an air of expectancy. The horses were quickly stabled, the mangers already being filled with the last of the previous summer's hay. Darkness fell quickly and the temperature dropped with corresponding speed. Most wore sheepskin jerkins over tunics often stained from working in the fields. This night, in their eagerness to share in the good fortune which had come to their Lord's family, men, women and children crowded into Udda's hall, faces alight with curiosity. Without delay the dishes were served and hunger sated with much appreciation before Udric was encouraged to tell his mother and sister about the land he now owned.

"The stream is clean and clear, as it is here. There is rising ground where the house will be and trees, although they are not as thick or well grown as the Uddings forest. We have found a site for the mill that I am charged to build. Apparently there are now so many people in Wymburne that the mills there can no longer provide all the flour that is needed, especially when the court is hunting nearby."

Men and women nodded silently agreeing with this fact but not a sound interrupted Udric's account. Even the fire settled in the hearth as if it too appreciated the highly charged emotion of the moment.

"We have marked posts on all the boundaries, you know, with two slashes for Udric's name." added Udda proudly. "It took until the sun was high to reach the furthest point where the stone comes to the surface. It will be hard work mind, to make fields for sheep or barley. I may lend you some field hands if Owen can spare them and they are agreeable." He joked, glancing at his most trusted overseer. Owen nodded, pleased to be consulted. Twice he had served in the army on behalf of Udda, returning each time with weapons and stories of skirmishes. Such evidence of skill in battle increased the respect and admiration of the community, and particularly of the women. He now walked proudly around Uddings and had caught many a maiden's eye on Sundays.

At the adjacent table the workers leaned forward to catch the conversation at Udda's table as more details of the scrubland, gravel and turf were all discussed. They nodded with approval when deer and boar were mentioned, wondering at the same time which of them would be asked to work on Udric's land.

Discussing the urgent need to break new ground before spring, Owen suggested that a cottage for himself, together with accommodation for any field hands, should be an urgent priority.

"I would like to take a young widow from Wymburne to join me. She is named Alana, and has two serfs who would be a useful addition to the labour force. Yes I know lord, you were about to say that no slaves would work at Uddings. Let me marry her first and then your dislike of serfdom can be explained when she is settled." Owen's sudden announcement that he intended to marry provoked cheers from all sides. Blushing deeply he had difficulty in continuing with the point he was trying to make. The field hands were temporarily far more interested in raising their beakers to him in a toast which he acknowledged cheerfully.

"If cottages are built on Udric's land he will need food for the workforce. What better answer to the problem!"

Udric laughed at Owen's matter of fact approach. "So you get a wife with two serfs and I get a cook for the field hands who will break the ground for both fields and hopefully a proper house. In time the mill has to be built, enough to keep us all busy for a while!"

After much discussion of the details and many jugs of ale, it was agreed that Owen would go with Udric as he had so much more experience with building cottages than anyone else. Since he had first come to Uddings and lodged in the lean-to against the huge oak tree he had built a succession of round houses for himself. Wooden spars pushed into the earth rot in time and need replacing. Thatch also became thin and leaky in winter weather. This too was replaced with freshly cut bracken, heather and alder laths woven in between the spars. He now trimmed his black hair and beard, both of which, although showing a little grey, shone with good health.

One of the young cripples who had found a welcoming home at Uddings had turned out to have a knack with working leather. Over time each worker had been suitably shod for his tasks at Uddings. Udda had first seen him one Sunday miserably watching all the other boys of his age practice at the archery butt. Remembering just how depressed he had been when forced to work at the beck and call of a slave master, without the companionship of familiar faces and kin, Udda had encouraged the boy to confide in him. It had resulted in the boy being released into Udda's care. Since then his skills had made him a valuable member of the household, held in affection by Udda's family and possibly more important to the young man, appreciated by those who worked more physically.

Owen kept his boots supple with grease, the thongs fastening just below his knees. His woman, Alana, would be made welcome and offered warm clothing if her own were inadequate. It was always warmer in a town so she might be unprepared for the winds which blew across open fields. She had already accepted his offer of marriage admitting that there had been little opportunity to learn about berries, nuts or wild fruits as her ingredients had always been purchased at the market. The approval of his announcement had left him with a warm feeling of belonging, of being needed and liked. "As far as I am concerned the cottages cannot be built fast enough. We need two immediately for my wife-to-be is used to her own chamber. Tomorrow we begin!"

The ox cart loaded with materials, food, tools and building poles and hazel rods left Uddings to start work on Udric's ground. The dry spell continued making the track easy to negotiate. The small party headed north as soon as it was light, most wondering if the land at Didlington would be as Udric had described it.

Under Owen's direction small houses were rapidly built on raised platforms and scrub cleared from the adjacent area. The beaten earth floors would dry out with the warmth of hearths which had been lit immediately.

"At least we'll have shelter, but for now it must be a communal fire for cooking. It will take many months for firewood to be stacked in any quantity. But you have a pleasant enough place here young master." commented Owen. "I shall get the children to cut bracken for bedding. At the same time they can keep a look out for berries or nuts which might grow around here. What will they say at court about the calluses on your hands?"

Udric glanced at his scratched and thickened palms, and then shrugged. "I have never pretended to be other than the son of a farmer. Well, actually, there was a great deal of teasing, particularly from the younger princes at first. Prince Aethelstan knows that I am never happier than when I am in the countryside. Young Edwin still reminds me of my humble birth at every opportunity but his barbed comments can be ignored most of the time.

At the same time, my loyalty to Aethelstan means that there are times when we have to spend time at the court with the King or his counsellors. Until now I had little of my own, even the horse I ride belongs to the King." Udric plucked his jerkin distractedly indicating that this garment too had been provided from the royal coffers. "Since my land will not produce any crops or new beasts no tithes will be charged. It amazes me that the collectors seem to know of every lamb or piglet on someone's land!

Presumably the field hands can take turns to help out here. The land is not nearly as easy to cultivate but no-one can say they have been bored."

Chapter Ten

It was with great reluctance that he set out to return to Court as promised. The charter had been concealed in the hollow trunk of the huge oak tree at Uddings, the protective roll of hard clay well wrapped in supple, greased leather. He had chosen the site for his manor house and the first trees had already been cut from the wood. Although it would be many months before his estate would be harvesting its own crops, the pigs were already putting heart into the first field. Their inquisitive noses shovelled earth in small ridges as they searched for slugs, worms, beetles and larva that might damage crops in the future. From the first ginger haired boar that his father had captured many years ago and the small pink pig which was one of the first purchases made at Wymburne market had come generations of mixed blood, but hardy swine. The determination to prevent in-breeding had led to several pig owners swapping boars without any money changing hands. Udric happily remembered one of the days chosen for the swaps to take place. Each man would drive his boar to market and return home with another's. It sounds so straight forward but pigs, especially boars, do not like being directed. One could arrive ragged and flustered, exchange a few greetings, then leave with one's allotted boar, being lucky to get home by nightfall totally exhausted! He was still smiling as he entered the stone gateway to Winchester, capital of Edward's kingdom of Wessex.

Attentive guards nodded to him, their weather-beaten faces smiling when he addressed them by name.

Returning to the Princes' quarters at court Udric was quickly re-established as their confidante and sometime peacemaker. All three had travelled on behalf of their father. They hardly waited until he had washed off the dust from his journey before regaling him with their activities during his absence.

"We, that is Aelfweard and me, we heard some court cases. Not important ones of course, but a divorce and some petty squabbles between neighbours." Aethelstan informed him proudly. Udric was shocked to notice that although Aethelstan was the elder, he sometimes demurred to Aelfweard who was rapidly realising the great responsibility that might be his as legal heir to the throne. Although Udric would still share a chamber with Aethelstan, Aelfweard had been given space adjacent to his father.

"There have been some changes here while I have been away," hinted Udric hoping to be told what had happened to cause the succession of his friend to be overturned. There was already less deference in the way people spoke to the eldest Prince knowing that he was no longer the heir.

"Well the Council was persuaded that my mother was not legally married to the King. It is a relief in a way but if Edwin had not stirred up a hornet's nest I dare say most people would have been quite happy to have me as King. I might add that Lord Algar would have none of it. He said that it was a pity that the Welsh system where the eldest male, legitimate or not, is the father's principal heir."

"There would be none better. Edwin has always been a little runt every since he came out of the nursery. My loyalty to you does not change. It matters not one iota that you are no longer the heir."

"Do not mention it in public will you, there is still a bit of rawness which will not heal if it is discussed too much. Come let us join the others. I am glad of your loyalty though Udric."

Watching his friend while he prepared to return to the hall Udric noticed his tired expression. A haunted look seemed to have taken root, Aethelstan's grey eyes were no longer so open, his smile no longer so spontaneous.

None of the Princes had mentioned hunting or other sports since his return, but instead the talk had been of travelling, courts and of course the likelihood of marriage for the older prince. Although he and his brothers frequently spent the evenings drinking or pursuing the wenches of their father's court, this latter activity had lost its charm for Udric. He waited with ill-concealed impatience for the return of Edith to the queen's retinue at court.

They teased him about his abstinence so that he was glad when the king sent them to the north and he could escape back to the relative peace of his land. The princes now had their own household bodyguards and led troops on behalf of their father so had less need of their childhood companion. All but Edwin were vociferous in their good wishes.

"We will come to Wymburne soon. In the meantime we have our own gift for you."

"I don't deserve more rewards," Udric hastily interrupted, "your father has given me enough already."

"Ah, but ours are really useful! We will not countenance your refusal. Come, they are in the yard."

A disgraced bodyservant and two slaves waited their fate standing patiently. All three lowered their eyes as Aethelstan and his brothers approached. Apparently they had been unable to pay wergild for their crimes at the recent court cases in which they had been involved.

"Here is your new master." This bald statement resulted in all three suddenly looking about them with a mixture of interest and dread. "You will live and work for Lord Udric in Dorsetshire. This is why none of you are branded, he is a fair master but he has the right to sell you to someone who might not be so accommodating."

All the men showed signs of great relief. In the time of the old King they would have been branded as slaves in addition to wearing an iron shackle. Knowing Udric's dislike of the practice of branding none of these men had been scarred for life. The custom now was to sell surplus slaves abroad rather than keep additional mouths to feed in the King's lands. One peered up, daring to look at Udric, his future master.

"But I must pay the fine for them." announced Udric searching for his scrip which had slid round over his hip. "The King's chancellor will expect fees."

"Oh, that has all been attended to. These men are yours. After all you need hands to tame that land of yours. It is beyond my understanding that you turned down the manor in the East. Anyway, it was your choice! Take them, for each owes twenty shillings which will take a life time to pay." Aelfweard's new found confidence still disturbed Udric. It would take time for the new ranking of the princes to become familiar and comfortable to him.

They parted with affectionate hugs and assurances of continued friendship. Udric was sorry that there had been little time to discuss Aethelstan's changed circumstances or his obviously declining health. Since he had not brought the subject up again when it could have been talked about in confidence, Udric had felt it might be tactless to dig into his friend's inner thoughts on the matter. Each of them was now a man, entitled to privacy of thought. He left messages with Lord Algar's household for the lady Edith when it was clear that she was still at her parents' house. At the same time he had asked after his good-father's health not having seen him since the Christmas festivities. On being assured that Lord Algar was frail but cheerful Udric asked if he could be informed when his sponsor returned to court. He left the outer chamber feeling more of an outsider than he had for years. It was tempered of course by the thought of returning to his new home. He shrugged, as if the feeling could be dropped off like an old jerkin. Breathing deeply he returned to the courtyard where the slaves stood.

Udric's horse was brought to him, ready saddled, the harness gleaming. He mounted, turning to look at the hall and up to the windows of the chambers which he had occupied for so many years. It felt as though a chapter of his life was closing and a new one opening. His life from now on would be different even if the princes had sworn life long friendship. The watery sun peeped from behind large grey clouds which threatened a storm. The dry unseasonal weather had to end sometime. Even the men at arms were putting on their capes which had been felted to shed rain more quickly.

How appropriate, thought Udric, that it should end today when his own life was changing. The Princes were accompanying their father and for the first time it had not been presumed that he would go with them. There would now be no hope of marrying the lady Edith. Such a match between himself, a small peasant landowner in Dorsetshire and the granddaughter of Thegn Algar would not be thought suitable. As the close friend of the heir to the throne it might have been possible. 'In my dreams!' he thought bitterly turning the horse towards the big gates. Even the weather mirrored his unhappiness, grey sky and lowering clouds dulled the brightest attempts by nature to enliven a dreary world.

Returning to Uddings with the men he discovered that one of them was a farmer from north of Oxford. Udda immediately suggested that, with Owen's approval, he be appointed in time as his replacement at Uddings. Owen had now taken up residence on Udric's land with his widow woman and seemed settled there. The two met often, sharing a mug of ale or cider while talking about developments on both estates. Having learnt many years ago to ride when the horses had first come to Uddings he made the short journey between the estates on a regular basis.

"Never thought I would be riding around one estate let alone two!" he joked. "Mind you, if lady Galena would share her recipe for honey cakes with my good lady I would be ever lastingly grateful."

Galena promptly fetched some for him to take back in the saddle bags which were permanently bulging. Sometimes it was only with extra clothes but often with borrowed tools or sweet-meats. Having the only bread oven she still baked for everyone, the loaves arriving at Didlington still warm and fresh.

"When Udric's mill is built our barley will probably be ground there. It is a nuisance having to take it to the mill in Wymburne. The king will still get his portion and the church their part so it will not change the amount we get back from the harvest at all." Ever practical, Galena looked out at the rain which had started to fall with unrelenting purpose. She sighed, thinking of the tasks which she had intended carrying out in the clearing in front of the house. The fowl huddled miserably in the lee of the bushes reflecting her own feelings. Aelflaed sat beside her grandfathers, a spindle whirling rhythmically as she teased the raw wool into thread. One by one field workers made their reports to Udda who had also retreated from the downpour, drops flying off the wolfskin cloak as if the animal had still been inside it.

"For heavens sake love, you'll soak us all. Put it on the peg and come to the fire." Galena admonished him tempering her words by drawing up another stool.

Udric followed his father into the hall. His brown hair was plastered to his head, drips running down his face. "I see the pond is full again mother. If anyone is making new pots or utensils we have great need. Owen's wife is a fine cook but ..."

Galena interrupted him, offering to provide ale and biscuits should anyone else be in urgent need of sustenance. Gratified by the chorus of requests for food, Galena and Aelflaed retired laughing to the kitchen leaving the men by the fire.

The slaves too had crept into the hall but stayed in the shadows. They had adjusted to their new life on a small farm. Initially their presence at Didlington had caused a stir. Now they worked on either estate but two of them would return with Udric. Each had skills which needed to be discovered with patience.

Dropping to his knees with gratitude the new steward-elect promised to serve Udda faithfully. His time in prison had been harsh, especially for one who worked in the fields. While not a free man he had raised good crops and eaten well. Now his face was sallow, the flesh having shrunk from the poor diet fed to him while waiting to be tried. His clothes were filthy so that Galena had been eager to provide a spare tunic rather than have lice-ridden clothes in her hall.

"Take that collar off Udric; I will not have shackled slaves at Uddings. All of them will have to earn their keep but my workers stay because they feel safe and are well fed, not because they are locked up at night and fear the whip by day. It has been my policy for many years. It will not be changed because they come from the prince."

It takes a great deal of trust to allow an untrained smith to strike off the bolt which fastened the metal ring around one's neck. Seeing a large hammer descend on the iron chisel held against the ear must strike terror into the boldest heart. All three men could not prevent themselves calling on Christ for aid, forgiveness and courage at their time of trial, much to the amusement of children who watched the procedure with wide eyes.

"Hold still, will you. You're not the only nervous one here! My father does not hold with serfdom but give me any trouble on my land and you will regret it." Udric was not aware of the tense edge to his voice but the men took his threat to heart.

With a sure stroke, the bolt was broken and the collar removed. In turn each man took an oath of allegiance to new masters. Technically they were still serfs, slaves, and the lowest form of human life but without the collar being a daily reminder of that status a man could gain some small measure of self respect. The farmer, a man in his early thirties, had been taken to his temporary home and then taken on a tour of the fields. The light was not good but the man had expressed his wish to start work immediately so Udda had taken him at his word.

The remaining pair went to Didlington with Udric. Accustomed to a more formal atmosphere the disgraced bodyservant had some difficulty getting used to Udric's country ways. Small cottages had already been built and some progress made with the hall but there was still much work and few to do it. Owen was wary of the well-spoken man and was rather pleased when Udric firmly announced that the Welshman would have overall authority at Didlington when the master was away.

"Owen is steward here and is in charge when I am away. All decisions will be referred to him. There will soon be a manor house here; you can see the shape of it marked out already. The sooner it is up and the kitchen built, then the sooner there will be opportunity for indoor work."

The man appeared mollified, apologised to Owen for his surliness and set to work with a will to bring forward the day when he could once again serve a master in a manor.

Each night the pigs had to be held in a hurdle pen in case the local boar decided to visit. Not only would young pigs and the resident boar be at risk but the sows would vanish into the forest with a new mate.

The weather now took a turn for the worse, a storm lashing the heathland. Lightning split the sky followed by thunder which reverberated in the earth itself. Respect for their master was hugely increased when it was found that Udric had gone out to the pig pen and secured the hurdles with strong posts and rope in the middle of the night. No torch could withstand the wind and rain so Udric had saved the pigs in pitch darkness while everyone else huddled beneath cloaks, furs and hides in relative comfort.

Owen expressed his shame and devastation that he had slept through the storm and not helped. Clothes were sodden from working in the rain which continued to fall during the day but good hot food and a series of racks erected by fires dried the worst affected garments. The ditches round the cottages kept floors more or less dry, the water being allowed to run off to a newly dug pond further down the hillside. There had been much grumbling at the huge efforts involved but when the bad weather finally turned to hard frosts the benefits became apparent. Water could be collected very quickly instead of undergoing the twice daily trek to the stream. On the whole the extended household was content. Responsibilities were allocated as fairly as possible, Udric being sure to back up Owen's decisions whenever he could.

Two years passed during which both estates prospered. Work on the construction of the mill was being supervised by the King's own mason and the new manor house neared completion. Aeflaed married her young man, Coran, living with him at his parents' household on the borders of the Danelands. She had gone to him with a dowry of household goods and woven rugs after a joyful wedding ceremony. Out of friendship to Udric, Prince Aethelstan had briefly attended the service and it was reported widely afterwards that had he known Udric's sister to be so beautiful he would have been tempted to offer for her himself!

Having stayed at the King's Tun just outside Wymburne the prince said that he missed having his friend around. He had asked Udric to accompany him back to court. "Even if it is only for a few days until someone thinks of something else I should be doing. There is nowhere here where we can talk privately. There are ears and eyes at every turn."

"I have missed your company even though there has been so much work to do at Didlington that my bed welcomes me every night!"

Ignoring the escort of guards which still accompanied the Prince when he travelled round the country, the two friends talked freely of the king's wish to see his sons married and heirs on the way. "T'is no fault of mine" grumbled the Prince, "every likely maiden appears to be already betrothed or have no dowry. My father may be persuaded to leave me nothing so I must look to my own future. Apart from two manors, neither of them rich, I live at my father's expense at court. Aelfweard will inherit our father's lands along with the treasury, to say nothing of the crown itself!"

"The kingdom will not be divided then? You already have much experience and have shown skill in battle."

"The lady Aelfled's father from Wiltshire secured a promise on oath that her children would be the legitimate heirs. My father could never break a sacred oath. My sister and I are deemed to be bastards as far as the church is concerned. His councillors urged him to marry properly but my mother died and for many years after your father saved me from the horses in Wymburne I went to live in Mercia with the lady Ethelfleda, my father's sister. It was only after another wife had been chosen that my return to court was really accepted."

Udric noticed the bitterness in Aethelstan's voice. They talked late into the night in their shared room. Aelfweard now had his own quarters as heir to the kingdom of Wessex. There were now thick tapestry pictures hung from the wall which had been made more substantial. While it gave greater privacy, there was only one small window to light the chamber. Smoke from the central fire in the hall no longer rolled across the partitions of the private chambers seeking cracks in the tiles through which to escape.

They wandered rather aimlessly round the stables and hall greeting people who had known Udric when he had lived at court. Conscious that there was an air of awkwardness when he addressed people even though he was clearly in the company of Prince Aethelstan it was not until he spoke to a servant in Algar's chamber that the true reason for people's change of attitude became clear.

"Young lord, my master is not at court this month or he would have scotched the rumours before now. Prince Edwin and Chester's son have been saying that you should not be so friendly towards Prince Aethelstan because of the difference in your status. The prince has told everyone that you are only a peasant, not fit company and that he is ashamed that he ever had lessons from the same tutor. Chester's backing him, saying that your dalliance with Lady Edith is disgraceful as she is more or less promised to him. My lord Algar knows that is not true but neither he nor the girls father are here to contradict the gossip. He would be very unhappy to think that his granddaughter was the subject of rumour."

Even as the manservant had been talking to him Udric's anger had been fulminating, a deep seated fury rising which would soon explode into full blown rage.

"The first thing I told my Lady Edith was that my birth was humble. She had every opportunity to discourage me from even speaking to her. Yes, she dances with Chester, and with others too and I am jealous but have never said one word against either him or Prince Edwin, well, not in public anyway," he added hastily remembering his conversation with Prince Aethelstan. "Since I was a small boy when first at the King's Tun with the princes, I have tried to do small tasks for all of them. For years my position was as Prince Aethelstan's bodyservant and it did not demean me to spend time in this capacity.

Thank you for your frankness. I have noticed strange looks since my lord Aethelstan invited me to return to court with him. My lord Algar suggested that Lady Edith might be a suitable match for me but now I see that even he can be mistaken."

Udric was relieved in a strange way that Edith had still not returned to court. Selfishly he feared that Algar's granddaughter might be an attractive bride for his friend should she be brought to his attention. Now that the court hummed with rumours that he was nothing more than fortune-seeking peasant he felt hurt and angry. Breathing deeply he thanked lord Algar's servant for telling him what was being said about him.

Although there was not even an understanding between them he had lost his heart to her more than two years ago. There had been a time, only moments before, when he had longed to approach her father and ask for her hand just as soon as his manor house was finished.

Sitting at a table some distance from the high table Udric noticed that men were staring and conversation around him was stilted. Earl Chester and his son were on another trestle close to the Princes. Edwin was pointing in his direction causing other men to turn and stare. Udric could feel his face reddening as heads turned. The food turned to sawdust in his mouth, he could not swallow. Trying not to draw attention to himself he coughed the half chewed mutton into his hand and dropped it casually on the floor. 'If I had been behaving like a peasant I would have spat it out and kicked the dog as well,' he thought angrily.

The interminable meal finally ended and men could leave the hall. As Udric stepped over the bench a man's foot deliberately tripped him. Fortunately he was blessed with excellent balance and was able to remain upright. He turned quickly on the offender, frowned and then strode off wordlessly.

The alarm bell sounded while the palace was in darkness. Only the guards peered watchfully from their lofty perches. No lights showed in case they affected a watchman's night sight.

Men tumbled from their beds dragging belts, arms and cloaks in total disarray. "Who sounds the alarm?" shouted the Captain of the guard as he arrived in the courtyard at a run. Dogs were running around excitedly getting in everybody's way and barking in a hundred different tones guaranteed to irritate the calmest man.

A soldier saluted briskly and spoke hurriedly, pointing to the shadows below the new staircase. A torch was passed wordlessly to the Captain and held aloft as he examined the crumpled corpse.

Prince Aethelstan and Udric joined the gathering crowd. Fully dressed and armed, a body of household guards stood in close formation around the Prince. Tall, burly men, all sworn to loyalty to the King and his family, their eyes flicked constantly from one side of the building to the other noting who was present, who was armed and who was a threat to their charge.

"What is going on?" muttered Aethelstan irritably. "The bell wakes us from deepest sleep but no one is on the walls and the archers have not been summoned."

"Captain, do you have a report for the Prince?" called Udric realising that his friend's temper was beginning to be tested by having been roused from his bed by such an imperious summons when no emergency was apparent.

The courtyard was now fully lit and danced with shadows as men, women and children surged around in mute anxiety. Even the dogs were now subdued as two soldiers lifted the body from the darkness of its hiding place and laid it down in the light of a dozen torches. Gasps of horror and indignation were mixed as the deep crimson cloak fell away from the face of the young man dressed in the livery of Prince Edwin. The face was frozen in anguish, suffused, bruised and mauve.

"For God's sake close his eyes," barked Aethelstan as he stared down at the revolting sight. "If it is true that the eyes show a picture of the murderer then we are all suspects. Where's the priest?"

Heads turned towards the King's chapel. A woman walked hurriedly away keeping to the shadows while the priest pulled his robes straight as he walked towards the crowded courtyard. The slap of his sandals on the packed earth and the familiar dry, scratchy cough announced his arrival.

"Bless my soul!" he exclaimed peering short-sightedly at the corpse before hastily crossing himself with greater reverence. The crowd followed suit, pressing round the guards holding the torches.

Nobles and their body servants pushed servants and kitchen slaves out of their way. The Earl of Chester's son used his considerable height to stare over a soldier's shoulder.

"Why is he lying on the prince's cloak? That's Lord Edwin's cloak, not a cloth for a servant's body." His comments did not produce any explanation or response from the Captain of the guard who was still examining the man's wounds, tutting under his breath as he held a torch at a different angle to inspect the knife more closely.

"Indeed it is lord, but he was wearing it and we have not yet turned the body over ….."

"Wearing the Prince's cloak? Where is Lord Edwin? By God's blood, what next, a servant wearing a master's cloak and the man is killed! "

The young man's freckled face was pink with indignation. He had run his hands through his red hair so that it stuck up in spikes. He looked round hoping to gain support for his opinions but was met with stony stares. Other nobles were now being served ale and sweetmeats by kitchen staff that had been called to order and drummed into service by the cook. Light spilled out from the open door transforming those who stood in its path to ghostly black shapes.

"Ho down there, what's all the noise?" The voice of Edwin, still in a state of undress, penetrated the buzz of speculation and chatter at the bottom of the staircase.

"Get dressed brother. One of your men is dead here. The Captain is looking at him now." Aethelstan called up to his half brother, his voice carrying easily over the heads of the soldiers and men who had identified the victim as one of the prince's servants.

"How can he get dressed?" queried Lord Chester's son looking around for support, "he has no cloak to wear."

"Oh do stop going on about the cloak, Chester. There will be some simple explanation, not a great mystery."

Udric stepped back a couple of paces as Edwin strode through the parted crowd to his brother's side and peered down at the dead man.

"He's my man. I sent him to the kitchens during the night. He must have used my cloak for warmth thought he would have been whipped if I had known at the time." Edwin's lips curled with distaste at the sight of the knife which still protruded at an angle from his chest. With such a stroke, death would have been instantaneous yet the absence of blood was puzzling the Captain and causing the delay in removal of the corpse.

A dog sniffed curiously at the body, yelping when a soldier's boot connected with its ribs. It slunk away into the shadows, crouching to lick its hurts.

Having muttered the requisite prayers and pleas for the man's spirit to enter the Kingdom of heaven, the priest rose from his knees, dusted off the mud from his robes and made his way out of the circle. Another man left with him and used the far wall to relieve himself.

Already the darkness was less velvety, the first glimmer of dawn appearing in the Eastern sky. The gates were open to admit servants and supplies for the King's table, the driver of each cart pausing to find out what was happening so that a queue developed and tempers flared.

"Pick the body up and take it to the church. You can carry on with your examination there Captain. Now we know why he was wearing Prince Edwin's cloak the Sheriff can deal with everything else."

"Yes, do that Captain and I want my cloak back. Not that I'll wear it until it has been cleaned," echoed Edwin, determined to reinforce his newly elevated position over that of his older half-brother.

Udric hid a smile at the obvious way that Edwin was determined not to be outdone or even appear less commanding in presence than Aethelstan. He too now needed to visit the midden and caught Aethelstan's eye as he left the courtyard.

Four soldiers now picked up the body using the rich fabric of the Prince's cloak as a stretcher. They faltered when a few stitches snapped, one corner suddenly lurching. Unable to march evenly, the corpse was rushed with little piety to the open door of the church. They laid the man on the cloth covered table where monks waited to perform the last services.

"Look at the man's throat!" exclaimed Prince Edwin who had followed the soldiers closely in order to retrieve his precious cloak. "His throat has been held and there is only one man I know who kills like that. He has attacked me with his thumbs until stars jumped in my eyes and the world went black. My father took his side when he nearly killed me but Udric must answer for this now."

Aethelstan gasped in shock and amazement. They were children when Udric and Edwin had fought. Yes, Edwin's throat had borne similar marks and he deserved each of them. "Don't be ridiculous Edwin. I doubt if Udric even knows the man. Why should he kill him?"

"That's the point brother," countered Edwin smiling slyly. "He thought it was me wearing that cloak. He has always hated me and now he has tried to kill me. Guards! Take that man." He pointed shakily to Udric who was returning from his visit to the midden and was still adjusting his trews.

"What!" he exclaimed as two armed guards grabbed his shoulders and attempted to hustle him from the courtyard. The crowd did not part to make their efforts any easier. Prince Aethelstan was arguing with his brother and the red haired Chester was supporting Edwin's argument but being ignored by the royal brothers.

"You can take yourself off Chester! It is not your concern even though you would love to have your rival for the hand of the lady Edith removed. It would be very convenient wouldn't it?"

Aethelstan's last comments caused the young man to splutter with indignation and muttering that his honour was being impugned he retreated to tell tales to his father who stood with many of the other leading men eating an early breakfast.

Udric's guards were still gripping his arms tightly. Their head's turned towards each of the princes as they argued, the crowd milling around listening avidly as Prince Edwin insisted that Udric be charged and punished as a murderer and Prince Aethelstan defended his long-time friend from the accusations which were undoubtedly based on spite.

"Your cloak lord," interrupted a nervous looking servant handing the offending garment to Prince Edwin.

"Idiot, fool! Get it cleaned. I can't wear it after it has been round a murdered man! Take it away!" Edwin was almost spitting with fury and vented it upon the hapless servant aiming a kick at the man's retreating back.

"Lord save us Udric. I know you did not leave the chamber last night. I also know that you do not harbour grudges, even against Prince Edwin even though he sets out to demean you at every opportunity. Go with the guards. At least that will keep you safe and out of my brother's reach."

Turning to the guards he gave clear, concise orders that Udric was to be kept safe, with dignity and that no one, absolutely no one from Prince Edwin's household was to be allowed near or to provide meat or drink.

"Do you understand? Thegn Udric is guiltless in this business but now I have to prove it."

Udric bowed to his friend and walked away between the soldiers.

He did not see the smile on Edwin's face nor the smirk of triumph on his rival for the love of Lord Algar's grand-daughter.

The sheriff arrived with his own retinue and strode quickly into the church leaving stable staff to deal with his horses. The priest was bobbing obsequiously, moving rapidly backwards to clear a way through the crowd until his sandal caught on an uneven cobble and he toppled over. The crowd laughed as his bare white legs were exposed, their amusement over this trifling incident serving to reduce the tension which had been building since Udric had been accused of murder. Many of them liked him and were taking Prince Aethelstan's side against his brother. Edwin was quick to notice their partiality and ordered those who did not move out of his way fast enough to make way for their betters. Ill concealed scowls met his demands there being sufficient numbers that he could not accuse any one of them of contempt.

"My lord Sheriff!" greeted Edwin pompously, determined to take precedence in the matter. "The murderer is already taken. He is under guard."

The Sheriff responded with a nod and pulled aside the sheet which now covered the murdered man. Pulling the man's head from side to side, he examined the purple bruises on either side of his Adam's apple. The well formed lips were drawn back in a grotesque parody of a smile.

Prince Aethelstan watched the law man inspect the cadaver, appreciating the thorough but quick movements as the body was turned this way and that.

"Prepare the body for burial," ordered the sheriff brusquely glancing at the monks who had stepped back to give him room. "Wrap the shroud well and leave it guarded."

The monks moved forward to complete their tasks without a word being said as they wrapped the corpse from head to toe in fine wool shrouding. The church emptied, men and women returning to their work now that the sky was now truly lightened. The carts still trundled through the high gates, bleating animals headed for the King's slaughter house and the smell of new bread wafted over the courtyard from the open kitchen door.

Prince Aethelstan strode briskly up the staircase his forehead puckered with concern. He knew that the Sheriff would question Udric and prayed that the man was as impartial as he was rumoured to be.

"Trust this to happen when father is not here. He would have seen through Edwin's spiteful tricks, although I cannot at the moment see how it was done. There is no way my father will sanction trial by combat, not with his precious son, but …" As the Prince pushed the curtain of his room aside a glimmer of an idea was beginning to form. At the moment it was a mere possibility at the fringe of his conscious thought. He sipped from the night ale and spat it out onto the rushes.

"Ugh! Yes! Why did my brother need food or drink last night. The servants always put more than enough in case any of us wake and need refreshment. Edwin had no need to send a servant for food." Now he was beaming and caught sight of his full blooded grin in the small bronze looking glass, a prized possession.

"Ha! Not so clever brother. And, come to think of it, whose knife was it. It was not Udric's for his is here beside the bed. Where's the sheriff?"

Guards spilled into his room when his voice was raised. They followed him to the guardroom where the sheriff and the captain were talking quietly.

"My lord Sheriff, forgive my interference."

The Sheriff and the Captain of the guard had both risen to their feet when Prince Aethelstan barged into the small room. Their breastplates creaked and smelt of new grease with every movement in the confined space.

"Lord Prince" muttered the Sheriff as he bowed quickly.

"My brother accuses Udric. It is true they fought years ago and Prince Edwin's throat was similarly marked. Father ruled that Edwin had provoked Udric so he was not punished as my brother thought he should have been. I believe he still harbours a grudge and feels that Udric should not be my friend and body-servant. Udric sleeps in my chamber and as far as I know never left it until the alarm bell was sounded. What puzzles me is, well, two things.

Looking down at his hands the prince held up a forefinger and paused before resuming his spoken thoughts. He looked up expectantly at the faces of the two men. The sheriff was regarding him seriously while the Captain's face showed a hint of a smile as if he admired the prince in his effort to clear Udric of this awful deed.

"Firstly, who knows the man? He wears my brother's colours but I do not recognize him. Secondly, and now I am guessing! Was the man killed elsewhere and then wrapped in my brother's cloak and put under the staircase?"

The Sheriff was nodding. The prince was only voicing his own suspicions but he had his work to do and liked to follow his own procedure. "Lord, some of what you say has occurred to me. There are several matters which need to be explained. I will question the man Udric shortly. Unfortunately if both of you slept well then neither of you can vouch for the other during the hours of darkness. Let me carry out my own investigation. It will be thorough and I will hear all sides in this tragic matter. Does the man have kin? A wife? Does he sleep close to Prince Edwin? All I know is that he is a servant in his household. When I know more then a trial can take place, if it is warranted. For now, you must let me perform my duty. The captain here has Udric under guard and we will go and see him. In view of your interest you cannot be there and neither can your brother as he is the accuser."

The Sheriff bowed to Aethelstan and he took the hint and left the guardroom. With every step the questions and possible answer tumbled randomly through his thoughts. He returned to the hall unaware of the greetings from people he passed.

The trestles were informally laid with bread, meats and ale. Men were standing around talking while they ate. A hunt had been planned but there were few signs of preparations. Dogs sat patiently hoping for dropped morsels. Servants refilled mugs and renewed dishes as they emptied. Prince Aethelstan picked at some mutton and walked away with a mug of ale before anyone could engage him in conversation.

"By Jesus' Blood, there has to be an answer to this…. My brother is blaming Udric and has deliberately revived memories of their childhood fight. Everyone in the King's hall is suspect."

Prince Aethelstan needed time to think, to put his thoughts in some sort of order.

"Is it true Lord, I mean …. Lord Udric is accused?" The stableman faltered; his eyes half closed, his face a picture of misery. Automatically he fitted the bridle and then the heavy saddle with its jewelled cantle onto the Prince's stallion. It turned its head sharply, yellow teeth bared as the girth was tightened. The stableman pushed it away with his elbow, grunting with the effort of buckling the last strap.

"Yes, but I am sure of his innocence. A ride will clear my head."

"Lord, where's the guard. You cannot ride alone. If young Udric is innocent then a murderer is among us. Let me come to guard your back. I will not bother you with chatter. A moment Lord..."

The prince never went inside the stables having a childhood fear of horses until he was safely astride in the saddle. He waited while the stocky stablemaster, the King's staller, fetched another horse. The stallion stood impatiently, snorting and stamping its iron shod hoofs on the stones. Its tail swished from side to side with annoyance.

True to his word the staller appeared fully armed with a seax on his back and an evil looking axe hanging from the saddle.

"There we are Lord, ready to go." He spoke brightly as if riding out as the sole companion of the King's eldest son was an everyday event.

With little ceremony he bent his knee for Prince Aethelstan to mount and leapt on his own beast with surprising agility for such a short man.

The stallion released wind noisily as they left the city walls. Both men laughed, Aethelstan's laughter subsiding into giggles as the tension left him.

Carts moved off the crown of the road to let him pass, but as soon as the fields appeared on both sides the prince kicked into a canter. With great strides the stallion covered the ground easily, the cool air rushing past its rider's face. Smells of clean earth and hints of household smoke came on the breeze, quickly overlaid by the stronger odours of horse sweat and leather. On the horizon small clouds scudded briskly in pale sunshine, chasing one another beyond the sight of men.

"Did you know the murdered man?" asked Aethelstan when the horses were once again walking.

The staller pushed his horse forward until its nose was almost at a level with the Prince's stallion.

"No Lord. I know he wore your brother's colours but he was a stranger. Of course, not all his servants would come to the stables, but most have been in his service this past year or two. Come to think of it, even though the man's face was swollen, he reminded me of the blind boy who came looking for work the other day. A singer I believe he was."

"What did you say? Blind! It would be easy to kill a blind man, put my brother's colours on his head, bundle him into the cloak and push the body under the staircase for the guards to find."

The stableman's sun burnt face grew pale as Prince Aethelstan's tumbling words reached him.

"You think your brother ordered him throttled, to blame your man?" he queried quietly, fully expecting an immediate robust denial of such an outrageous suggestion. He prepared to duck if the prince felt he deserved a blow for voicing such suspicions.

"Mm.., but you must not breathe a word. You put yourself in danger with such thoughts let alone saying what you have. I must go back. The young man would be with the monks. If he cannot be found then I fear you may be right. Do nothing different to your normal work. I have already endangered you and am heartily sorry for that."

They had already turned the horses back. The high walls loomed ahead of them, the great gates still open to admit all those who passed the scrutiny of the guards.

"Here take the horse. I will enquire after the singer and then see the sheriff. Thank you for your company Master Staller. God go with you."

It was small gestures like this which made the oldest Prince so popular with the King's servants. As the stableman took the stallion's reins he sat that little bit taller in his saddle as he made his way back to his own domain and charge, the King's stables.

The slight increase in warmth brought out the familiar smells of the city as the Prince strode towards his quarters. A pig wandered about cleaning up the leavings and waste already collecting in the courtyard.

He turned suddenly as if he had just remembered something and walked briskly towards the monastery.

It did not take long to ascertain that the singer was missing, presumed to have continued his wandering lifestyle. Sure now that the staller had only voiced what he himself was afraid to even think, let alone put into words, he ran his fingers through his blonde hair then gripped his lower lip between his teeth.

The niggling suspicion, the small core of black thoughts was growing until he was almost sure of the course of events. Would Edwin just demand or would he pay someone? Who had more money than he should have? Could the sheriff order a search?

Within days one of Edwin's servants was forced to admit to the killing for which he had been paid but even when threatened with torture, he would not say by whom. The smith had talked in his sleep and had been overheard by his apprentice who had reported his suspicions. The man was arrested and quickly admitted his guilt when a fortune in silver pennies was found in the smithy. Staying silent was the only way he could protect his wife and children from retribution.

He was hanged, but not allowed to drop and break his neck despite trying to jump from the cart in an effort to do just that. Prince Aethelstan was familiar with such a death sentence but found himself disgusted by the giggling and laughter of the crowd enjoying the spectacle of a man's death throes.

Udric gently suggested that they had seen enough. "He may have done it, killed the man, but we only have our suspicions that Edwin was behind it. The sooner your father sends him to Wales or to the borders the better pleased I shall be."

"Amen to that Udric. I'm hungry; let's see if we can find a meal. All of a sudden my appetite has come back!"

In the hall everyone was smiling. Gone were the furtive glances, the whispered innuendos and turned faces. Udric breathed deeply, happy to smell the first oily smoke from newly lit candles and torches. Sitting in his cell with nothing to do but think, the hours passed slowly, each night an endless time of darkness. Now he was delighting in the sights and sounds of the King's hall, the smell of male sweat, the odour of wet dogs and the heady scent of the baked apples in honey which were in the dish before him.

CHAPTER ELEVEN

Because Mercia was now under King Edward's control the Council had suggested that its governance was a suitable task for Prince Aethelstan. Udric watched the Prince leave Winchester with a suitable entourage until he could no longer recognise his friend's blond head among the pennants and upright spears of the guards.

He returned to Didlington thoughtfully, guiding the horse over Cranburne's rolling hills where the path across the grassy common land was still marked by white-painted stones. The tumuli stood as silent reminders of an age long past, sheep not fearing to awaken the sleeping spirits within.

Owen's wife had surprised everyone by giving birth to a healthy boy child, a cause of great celebration as it had been thought that she was barren. Although their courtship had been brief she now revelled in her position of authority at the new manor and held her head high on the regular visits to Wymburne where she had previously been an object of pity.

It was into this cycle of seasonal activity at the start of a new year, nine hundred and twenty four years after the death of the Lord Jesus that the dramatic news of King Edward's death was brought by messenger to Wymburne. All men of thegn status or landowners were to proceed to Winchester with all speed. Udda and Udric were stricken with grief, each having received favours from the dead king. Now his legitimate son, Aelfweard, was to be crowned as successor. First the funeral and then the crowning, attended by the highest and the lowest in the land, some of his slaves hoping for freedom in the time honoured way.

They left together wearing the best clothes Galena had hastily prepared. Fur lined cloaks would double as bedcovers for there was no doubt that accommodation would be in short supply. Udric knew from experience that the king's hall was not as snug as his father's house or his own with its braziers.

In contrast to the purpose of their visit the sun blazed from a clear sky as if the world rejoiced. In the distance a few feathers of cloud caused momentary shadows on the rich pasture. It was not warm but fine weather lightens the heart. Udric hoped that he would no longer be the subject of tittle-tattle. There had been no opportunity to discuss the matter with Prince Aethelstan who had been elated over his new appointment. To a certain extent Udric knew he had allowed the matter to fester, but this would not be the occasion to allow his hurt and anger to surface.

On arrival at Winchester, a city in mourning, they found Prince Aethelstan and offered words of comfort. He had changed from his usual flamboyant dress to sombre russet tunic and leggings, only the narrow circlet of gold, a jewelled belt and gold trimmings pronounced his royal status. Aelfweard too, showed obvious signs of grief; the last vestiges of boyhood had been shed overnight. Already the firm chin and high cheek bones were evident, the chubbiness of childhood stripped from his features. He gripped Udric fiercely, a familiar and friendly face to whom he could voice his fears of the future without loss of pride. Udda stood a little to the side, not wishing to intrude on these confidences until Aelfweard turned to him.

"We do not need introduction Udda, for Udric is your image. You will continue with your work with the horses won't you? My father lies unburied and until that is done and the crowning finished, I cannot accept your oath. He valued your healing skills and work with his stallions greatly. I would do likewise."

Udda bowed deeply, muttering his thanks for the continued patronage then withdrew to see to their own horses.

Seated on the same bench in the courtyard where he had talked to Lady Edith a life-time ago, Udric discussed the funeral arrangements with Aethelstan in subdued tones while guards prepared the torches for the procession. "His body has been brought back from Farndon in Mercia. It will be carried by his personal bodyguard to the tomb, closely followed by my father's widow, Eadgifu. She grieves and is again heavily pregnant poor lady. Behind her, in order of precedence will follow the aethelings, so I will be at the back," joked Aethelstan. "Then the kings of Scotland and Wales and the thegns of the kingdom. My brother Aelfweard asks if you will take your place as our body servant. I miss you in Mercia, my chamber is large, servants sleep across the door but I shall soon be reduced to talking to myself!

Anyway, to get back to the procession to the church, after the Kings and thegns the free landowners fight for position. There will be ushers and my father's seneschal will be there to keep order but there is no precedent for degree or size of holding.

You will walk with other important household servants like Odo the treasurer who has a manor at Hame, immediately behind the royal party."

It was this favoured position which placed him almost alongside his beloved Edith who had been recalled from her father's household to act as handmaiden to the Queen at this time of mourning. Heavily encumbered by her pregnancy and her grief, the late King's wife could barely see for swollen, red-rimmed eyelids. Edward's heir hastily put his arm around her, helping his step-mother to take her place at the front of the church almost touching the huge coffin which held his father. The body of the church was lit by a thousand candles, their smoky plumes rising in curls to the rafters where birds had made their homes. A young acolyte swung a censer of incense wafting heavy, musky perfume amongst the mourners. The atmosphere quickly became fetid, the aroma of several hundred bodies crowded together causing the Queen to sway dangerously. Udric followed the lengthy Mass, crossing himself devoutly. He had not been able to see where his father stood among the lesser landowners but could see Chester and his son some distance away towards the wall. Prince Aethelstan turned briefly as if to assure himself that Udric was still there. He smiled then returned his attention to the Archbishop's lengthy eulogy of his father's virtues.

As soon as a decent interval had elapsed Udric determined to ask permission of the new King to wed the girl, especially as his hall was now fit for her to live in. He would pay no attention to Prince Edwin's dislike of him, or the scorn of an earl's son. For now he had to attend to the matter in hand and collect the tokens passed to him by the princes as archbishop Athelm intoned the last part of the funeral mass.

The body of the king, wrapped in mauve robes of finest quality wool was solemnly covered while priests chanted prayers of intercession for the dead. Six strong bodyservants slid poles beneath the coffin and marched towards the prepared tomb. A few moments later the procession left the church and wound its way back to the royal hall, the sun shining brilliantly on the robes and crowned heads making the fair hair of Aelfweard seem paler than usual, and highlighting his waxen pallor.

The legitimate princes retired to their private quarters leaving Aethelstan to accept the condolences from the gathered nobles. For a few moments Udric could speak to Edith before the funeral feast began. Her father was attending court and on seeing the couple together edged his way towards them. It had always been his intention to wed his daughter to the son of a great lord. He had discussed his hopes for such an alliance with his father, Edith being a very attractive maiden, biddable yet having self-confidence. It was the only time he had seriously quarrelled with his own father, Lord Algar, the latter insisting that Udric's personality alone outweighed all other considerations.

He had even enquired among other thegns at court as to their opinion of the young man with whom his daughter had obviously formed an attachment. Not one had mentioned any vice or fault which would support him using a father's right to forbid the girl to have any further contact with a particular young man. Only the Earl of Chester had spoken disparagingly of Udric, pointing out his low birth and correspondingly poor prospects. It was the only time lord Brihtric had snubbed an earl and thereby made an enemy.

If the new king was agreeable, then he would raise no objections to their betrothal. He wished to acquaint himself with the family of this young man who he already knew had been the close friend of the princes for many years.

'I have never quite understood why my father stood as sponsor but he never does anything without good reason,' thought Brihtric as he approached Udda. He had the opportunity to study the man from a distance. True, there was no rich gold embroidery on his tunic, nor was his cloak lined with expensive furs but he was clean shaven with just a sprinkling of grey among the dark head of hair. Having introduced himself, he was pleased to see that Udda's nails had been trimmed, his boots shone with lanolin-based polish and that he did not avoid eye contact.

"Edith is my only daughter," announced Brihtric. "My father, Lord Algar speaks highly of Udric. I know he was granted land a few years ago and has spent more time there than with the princes but is there revenue from this land? It is close to yours isn't it?"

"Indeed lord, it abuts Uddings and the two estates can be run as one when needed. The land amounts to six hides; Uddings has one large holding of some two hundred and forty acres, while Didlington is five hides. Already there are sheep and income from the wool. At Uddings, as you know, we breed horses for the king. Well, the late King I should say, although our new Lord Aelfweard has already asked if I will continue in this service. Udric is equally skilled so he may be appointed in due course. What do you suggest the lady Edith brings to the union with Udric?"

Momentarily astonished by Udda's directness, Lord Brihtric tugged his small beard thoughtfully. 'Here's a man who has a look to the future. Hardly the peasant his son is supposed to be!' If possible, his father would never hear the disparaging comments which had circulated about his good-son. Having heard the details from the same manservant who had informed Udric of the gossip, he had discovered that Prince Edwin had long harboured a hatred for Udric because he had been punished many years before, the shame having turned to bitter loathing over time.

The tenuous approach for Brith's hand in marriage by the Earl of Chester on behalf of his son had been rebuffed after their previous encounter. Looking now at Udric's father, he could see which physical traits had been inherited. They both had the same open face, expressive and without deceit or guile.

They carried on their conversation, Brihtric commenting that his precious daughter had been recalled to the queen's household while preparations for the feast continued behind them. Servants erected the trestles then covered them with snowy white covers. The salt was placed carefully at the top of each minor table the seneschal unlocking each container with ceremony.

The top table was provided with gilt dishes while those on the lower trestles made do with wooden ones. The candles guttered in the draught as teams of servers rushed past carrying decorations or cold dishes for the diners. A gong announced that all should make their way to the hall.

"Until later then Udda, I find your conversation refreshing. No doubt the top tables will be full of flatterers and chatterers! I look forward to our meeting." Thegn Brihtric bowed to Udda, according him the respect due to one of much higher status. Udda hastily returned the courtesy, a small smile playing round his lips.

An usher must have noticed the encounter for he showed Udda to a seat far higher than he had originally intended. "After all there's no harm in giving a man helping hand. A friend of Thegn Algar's son is a man of good character, for the family chooses their friends carefully," he muttered under his breath looking the next landowner up and down to see what sort of standing he should be accorded on his seating plan.

Udric smiled when a small page offered him a bowl of water and cloth with which to clean his hands. He whispered his praise to the frightened boy who blushed and smiled shyly as he moved to the next man.

The hall was well lit, wall torches casting shadows among the diners. Men at arms crossed their reversed spears in front of the doors; their stern faces seeming immovable, granite features adding to the solemnity of the occasion.

The Lady Eadgifu attended the feast briefly to take her place next to her stepson but soon retired to her room. She was only a small lady, her headdress adding at least a hand-span to her height. She too had dressed in duller colours than usual, her veil shading the puffy features which child bearing can cause. Aelfweard himself sat on the right hand side of the empty chair which had been his father's and could not be persuaded to use the padded seat until he had been formally elected by the Witangemot, the highest court in the land. He too left the hall early complaining of sickness and fatigue. He signalled Udric that he needed him to accompany him to the private chamber next to that of his late father. Udric extricated himself from his seat between two large diners, apologising for interrupting their meal. In Aelfweard's quarters he wrapped the young man in furs against the chill of the room. Despite having been told some years ago that he, not Aethelstan was to be King Edward's heir, his quarters were almost spartan with bare walls and plain shutters. A jug of ale and some biscuits had already been placed on a table, patterns in the dust showing where previous night dishes had been laid. Udric drew his finger through a mark, wiping his hand on his thigh.

"Have you heard the rumours that I am not the choice of all to be king in my father's place?"

Udric truthfully reassured him that no such thoughts had entered his own head and that he had heard nothing to support such worries. "As the eldest legitimate son of King Edward, God rest his soul," said Udric, crossing himself rapidly, "you are surely the rightful heir to the kingdom. Your brothers and half brothers have long accepted that you will be king in your father's place."

Beads of sweat now showed on the prince's forehead, his lips pursed with pain as he lay down, both hands clenched around his stomach. The much admired blond hair was already becoming lank and dull. Tactfully Udric brought an earthenware bowl and placed it on the stool beside the bed. "Do you really have fears for the future? Has someone threatened you? It is not my place to ask, but are you nervous of the Council?"

On getting the merest grunt in reply Udric offered to stay with him. "I will use your spare cloak, for the room is cold. The servants grieve but seem to have forgotten to care for the living."

In fact Udric stayed all night, the Prince frequently waking to voice his doubts about his own suitability to be king. He worried that he might not be elected in preference to the oldest prince, despite Aethelstan being illegitimate. The council would have the final say as to whom they would accept as king but that gave little comfort in the dark hours of the night. A servant fetched a small brazier to warm the room, its deep glow casting shadows. Udric wrapped himself in the prince's cloak. Being fur lined he was able to doze on the body-servant's bed, the man having been dismissed earlier as the prince did not want his weakness to be spread abroad.

The full Council met in the great hall which had been cleared of trestles to make space for those who would attend. Cushioned chairs had been placed on the dais for the Council members. Below them, benches were arranged in rows so that many of the thegns and nobles of the land could sit and watch. The household guard, still wearing the dead king's colours, stood beside the doors, their spear heads in the rushes. Opening the proceedings, the Archbishop now dressed in his finest cope of golden cloth, ordered Aelfweard to stand before the assembly. He stood there alone, his head bare and listened to the prelate reading the will of his late father appointing him ruler of Wessex. When the assembly was asked to approve the appointment, Udric noted that the cries of 'Aye' were not exactly deafening, but there had been no shouts of disapproval. In a strong voice, despite his sickness, the new King made his oath to rule justly and fairly. With one accord, the guards reversed their spears and banged the shafts noisily on the ground. A King had been appointed. It was the first time Udric had attended such a council having found a place within sight of the other princes but not so close that more important people might be offended.

'Come to think of it, many present have not seen a King elected for Lord Edward ruled for twenty five years,' thought Udric as he studied the men in the crowded hall. Some had already crowded round Aelfweard, jostling for position.

No-one could possibly leave court until the hallowing had taken place for fear of being impolite, or at worst thought disloyal. The hall was full to bursting, small groups talking or arguing so that the noise was tremendous. Few had discarded their cloaks before entering and were now unpleasantly warm, an odour of rankness mixing with the smoke from wall cressets.

"T'is the din, everyone talking at once," complained Udda who had gladly escaped outside to the cool of the courtyard. "Church on Sunday is noisy enough, but this is deafening. I shall be glad to return to the quiet of my own hearth."

Accommodation had been hard to find but the stableman, having often accompanied King Edward to Wymburne recognized him and had quickly found a snug corner. The two of them had spent an enjoyable evening discussing the future breeding of the mares over several mugs of strong ale. The fact that his head was still throbbing probably had something to do with his intolerance of the cacophony of raised voices in the King's hall.

"I have the king's permission to marry Edith." Udric whispered to his father. "I only wish mother could have met Edith before it became public, but she will like her. Everyone speaks highly of her. Lord Algar is pleased for us. He sends his good wishes to you and hopes to see you before you leave. But we must go to the hall now or there will be no place for us." His excitement was infectious. Udric embraced his father roughly then let him go when Udda complained of his son's strength.

"I will bring Edith to meet you after the feast. God willing it will not last overly long and she will be excused if Lord Edward's lady retires early."

They hurried in and found a bench far from the high table where other lower ranking men were seated. From there they would easily be able to make a discreet exit without giving offence to the new King or his family.

In the great hall Aelfweard, dressed in deep purple and wearing his father's circlet now insisted that his food was tasted prior to eating it himself. He seemed to be suspicious of everyone including his half-brother, and after pecking at his meal he left the hall. Everyone rose to their feet but he waved his hand to indicate that the diners should continue to enjoy his hospitality. Only a few minutes later the King's bodyservant came to Udric whispering that the King wanted him. Excusing himself from the other diners, but looking longingly at the dish of fowl which had just been laid between them, Udric apologised to his father, and discreetly followed the king to his quarters.

In the privacy of the king's room which Aelfweard now occupied, the new King sat dejectedly on a stool his head in his hands. The royal robes and circlet had been discarded on the bed, a larger and more luxurious version than his previous fur covered cot. Having offered to pour ale and been ignored Udric presumed on their long standing friendship to offer advice.

"It is still light. Why not ride out with friends or the guard until you are tired enough to sleep. You have eaten very little for days now and need your strength for the task ahead. I will get food and put it on the table for when you return. My lord you must try to eat and then rest"

The king raised his head acknowledging Udric's practical suggestions. "I am already sick of people asking for favours, appointments, or other attention. I need time to adjust; after all, my father was not sick. There was no warning of his death. Next will be the crowning and the taking of endless oaths. Time on my own would be a luxury."

He rose from the stool enthused with the idea of a solitary ride, picked up his warmest cloak and strode out with new energy. As he followed the king out of his room Udric heard Aelfweard call for his horse, refuse the offer of a companion, then watched him leave on his late father's stallion.

He found Edith in the hall talking to Aethelstan. Neither of them saw him approach. The prince was holding her hand and looked up guiltily when Udric strode up to them. Jealousy rose like bitter gall in Udric's throat. He did not notice the elegant blue gown she was wearing or the pretty veil which partly covered her long dark hair.

"We were taking of my late father's wish that I marry suitably," stated Aethelstan almost unnaturally quickly. "Now that the succession is settled my need to marry is less urgent. The lady Edith here ..."

Udric interrupted rudely, his long friendship with the eldest prince temporarily forgotten. "Is mine, betrothed to me with your brother's blessing and her father's permission."

Edith quickly moved to stand beside him but her attempts to soothe him were brushed aside impatiently.

"Oh I know all that. Your woman is safe with me. She is pretty I'll grant you, as your own sister is, but I find myself unmoved by beauty at this time. It's a curious feeling, especially when I have wenched and boasted of my prowess with the serving women. My young cousin Aelfwyn, from Mercia, eyes me speculatively and also the daughter of a Welsh lord, but my brother now has the choosing of my wife if he cares to bind a contract with it."

Knowing that he spoke the truth, as only recently the late king's sister had been forced to marry the Northumbrian earl for reasons of state; Udric's anger subsided as quickly as it had risen. Now feeling awkward he stepped back, colliding with a stool as he did so. He fell clumsily, arms and legs waving wildly in an attempt to save himself. As he lay on his back in the rushes both Edith and Aethelstan laughed at his discomfort before offering a hand to pull him to his feet.

"Thank God the rushes seem to be fairly clean!" Udric scowled as he brushed the straw from his best tunic and braies.

In a moment the old camaraderie returned, the misunderstanding swept aside as they all embraced, giggling unrestrainedly.

Aethelstan called for wine and sweetmeats to be taken to his room as with linked arms, the friends negotiated their way past the trestles and stools to the doorway. Without separating, the lady Edith, having waved away her maid, turned the trio sideways so that they filed through, Udric attempting to hold her overskirt so that he did not step on it. Prince Aethelstan brought up the rear still laughing at Udric's embarrassment.

It was some hours later as night was falling that guards returned bearing the body of the uncrowned king. They admitted to having followed him at a discreet distance but he had galloped away from them and been knocked to the ground by an overhanging branch. The bruised corpse was laid out and wrapped in his woollen cloak before being placed on a trestle in the centre of the hall.

"Lord forgive me! I persuaded him to ride out!" Udric was smitten with guilt for having suggested that Aelfweard tire himself and then eat the food which he had already placed in his chamber. The sweetmeats were a special favourite of all the princes and the leg of fowl was succulent, inviting even the most jaded appetite to taste it.

The court was alternately in uproar or hushed disbelief. Men gathered, arms waving in extravagant gestures. Preparations for the crowning were already well in hand, the food for the feast prepared in the kitchens. Now the cooks would be laying it out for a funeral wake.

Aethelstan took charge of the situation, announcing that his half-brother would be buried alongside his father on the following day, and that the Witan would then meet immediately. Aelfweard had only just been chosen but not yet crowned. Nor had he named his own successor or made a will.

"I had to take charge, they were all running round wailing and saying there was a curse or some such nonsense."

Udric was almost too shocked to make a suitable reply. One minute he had been encouraging the King to take exercise before getting a good nights' rest and the next he was dead, purely by accident. It was known that the prince did not have the best sight out of doors, preferring books to hunting or feats of arms. Someone had to take charge and who better than the eldest of King Edward's sons.

"I feel so bad, almost guilty that he wanted to talk but I suggested he have some air and exercise so that he would sleep better. May be if...." Udric's voice trailed away when Aethelstan embraced him.

"Jesu friend! There are enough regrets without you adding to them. Bear up for I shall need friends more than ever now. Edwin is already prancing round claiming that he is next in line of succession."

Looking round quickly to assure himself that there was no-one within earshot Udric muttered "God forefend! The Council knows that he is a bad choice."

Once again a solemn funeral procession made its way to the church led by a deputy prelate, the Archbishop having already left the court to prepare for the crowning. The body was lowered reverently into position next to King Edward's tomb, the long mass dolefully conducted. Many had hardly had time to don their less colourful tunics. Few seemed genuinely upset by the demise of their newly elected ruler.

The return to the hall was less dignified as thegns, noblemen and landowners rushed to obtain the best position from which to observe the Council. Immediately it became apparent that there were two groups, those supporting Aethelstan as the eldest prince, son of King Edward's handfast woman, and those who supported choosing the very young but legitimate heir, Edwin. Being not yet of age he would need a council of protectors until he became of age, but now he stood before them cleaning his nails on the rim of his large shoulder pin.

"No doubt some are hoping they could take advantage of his youth", thought Udric with uncharacteristic cynicism. "He was always a bit of a sneak when we were young. Blame anyone else, frequently me, if things did not go according to plan. I got the birch on his behalf more times than... oh well, little point in looking back now. Gods' blood! My voice will not be heard but Aethelstan is by far the nicer person, his birth does not matter one iota to me, nor to many others I'll wager."

The two oldest councillors, Waergan and Algar opened the proceedings. As usual both wore dark gowns which on this occasion served to emphasise the gravity of the occasion. Both needed help to walk to their seats but Udric's heart filled with pride as his sponsor slowly scanned the assembly sternly impressing them with his authority before sitting down. He had managed to tuck himself into a corner so closely packed that none of them could move without discomforting his neighbour.

Naturally the fact that Aethelstan was not of full royal blood was emphasised by the faction who supported Edwin.

"His mother Ecgwina was only the daughter of a shepherd," challenged one noble bluntly, repeating the well known tale. His face mirrored the scornful, belittling comment. "Just because she dreamt that a globe of light shone out of her body illuminating the whole of England, like the moon, and was adopted by our late king's nurse before becoming Lord Edward's mistress does not make lord Aethelstan a truly royal prince."

Thegn Brihtric, wearing a midnight blue robe with silver trims to the hem and sleeves, took the floor when the previous speaker had sat down, a self satisfied smirk on his face. He announced that he was a supporter of the eldest prince before furiously denouncing his disparaging comments. He countered by reminding those present that some of them had also risen from the lower orders. He stood in front of the two counsellors, hands on hips, glaring at the senior lords and thegns who were seated. Some, having the grace to look shame-faced, found their shoes terribly interesting when they could not meet the thegn's eyes. Udric noticed that Lord Algar had concealed his face behind his hand, ostensibly wiping his rheumy eyes. Just the hint of a smile lurked in the corners of his upturned lips. He returned his attention to his future father in law when Brihtric spoke again.

"Just because he is the son of the king's first love he has nevertheless been brought up to be a prince and to lead forces in battle. Many a time he has held court in the absence of his father. We need a strong king, one who has some experience and has already proved himself a leader of men, not a child who is scarcely out of the nursery."

The arguments continued heatedly. Edwin was allowed to leave having loudly objected to his half-brother's presumptuous claim. It was emphasised several times that he had spent the previous evening in the church and was tired.

Aethelstan, bareheaded and modestly dressed, continued to stand silently in front of the court. The only occasion he could speak on his own behalf would be if he was offered the crown of Wessex.

Udric found himself becoming acutely uncomfortable. His friendship with both Aethelstan and Aelfweard had been close. When Edwin had joined them his youth and inexperience had always meant that he had often been left out of their escapades. The venom in the voice of the champion of young Edwin as he derided his half-brother had shocked him acutely. Now it seemed that anyone could voice his opinions with impunity, regardless that one of those discussed still stood before them, with no right to protest or correct a mistaken fact.

When everyone seemed to have exhausted their partiality, the room became quiet save for the low tones of murmuring.

At length Algar turned to his old companion before demanding silence by banging his gavel on the oak table.

"Are we all said on this matter?"

There were a few assenting grunts but no-one leapt to their feet to make final pleadings for either choice. "Then the time has come to make your choice. Will all those who favour Edwin to be our King stand up? Sergeant; a count if you please."

A whispered figure was delivered to the two councillors as the second vote, in favour of Aethelstan was called. It was obvious who had been chosen but the soldier again whispered his total to the elder statesman before returning to his position by the main door. The elders' vote would not be needed but they still talked conspiratorially in low tones before Algar rose painfully to his feet. He supported himself on the table before looking directly at the assembled men before turning to the solitary prince.

"Prince Aethelstan, you have been elected king by the majority. In the presence of this council, will you accept the rulership of the kingdom?"

Unknowingly Udric, along with many others, had been holding his breath. It was released with an audible sigh of relief. Now his friend was within moments of becoming king. For ages he had maintained his composure in front of them all, now he was swearing to rule the kingdom and people with the help of almighty God. The Archbishop of York now stood to beseech the Almighty to give wisdom and other moral guidance to the newly elected king. He brought his prayers to an abrupt end when signs of impatience interrupted him. Cheers erupted as senior noblemen who had been sitting closest gathered round Prince Aethelstan. Once again the guards reversed their spears to the upright position and thumped the hall floor. The doors were opened wide revealing a crowd of servants who had been eavesdropping.

Amid the commotion Udric saw his sponsor gather up his sticks, bow briefly to the new king and them limp from the raised platform. Udric made his way quickly through the crowd to help the old man.

Clearly exhausted, Algar remonstrated that Udric should be with the king. "He will need his friends, stay close to him. I will see you tomorrow, God willing! Bring my granddaughter with you." He added with a sparkle in his eyes.

Reluctantly Udric watched his sponsor struggle painfully across the courtyard to his quarters before returning to the crowd which surrounded Aethelstan.

His first announcement as King was to order the court be moved to Kingston on the Wessex, Mercia border. Here he would be hallowed by Frithstan, the new Archbishop of Canterbury, then accept the homage of his thegns.

Udric followed the king from the hall, the royal cloak over his arm. Either man could have left wearing the late King's garment which had been laid on the table by the two council leaders. He caught sight of Edwin talking heatedly to one of his erstwhile supporters who strangely had been among the first to offer his loyalty to the new King. Udric hesitated, looked round for his father, and then continued on his way to the royal quarters.

At the feast that night he sat with his betrothed just below the high table. He related the events of the day to her, pleased that she genuinely appeared interested. No women had been allowed in the hall to witness the election. Normally they would be told few of the details as the matter did not concern female ears. He looked forward to his marriage, longing to show her the immense efforts which had been made to tame his land.

"There are few comforts there now but these will be added. Perhaps you will guide me as to what you need in the solar, for I am determined that there will be a private place. We could be married soon since everything has been agreed, although it would be correct to ask permission from Aethelstan I suppose. He would be mortally offended if we went ahead on the basis that Aelfweard had already consented."

They talked quietly between themselves, sharing a trencher, ignoring the other diners and the musicians who had come to play for the new King. Neither of them really appreciated the delicious dishes placed on the tables, the spicy sauces to pour over joints of meat or tart jellies to freshen the palette. Apart from the occasional polite greetings to those who sat either side of them, Udric and Edith were cocooned in a private liaison amidst the organised chaos as servants scurried around refilling drinking mugs.

Later when the trestles had been stacked alongside one wall his father joined them. Edith greeted him respectfully and asked if they would like her to leave them alone. Both men chorused that she should stay, her company lightening the atmosphere. Many other small groups were forming, the events of the day providing gossip and food for discussion. Udda admitted that he was anxious to return to Uddings.

"I miss your mother and the quietness. Besides, the new steward may need help. There is still considerable ill-feeling as far as Thomas;

the butcher from Wymburne is concerned. You were not at the moot, being with the Prince, but he swore he would get even. I don't trust him and many of us felt the same. Twice Owen has gone in my place which is perfectly legal but some men obviously feel that my work is less than theirs. The fact that I am a landowner when most of the other men own no more than an acre and also work for a master does give rise to jealousy.

Will Prince Aethelstan, the king I mean, still require me to look after his horses? No matter, it's late; there may still be space for me to bed down in the stables. Good night son, Lady Edith."

He smiled as Udric escorted Edith to the womens' quarters. He was sure Galena would like her, his only concern being that the girl had probably been brought up in a large household with many servants. She would have to adjust to a small estate with a few bondswomen to help her.

He shivered in the cool night air. Stars peeped distantly from the blackness above the roof of the King's palace. Occasionally the light from the hall briefly spilled out through the open door illuminating the courtyard. The sound of revelry coming from the hall where musicians were playing a rousing dance was abruptly muted when the heavy doors slammed shut. Men were relieving themselves in dark corners shouting greetings to others who had come out for a breath of air.

Making his way back towards the stable buildings Udda passed the store rooms. A man drew quickly back into the shadows. Memories of the attacks on him many years ago flooded back as he broke out in a sweat. For years he had lived peacefully at Uddings, the injustices of the past receding in his memory thanks to Lord Algar's efforts. An owl hooted as it flew silently on its hunting mission, the haunting sound increasing Udda's fear.

His father's health had never recovered from the ordeal but since his death, thoughts of regaining ownership of the family farm at Woodcutts had died too. With a rush, the whole episode of the trial and expulsion from the farm returned. Images of the new occupant of the land flashed before him as he fumbled for his knife. A slave approached silently, hesitantly offered him a torch.

"Come with me to the stables," instructed Udda more tersely than he intended. His nervousness had added an edge to his voice. He felt slightly ridiculous asking an unarmed slave for company but could not prevent his eyes trying to penetrate the darkness beyond the flickering ring of light afforded by the torch.

There was no sign of an assailant in the shadows but he heard rapid footsteps receding and knew he had not been mistaken. Once safely inside the wooden building he dismissed the slave with thanks and made his way to the stall used by the stable staff. He found a space between two of the young men, wrapped his cloak around him and lay down.

It was a long time before he slept. Several of his companions snored while others were restless sleepers. In the morning he woke un-rested, feeling distinctly apprehensive. The thought of making his way back to Uddings on his own was not a journey he relished. He was nervous and went to the midden to relieve himself looking over his shoulder while he did so. Every man had a knife but few came to court fully armed. Seax, the Saxon's weapon of choice, spears and bows were all given up to the King's steward on entering the palace precincts. No one entered the King's presence armed. His small weapon would be no defence against a determined assassin. 'Although God knows I am not carrying anything worth stealing! Why on earth should there be any trouble?' Udda's thoughts were jumbled. He brushed a few bits of straw from the heavy folds of his cloak in order to smarten up his appearance. The shoulders were padded with the last of the ver skins which had lined the cloak belonging to his long dead master. They added much needed warmth when the cold winds blew so that it seemed to penetrate the very bones of a man.

Edith too was up early and greeted her future father in law respectfully. She too was wearing a cloak of green wool with a fur lined hood. Together they collected a manchet of bread and ale on the way to the hall where a few trestles had been erected between the still slumbering men.

They sat companionably on a bench. Slices of cheese and cold meats had now been laid on the table. Admiring her blue eyes and eyelashes which lay like fans on her smooth cheeks without staring at her, Udda ate sparingly. He felt unaccountably nervous and the food lay heavily.

"I would like to take my leave of Udric. Do you know where he is?" Udda asked casually, not wishing to burden the girl with his worries.

"He has gone to the stables with my lord Aethelstan. They go hawking this morning. The late king's gerfalcon is fretting in the mews. A message was sent about it last night I believe."

Udda jumped up spilling his ale. Hastily apologising for his clumsiness Udda hurried to the mews. A nauseating feeling of dread swept over him like a blush which starts in the guts and rises unbidden to one's face. He ran across the courtyard, ignoring the puzzled looks that such haste engendered in others who walked at a more leisurely pace.

Prince Edwin and his companions were already there in the semi-darkness apparently discussing the merits of each bird. The great gerfalcon eyed the intruder briefly before hunching down on its perch again. Noting that it did not look the least distressed Udda left quietly, bidding the men good hunting. He made his way to the stables in search of Udric. He breathed deeply to remove the acrid smell of the mews from his nose. "God's Blood! I am getting like a feeble woman fancying phantoms and devils in every corner!" he muttered trying to recover a small degree of poise before anyone saw him.

In the stables several horses were being harnessed. Aethelstan, who was standing well back from the stalls, would ride his father's stallion, a large dappled grey with yellow teeth. Udda stroked its formidable forehead affectionately waiting until Udric, who was talking to the prince noticed his presence.

"My lord, my father has attended your late father's sick and breeding horses for several years. Shall he continue in your service?" The request was so timely; Udda could not avoid grinning at his son's choice of phrase.

Aethelstan pretended to think seriously for a few moments before clapping Udda on the back heartily. "You saved my life when I was but eight summers old and for this reason alone I owe you thanks. My father trusted his horses to you and I shall do the same. Will you have me as your lord?"

Dropping to his knees, Udda spoke his oath of homage slowly and clearly, his hands between those of his king. The horses looked on quietly, their fidgeting still for the moment. As Udda rose to his feet and dusted off the straw which now clung to his leggings the king spoke briefly to his stable master. A few moments later he returned leading a finely built roan mare, completely harnessed with quality leather saddle and bridle. The king's colours had been placed on her browband. The ribbon tossed as she walked, stepping daintily passed the big stallion which eyed her greedily.

"Take this mare for your own as a token of my trust in you. If you breed from her let me know. She is young and untried but should serve you well, as you served my father."

Concerns over the man he had seen in the shadows momentarily forgotten, Udda stroked the mare and gave her a small piece of the bread he had kept for his journey. Unable to prevent himself from grinning widely he thanked the king for his generosity. He was still admiring his new horse when Udric and Aethelstan left the stables for the mews. Out of the corner of his eye Udda saw them enter the gloomy room, ducking under the low doorway.

Chapter Twelve

A man screamed in pain startling the mare. Udda's head jerked up suddenly. Throwing the reins over a peg he ran to the mews to find his son bleeding profusely from a knife wound. On the point of attending to his son's injury his eyes adjusted to the dim light inside the mews. At the far end of the building the king was being held firmly by two men while a third held a hot iron in one hand. At a glance Udda saw that Aethelstan's struggles were ineffective against the brute strength of his captors. The birds were screaming on their perches adding to the fearful atmosphere. Udda pulled out his knife and lunged at the nearest man. The blade struck home causing the ruffian to loose his grip. A well aimed kick in the groin completed the man's submission as he rolled in agony amid the droppings. The gerfalcon clawed at his face, its leather thong stretched to its limit.

Attacked now by the hot iron, it caught Udda on the arm. The pain caused him to drop his weapon which was immediately kicked beyond his grasp. Blows followed rapidly as he bent down, scrabbling in the dirt to retrieve it. Dizzy from their force he heard a voice saying that the iron would have to be reheated to take out the king's eyes. In the horrified silence which followed Udda struggled to martial his wits. A further attempt to grasp his knife brought an agonising blow to his head so he lay as if stunned waiting for his chance to attack. With a quick lunge he snatched it, rolled onto his back and threw the knife. The blade struck just below the man's breast bone. He sank to his knees falling across his comrade who had been so savagely ripped by the falcon. He died moaning, face down on the filthy floor, his blood dripping slowly from the mortal wound.

Now unarmed, Udda sprang at the last of the assassins oblivious to any danger to himself. His fury leant him a God-given strength far beyond his normal capacity, a temporary feeling of invincibility. Lashing out angrily, and landing several hard punches, the man fled leaving his companions, dead and alive. Panting with the effort and emotion, Udda un-gagged the king and cut the ropes which held him before sinking to the ground exhausted. Sweat had broken out all over his body despite being a relatively fit man from the physical activities he did during the working day. He wiped his face with the sleeve of his robe, shocked by what had been intended. A feeling of dizziness and nausea forced him to remain on his knees until the sickness passed.

"Ho, guards, to me guards!" shouted the king rubbing his wrists and flexing his arms where the ropes had bruised him. He was white faced except for two high spots of angry colour on his cheeks. Clenching both fists in an attempt to control his rage he leant against the gerfalcon's perch.

The soldiers rushed in, stopping in confusion at the carnage which met their eyes. "Chain them up," commanded the king pointing to the two would-be assassins who lay still on the soiled straw. He was unaware that one of them was already dead. "I will question them myself."

Somewhat shamefaced, as they had been chatting among themselves in the courtyard, the soldiers pulled the two men brutally out of the mews tearing fabric and skin as the bodies bumped over the threshold.

Udda bent over his ashen-faced son using his headband to staunch the blood which still flowed from the chest wound, cradling the boy's head in his arms, willing him to live. Udric's eyes were closed, his breathing ragged. Now that there was some light Udda could see some of the damage the knife wound had done to his son.

Aethelstan quickly recovered from his own ordeal when he saw Udric's pallid condition. "My own hurts are nothing to Udric's. He entered first and was dragged to one side before he could even stand up. Carry thegn Udric to my own quarters. Send physicians to him. Go with your son Udda. I will come soon."

His bodyguards hurried to obey, picking up Udric's limp body with surprising tenderness.

The keeper of the mews, a weedy man who had no need to duck under the lintel of the low door, returned to his charges wringing his hands. On being accused of being absent from his post he hastily explained that he had received a message from Prince Edwin's man that he was to attend the king in the hall where he had waited for some time.

Convinced that the man lied, Aethelstan roughly seized the keeper by the throat, threatening him with a painful death unless he spoke the truth. As grim faced house-carls prepared to remove the man to await the awful punishment the king had mentioned, the man drew breath with difficulty, sobbing that he told the truth. "He wore the prince's colours lord; I would not leave my post. The birds know me and no other." The gerfalcon indeed recognised her keeper's voice, mewing for him. The king relaxed his grip allowing the man to calm the bird and untangle the jesses from its legs ending in claws nearly as long as the breadth of a man's hand.

"She has had enough sport for one day," commented the king dryly having seen the mess she had made of his would-be assassin. He strode from the mews, ignoring the crowd which had now gathered in the courtyard. Regardless of concerned councillors and thegns, the King returned to his own quarters where Udric lay apparently lifeless on a pallet beside the royal bed. The bleeding had been staunched but the physicians held out little hope for the young man's recovery. Udric's chest rose slightly, each breath an effort. Apart from bleeding a man, and this man had obviously already lost much blood, most doctors were not very skilled in other healing methods. Poultices often consisted of goats' droppings and similar material guaranteed to introduce infection. Fortunately on this occasion, probably because they thought his case was hopeless, the physicians had agreed to merely bind the wound with relatively clean strips of linen provided by the steward's wife.

Udda had never professed to being a religious man, but when the king entered he found him on his knees whispering prayers on behalf of his only son. Aethelstan laid his hand on Udda's shoulder dismissing the two black gowned men who appeared to be doing little more than wringing their hands and sighing over the loss and waste of a young life.

Edith brought a jug of ale, hesitantly pulling aside the heavy curtain of the royal bedroom. She placed it on the settle between the two men before calmly laying her hands around the pale face of her future husband, willing him to recover consciousness. Neither man thought to criticise her daring to enter a man's quarters, let alone enter the royal presence without permission.

"Tell me what happened Udda. All I know is that Udric entered the mews first. As I went in I was seized and bound before my eyes could see in the darkness within."

Udda told how he had found his son lying mortally wounded by the door and how he too had been attacked. "My lord, I have killed a man, I ask your pardon," finished Udda softly, unwilling to disturb Edith's prayers. She knelt beside the pallet, ignoring both the King and her future father in law whom she had just addressed in such a familiar manner. "When I was young I practiced throwing my knife to kill wild fowl. This time my aim was true."

"It's no more than the traitor deserved," muttered the king clenching his fists, "the other will wish he were dead too when I catch him. Would you know him again Udda?" He strode out angrily not waiting for a reply. Udda followed respectfully leaving Edith to nurse Udric without a care for propriety or convention.

One villain was now lying firmly bound in the guard room. He might be somewhat recovered from the blow to his body but the gerfalcon had done her work well. One eye was missing from its socket and his face was a mass of open wounds, the drying blood attracting flies.

"Bring the brazier closer and fetch an iron," commanded the king savagely pressing his dagger to the prisoner's throat. Convinced he was to die, the man confessed that three of them had been recruited by Alfred, a thegn who supported Prince Edwin's claim to the throne. They were to blind the king but not kill him. In a further effort to save himself the conspirator divulged the names of his companions. Guards left to find the third man as the king turned to him with the hot iron. The prisoner quickly realised he was to suffer the same fate as he had intended to inflict upon his king. Despite his desperate protestations of everlasting loyalty in the future, the King would show no mercy. There was already a smell of sweat, but now the man's bowels evacuated in his terror. King Aethelstan ignored everything except inflicting punishment on the man who lay helpless before him. Soldiers watched impassively, arms crossed beneath uniform cloaks.

Udda left the crowded guardroom breathing deeply as the man's screams faded to moans, then silence. His own head still hurt from the blows he had received and he had no wish to witness more violence. Aethelstan came out wiping his forehead on the sleeve of his tunic. There was a grey, pearly sheen to his face which increased until his eyes were mere slits. He suddenly vomited into the weeds beside the wall. Udda looked round quickly, unsure whether to call for help or to protect the King's privacy.

The King staggered, reaching out for Udda's arm. "We are told the Bible says 'an eye for an eye' and then that the Lord God will take revenge. What was I to do? The guards did not think I would actually do it. Imagine what they would say if they had been made to do it in my stead? That the King was not man enough?"

"My Lord, I cannot pretend that my knowledge of the Holy Book is a match for yours. Surely there are priests who can advise you on this?"

"Yes, hundreds of them, but most are milksops and would have me on my knees several times a day and there is no time for that. I have to rule Wessex and Mercia in a way that makes men obey me. If that means that they fear me at the same time, so be it. No-one must think that they can commit a crime and get away with it. There have to be consequences. On this occasion, a harsh one."

Aethelstan stood up and breathed deeply. He took Udda's arm as they hurried back to Udric's bedside where Edith still kept her vigil. Her long hair fell in a thick plait which she flicked over her shoulder whenever it came between her and her unconscious patient. Apart from glancing quickly at the King when he returned, her attention was entirely taken up with nursing Udric. The afternoon hours passed slowly. Not one of them noticed the sun passing its zenith then falling down in the Western sky, a pink glow promising good weather to come. Servants tip-toed in and closed shutters or restocked the brazier to keep the chamber warm. Many knew Udric and mumbled prayers for his recovery as they went about their duties.

In the King's hall there was an air of suspicion, each man keeping his own counsel instead of chatting. Although Earl Chester had left court, his son was surrounded by young men of a similar age.

"He's only a peasant for God's sake! Why the fuss? I would not give up my bed for him as the King has done." Chester's son's face was a picture of derision, his head slightly tilted upwards so that profile could appear more noble to his friends.

"What if he was the bait? He was to lead the King into the mews so that he could be attacked. It is known that Aethelstan trusts the man. He needs money doesn't he?"

"If he dies, my suit with the Lady Edith will be successful. Her father will not turn me down again. Udric's injuries are said to be fatal and he is already close to death. He may indeed have been involved and was silenced for his knowledge of the scheme despite having been friends with Lord Aethelstan for many years. Money can do strange things."

"Especially if you are short!" quipped his companion finishing another mug of ale.

The young men left the hall laughing and teasing each other about their success or lack of it with women. The late King's seneschal looked thoughtful. He had overheard much of their conversation and it troubled him.

Prince Edwin sat at the high table, appearing shocked by the attack on his half-brother. Men acknowledged his presence but few sought his company. If any of them had been involved it was not obvious for there was an unusual quietness, broken only when servants replenished ale mugs or brought new dishes to the tables. Torches were lit as the light faded, men leaving the hall in groups rather than singly in case assassins still lurked in dark corners. Many wore daggers openly on their belts, hands never far from the hilt even when crossing from the hall to private chambers. The very air seemed charged with fear, nervousness and suspicion.

In the King's chamber they ate sparingly from platters on the royal coffer while another pallet was fetched, the king refusing to allow his friend to be moved out of his own room. Promising to call Edith if there was any change to Udric's condition, Udda gratefully lay down on the fur covered paillasse, pulling the thick covers over him. He sank into a deep sleep, exhausted by the traumatic events of the day.

The planned move of the court to Kingston was delayed. The third would-be assassin was caught, questioned and punished in the same way as the other survivor. Few except the perpetrators and the victims knew the gory details of the attempt on the king's life but many were aware of the attack on Udric. Udda was amazed at the number of people who offered sympathy and prayers for his son's recovery. Apart from quick visits to the stables to check on the horses and a short ride on his newly acquired mare, Udda spent the next few days in a state of constant anxiety.

It was on his return from one of these inspections that Udda discovered Edith sleeping beside Udric. She had obviously lain down beside him to provide his body with her own warmth and fallen innocently asleep. Udda gently covered her with furs from his own bed drawing up a stool to keep watch. The skin around the wound had not festered for which mercy he gave thanks to God. He watched his son's shallow breathing hour after hour and made little of Edith's embarrassment when she awoke beside Udric. Momentarily bemused by sleep, she reddened at the impropriety, leaving hastily to change her creased clothes.

"Father, is that you?" whispered Udric through cracked, dry lips. "I'm thirsty."

"Thanks be to God," exclaimed Udda rushing to the door to order small beer for his son. Supported by strong arms, Udric was helped to take a few sips. The effort clearly exhausted him so they lay him down gently. "I thought for one moment that a priest would be needed!" joked Udda. Relieved by the normality of his son's request for a drink, Udda would not usually have reacted by finding anything remotely funny in someone's request to attend to their immortal soul. Silently he asked the Almighty for forgiveness for such levity.

Between them, Udda and Edith nursed Udric in the royal quarters. At first Udda had attempted to remonstrate with Edith, remembering that it was not perhaps proper to allow a young maiden to see a naked man. Edith however, had not let her initial shyness deter her from washing and cooling Udric's body as a fever burned in his lungs. Each breath was harsh, his face and lips grey with the effort of drawing air into his damaged chest. Occasionally he opened glazed, fevered eyes, unrecognising and unfocused.

"He is to be mine shortly. He will not die for lack of care, but needs me here when he is lucid. Let me stay and help, after all you cannot lift him and wash him at the same time!" she added mischievously.

Aethelstan refused to stand on ceremony, forbidding his friend to be moved from the comfort and privacy of his room. The king had in fact been too busy to make much use of his own bed. On hearing of the death of King Edward and his immediate heir soon after, the Danes of Northumberland had taken the opportunity to raid the northern borders of Wessex.

Four hundred Mercian soldiers had been mobilised to attack the enemy's territory where they had plundered and scattered the population forcing Sihtric, their king to sue for peace. The two kings would meet at Tamworth on the last day of the month when Sihtric had agreed to be baptised into the Christian faith. To further seal the peace, Editha, the king's young sister would be given in marriage.

The court once more hummed with activity. Preparations for the delayed move to Kingston upon Thames followed a well tried formula, the huge wagons rolling into the courtyard to await loading by a steady procession of servants. The oxen stood patiently chewing the cud. Huge stacks of bedding, household goods and coffers were loaded. Clerks bustled round checking lists whilst cooks put closed bowls of sweetmeats into hay padded boxes for the journey.

"I am loathe to leave Udric but my need of him is as nothing to his need for rest. God willing he will recover his health and strength for I have need of friends. Instructions have been left with the captain of my guard that a message be sent to me if there is any news. I must be crowned so that my authority is not in doubt and then the whole matter will be investigated. On my oath Udda, the men who did this will be punished, not just the three ruffians, they were not alone. It was not their idea to disable me. I will have answers and God forgive me, I will have revenge too."

The king left for Kingston with most of the thegns to be hallowed by Archbishop Frithstan who he had confirmed in office. The resources of Winchester were running dangerously low. Crowds had come for the funeral of the late king followed by the meeting of the Council to choose the successor. More had arrived too late for the first ceremony but determined to be present at the election of Aelfweard, now also dead and buried. Every day carts of food had entered the city until merchants grumbled that their barns were now empty. The privies were full, the rushes filthy. The King's palace desperately needed to be cleaned and refreshed after such a long period of use. The cavalcade had left noisily with trumpeters blasting their single notes into the skies. Guards rode close to the King, the horse carrying his grandfather's gifts to him immediately behind. King Alfred had given the young boy a purple mantle, a jewelled belt and a golden seax in an ornamented scabbard. These had never been worn but would be put on at his crowning. For years the gifts had remained in his coffer, secreted away from prying eyes, especially those of his half brother Edwin who rode in his coronation procession. "Jealousy is an evil worm, eating into the heart of a man," muttered Aethelstan as clouds passed over the sun. "He has always been wild, cruel and true only to himself. Had he known of my grandfather's hopes for me when we were children then God knows what he would have done."

On the fourth of September, in the year of our Lord nine hundred and twenty five the King stood upon the sacred rock where so many of his antecedents had been crowned. The Archbishop blessed the newly crowned ruler, calling on God to guide him. With his late father's crown firmly on his head, the jewelled belt and sword at his waist, King Aethelstan accepted the homage of his nobles and landowners, a tedious ceremony as each man repeated his oath before God and the king. It was after this ritual that the King called for silence. Rising slowly, he scanned the expectant faces before openly accusing Thegn Alfred of being behind the attempted assassination in the mews.

There were horrified gasps from the huge assembly of men who only moments before had knelt before their purple robed King. Silently, the men parted to expose the accused to the full glare of the King who grew in stature before their very eyes. A shaft of light from an open window lit up his blond hair like a halo beneath the golden crown. Hands reached for empty scabbards, Aethelstan having insisted that no weapons at all would be allowed in the nave of the church. Guards stood at every door, every face schooled in watchfulness.

As Udda and Udric were later told by Thegn Brihtric, Edith's father, Alfred had apparently gone white, blustering his denial of anything to do with the dastardly deed. Amid mingled gasps of astonishment and embarrassment, he offered to take a sacred oath to affirm his innocence in front of the Pope in Rome.

"Very well! You will depart immediately. Guards! Escort this man from here. You are not to stop until you reach the port of Hamtun. From there you will accompany him to Rome where he will make his oath on the Holy Book, in front of the Pope. You will return and report to me that he has sworn his innocence in any part of the attack on me."

A detachment of guards formed up around the accused thegn. Alfred had no alternative; he left the hall followed by the four armed soldiers and was heard cantering off to take ship from Hamtun. The other nobles and thegns looked on in astonishment. For many it was the first they had heard of the attack. There was a great deal of whispering among them as the ceremony drew to a close.

"My son has heard that the King's peasant friend was involved. He was attacked and is close to death. He lies in the King's own chamber so I'm told!" bragged the Earl of Chester in much the same tones as his son. From the attention his words were getting he was telling the other thegns something new. Their faces reflected total surprise. Many of them admired Udric, a young man much favoured by Lord Algar, the leader of the King's Council. That the young man was so badly injured saddened them and many spoke in his support.

"Well, he was there when the King was attacked and did nothing to help," countered the Earl realising that his companions were not of the same opinion as himself.

"No, he did nothing to help the King because he was attacked first and left for dead. Excuse my interruption lords, but young Udric probably took the blow intended for the King. Even now the doctors despair of his recovery and the priests have attended him." The seneschal bowed gracefully to the nobles and backed away. The Earl of Chester had the grace to look crestfallen, reddening under the weather-beaten skin of his face. The other men very quickly found others to talk to, ashamed of their attention to Earl Chester's accusations.

Content that his daughter was in good hands, Edith's father prepared to leave for his own estates. Udda gladly agreed that he would care for her since he too was reluctant to leave Udric who was still too weak to defend himself.

"The Queen has left court. My father has returned with Lord Aethelstan to lead his council. He will arrange for an escort to bring you home. I have heard that the Earl of Chester has returned to his manor. He was heard to suggest that your young man might have been involved in the attack on the King. No, daughter, do not interrupt me, for you should know what is being rumoured at court."

"Udric was almost killed father. He would never have threatened Aethelstan. The two have been friends since Udric was only a child. How could he have been involved?"

"Chester's son is not a friend of Udric. He wanted to have you for his wife. Jealousy does strange things to a man's judgement and that is probably a kind description. You turned him down and I refused him on your behalf. Stay with my father for they may look to question your virtue. That family has tongues like vipers and spread poison without a thought for anyone's good name. If you have found happiness with Udric and are content then my father and I will protect you as best we can. Bless you daughter! If Udric survives, it will be God's will and the marriage should go ahead. Udda will not leave his son and it would be a hard father who would deny his daughter the right to nurse her intended." Lord Brihtric stroked his daughter's face and kissed her lightly. He bowed quickly to Udda and left the King's chamber, pulling the heavy curtain across the doorway.

Udda put his arm around Edith's shoulders. Her cloak lay discarded on the bed.

"I agree with much of what your father said. Lord Chester is forgetting that when the King and Udric went into the mews, I was on the other side of the courtyard. I heard him cry out and the screaming of the birds. There is no truth at all in the lord's accusations. Many a time Udric has protected Aethelstan from harm. Now that he is King he will have skilled and learned men to advise him. Udric can return to Didlington, finish his house and get married as you planned.

Having been a witness to the attempt on the king's life he could still be in danger from Edwin's supporters should the matter come to trial. The assailants themselves can harm no one. The King tells me that they are being kept as chained slaves until they die of exhaustion or old age."

It was more than a month before Udric took his first unsteady steps outside. Blinking in the unaccustomed light he leaned heavily on his father. His normally bronzed features were grey with pain, the sunken cheeks altering his appearance so that few recognised the young man walking slowly around the courtyard. Dressed in borrowed clothes, for none of his own tunics fitted, Udric breathed in the fresh air.

The autumn air had a slight chill which reduced the odours of the old rushes which were being changed. The King had gone to meet the Danish King taking a full complement of guards and nobles with him. In his absence servants cleaned and swept every room. Middens were emptied by slaves who stumbled round in shackles. No-one stayed in the capital unless they were forced to when the cleaning process was being carried out.

"The sooner you get some good Dorsetshire air into you the better. This place stinks and the very air is full of poisonous fumes."

It took several more days for Udric to walk unaided. Edith and Udda took turns to accompany him talking of their plans for the future. His appetite returned gradually, the hollows of his face becoming less pronounced.

Udda found a messenger who was returning to the King's Tun at Wymburne and asked him to call at Uddings to warn Galena of their impending return. She may have already heard of her son's terrible injuries and be anxiously awaiting further news. Many of the Wymburne guards and workers knew Udda and were pleased to oblige him. Galena's honey cakes were legendary and visitors were often offered some. The rider, wearing the King's device on his tunic set off cheerfully, promising to deliver the message safely.

Dressed warmly, Edith joined Udric in the courtyard. He had only just started riding again and was still flushed from the wintry air beyond the city walls.

"My father has sent an escort for me. It is a tedious journey back to Suffolk but I cannot keep the men waiting my love. You must get well. You can best do this at Uddings. As soon as you are fit the marriage will take place. I have promised to call at St Agatha's on the way home. She answered my prayers for your recovery. Go now my love or you will have me in tears. God knows, I have shed enough of those when you might have died. Go with God Udric."

They kissed, holding each other closer than might be acceptable to matrons and churchmen, only breaking apart when the saddled horses were brought close-by. Heat suffusing his whole body, Udric stood and watched Lord Brihtric's guards form a protective shield around his betrothed. The cavalcade trotted down the road to the guard tower and out of his sight.

The homecoming was a time of celebration. In glorious winter sunshine the two riders passed the burial mounds of the long dead and dropped down to the heaths of Holt and Uddings. Horns blared as soon as they were spotted. Smiling fieldhands cheered, dropping their tools to run to the bank which edged the track down which Udric and Udda rode. The former tried hard to return the greetings of people who had watched him grow up but it was obvious to his father that Udric was exhausted by the ride. As the mare which Udda proudly rode was so young and bearing in mind the state of Udric's health it had been thought a sensible but reluctant necessity to break their journey at Cranburne. Not a place which had endeared itself to Udda, their stay in the guest house which was still very spartan, had been as brief as possible. The ale served with the meal that morning had been tainted so neither had drunk more than a few sips. Instead they had watered the horses in a small stream running between two hills on the chase and drunk some of the icy water themselves. Being close to the source it was hoped the clearness also indicated its purity. As the journey progressed at a steady walk in the almost heatless sunshine, neither of them had suffered any ill effects. They would both be glad to return to the safety of Uddings, to the stream which flowed along the boundary. There were no mills or other homesteads up-stream to foul the water. Two rough coated dogs rushed out to meet the riders, tails working rapidly from side to side. With open jaws they appeared to be smiling. Udda dismounted and patted both of them. A boy, dressed in serviceable brown tunic and trews took the mare's reins, his eyes wide with astonishment when he saw the quality of her harness and the royal colours on the browband.

Affectionate greetings were the norm at Uddings. It was a working farm, not by any stretch of the imagination a manor house where more courtly manners and stiff formal greetings would be more acceptable. Galena supported her father who moved stiffly but was anxious to see the new arrivals. Gerhard's hair was now thin, scarcely covering his scalp. His body beneath a heavy wool cloak was thin and frail, racked with stiffness probably caused from his previous occupation as turf cutter, out on the heath in all weathers.

Despite his pains he remained cheerful, most often to be found beside the kitchen oven doing small tasks when he could.

Galena, in contrast to her father, radiated good health and well being. She was now of matronly proportions, emphasised by the white cloth tied around her rather ample waist. Regardless of how carefully her wimple was arranged in the morning, by the time Udda returned curls escaped to frame her smiling, rosy face. She kissed him enthusiastically making no secret of her love for him. No one was embarrassed by such a show, it was normal here. She beckoned a young girl to come forward with some of her best ale.

"Aye love, a wholesome, full bodied drink, not like that mishmash served at the Cranburne guesthouse!" Udda pulled a face which made the little girl burst into peals of laughter. Once again he hugged his wife passionately, whispering endearments that only she could hear. "We have much to talk about and Udric needs your care so he will stay with you. Owen wants me to see the stock as my absence was much longer than planned. Your suggestion of having a feast is timely. Did you notice the new mare I was riding? - A gift from lord Aethelstan, now King. So much has happened but first the beasts need to be checked while there is light." Planting a loud kiss on his wife's cheek Udda threw off his best cloak to exchange it for a more workaday garment.

While Gerhard and Galena fussed over Udric, Udda inspected his stock with Owen who had been in overall charge of both estates in their absence. The feast to celebrate their return, in particular Udric's survival of a terrible wound would be for all, regardless of status. A barren ewe was marked for slaughter to provide meat for everyone. Those on Udric's land would come by cart only leaving a couple of volunteers and the dogs to see to the safety of the beasts. They would have their turn to celebrate later but would get parcels of food brought back for them.

Sitting on a bench outside the steward's cottage, now occupied by his deputy, Udda told Owen of the attacks and of the danger which now faced Udric as a witness to the attack on the King. He was appalled, his brow immediately furrowing with concern. "Then from now on I suggest that all strangers be accompanied to the homesteads whatever their reason for visiting." Udda nodded his agreement to Owen's proposal. "And the dogs should be loose at night. They know all our people and would give advance warning of any strangers. You say Udric was stabbed through the chest? He is a lucky man to survive such an injury."

Despite the hardships of his early life as a slave and survival of several skirmishes in the King's army, Owen's hair remained totally black. Apart from being weather beaten, his face remained open and trusting, brown eyes unafraid to look directly at his lord. A few late withered leaves blew past him then lifted once again by unseen forces to swirl round and move on. He watched them thoughtfully, considering the chances that a man so mortally wounded had of returning to life. "The young lord was lucky. I would have added my prayers to yours had the news come sooner."

Putting down his wooden beaker of ale Udda ran his hands through his own grey hair which already showed signs of thinning. It had been barbered while he nursed Udric at Winchester so still looked neat. He replaced the band carefully, ensuring that the King's colours showed prominently on his brow. Owen adjusted the motif so that it was central.

"So Udric stayed in the king's chamber all the time?" he asked curiously. "What about his lady? You say she was there too, in the room with you."

"That's right! All the normal rules and petty ugly thoughts were forgotten. Everyone prayed for his recovery, well not everyone of course. I understand that the King accused thegn Alfred of instigating the attack on behalf of Prince Edwin. He was sent off to Rome to make his oath before the Pope. This was after everyone had taken their oath to the King which went on for hours I tell you. Thegn Alfred looked so surprised when he was packed off immediately! Of course Edwin is the next legitimate heir but much younger. I wouldn't trust him at all. He has always been a spiteful boy according to Udric. A tale bearer too which never makes anyone popular. The plan obviously came from him or his supporters. No doubt they were marked when the voting was done. Aethelstan won easily; after all, he has been tried in battle and tested in the courts so he has much more experience than the younger prince. There is sure to be a trial, but of whom I wonder. Will the King try the prince? No doubt we will hear in due course. Is that jug empty yet?"

Sunday church services were still the occasions when townspeople and the farming community mingled. News of births, deaths and marriages was circulated together with gossip brought back by men serving in the fyrd. On this day, at the beginning of advent Udda took his family and those who wanted to ride with them on the ox cart to the town. After Mass was over the young men dutifully went to the butts to practice while the women sought to purchase their household needs.

The noise emanating from the market place in Wymburne was enough to penetrate the hearing of even the deafest townsman. In the far corner the butcher reached for the next unfortunate victim of his skill. The air was rent with the scream of the pig until it was abruptly cut off as the knife flashed in the autumn sunshine. Small children watched in awe until its death throes had ceased.

At the stalls, many had already become hoarse from shouting their wares. Leather belts, straps, head-collars and harness for horse and ox carts were suspended from the framework, while next door a farmer's wife with a cheerful red face, tried to sell her surplus cheese, eggs and butter.

There were stalls selling iron pots, ladles, knives, saws and strainers, the smith's apprentice in his leather apron disappointed that so far he had few customers. His master would be annoyed if the sales were not worth the fee of two pennies charged by the warden of the Wymburne market.

This individual, flourishing his staff, charged each stall holder. He also charged a fee for each animal brought to the pens, whether for sale or to be slaughtered.

Cages of fowls, ducks and squirming piglets added to the cacophony of noise. The occasional escapee introduced an air of levity except to the owner who chased the animal through a maze of legs, barrows and alleyways encouraged by bystanders and hampered by the children who had now become bored with watching the butcher.

Other stalls displayed colourful lengths of woollen cloth. Housewives fingered the texture, before pointing to the piece they needed to buy. A few ready-made garments hung from the horizontal bar. Only the wife of a burgess could afford to purchase a luxury item such as a ready sewn tunic or kirtle. She might not have an upright loom in the upstairs room of her house but few did not sew their own clothing.

Needles, ribbons, pottery items, brass buckles; everything needed for the household was on sale. Then of course, were the foodstuffs, normally occupying one row of stalls and competing loudest for the attention of the frugal housewife. Beans, dried peas, root vegetables, together with bunches of herbs and wizened apples ranged alongside the sellers of meat whose stall attracted swarms of flies. A boy waved rather ineffectually at these pests, any faltering being rewarded by a cuff round the ear.

Salt had to be kept dry and was sold in blocks, often wrapped in hides which seeped a grimy discharge. Women in Wymburne had no access to the sea and were forced to purchase supplies at the one stall licensed to sell the valuable and essential commodity. If they wished to preserve meat from the November slaughter, they needed to buy salt and the seller was aware of this so had little reason to shout his wares.

Occasionally the two Wymburne fishermen sold fresh river fish so that people could observe meat-less Fridays. There were barrels of preserved herring for women who could not afford to buy the fresh carp or pike caught in the river Stour. Most of their catch was already sold to richer folk and taken straight to their kitchens.

Honey, the only sweetener available was sold in rough unglazed earthenware pots, the surface sealed with molten beeswax. Any self respecting housewife collected this to make a small rush-light which would burn pure and bright in the winter darkness.

Beggars were discouraged, often ending up in the stocks surrounded by the mob of unsupervised children throwing mud and worse at the poor offender. The town constable would look on, often with a jug of ale sold by the church. After all, it was hard work patrolling the stalls along the Shambles, settling arguments and protecting the market warden with his fat purse.

At the Hundred Moot the reeve from the King's Tun announced that King Aethelstan had introduced a measure to ensure that the poor and destitute were cared for by each town's officers.

"Another tax!" complained one man just loud enough for the reeve to hear.

"I hope you are never in need of aid from such a fund." The reeve retorted staring fixedly at the cordwainer who promptly blushed with embarrassment, staring fixedly at the polished leather shoes which served as an advertisement for his trade.

"In Wymburne you are lucky. A man can get alms from the monastery and a monk will physic him if he is ill. There are many towns where they have no facilities and people starve for lack of care and compassion. From now on the poor and sick will be cared for by the town. The priest will keep records of the monies. You trust him don't you?"

Men nodded hastily and were about to discuss the matter when the reeve once more shouted for their attention.

"The second measure my lord King has made law is that each year

I am entitled to free one slave. Not a prisoner of battle, nor a man who has killed unlawfully, but a man who has been sold because he was unable to pay the fine. Great King Alfred set out the wergild for every crime and it remains the same today but many have not been able to afford even the smallest amount and have therefore become churls or slaves. My remit covers the whole of the royal estate here in Wymburne. If you know of a man who deserves such release you will tell me, either here and now or later in private.

There was silence as each man looked at his neighbours wondering who might know of such a man. Udda and Udric no longer had any slaves, the last of the three being freed before the birth of his child. Neither of their estates were within the boundary of the King's Tun. Apart from royal servants there, and a few of the Cheneford workers on the far side of the River Stour, they knew few who might qualify from the King's bounty.

Men struggled to their feet, most dressed in warm fleeces for the winter days were short and cold. Fortunately there had been no accusations of light weight loaves or dyed fabric which did not keep its colour to be dealt with. They walked briskly back to the town hoping that their wives and workers were ready to return to homesteads before nightfall. A crescent moon was already rising, highlighting clouds which looked dark against the sliver of light. Udric shivered beneath the cloak he wore. He was still gaunt, exhaustion etched into the brown hollows beneath his eyes. Cold air seemed to aggravate the scar tissue but he had been keen to attend the meeting. Many had heard the rumour that he had been close to death. News like that could not be kept secret, nor could the cause of his injuries.

"The more men who see me alive and well, the more pairs of eyes will take note and remember strangers who enquire for me. I have noticed though Father, that the jealousy that was so evident at my first moot as a land owner seems to have evaporated rather quickly when the quality of the land involved was described. I think many of them pity me trying to tame heathland!"

CHAPTER THIRTEEN

Udric's manor-house, erected on a small rise, now boasted a private bower for his wife-to-be. The chamber was little more than one end of the hall with upright beams with interwoven hazel wands forming an interior divider. The wooden walls had been ribbed so that plaster could be spread which in turn would help to keep the property warmer. The kitchen had been built a little distance from the house with store rooms close by. Two of the field workers' wives were offered promotion to work indoors. They would help with the cooking, the stores and any cleaning or washing required. They would spin or weave if that is what their new mistress asked them to do but as yet the hall was bare of all feminine accessories.

Although bonded, his outdoor workers were not slaves and had small, round huts of their own, receiving a share of the produce from the fields, both in grain, wool and meat as well as clothes in return for their labour on Udric's land. They could not work elsewhere without breaking the bond and technically any children would also be bonded to the same lord. Little different in status from serfs but un-free, shackled slaves were an abhorrence to Udric as they were to Udda. Similarly when a child was expected by the slave given to him by the princes, he gave the man his freedom so that the child would be born free and in time could barter for his labour. In return the man gave his oath to Udric having him for his lord. Although the event had not occurred many times they had been emotional occasions, rewarded by fervent thanks and devoted service from then on. Now a year after the three slaves had been gifted by the Princes, all of them were settled and free men. The house-servant who had initially been unable to hide his disgust that he would be expected to do manual labour could hardly wait for the arrival of his lord's wife. He understood that she was a thegn's daughter and would therefore need comforts in her home. A house servant of his standing would direct others to carry fuel for the hall fire, close or open shutters and all the other tasks which were done indoors. He smiled in anticipation of the young lady's arrival. No harm would come to Udric or his family while he was there to care for them. He sniffed, wiping his nose discreetly on his sleeve, hoping that the odour of the plaster would fade long before the wedding. His hands were still rough from helping to apply the muck made up of clay, ox dung and gravel. He shuddered dramatically even thinking of the demeaning task he had helped with!

Owen had emphasised his instruction that anyone visiting either Didlington or Uddings was to be escorted from the outer boundaries regardless of what work someone was doing. He had explained some of the reasons for this hostile approach to visitors, providing horns so that warning could be given before two-legged or four legged intruders could get close to their master. There were a few false alarms but these interrupted what would otherwise have been a routine and possibly boring day.

The construction of the mill continued apace, the most difficult part being the harnessing of the small river Wym which some called the River Allen in these parts. Several times floods had swept away the boards which channelled part of the flow to the sump where the wheel would be hung. Two stories high, the building rose steadily round the tallest timbers which the woods at Uddings could supply. The poor ox had struggled to pull the weight of each trunk, a small boy armed with a hazel twig urging the beast to greater effort round the hill to the river.

Udric had not long been fully recovered when he was summoned to attend the king. Since King Aethelstan had thoughtfully provided his son with an armed escort, Udda was less worried about the journey back to court than when they left several months ago. Once again the workers waved and wished him Godspeed, a fact which astonished some of the soldiers who were to ride with him. They were far more used to surly looks and a total lack of interest when a lord left his land.

"Glad to see you recovered Udric," declared the officer of the guard. "Nasty business that and you were caught in their web. Lord King Aethelstan has acted quickly. He also ordered the coastal shires are better guarded against invasions. Those cursed Norsemen cause trouble despite being chased back to their boats."

They chatted most of the way, even when the grey sky delivered a fine drizzle for most of the journey. Udric looked about him noticing that the road had been repaired since he had ridden out, barely clinging to the pommel of the saddle. He longed to ask if the lady Edith was at court but held the question back knowing that he would find out soon enough.

They rode straight through the outer guard house saluting the housecarls who recognised Udric and welcomed him back. There had been an attempt to infill between the inner palace buildings so that guards could be more effective. There were no longer shadows between storehouses where assassins could lurk. New torches had been mounted in iron mouldings. Obviously the King was not going to give anyone another opportunity to attack him.

Udric mounted the staircase, paused to survey the familiar scene and entered the King's chamber where he was embraced heartily. Wine was poured into glasses, its deep ruby colour slightly muddied by the crackled surface of the vessels. Udric marvelled at them before grimacing slightly at the unaccustomed taste. King Aethelstan drank his quickly before indicating that they should both sit beside the brazier.

"Udric, you are a true friend. You have asked for no reward for saving my life and offer your loyalty and service to me freely. I would show my gratitude in a proper fashion, but first let me tell you news of the traitorous Alfred. As you know he went to Rome under escort, made a vow in front of the Pope swearing his innocence in any part of the plot to injure me. Immediately he fell down in a faint. Well more than a faint, he never recovered his senses and died three days later! The pope asks what he should do with the body. The papal messenger awaits my decision. Should he be granted Christian burial or shall I tell him to throw him to the wild beasts? In ancient Rome bodies of criminals was thrown from the edge of a cliff onto the city midden!"

Startled by the directness of the question Udda was speechless for a moment, his emotions in turmoil. He was many summers younger than Aethelstan and had never made decisions of the like.

"My lord I am not qualified to advise you in these matters," he replied diplomatically. "Surely you have councillors more used to such weighty matters."

"Indeed I have, several have recommended that the death be used as a warning to others who have treasonable thoughts. The Bishop of Bath on the other hand points out that God will judge Thegn Alfred's soul and it is not for men, even a king, to condemn the dead."

"I rather agree with the Bishop. To deny a man a proper burial seems to make us no better than the beasts of the forest. They walk away from the fallen and in some cases use the carcass as the next meal." Udric frowned at the weighty words he had just used, his eyes narrowed in concentration.

There was silence as Aethelstan considered his friend's reasoning.

"You have deep thoughts for one so young," commented the king lightly, "come we will give the messenger his answer. I shall not benefit by one hide of the traitor's land. It shall be given to Malmesbury monastery, which is closest to his manor, where they shall pray for his soul from hereon."

He swept out of the room, his cloak billowing behind, leaving Udric adjusting his diadem as he followed the king through the guarded doorway. He had intended asking Aethelstan when he might be permitted to marry the lady Edith but was forced to wait while business was conducted in the king's hall. When he finally found the right moment to ask, as a matter of courtesy, if the wedding could be soon the king was enthusiastic.

"Ah yes, the lovely Edith! She cared for you here you know, without a thought for her own reputation. She loves you well." He added a little wistfully. As yet he was unmarried despite the urging of his council to secure his succession by producing a male heir at the earliest opportunity. "All Saints Day would be a propitious day. It should be held here at the Minster, after all Lord Algar would not want to miss his young body-servant's wedding to his grand-daughter. Had it not been for his persuasion she could have been espoused to Chester's boy, a ninny and not half the man his father is. Alas Edith's grandfather can no longer travel very far, but he will want to hear all your news. See you in the hall at dinner."

Dismissed, Udric crossed the courtyard to find Lord Algar. As the oldest man at court he was entitled to many privileges, not the least of which was a brazier burning brightly in the centre of his room. He was unable to rise to his feet but greeted Udric with joy, spontaneously sending for ale and food.

Udric dropped to his knees before the man who had given him so many opportunities. He was immediately waved to a stool, the old man's hands spotted with age stains on his pale skin. Initially shocked by his frail, cadaverous face, Udric took a moment to re-establish his composure. They talked of the family at Uddings and how Udda had turned the land into good pasture. "As you know much of the ground at Didlington was poor. Father's pigs were folded on each part in turn to put heart into the soil. It would have needed more than one plough to do the work. The land is scrubby, mostly heathland and unkempt woods! There are men working on the mill which has to be built according to my charter." he added proudly.

Algar nodded, vaguely remembering the day Udric had chosen the land north west of his father's land instead of a re-possessed manor the other side of the Kingdom.

"Tell me of your house. Brihtric is concerned that Edith will not have the comforts she is used to."

"Hopefully we have thought of everything. All my workers know that I hope to bring a wife to the house. It is longer than my father's house, with a private chamber at one end which will be Edith's solar and our bedroom." Udric blushed but continued when lord Algar looked up enquiringly, obviously expecting more details.

"There are two windows in the solar and three in the hall itself, all with shutters and a bar for security. The smith in Wymburne is forging a brazier, rather like the one you have here." He pointed to the burner which glowed red above a shallow layer of ash. It settled gently allowing a few small flames to ignite.

"The hall will have a central hearth but the stones had to be brought from further West as there is only gravel on my land. We used the gravel on the floor and then cut bracken but there will be no using the floor for er…. personal reasons," finished Udric lamely.

"Oh Udric, you are so easily embarrassed! But I agree with you, men who cannot use the midden must live like pigs in their own homes. Personally, I find the odour of dung in some of the halls the King visits is enough to make one's eyes water. I may be old and doddery but there is nothing wrong with my sense of smell!

A little later Udric told his sponsor of the king's suggested date for the wedding, hoping that Lord Algar would be well enough to attend.

"I take that as my invitation! No doubt Brihtric will also send word on Edith's behalf, but in the meantime I need to rest before dinner. My thanks Udric, for all your news. Much of my world now has to come to me. I have lived more than my four score years and ten, but hearing of your recovery and what is going on at your father's farm and Didlington makes me feel, well, as if there is a real connection between us."

Very gently, Udric hugged the old man, conscious of his thin shoulders beneath the warm cloak. He bowed and left Lord Algar looking dreamily into the fire.

As the days grew shorter Udric divided his time between his small estate and the capital where a room in the palace, close to the King's quarters was to be set aside for his family during the wedding celebrations. There was little heat in the sun if it managed to break through the blanket of grey cloud and mist which had settled over the whole land. The trees were bare of leaves standing like sentinels on the sky-line. Men hunted for deer or wild boar to add to the larder, King Aethelstan taking the gerfalcon out with him in an attempt to provide herons for those days when the church decreed that no red meat should be eaten.

"It is strange that I felt no guilt when she damaged a man's face, yet pity smaller prey when she falls from the sky to kill." He stroked the smooth feathers on her speckled breast conscious that her enormous talons were gripping his arm through the thick gauntlet. The bird cocked her head listening to the man's voice, reacting suddenly when the huntsman shouted that a suitable quarry had been spotted. "There you go girl! Fetch the dinner!" with one fluid movement the King launched the hawk towards the hapless heron which flew low over the river in the distance.

In Dorset, where the pace of life was always slower, the new horses the King had ordered from Northern France had arrived safely at Uddings. Shipped across the channel in boats relying on sail and oars, the beasts needed time to settle in their new home. Udda was charged with selecting the mares to be used for breeding in an effort to improve the size of the native British horses. True, they were sturdy animals, easily trained and cheap to feed. Many could survive the harshest winter weather on moor lands and open heathland. These ponies however, could not be used to carry a man and his weapons on a long journey. It was still the case that only the wealthiest men could afford the larger, imported horses. King Aethelstan wanted more but was loath to pay the vast sums demanded by Norman lords plus the costs to ship them to Hamtun. The matter had been discussed in detail during the long days when Udric had been in the King's chamber recovering from the stab wound and Aethelstan had spent so much time visiting his sick friend.

It had been reluctantly decided to purchase suitable new horses, a knowledgeable man being sent over to conduct negotiations. It was only when a messenger arrived to say that they had actually been landed at the port that hasty preparations for their arrival were made at Uddings.

On their arrival Udda left them in the largest area of grazing land to settle down, putting his own roan mare in with them. If she was got in foal by either of the stallions he would be delighted and closed the hurdle gate watching her flirt with the big horses.

When the message came from Udric asking them to attend his wedding on All Saints Day, Gerhard volunteered to stay at Uddings. "I rarely even make the journey to Wymburne now; the jolting of the cart causes agonies to my old bones! My hands shake but God willing the dogs would give me enough time to make a nuisance of myself."

Galena had noticed how frail and thin her father was becoming. His hands shook so that he sometimes needed help with the simplest of tasks. She no longer barbered his thin white hair, although the darker beard remained thick and full giving his face a contradictory appearance.

"You will not lack for company," she said thoughtfully, "but Udda feels that the horses should be better guarded while both he and Owen will be absent. The King has paid for them but that would not stop thieves taking the beasts. Udda will tell you what has been arranged, both for the security of Uddings and the stock. Every man has a horn now and most of them have been practicing with slings and shot. After all there are plenty of small stones at Didlington."

Secretly pleased to be asked to accompany the family party as their bodyservant and guard, Owen was confident that the Uddings steward could cope with both estates during his absence. He hastily had his hair cut, and helped his wife cut out a sheepskin jerkin to fit across his broad shoulders. Alana could not stop talking about his forthcoming visit to court. She made new leather garters and greased his boots so that they would keep his feet dry however wet the weather became.

He was then persuaded to let his wife measure him for a new tunic and to allow the house- carl to redress his old woollen cloak. The leatherworker produced new gloves with ornamented stitching. Owen was sure that his appearance would not let the party down.

Galena, plump and comely in middle age, hastily sewed a new cloak for herself together with a matching kirtle and overdress with contrasting sleeves. She had no way of knowing that fine lines beside her eyes and mouth had developed over the last few years for she had no mirror. Fortunately her mouth turned upwards at the corners quite naturally giving the appearance of a ready smile or laughter. Her youthfully rounded cheeks often dimpled girlishly when she was amused, a trait she had passed on to her daughter.

Udda too was to have a fine new outfit with a tanned belt and sandals. He had once seen himself in the King's mirror. At first he had been shocked by the face which looked back at him. He saw his high cheekbones above a strong chin and full mouth, all inherited by Udric of whom he was so proud.

"Vanity is a sin but surely God did not intend us to be blindly ignorant of how a man looks. I see others and note the colour of their eyes and whether their teeth are rotting so it cannot be too wrong to know that most of mine are still in my jaw. The good Lord will forgive me this once for we are told that he sees our every act and thought. Perhaps he will put it down to innocent curiosity!" Udda mused on the teaching of his childhood priest at Sexpenna Hanlega whose words had been far less about hell fire and eternal damnation than the untidy and slovenly priest at the church in Wymburne.

Owen was agog to see the king of whom his lord and Udric had spoken so well. His wife was invited to accompany Galena as companion and maidservant. They would travel to the celebration leaving their son in the care of the steward. The boy had shown skill with the horses at Uddings and was to be given charge of them during Udda's absence. The steward had never overcome his fear of the great beasts but assured Udda that the boy was conscientious.

"You are to sleep with them while I am gone," instructed Udda firmly. "Keep a dog with you at all times. These are the king's horses. Choose a companion to stay with you. If you need to summon the steward or Master Gerhard, send the boy. Do not leave the horses for any reason."

The young man was thrilled to have the responsibility, muttering "yes master" or "no master" at the appropriate times. He darted away to select a young lad who he could impress in turn with his own authority and seniority. Udda smiled to watch him grow up in the course of just a few moments. "If only they knew, by the time I was their age I had travelled the country, served a prince and become an outlaw! I must be getting old to hearken back to those days!"

Udda rode his mare, hoping that she was already in foal while Owen drove the cart loaded with gifts for the newly weds and special tokens for Algar who remained his friend despite the difference in their status. The fact that the gifts would then undoubtedly also make the return journey as the newly weds would be taking up residence in Udric's new house did not prevent Udda from taking them to the ceremony. Udric had pointed out that gifts were often exhibited on trestles so that others could admire them.

"Let no one say that Udric's parents have been grudging or tight fisted with wedding goods. We will hold our heads up with the best of them for my wife's sewing and weaving is second to none."

Having heard some of his boasting, Galena had blushed with pride, her heart almost bursting with love for this man who had never strayed nor punished her for small faults. Gossiping with other women in the market place she had seen many a bruised face or arms, usually inflicted by husbands whose tempers were allowed free rein.

Galena made her self comfortable in the ox cart among the straw beside Owen's wife, who was somewhat conscious of her new position. Alana sat with her back to Owen who held the reins of the cart. Soon they were all chatting and much more relaxed. As if joining in the occasion the sun shone brightly through leafless trees, the overnight chill quickly giving way to the crisp coolness of an autumn day.

Their entry to the capital through the huge gates set in the forbidding stone walls was slow due to the number of other vehicles trying to find a space in the courtyard. They noticed that some carts were pulled by native horses, the shaggy manes and feathered legs so different to the clean lines of the Norman horses in the paddock at Uddings.

Udda glanced at the stockade as they passed, muttering a prayer for any who were inside. Outwardly he remained cheerful, pointing out the King's exchequer and the bishop's house as they made their way to the palace. Many buildings had been freshly whitewashed, partly to combat disease and in part to remove deep shadows. King Aethelstan demanded that the streets of his capital were torch-lit even though there was a curfew. Galena and Owen's wife marvelled at the size of the buildings, the bright colours of the soldiers' tabards and the width of the road through the capital.

Having kept watch for seemingly hours, Udric leapt out of a doorway when he recognised his father and then mother on the cart. His face betrayed his inner happiness; his eyes alight with joy, infectious among all who saw him that day. The cart and ox were looked after when all the bundles had been removed, the young mare pretending to be skittish and high stepping when the stable lad drew her towards the stalls.

"I have never seen buildings like this," whispered Owen's wife who had blushed to the very roots of her hair when Udric had embraced her as a treasured guest rather than the wife of his steward.

"He's never been one for allowing rank or status to interfere with life at Didlington. Here though, perhaps he ought to show a tiny bit of dignity. I look forward to seeing the lady who has captured our young lord's heart. She must be very special indeed for he never mooned after girls when he was a child!" Owen spoke seriously, hinting at his long association with Udda's family, for he had been there when Udric had come into the world. He had helped him take those first tottering steps, saved him from being stuck in high trees and taught him to use a bow.

True to his word the king had allocated a handsome guest chamber for Udda and his family. Udric proudly escorted his parents through the endless rooms of the Kings palace. "Edith and her father are staying in Lord Algar's quarters. He seems rejuvenated at the prospect of the wedding. He constantly reminds his visitors of the part he played as match-maker! Honestly, Lord Algar has a real twinkle in his eyes. He deliberately made Edith blush; reminding her that he wished to see a great grandson which I thought was quite mischievous of a man who told me last time that he was more than seventy years old."

The wedding was a social event at which anyone present at the court could attend. Dressed in her best clothes, the bride had a delicate veil of French lace around her face, which in no way obscured the burnished sheen of her hair, hanging loose down her back. There was a delicate blush on her cheeks below well arched eyebrows which gave her face a vague look of surprise. Udric smiled until his face ached with happiness. The vows were made in the porch of the church, witnessed by close relatives, their retainers and as many other folk as could squeeze into the church yard. Inside the church, lit by a myriad of candles, their union was solemnly blessed by the Archbishop of Canterbury, a further sign that Udric, nine years the king's junior was indeed a highly favoured friend. The wall paintings had been newly refreshed so that the colours seemed to glow, the gold paint used to highlight faces and clothes, sparkling in the side aisle. Aethelstan himself attended with his sister Editha and a younger half brother, son of the late king's third wife. Unaware that there were some who thought the child might one day be a rival for the throne, the boy followed the king, acting as his page, but visibly copying the mannerisms and walk of his elder half-brother. Algar beamed at everyone, kissing both his granddaughter and Udric, now related to him by marriage. He had been brought into the church in a specially converted and padded chair. Four lusty guards stood behind him awaiting the command to lift both the chair and the frail old man into the hall for the more fleshly celebrations.

With memories of their own hasty marriage at the whim of the present King's father recalled, Udda and Galena embraced the newly wed couple.

"Edith at least had a veil of her own," laughed Galena who was delighted with her new daughter. "I was lent one by the king's wife and gave it back afterwards."

Amid all the happiness the King's sister was noticeably thoughtful, no doubt wondering if her own forthcoming wedding would be so happy. When she thought no one was looking her eyes reflected the fears she felt, concern at leaving all she had ever known behind and going virtually alone to a stranger and a foreigner. She was contracted to wed Sihtric of the Danelaw lands, an alliance arranged by her father Edward, King of the Old Saxons, purely for political advantage. Editha knew that her own opinion carried no weight and shrugged off her momentary concerns to escort the happy couple to the feast.

It was a sumptuous affair with many courses laid on the trestles covered with snowy white linen cloths. Owen and his wife, on a lower table looked around them in awe at the surroundings, hardly able to eat for excitement. They marvelled at the tapestries on every wall highlighted by torches. "Many of the dishes are strange to me," murmured his wife, sampling a little from each in case she could copy them. "I can hardly ask the cook for the recipe in such a grand place, but I did promise to take a treat home for Owenson. See, we can wrap a piece in this cloth!" Discreetly the sweetmeat was wrapped and stowed in Owen's scrip while his wife placed yet another tasty morsel on their shared plate. Servants moved dishes and filled ale mugs without interrupting the flow of conversation among the diners, most of whom had stopped to admire the increasing display of wedding gifts on a table below the raised dais.

Everyone was interrupted when the king loudly banged his drinking horn on the high table.

"Hear me, hear me."

The minstrel abruptly stopped playing and the diners paused abruptly in their hearty eating causing one or two to scowl momentarily in annoyance as a tasty morsel dropped to the floor where dogs hastily snapped up the unexpected gift.

Udric was ordered to stand in front of the King's chair, in the small gap used by the servers. The king used a tone of voice which did not brook disobedience, demanding that everyone was to bear witness.

"Do you bear me loyalty and service Udric?"

"I do my lord, I have sworn an oath to fight for you, to hate those you hate and to die for you if necessary." replied Udric somewhat puzzled, utterly discountenanced and embarrassed by being singled out at his own wedding feast. Warmth was spreading up his neck but he restrained himself with difficulty from loosening the ties of his tunic. A glance at Edith convinced him that she was as mystified as he was. When Aethelstan continued, Udric brought his attention back to the present.

"Aye and you nearly did die for me not long ago. I now wish to raise you. You will be Thegn Udric from henceforth. Thegn of Chalbury sounds good. My clerk has the documents ready drawn. Will you accept and sign with these people, guests and family as your witnesses?"

"My lord, I accept with all my heart and will repay your trust a thousand-fold." His words were pronounced in total silence. The raising of a villein to a higher status was an unusual occasion. It would be talked about for days, as would the wedding in the King's presence, of a Thegn's daughter to such a villein, an upset in the strict status system of the time. A man born a villein normally stayed in that capacity for his life, his sons following in his footsteps.

Udric was given time to recover his composure as the small page brought the deed to the king's table where it was unrolled. The salt pot held one end secure while another diner hastily placed his eating knife on the other end, the point carefully pointed towards his own body. God forbid that his knife should swing round and point at the King. Everyone was still conscious of the attempted assassination of their lord, King Aethelstan. Pointing a knife, however blunt towards another was now held to be extremely bad taste. As the signing was completed and the signatures sanded, a cheer rose from those in the hall who toasted the new thegn.

Udda and Galena looked proudly on, the honour to their son beyond their wildest dreams. "This day is one to remember for the rest of our lives and to recall for the grandchildren," croaked Udda, his throat having tightened with emotion so that he found it hard to speak. Galena openly brushed the sleeve of her new gown across her eyes leaving teary streaks on her flushed cheeks. Forgetting that there was an audience to their embrace, Udda and Galena were for a moment in their own bubble of joy.

Owen, with his widow-wife at the lower end of a table, was already the worse for drink. He would no doubt end the day sleeping below the trestles but for now he did not care who knew that he had served the new thegn from the day he was born. The palace dogs crept up to him sensing a diner who might be generous. He passed a piece of cold meat down to a bitch who was obviously nursing a litter somewhere. "Wife, this is the proudest day of my life!" he expounded, enunciating carefully as those who have imbibed a surfeit of ale tend to do. His surprise when she playfully slapped him was instantly sobering. "What now? It is indeed for …."

He got no further for his wife's blood was now riled and she was going to have her say here and now.

"Owen, the proudest day of your life was when I became your wife. This is the second proudest day. Wait 'til I tell our son of your fall from grace." She emphasised certain words to add gravitas to her complaint. Owen looked sheepish, a rather silly grin on his normally sober and straight face. To return to his wife's good opinion he took her face in his work roughened hands and kissed her squarely on the lips.

Much laughter and ribald jokes accompanied Udric and Edith as they were escorted to bed. Even the venerable Algar could not resist reminding the couple that he wanted to live long enough to see his grandchild. Blushing, the pair closed heavy leather curtain in the face of the traditional crowd of young men who encouraged the groom to do his duty.

The young couple embraced closely, Udric hardly able to contain his natural impatience. With exaggerated care he removed the delicate veil allowing her hair to fall freely. Taking a handful he buried his face in the luxurious scent, sensing a cleanness with hints of citrus, a rare and expensive fruit from warmer climes. Feeling strangely emboldened, Udric unlaced the ties of her gown, kissing her face and neck as he did so. Edith responded to his passion, a warmth building from her inner core, inside the hidden female parts which had been protected for so many years. With trembling fingers she untied his tunic then the buckle of his belt which fell to the floor and lay between them unnoticed. When both were naked, he carried his partner in life to the ready made bed and gently took her maidenhead.

Udda and Galena gave them a couple of hours of privacy before they too crept quietly to their pallet in the same room. The brazier had died down but the chamber was still pleasantly warm and perfumed from the lavender which had been scattered on the floor. Each step had released the fragrant oil into the air. Heavy rugs of coarse wool kept the coolness of the night from disturbing the slumbering guests.

At dawn the following day the Lady Editha prepared for her journey north for her own marriage with much less enthusiasm. The pack ponies carried chests of jewels and money for her dowry, while ox carts were loaded with richly embroidered clothes and household goods. King Aethelstan, dressed in his finest clothes was to escort his sister on her journey accompanied by an impressive number of soldiers. The colourful procession left court on its way through the old roman streets to the city gates where crowds bade her farewell. Among them were Udric and his new bride hand in hand. Editha had waved in their direction, possibly recognising them but it was well known that she was short-sighted.

"Poor lass, leaving her home like this," commented Galena who had come out to watch the preparations. "It may be for the affairs of state about which I know very little, but the man is a stranger to her! He's a Norseman too!" The after-thought reminded her of the often repeated prayers in church to keep the town safe from such men who were known to be ungodly, cruel and rapacious.

Turning back towards court Udric proudly linked arms with his wife. "It's time to go home. We have much to do and a day's journey ahead. Will you ride with me or travel in the cart?"

"I would prefer to ride. Do you have a pillion? No matter, if we ride we can still be together. I must bid my grandfather farewell. Father said that he had enjoyed the day but was exhausted. Being raised to a thegn was as much a shock to him as it was to you. Did you know that you blushed?"

Edith looked up at her new husband admiring the firm set of his jaw which was clean-shaven. She caught his eye, laughed and squeezed his arm which rested lightly around her narrow waist.

"Not half as much as you did last night!" reminded Udric grinning proudly. "We'll go and see your grandfather and tell him all about it."

"Udric, you can't mean all?" Edith emphasised the last word as she patted the new net around her hair. As a married woman her hair would be covered by suitable material or mesh. It gave her status and because much of the length had been plaited and lay on top of her head, she had suddenly grown in height.

Udric found Owen who had only just recovered from a bad head followed by an attack of biliousness brought on by an excess of feasting. His wife tutted at him, embarrassed that he had snored noisily, stentoriously throughout the night which they had spent in the hall.

Every response to Udric's questions was followed by 'My lord, Thegn Udric' until Udric laughing loudly, told him to just get on with harnessing the cart.

The journey home was uneventful as they made their way steadily southwards across deserted heathland then across Cranburne Chase. The slanting rays of the winter sun were in their eyes as they travelled steadily westward. Unusually for the first few days in November, the track was not yet a quagmire of mud. Isolated gorse bushes exhibited a few bright yellow flowers, the only colour in the grey-green countryside. Small birds rose up in unison, twittering as they approached and settled back in their thorny shelters when they had passed. Edith studied the land on either side wondering what her new home would look like.

Udda's roan mare was decidedly skittish, almost definitely pregnant much to his delight although he could not say which of the two stallions was the sire. The ox cart was piled high with Edith's dower gifts under a waxed leather cover leaving little room for Owen's wife who elected to sit beside her grinning husband. Galena drifted in and out of sleep, reliving the moment her son was raised to thegn status. She heard snatches of conversation but as none was addressed directly to her, the memories continued, some in slow motion and others passed in a blur of colour and activity. The newly weds rode matching long and slender legged horses, their wedding gift from the king. Udda could not help looking to the future when the mare might be put in foal to one of the Norman stallions. In his mind's eye, the resultant colt would have the best features from both breeds, the slightly dished face of the Arab, with the weight carrying properties of the stronger boned stallion. There was little point in discussing the matter with Owen, for he was still living in a cloud of euphoria more than likely fuelled by the amount of alcohol he had consumed and Udric most definitely had other things on his mind. Udda found himself consumed with impatience and longed to be back among the familiar people and beasts at Uddings.

Edith exclaimed with pleasure at the preparations which had been made to make her feel welcome in her new home at Didlington. Her easy manner and pretty looks endeared her to the two house-servants, especially when she admired the new baby snug in its box cradle.

Accepting only brief hospitality at Udric's manor house, Udda and Galena made their farewells and left for Uddings.

"He has indeed improved much of the land. His field hands look well. I saw no sign of ill-fed children or ragged tunics. Perhaps he will be able to make pasture out of some of the heathland; for all that it looked like an uphill task when we first saw his land."

Surprised that Udda should notice things like torn clothes Galena could hardly suppress her pride in Udric's achievements.

"Never in my wildest dreams did I think I would go to the King's palace at Winchester," she commented lightly. "His palace here in Wymburne is a poor building in comparison. There is so much to tell father. He is so frail that I fear for him when he is left. Just to think that our son is a Thegn! It makes my heart beat faster. Lord forgive me, for pride is sin but I never thought that my little boy who went off to join the princes at their lessons, would be a noble. I fear that Owen was fit to burst with pride when he saw the ceremony." Galena's mind was jumping from one marvel to another but her smile was nothing short of radiant.

"You were the one who had doubts about him joining the princes!" joked Udda rattling the reins of the ox cart. The last rays of the sun fell on the woods around Uddings as they approached. Horns blew in welcome even though the workers had finished for the day. The landowner and his wife were greeted with rewarding enthusiasm by both workers and Gerhard, all anxious to hear the news. The old man's breathing had worsened while they were away. He wheezed like leaky bellows but still managed to look interested, despite being grey-white with the effort of drawing air into his diseased lungs.

Although he was tired, Udda excused himself to go to the pasture where the horses grazed peacefully in the rapidly fading light. The young boy leapt to his feet when he saw Udda approaching. Over two nights he had conquered his fear of the dark and the sounds of the night which can undo the strongest man.

"Well done youngster, I hear you have done your work well in my absence. Stay with them one more night and in the morning we will inspect them together."

The boy nodded, beaming with pride. Respectfully bidding Udda a good night's rest he hunkered down in the shelter of the hurdles. Udda pulled his cloak round him before hurrying back to the warmth of the house where the meal would be waiting. A young lad hurried past him carrying a pot of hot food wrapped in a woollen cloth on its way to the young horse guard. Udda smiled with content and joined the diners already at the table and told them of his son's new position as Thegn of Chalbury and the wedding to Lady Edith at which King Aethelstan had been the principal guest

.

The winter months of frost and cold winds passed without incident on both estates. The annual slaughter of beasts had ensured that both larders would be full of meat and skins would be tanned or stretched for new clothing. Udric had briefly travelled north to attend the king at the marriage of his sister, and Sihtric. Although the formal betrothal, which had taken place months ago, was as binding, Lady Editha had seen little of her intended husband, reportedly a dour man. She had been kind and attentive to Udric's new wife at their wedding. Now he returned the favour and wished her well in her new home.

Since arriving at his court however, she had unexpectedly become fond of her husband. The event became a happy one, only soured by the absence of her husband's two sons by a former marriage. They were reportedly sulking in their father's stronghold. After the feasting and interminable toasts to the bride and her new husband, Aethelstan had embraced his sister affectionately as his party prepared to leave shortly after dawn the following day.

"They must be hardier than us," commented one man glad of the sleeves of his jerkin and heavy woollen cloak. "All the Danes had bare arms, laden with gold and silver bracelets. Most of those were probably made from looted treasures. But I shall be glad to get home. I swear it is warmer in Wessex! "

In the king's quarters back at Winchester Udric sat on a stool waiting for his friend to speak, knowing there was something on his mind.

"I intend to hunt in Wymburne in spring. Tell your father to bring any fit horses to the palace stables. I must admit they were not supposed to stay with him so long but events have overtaken us recently." Aethelstan laughed cynically as he gripped Udric's wrist affectionately. "I need loyal thegns like you to assist in the ruling of the kingdom, a council of men dealing with local matters. I have in mind calling a meeting to discuss the idea." He would have enlarged upon his idea but a small page tugged at the King's sleeve.

"Yes, yes," the king snapped irritably, "one moment and I will attend to you." His belly ached with the rich food so that his temper was becoming noticeably shorter.

Udric grinned as the page looked crestfallen remembering his own time serving Algar. "Never mind lad, I will not keep the king a moment longer from his meeting." Ruffling the page's hair Udric bade his friend and King farewell. They embraced roughly before pulling apart, studying each other's faces, the one long and thin, and the other broader with bright eyes beneath well formed eyebrows.

"God speed thegn Udric. I look forward to hearing that a godchild is on the way."

Even though the king had smiled broadly, Udric felt his face flush with embarrassment. He took the reins of his horse before vaulting onto it, urging it to a gallop. Moments later he drew it to a walk mulling over the idea of a body of men assisting the king in the administration of his realm. Even such a simple matter as to the movement of a herd of horses had been overlooked because there was no one in charge of the king's affairs in Dorsetshire. True he had sheriffs who he sent to mete out justice and deal with major disputes, but no one stayed in the county organising the army or overseeing the building of defences. The sheriff lived in Wareham, a fortified town. His deputies brought prisoners to him, carried taxes and tributes, and acted as guards when the sheriff journeyed to the capital. Acting as overseer for the repairs on a bridge or the clearing of undergrowth from the king's highway was not thought to be within the remit of the deputies. The King might order things to be done but often had to visit personally to check that the work was really being done.

"Yes, I do believe he has given great thought to this. There is no-one who works for him on local matters. We have the King's reeve at his palace in Wymburne, but what about the other towns and villages where there is no royal presence?" Udric was thoughtful as he rode away from the smells and sounds of the city.

During the spring travellers arriving in Wymburne brought news of uprisings put down by the king's forces. They also spoke in hushed whispers of the king's revolting eating habits. His apparent inability to swallow food properly and the violent stomach cramps which occurred without warning fascinated the caring while causing fear among the ignorant. A few remembered that the king's father had apparently suffered in the same way.

"I believe King Alfred also had a weak stomach," commented Udda frowning. "When my father was sentenced the king was in great pain and died only a day or two later, but by that time my father had been banished. I heard rumours of this when Prince Aethelwold was strutting round the court expecting to take his place."

Udric grunted and made a non committal reply, unwilling to divulge the confidence of his friend who had already told him of his concerns. "For the moment there are greater concerns than gossiping about the King's health. I am far more worried about providing fodder for the over-wintered stock, the completion of the mill and the fact that Edith is now pregnant."

"Indeed son, you are right. It is a worrying time, but Edith is young and healthy. God willing she will give you a healthy infant and recover from childbirth herself. Have you women who can help her? Owen's wife may offer and your mother would welcome the chance to become better acquainted with her daughter in law."

Several cottagers from the Chalbury side of the track had recently professed their loyalty to Udric, working part of each week in return for his protection. They came to his hall for the main meal of the day. Occasionally they would bring eggs or surplus edible roots to contribute to the common stores. The hall would be filled with trestles and benches, the women taking turns to dish up the meal.

Winter was always the harshest time of year when joints ached and chilblains split. Coughs and colds spread among them easily, the children suffering worst despite being dosed with herbal cures and remedies.

Owen's wife had become quite moody with the shorter days, complaining that her whole life now revolved round cooking and feeding everyone. Smoothing her work-roughened hands down over her stomach she could feel the hard lump which grew day by day. A niggling pain brought further irritation and shortness of breath. There had been no further children since the birth of Owenson. Other women whispered that it was nature's way for older mothers as everyone knew that giving birth was a risky business.

Normally a man of even temper Owen became short with her. "You work hard here, we all do, but few are lucky enough to accompany their lord to the King's capital. The lady Edith is a good woman and will need your help soon. Owenson is growing up fast and working with lord Udda's horses. Neither of us gave thought to having children but he is a credit to us, and we have much to be thankful for. You are the Steward's wife; other people look to you for daily guidance in running Thegn Udric's manor-house. The lady Edith relies on you to run her kitchen for I doubt her cooking skills compare with yours. Cheer up my love, for winter will be over soon and the days longer."

He hugged her matronly proportions affectionately, wiping her tears away. She was not much comforted by his un-practiced efforts at flattery and cajolery but did stop complaining for a few days.

Edith wove hangings for the hall and made woollen cloth for her child, a picture of contentment which affected all who worked on the estate. Already she had introduced comforts to their hall. Heavy curtains which had been part of her dowry cut down draughts and added colour. They also had two glasses, a gift from her grandfather. These were kept on a high shelf so that there was little likelihood of their being damaged when the trestle tables were erected for meals. Even weak ale tasted different when supped from a glass beaker.

Very respectfully Owen asked her if his wife might be involved when it was her time to give birth. He had reddened at his temerity as childbirth was not a subject normally discussed by men. Standing before her, twisting his huge brown hands awkwardly his embarrassment was almost tangible.

"Of course I shall need Alana when the child comes. I have been remiss in not asking her before now but it is still many months…" Edith smiled at him, hoping to put her husband's tongue-tied steward at his ease. "She has been wonderful and teaches the other women many of her skills in the kitchen. Cooking is not something I did at home but I see now that my mother did me no favours. Every woman should at least try making her man's meals! Let me approach her in my own time for she would not be pleased to know that you had reminded me."

Owen could hardly prevent himself from bowing himself out of his lady's solar. Edith was a beautiful young woman with a kindly way of talking to everyone. He was not the only man to feel that strange mixture of respect and desire when in her presence. He had overheard field hands voice their admiration of their lord's choice of bride and provided their gossip did not degenerate into vulgarity he affected not to hear them.

Uddings too was thriving, many of the fieldworkers now having wives who worked under Galena's direction. They sang as they cured hides, spun wool for clothing and cooked huge meals for the hall. New trees were planted to replace the original boundary posts now rotting while the old clay pit from which Udda had taken material to fashion his first pots had filled up with water. Birds often visited the pond where Gerhard liked to sit, sometimes taking a water fowl to add to the stores. The water was pure, filling up from natural dew, a valuable source when the stream was low.

"I for one will be glad if the water remains clean," declared Galena. "We need only fetch stream water if the pond dries up. The constant carrying of water jars from the stream has always irritated me, especially on those days where everything is rimed with frost and ice has formed in every puddle. Except in an emergency the pond is much closer and it is some distance from the midden so should stay pure."

Udda spent time breaking in the horses for riding. As they had been handled since birth this was not too difficult. The buyer of course, would then introduce the specialist skills needed for use in tournaments or in battle. Many mares were in foal and had to be kept apart from the stallions. The pretty Arab mare given to Edith by the King had also proved fertile. Since she could not ride herself at this time, trusted opinion being that no woman carrying a child should sit upon a horse, even if the beast was well trained. He could hardly contain his excitement watching the swelling belly of the mare as she grazed contentedly beside the other mothers-to-be.

The best young stallion was being trained to be a safe ride for the king. "It has a nobility of carriage even at this young age," thought Udda as he gently placed an old saddle on its back. He rode it carefully using the new reins cured from the hide of the old ox which had finally reached the end of its days. Later the young lad who had guarded the horses during his absence was allowed to sit on the stallion while he held the end of a rope. "Sit up straight; flex your back as he walks. Now press your heels for faster. If you can ride him, he'll surely be safe enough for the King. Stop now, pull gently back. No back, tell him you want to go back."

And so the lessons went on until the horse had learnt to turn, trot, canter and step back when asked. He had to get used to pennants, weapons, bells and crowds. Udda tried to introduce new experiences, some of which caused great amusement. He asked the field hands to run towards the horse cheering or shouting, but since this was a break from weeding or some other task in the field no-one minded the interruption. Leaving the oxen placidly chewing the cud men were asked to flap cloaks, bang drums, blast the horn; all the hazards which might be met by a horse carrying the King. In the evening people made suggestions of further events which might occur, none was too ridiculous to be considered.

Few people in Wymburne owned a horse and of those none had trained their own beast so the novelty of Udda's methods was discussed by anyone who had ever ridden. Some were little short of derogatory, voices becoming hard with sarcasm.

"After all, the man knows nothing of horses for all that the late lord Edward, God bless him, appointed him to heal them. Doctoring a beast is very different to taming one so that he is safe to ride. No, Udda has become puffed up with pride, thinking he can befriend nobles with wily ways."

Unfortunately for the speaker, Owen's wife overheard these offensive comments and for once, moodiness put aside, totally lost her temper. She had been in pain all morning, each breath lancing through her chest but had determined to do the household shopping in the market herself. Now she drew herself up, puffed out her considerable bosom like an enraged turkey cock and screeched at the woman. Using words that a lady, particularly not one who had a position to uphold should use, Alana released the last dregs of bitterness which had festered in her soul. "You vile, vicious old whore! You know nothing about the man or about his skills. Udda is one of the gentlest men I have ever met. It makes me sick to my stomach to hear you criticize his methods of training when you have not even seen him gentling the wildest stallion hour after hour. How dare you accuse him of deliberately befriending nobles when his own son is now a Thegn!"

To say that the womenfolk of Wymburne were astonished is an understatement of huge proportions. There was total silence, both from the woman who had passed judgement on Udda from a platform of ignorance and Alana, who was now gripping her chest. Sweat had broken out on her brow beneath its matron's wimple; her head was thrown back following the line of her arched back. It was clear that the woman was in great pain but not a hand was lifted to comfort her in this time of need.

Slowly her legs lost their strength. All her weight descended in slow motion to the beaten earth of the market square. Her wimple fell into the mud but her glazed eyes were unfocused while knives twisted and prodded within her chest. Children in their innocence started to gather round until one youngster, braver than the rest, rushed off to find the priest. In his uneducated mind the personification of the Lord Jesus, to whom all prayers were addressed, was the only person who could help this woman in her distress.

His arrival quickly dispersed the hard eyed women. Their colleague who had been so insulted by Alana muttered curses safely beyond the hearing of the young priest. He possessed surprisingly wiry strength, for with only the help of the little boy; Alana was lifted from the detritus and ordure of the street and taken to the church.

News of the drama in the centre of town was spread, the initial cause of the exchange being overlooked as the tale was exaggerated by each successive gossip. "She has an exaggerated sense of her own high standing in society. When she was widowed so young we felt sorry for her even though there were slaves to do her bidding and wealth to buy more than we could afford. Now she is wife to a steward, the position has swollen her pride beyond endurance. We should complain!"

Many voices agreed with the hasty judgement but after their menfolk had become involved the origins of the heated argument had come to light.

"It is not right to condemn a man for trying to better himself. If we were able to doctor someone and were successful then people would want that help. Even now we go to the monastery because they have skills. Udda has never offended anyone, nor has his steward, that ex-slave he promoted. The woman is clearly sick, perhaps in mind as well as her body. Did you see the way her back arched?"

So the discussions, debates and tales went on, even the woman whose virtue had been cast in doubt becoming more rational as the hours passed. The priest suggested that all those involved look into their souls to see if they were innocent of casting aspersions and at the very least lacking compassion for a woman in such pain. A few were red faced, quickly purchasing their immediate needs and retreating into the familiar gloom of their dwellings.

A new cow had calved so that hard and soft cheeses had been made from the rich milk. Owen too, had more time, his overall stewardship being less onerous now that the fields were well established. Crisp edges denoted the boundaries between crops while those which provided pasture for the horses had permanent fencing into which self set bushes grew. Additional oak, beech and even birch saplings were planted if one was found in an inconvenient place rather than being wasted on a fire. He purchased a saw from the forge master at Wymburne. The new tool, with its serrated cutting edge, made short work of forming planks and bench seating for the halls. One of the young men who still lived at Uddings made spoons, ladles and bowls with great skills from waste pieces of wood. He also scoured the woods for odd shaped branches from which household items could be made. His limp prevented him from doing much of the communal field work but by contributing leatherwork and carved items it was felt by everyone that he was a useful member of the homestead. For years as a child, such a handicap had been either a source of pity, scorn or ridicule. Here at Uddings the boy had matured knowing that he was valued. He spoke little of his parents still living on the fertile land towards Walford where his father and his physically perfect sibling farmed, growing barley for the royal estate.

CHAPTER FOURTEEN

At night after Udda and Galena had enjoyed the close contact of long married couples, they often whispered of their good fortune, conscious that Gerhard was in the same house. He was now more than sixty summers' old but showed little sign of the idiocy which sometimes affected old people. His breathing became worse in damp chilly weather and felt the cold so even in summer wore many layers of wool over a linen under-tunic which Galena had purchased for him at the market.

Two carts were now needed on Sundays if everyone wanted to attend church. It was on these occasions that gossip was relayed and often further distorted. Alana used one excuse or another to avoid going in to Wymburne. The painful spasms she had experience on her last venture to the market had left her exhausted. Edith and the other women had purchased their needs from the stalls, the former now glowing with that peculiar well-being unique to those carrying a child. Her cheeks were rosy, the blue eyes bright with mischief. Occasionally the child moved within her, the tiny fluttering little more than the beat of the wings of a butterfly then stronger as the weeks progressed.

The young men courted blushing girls while the children played among the stalls in the shambles. Strong ale, brewed by those licensed, was sold in pot jugs after the service. Even the church had ladies who vied with each other to provide the best beer.

Twice a year other ladies baked cakes on behalf of the church, a luxury which few made for themselves. Flavoured with imported dried fruit mixed with honey, the children pleaded for a taste before running off to play with friends who only met on Sundays. Those who imbibed too much had time to recover while Udda attended the moot held on the king's land. Udric too sometimes made his way there where he was accorded the respect due to a thegn, much to the satisfaction of his father.

"Congratulations Udda, your son has done well. Lord King Aethelstan has been kind to your family, as the late Edward was to you I am told. My father used to tell me stories of this young man who was married at the King's Tun. Was it really true?"

"It is long ago now, but yes, Lord King Edward, blessed be, was a witness at my wedding there. I healed some horses for him, or for Lord Algar to be more accurate, and the King gave me a position and land to look after his beasts. My son will do this after me, God willing!"

"You heard of the fracas in Wymburne? Your steward's wife insulted a trader's wife when that woman accused you of self aggrandisement. It was uncalled for and many of us feel that you were wronged. The steward's wife was ill I'm told. Is she recovered?"

Udda was on the point of replying when the King's reeve interrupted the chatter.

Thomas the baker had died, some said of pains in the head for he had been seen striking his forehead against the doorpost of his property. No-one seemed to grieve over his absence from the gathering. He had never been guilty of selling underweight loaves but his abrasive manner had not endeared himself to other shop keepers in Wymburne. Everyone dutifully mumbled the requisite sympathies for his widow as the reeve continued to give the men news or complaints that needed their attention.

"The practice of archery is supposed to be the young men's activity after the service has fallen into disuse. Only a few are visiting the town butt above the farm at Walford. It is to be hoped that you will encourage your sons or young workers to use their bows.

The king comes to Wymburne in two weeks. All rents are to be taken to the palace before that day. Let it not be said that the people of this burgh cannot provide food for their king generously." The men parted thoughtfully, most of them having the quantity and detail of their rents set out clearly in the terms of their leases.

The priest made many such announcements in the church. He had been told of Lord King Aethelstan's proposed visit by the Bishop visiting the nunnery. Only that morning he had preached a parable story concerning giving while fully aware that his congregation immediately started talking among themselves of their dues to the king and how they should meet his demands. Not all felt that their rents were equal, especially the man whose dues were paid in honey and wax for candles.

Because Udric wore the king's colours on his headband he was presumed to have the royal ear, even in the matter of rents. The honey collector, a thin wiry man, headed straight for Udric when the church doors re-opened.

"Tis too much! I have to search all year for bees' nests in the forest. I get stung for my pains. My son was killed in the war so he is not here to help. It is a painful task for little reward." complained the man pulling up his sleeve to demonstrate the small pits resulting from the bees anger when they were robbed. Udric immediately felt compassion for the pain the honey collector must have suffered but could offer little hope that the King's reeve would listen to excuses if the requisite number of jars did not materialise on the due day.

Others nodded sympathetically but offered no solution. They too had problems of their own. Some had to supply a young ox, sheep, pigs or fowl and there was only two weeks to select and fatten suitable animals. As usual little flour remained from the last harvest but some were obliged to provide barley, horse-feed or loaves for the king's table.

Udda quietly left the gathering. The business of the day was over and he was uneasy at the volume of unrest. "There seems to be more resentment over the payment of food rents this time. Those with skilled trades only provide their services while those who farm have to provide a portion of their crops or livestock. If the harvest was bad or animals sickened .... do we have any surplus honey?"

Galena, somewhat startled by the abrupt question, admitted that there was more than a season's supply safely stored and wondered why he wanted more.

"There is a man whose son was killed in the fighting. He has not gathered the jars of honey he is obliged to pay. I noticed there was none for sale at the market either."

"Let him have some of ours, it is bad enough to lose your son without being further punished for non payment of his dues." Udda admired his wife's compassion. He sent a message to tell the unfortunate man to call at Uddings. Anxious to return to Edith, Udric embraced his father before riding north to Didlington, leaving his parents to deal with the shortage of honey.

Striding up the hill from Wimborne, his eyes darting around in case he should spot suitable sites where bees had built their honeycombed nests, the collector made his way to Uddings in the early spring sunshine. As yet there was little heat in the sun but the clear sky promised greater warmth later in the day. This area was not on his normal patrol and he was astonished to find orderly fields, fenced sties for pigs, contented fowl working through the leaf-mould and the much vaunted horses belonging to the King. "Well bless me! I never knew all this was here. It is a veritable hive of industry, not unlike the activities of the bees whose nests I rob!" Galena laughed politely handing him the jars of sweetener so vital to a cook's fantasies and desserts.

His gratitude was moving. Not only was he relieved to be offered the necessary honey but he would avoid a fine levied at the moot would add to his public shame. He left Uddings with the precious food, promising to replace it as soon as he could.

As the day for the king's arrival at Wymburne drew near Udda prepared the Norman horses for their short journey, grooming the stallion until its coat shone. The boy, Owenson, now growing quickly with a dark shadow of downy hair on his upper lip, would walk behind, leading the other animals which would follow the stallion meekly enough. Only the mares and foal would remain in the Uddings fields, one of them pregnant by the beautiful horse intended for the King's own use.

Owen had given so many instructions as to how the boy should behave at the royal palace that the young lad's head was spinning. To think though, that he had ridden a stallion belonging to the King! He walked tall, fearless even with unbroken animals who offered him no harm.

Udric too, readied himself to see the king. His tunic was brushed, boots oiled until they gleamed. Edith had given birth to a healthy son which they had named Odda, a slight variation on his grandfather's name in the local dialect. Udric intended to ask the king to stand sponsor for him, something which had already been suggested by Aethelstan himself. Both parents were proud of the baby, born with wisps of blond hair and deep blue eyes. During the birth Udric had paced up and down fretting with anxiety. Galena had supervised the women who helped in the private room; Alana insisting that clean cloths were worn over their workaday kirtles. She bustled round importantly, flinging her commands for the mid-day meal casually over one shoulder before drawing the curtain of the chamber. It was normal for men to be excluded from the birthing chamber. Indeed the sight of a woman's agonies would have been too much for many to bear, let alone contemplate. Fortunately there were no complications and the new little soul slipped into the world amidst smiles and rejoicing. Wiped clean, bound in the softest wool swaddling, Galena had been proud to present her son with his heir.

"Yea, he's a delight to my eyes, but Edith? How is she? I heard such noise that I stopped my ears. Is Edith well? She is not bleeding?"

"No! and yes!" she giggled, the dimples showing only shallowly in her plump cheeks. "It was a fairly easy birth although as you see, the child is well formed. Your wife is a small woman but it is done now. Will you come to her now? Shall I carry the baby?"

Passing the sleeping child to his mother, Udric sprinted to their private chamber where Edith lay, exhausted but smiling. The room seemed over-hot to Udric. There was an unpleasant odour of sweat, blood and birthing liquid. He paused, watching the women crowding round his wife and the child. Edith greeted him brightly, her voice slightly forced above her tiredness.

"Are you pleased? He is perfect, but by God, I'm tired. Sit with me until he needs feeding which probably won't be long. There is no need to send for a priest. His christening can wait. I feel sure he is healthy."

The two parents embraced, whispering intimate phrases known the world over, while the women quietly withdrew to give them a few moments privacy. As Edith had thought, it was not long before the newborn advertised his displeasure, his hunger, with a wail which belied his size. The ear-piercing shrieks brought her milk in, just as nature intended so that she was glad to offer a full breast to the child. While he suckled, Udric stroked the blond curl on the crown of his head. He only left the room when Edith fell asleep, the baby contentedly snuffling at her breast.

Having talked at the last quarter's meeting at Badberie, which involved all the adult men of the parish of Wymburne, of the king's intention to delegate some local affairs to thegns of each shire, other landowners had approved the idea, with one drawback.

"Will it mean increased taxes? A man is hardly going to leave his own land without some reward. How will he be compensated for going about the king's business instead of supervising his own manor?"

"We should ask the king," replied Udric decisively. "It is his idea to have 'shire reeves' as he called them. He already has justiciars or sheriffs to see to general law and order and they receive part of the fines levied. The officials he wants to introduce are to see to the roads, defences, and any other task which needs an overseer to ensure it is completed as the King would wish. Perhaps a grant of land to be rented out could raise income."

All thoughts of discussing the matter in greater detail were forgotten when a latecomer, breathless with exertion and excitement, brought rumours of the murder of Prince Edwin. The man's eyes were glittering, and from the expressions on the faces of the large assembly, he was the first with the information. Puffed with importance and fleeting pride, the dreadful details were relayed to the astonished freemen of the Parish. This awful news preceded the arrival of the king by a few days. Although Udric knew his friend to be single minded in his pursuit of kingship and the increase of territory under his control, he found it hard to believe that Aethelstan had actually set his young half-brother adrift in a small boat.

"There has always been a faction which supported Edwin's claim to the throne some seven years ago. Their support of the legitimate heir even extended to the attempt on the king's life as I well know." Udric rubbed the sensitive scar on his chest remembering his fight for life.

"I do not understand his actions. From the beginning of his reign he continued to welcome all the aethelings at court. There are also the foreign princes learning the art of kingship. My Lord Aethelstan's court is one of the most widely respect in the Christian world."

Udric reflected that it was unbelievable that his lord had carried out such a punishment without good cause. From a friend he heard that another aetheling had been the accuser. This had resulted in him too being executed. The king must have felt that his throne was threatened. He sighed, remembering the boy Edwin, trying so hard to outshine others in lessons in order to impress the eldest prince and his cruel jibes and feigned indifference to punishment. His rudeness was calculated to hurt and belittle those below his own status and most of this bitterness had been directed at Udric, a handy whipping boy.

Everyone was discussing the matter, albeit discreetly while the palace hummed with extra activity. After the day's hunt was over huge feasts were held to feed everyone, trestles placed on every available surface. The people of Wymburne had provided all the necessary food to feed the King and his court for the obligatory number of days.

It was clear to the discerning observer that the king did indeed suffer from the same malady as his father, most pretending not to notice when he spat out the solid food, feeding it to his attentive dogs. He left the table, holding a napkin to his mouth, after announcing that Bishop Brynstan of Winchester would hold a mass the following day.

A noble, dressed in robes of deepest red with small jewels sparkling in the torchlight, who had been sitting on the high table announced loudly that a council would be called afterwards, those required to attend would receive messages. There was no sign of Edith's grandfather, the venerable and aged Lord Algar. Udric and Udda looked at one another wondering if this was the discussion on delegated authority they had been waiting for. They left the crowded hall wondering if they would be summoned. It was a relatively large room with fresh straw covering the earth floor. Now it was filled with bodyguards, knights, soldiers and servants so that every colour of tunic mixed together in a heaving mass. "If the king feels his throne is under threat he is hardly likely to let any power, even in the outlying areas, pass to another. It will be a salutary lesson to the other brothers. They were only babies at the time," Udric reminisced, wondering if his friend would summon him.

Udda checked the horses he had brought, feeding the big stallion a titbit from his scrip. Despite its size, the soft lips caressed his hand, taking the tiny piece of fine white bread from his palm. It rested its head on Udda's shoulder while he stroked the smoothly muscled neck. He whispered that he would see him again shortly but wanted to return to Galena while the light held. The stablemaster chatted for a few moments as Udda mounted his mare. He rode off, his mind more on domestic matters than the recent death of Prince Edwin at the hands of the King. The fading sun was lighting a golden path across the land as Udda crossed the ford outside Wymburne and made his way back up the hill.

The meeting King Aethelstan had called for the freemen of Wymburne was held after the hunting party had left for Cranburne forest. Most of the hunters were members of his council or had large estates for which they already carried out an essential service as well as supplying armed men for his army. They would be away all day and might stay overnight at the guest house if the sport was good. The ground was still hard with the chill of the night but there was a promise of sunshine above the tiny leaves unfurling in the woods. Most of the horses, servants and dogs had also gone, leaving only those who were to attend the special assembly, some of whom would far sooner have gone hunting. After all, the King's hunting enclosures could not be entered by those who had no business there and no-one could take game without risk of dire punishment. Taking a deer which grazed on one's own crops was risky enough even if the damage it caused threatened the yield at harvest-time.

Aethelstan had dressed with care, his usual diadem replaced by the gem studded circlet which had been given to him on the marriage of his half-sister Aethelhild to Duke Hugh of the Frankish kingdom. He seated himself with care on the padded throne looking down his long nose at the expectant faces below. The hall was silent apart from men scratching at flea bites or other irritations.

"Many of you are aware of my intention to appoint supervisors for the various parts of my realm. For years, training of the army has been unreliable, building of fortifications is unfinished and many other tasks that have been ordered have never even started. The fyrd demands forty days of each man's time. A villein needs to be trained to bear arms properly, not in a haphazard way that is a danger to the man next to him. Skill with a spear must be taught not left to chance so that in battle a man is useful not a liability."

Some of the younger men giggled at the picture the King's words so vividly portrayed. They were hastily silenced when he continued, ignoring their mirth.

"I would hear your counsel on the matter. My Lord Bishop obviously has opinions so let him be the first to speak."

Pompously the bishop rose to his feet, adjusting his cap which had slipped askew.

"The Church is against putting authority in the hands of a favoured few, prey to jealousies and greed. You already have a Christian fellowship of senior churchmen in each diocese to oversee secular and lay obedience to your laws. If you gave more authority to them, which they would welcome, it would only add to their burden, not create another level of thegn or noble."

When the bishop looked as if he was going to expand further on his opinion the King raised his hand, stopping the flow of righteous and rather pompous rhetoric. Aethelstan nodded, considering the advice before signalling another to put his point of view.

The debate continued far into the night interrupted only by servants discreetly providing meat and drink. Men bowed themselves out of the royal presence when nature's calls could no longer be ignored, slipping back into the circle with equal unobtrusiveness. No conclusion having been reached it was scheduled to reconvene the following day after a night's rest and consideration.

The hunters had returned at dusk exhausted, their kills being taken straight to the butcher in his hut at the far side of the compound. They ate their fill, told exaggerated stories of their prowess and retired, leaving the court almost silent save for the snores of the sleeping men. Owls hooted over the newly burgeoning woods, horses stamped in the stalls and the hunting dogs twitched with dreams of their chase.

The peace of the night was shattered by trumpet calls soon after a messenger brought the news that there was a rising on the Scottish border. Although it was almost dawn and the kitchen staff were already at work men tumbled from their beds bemused by sleep but alert enough to send servants for their horses. Belts were fastened, swords slid into their scabbards and secondary weapons according to a man's skill, slung over his back. The younger men took up their lord's colourful pennants and nervously mounted their hastily saddled horses. Many of these beasts had only just been brushed down to remove the mud collected during the hunt. They were moody and skittish as they circled in the courtyard lit by smoking torches. Servants brought last minute items of clothing or tack which had been forgotten in the haste to march north to defend the border. Men shouted commands, each trying to gather his men to form some sort of order. The courtyard was full of the jingle of harness and the swearing of riders when something was dropped. Messengers were sent off to raise the fyrd in the more northerly shires.

The king's horse had unfortunately been lamed by a smith shortly after his arrival.

"I should have your hide for this master smith," yelled the King when the reason for his horse's non appearance had been explained. "As God is my witness you will suffer for this."

The smith was already on his knees, his huge muscular arms knuckled on the ground in complete subjection to the King's fury.

Udda rode into a scene of complete chaos. Not knowing when the meeting of Wymburne freemen would re-convene he had left Uddings while the stars were fading from the darkness and a pre-dawn light shone from the East. The head stableman was scratching his head in bemusement closely allied to panic. There were no spare horses except the young stallion. Already many of the hunters were riding their second choice beasts because they had exhausted or injured their best during the hunt.

"Well he'll have to use him," argued Udda. "Tell him the horse has been ridden by a seven year old boy."

"You tell him that and he will probably knock your head off!" exclaimed the stableman. "He has more pride than a turkey cock. You will have to tell him that there is no choice and do it now while he is still issuing orders to the councillors." The stableman left Udda no choice and stalked off to the stalls to fetch the stallion.

Udda shrugged wearily, wishing he had stayed in bed beside Galena until the dawn had well and truly lightened the skies.

"My lord King, you asked me to bring the fit horses to your stables here. Among them is a young stallion, fully trained for a rider, but not for battle or the chase. The circumstances are by no means ideal; No saddlery or harness have been made to fit, nor have you ever ridden him. I believe he will serve you well if you are gentle with him. My lord, he is called Thor!"

The King burst out laughing causing a stir among the riders and servants milling round aimlessly in front of the palace. The mud was rapidly being churned up and mixed with horse dung from nervous beasts.

"Once again Udda, you may save my life! Bring 'Thor' to me now."

While they waited for the stableman to bring the horse, Udda could not prevent himself from reciting prayers to which ever God was appropriate, or listening, that the King would not fall or be injured while riding the un-tried stallion. He could feel the unpleasant smell of his own sweat breaking out from every pore. He was hot but this discomfort was ignored when the stableman brought Thor to the King.

Even lord Aethelstan could not prevent a moment's admiration for the glossy coat and well muscled quarters of the stallion which looked down at him and then appeared to bow, scratching his nose on one foreleg.

"He's magnificent Udda, I thank you once again."

King Aethelstan, taking Udda's word that the horse was ready for use, mounted smoothly and cantered out of the palace followed by those who had been able to ready themselves.

Needing the stableman's support and taking great gulps of air, Udda staggered to the stables. He had held his breath when the King had mounted Thor, when a catastrophe could have occurred before the court as witnesses.

Others were still shouting for their servants to take the tents down while oxen were being hastily put to the baggage carts, all hindered by dogs which milled round in excitement. Servants had put torches in the iron loops but these smoked foully until the flame had fully ignited the tarry sticks.

"I must follow the king," shouted Udric as he ran passed his father tying his belt awkwardly. "Look to Edith and the child for me."

"God go with you son," called Udda as more riders clattered through the gates, "and God guard the king on an untried stallion." He added to no-one in particular. "The beast should have been tested at mock combat here, not been taken out to battle."

While the meeting had been going on, Udda and the stablemaster had inspected the new horses which had been led from Uddings. They had talked long into the night with jugs of barley ale, listening all the while to the shuffling and munching sounds which came from the stables below their sleeping accommodation.

By full light the court was deserted save for household servants. "We'll restore order here then see if the kitchens still have some food for us lesser mortals," joked the stablemaster. "You there, brush out that stall. Shift yourselves!" The stable lads grinned at their superior even while they hastened to obey. Each of them had found a reason to peer into the new stallion's stall. The big horse had enjoyed the fuss, breathing down his patrician nose at the little people hovering below his great height.

"Have you heard what happened at the meeting?" Udda enquired as they walked to the kitchens. "Only that our lord king wants to put men in charge of getting things done and the Bishop wants the church to be paid for it," came the grunted reply. "I've no time for those who cannot work without someone kicking their backside all the time. I've spent my forty days mending roads and a bloody waste of time it was too! A man should do what he is trained for, what he is skilled in. My hands were ruined for weeks."

Udda gently announced over their bread and cheese that he would take the injured stallion back to Uddings if that suited for he would not be sound until the nail wound had properly healed. The stablemaster obviously felt very strongly that his abilities had been belittled by spending time repairing roads. Not wishing to prolong the discussion which had devolved into condemnation of the current fyrd-service, Udda was anxious to change the subject. He made his farewells and walked slowly through the gates leading the king's horse. Its front hoof was wrapped in a linen bandage, padded with moss to lessen the impact. His own mare followed obediently giving breathy invitational whinnys at her unexpected companion. From Uddings he could quickly send word to Edith. Udric had only expected to be gone for a day. As he was one of the people in the area who could read and write Udda thought it was possible that he would be asked to supervise local projects. Now he could be gone for much longer.

Galena had waited anxiously for his return all day. After hugging Udda with surprising strength, she had listened to his news about the young stallion with some alarm her nerves further disturbed when he told her that Udric had gone to war with the King.

"I would rather she heard that Udric has gone with the King's forces against the Scots from me than hears rumours in Wymburne. You know how quickly news gets around. They did leave in a hurry but Aethelstan has always reacted immediately. Hopefully that horse will carry him well." Udda sent the messenger to Didlington getting the boy to repeat the words back to him. Now he and everybody else would have to wait. Even while birds sang and mated in the newly green trees, he could settle to nothing but prowled round restlessly. By the end of the day his grizzled hair was standing on end and his eyes were narrowed with concentration.

Galena, understanding his fears held him close. Most of the field-hands had already retired for the sky darkened quickly at this time of year. The firelight flickered, casting shadows around the room. Her father had gone to his bed some time ago although he was probably still awake for he slept often during the day. They went quietly through to their private room, divided from the main area by a wattle and daub screen. Udda was wakeful, worrying about Udric riding off to a battle and about the horse he had so glibly declared was ready for the King to ride.

At Winchester inside the walls of the town, the king marshalled his forces, all eager to put the Scots in their place and share the booty. The Welsh princes brought their hill fighters, the Danes from the East came with iron clad soldiers. The leaders were lavishly rewarded for their support. The king gave a small Kentish estate, previously owned by his half brother to one thegn who had arrived with twenty armed men. As the town filled with men and store wagons, the clerks were busy recording the gifts. Pens scratched on virgin parchment; wax was heated to apply the King's seal beside his signature and those of the many witnesses.

'…anyone infringing the rights of the estate would burn with Judas the committer of impious treachery. Signed this day in the name of Aethelstan, King of the English, elevated by the right hand of the Almighty which is Christ, to the throne of the whole Kingdom of Britain.' intoned the clerk before placing the document on the table for the king to sign.

"A little over enthusiastic there I think, young man, but t'is well written nevertheless!" said Aethelstan as he held the pen up for the deed to be witnessed.

There was an unseemly rush to add their names to the deeds lying on the high table, as if by doing so their loyalty would not be doubted by the king. Memories of his darker moods were still fresh in many minds. The clerk rolled each document up carefully. They would be kept securely to await the return of the thegn or locked up for his heirs to collect if he fell in battle.

The mixture of languages, colours and assorted weapons added to the almost festive feeling which prevailed. The sun shone on the gathering as servants packed and repacked wagons. Brilliant sparkles of light reflected off polished iron and silver as men checked their personal arms. Enormous quantities of food for men as well as horses needed to be loaded for the journey. The population did not look kindly on soldiers stealing their stores. Messages had already gone out to the county sheriffs to prepare camps for the King's forces. Strong boxes from the treasury accompanied the king wherever he travelled. These were guarded by the tallest and strongest men whose loyalty was beyond question. Even a tall, evil-looking slave could gain a form of freedom if he was selected for this task. If he failed he would be dead anyway so it behove him to fight well, guard the King's money from the opposing forces and possibly gain freedom if he returned fit and well with the money in its iron-bound chest.

The army headed for Nottingham, marching rapidly beneath their colours ignoring spring showers and blazing sunshine. When the Archbishop of York sent word that his soldiers would also join those of the King, he too was rewarded with additional estates in Lancashire. By the time the King reached the Scottish border he was leading soldiers from two Archbishops lands, three sub-kings, the Welsh princes, sixteen bishops, seven ealdormen or nobles, six Viking earls, eleven thegns, Udric among them, and retainers from thirteen other landowners. It was one of the mightiest armies ever gathered and the King was justifiably proud of his subjects.

Few had time to admire or disparage the state of the fields beside roads they travelled. Men sang as they marched, the cheerful sound being echoed further down the long line of spear-men, archers and mounted warriors. Even the contemptuous glances from the Earl of Chester and his son could not dampen Udric's spirits. He rode behind the King at Aethelstan's request which may have been the cause of the revival of hostilities between himself and Chester's son. The fact that both were now married had not annulled the hostile glares from eyes black with hate. When the army camped for the night Udric stayed far away from the men who obviously still wished him ill. "Who would notice in a battle if a man's wound was in his back not bravely to the fore where he had faced the oncoming danger?" muttered Udric while helping Aethelstan to remove his armoured breastplate. The hastily erected tent only provided basic facilities. King Aethelstan was not fussy about fancy beds and braziers when he was travelling with his army. The King enquired if there was some particular point to Udric's enigmatic comments. "Sorry lord, you have enough troubles. I'll just put a bit of grease on this strap."

The inhabitants fled at the sight of the enormous host. Livestock roamed uneasily in the empty streets, the smith's forge still glowed redly through the open door. King Aethelstan was now in a position to order fortifications to be raised immediately. He commanded that soldiers take charge of the town and then garrison the keep when it was completed. Men marched off to carry out his orders and no doubt to loot and steal when his eyes were no longer upon them.

As soon as the new walls were started the King felt confidant enough to return to Wessex, visiting Mercia on the way. As each of the commanders left to travel to their own homes, promises of continued loyalty and support were recorded. Above all, Aethelstan desired peace within his own kingdom.

"God knows there is enough fighting on our borders without feuds and jealousies at home. There is always one who covets another's land, or his wife, or wants the favour I have just granted to someone else! I spend more time pacifying my own people than seeking out injustices or inspecting the forts. Do you know, Udric, there are one or two who almost come to blows over who sits closest to me at high table!"

"I have noticed Lord, but the Seneschal should direct them to seats not leave you to be peace maker! Actually, you do not have to sit on the high table to be involved in feuds or jealousy!"

The king feasted with the nobles when the royal entourage broke their journey south each night. It seemed that each town tried to outdo the meal provided by the previous hosts.

"You do not push yourself forward Udric," commented the King after he had been forced to listen to endless speeches while his food grew cold on the plate. "Are you my friend whether I had become king or not?"

"Yes! Since we were children we were good friends. My bed was beside yours, not outside your chamber. We were always the favourites of the cook at Wymburne. Mind you the very thought of him with his enormous ladles is the stuff of childish nightmares! First you were the heir, with everyone bowing and scraping, then you were not, for your mother was deemed to be your father's mistress, not his lawful wife. Then the Witan-elders met in council again and this time preferred you to your half-brother. That caused problems if you remember!"

The two men reminisced about the developments of the past few years. Riding companionably beside the King, Udric was finally able to ask the favour he had been itching to put to the king since his child was born. The subject had been mentioned before by the King but could have been one of those thrown away comments of little weight.

"My lord, my son is safely born now. Would you honour Edith and me by standing as good-father?"

"Before your marriage had even been formalised I put forward my name as the child's sponsor in God. Delighted, oh yes indeed friend, I will stand for your child – a boy you say?"

"We have called him Odda, because in Dorset the 'U' sound is more open than in Wessex generally. If you are returning to Wymburne then the priest will name him after Mass is finished.

CHAPTER FIFTEEN

Odda was duly baptised some weeks later with the King standing as sponsor. Inside the church the townspeople shuffled and chattered, paying little attention to the priest who had been given very little warning that his King was to be present. Fortunately he had used that time to change his black woollen robe which showed evidence of many meals and spills, for a clean one of dyed linen. The day was only marred for Udric by the fact that his grandfather, Gerhard, had recently died. He had lived quietly and departed in the same unostentatious manner, in his sleep, a hint of a smile on his face.

The body had been taken to the graveyard near Wymburne where it was reverently interred. The old practice of burning the body was no longer practiced, the pagan rites having been forbidden for many years.

"It makes me aware of my own age," commented Udda as he comforted his wife. "After all, I have seen almost forty-nine summers now and every bone in my body aches in the winter. Either I am getting weaker or the horses are getting stronger!"

Galena smiled affectionately at her husband's attempt at light-heartedness. She too now suffered from aching bones, especially in her fingers although she still spun the wool for Udda's tunics herself and made swaddling clothes for Edith's second son called Alfred in honour of the King's grandfather.

It was in the New Year of nine hundred and thirty seven that the King called the biggest council ever held in living memory. He had ordered a huge purpose-built hall to be constructed on the high ground in Dorchester. Two hundred of the highest magnates in the land could be seated within its vast beamed expanse. Aware that her father would be attending Edith insisted on accompanying Udric to the meeting so that Thegn Brihtric could see his grandchildren for the first time. Seating Odda on a pillion pad behind his father from which height he pointed stubby little fingers at all the new sights now available to him, Udric led the way southwards.

The new baby was wrapped up warmly in a shawl fastened across Edith's shoulders, its tiny head protected by a woollen blanket. In clear air, blown straight from the Dorset coast, the hall could be seen from a considerable distance. Butterflies danced from flower to flower, settling only for a second before continuing their silent flight. To the young boy, clinging to his father's belt, everything was fascinating, new and worthy of question.

In the quarters set aside for him, thegn Brihtric relaxed in a carved chair with supporting arms and back. A colourful tapestry covered the walls and the seat of the chair had been upholstered with a smaller version. As each child, dressed in their best clothes was formally introduced to him, Odda bowed as he had been taught while little Alfred played with the jewels on her father's chain. Udric made his own formal greeting before apparently remembering some small task, leaving Edith and the children with her father.

"Our hall is being enlarged yet again and now that the fields are productive, Udric has cottagers who labour for him." Edith said proudly, hugging her father closely. "Perhaps you will visit us one day and see for yourself the work that has been done. The curtains you gave me are beautiful. You were so generous. I have all the help I need. Indeed there has been time to make a tapestry for the wall. My lady mother taught me well. You will tell her that I miss her and my brothers and sisters won't you Father. We had not intended to have another so soon after this little one, but it's happened!" She shrugged, holding a child in each hand, the toddler still reaching out for the shiny baubles just beyond his reach.

She knew that her father was now one of the richest men in the kingdom, owning vast estates in both Suffolk and Winchester having inherited lands from Lord Algar. His dark hair was now liberally sprinkled with silvery lights, not detracting one iota from the handsome face and broad shoulders she remembered from childhood. She sent loving messages to her mother who had not come to Dorchester and received Thegn Brihtric's blessing before leaving him to his business affairs.

Some men made no secret of their jealousy, that Udric had been a close confidante of the King for twenty years. He was sure the ill-feeling was being deliberately fermented by allies of the Earl of Chester or his kin. Many times he had felt the penetrating disdainful stare that men cast towards cripples and lepers. On several occasions he had turned, involuntarily, towards the perpetrator to find an unknown petulant and hostile face. Udric was careful to take only his rightful place at the lower table, never presuming that his long standing friendship entitled him to exert influence over matters that did not concern him. More than once he had overheard men mutter that his grandfather had been banished for murder. It had angered him but as no one had ever been bold enough to repeat the slur to his face he had never had the satisfaction of thrashing the culprit.

With some difficulty Udric brought his attention back to the matter in hand. He was seated some distance from Aethelstan and listened intently to his friend as he told them the purpose of the meeting.

The council was to elect governors to rule sub-kingdoms or shires under the King. The Bishop of Salisbury was elected to take responsibility for Somerset and Dorsetshire having lands in both counties; Thegn Brihtric became the king's man for Suffolk. In this way the King divided the shires between Churchmen and lay magnates. They would make sure that work on defences, roads, and bridges was carried out on a regular basis. When necessary they could punish people who did not complete the forty days due to the King, or worked half-heartedly. It would mean absence from their own affairs but as they had their own income it was hoped that they would not fall prey to bribery. The meeting broke up as small crowds discussed the King's proposals and how it would affect them. Udric had been invited to Lord Brihtric's chamber for refreshments. Udda, who had not attended the meeting but been asked to bring another horse for the king to give as a gift to a favoured magnate, joined his son.

Like his father, the venerable Lord Algar, Edith's father judged a man by his deeds not his education. "I care not whether a man is literate, peasant, villein or well-born as long as he is honest. The effort your father has put into making Uddings into a happy homestead is admirable. My father often told me of his first meeting with Udda, when the horse had cut its leg. How he had been offered a meal and shelter even though the house was far from finished. He was proud of your achievements Udric. I think he thought that many a lad would not have got to grips with Latin, especially if he saw no need for it in the future. He was always telling people that his good-child was making the most of the opportunity. Of course, some knew that it was he who had suggested the whole scheme in the first place. But it worked well. We have young lads even now taking lessons with the younger children. One tutor can teach several at a time. There is more competition, just as there is in real life."

The three men were making their way to Brihtric's chamber. Guards stood aside for them to pass. The smell of the new wood was so novel everyone was remarking on it. Everything was new in this purpose built hall. The thatch over the porch was still bright, the underside of the roof tiles unstained by smoke drifting upwards from the two fires.

'It's a big responsibility to take on son. The King is asking for personal supervision. I have stewards of course at each manor but as you know yourself, most of the decisions are made by the lord. Only last autumn ….'

He was interrupted by Udda's gasp of shocked surprise. Tugging urgently on Udric's sleeve, he begged forgiveness for his rudeness and asked for them both to be excused from Lord Brihtric's company.

"We'll be back shortly and explain all to you, but this is urgent my lord." Having seen the horror in Udda's face, Udric gabbled his apologies to his father in law. They drew into the shadows beside the shutters of the window.

"I have just seen Garth! - The man who now owns Woodcutts farm, my father's farm. Surely it is him, much greyer now and stooped, but he was at court the night before you were nearly killed. He must be in his fifties now. What with the attack on the King and the guard shouting, I never thought to mention that I had seen him again."

Udric followed his father's glance and turned back quickly, his face blanched with distress. In a fraction of a second his normally gentle eyes had taken on the hue and hardness of flint.

"He attacked me! I'm sure of it. Does the king know he is here?"

"He must do, after all, didn't your father own the land directly from the king? That was probably why he was accused, petty jealousy surely, nothing to do with your neighbour having discovered the body. It follows that the same man must also have seen the rape of your sister. God knows how Garth got news of your father's arrest but you say he came to the farm and took over the day you were turned out. We must go to the King. Are you armed?"

Both men discreetly pulled their knives from their scabbards and left the hall, arms linked affectionately so that no one remarked on their departure. A few heads turned, nodding a greeting but most men were still involved in discussing the merits of the men elected to supervise the King's work in the Shires

Outside Aethelstan's private quarters they had to wait while other business was conducted. Udric found the delay hard to cope with, sweating under his leather jerkin. Storm clouds were building, the sun now almost hidden behind the bank of greyness, clouds building and folding in great swelling towers towards the heavens. The tension in the sky was mirrored by his own emotions as they were forced to hang around the ante-room for the King's attention. As yet only a whisper of wind ruffled the pennants flying from the stands. Udda wished he had not left his riding cloak in the stables. He could feel the sweat drying coldly beneath his arms and shivered as if someone had walked over his grave.

When at last they were admitted to the King's presence, a small chamber with a table and stools but little luxury, Udda boldly suggested that what they had to say should be revealed in private. Intrigued, Aethelstan waved his clerks away so that they were beyond hearing what Udric and his father had to say. He had immediately been aware of the urgent, tense atmosphere that accompanied them.

"One of the assassins is here lord. I saw him." Udric's bald statement momentarily produced a stunned silence.

"Surely not! They are all dead or soon will be." Obviously puzzled by his friend's abrupt announcement, Aethelstan suggested that the whole story would make more sense. Both men turned to Udda who breathed deeply before explaining what had happened.

"The land of my father, Woodcutts farm, near Sexpenna Hanlega in North Dorset, was given to a distant relative by Edward, King Edward that is. I will try and be brief, but er ..." he faltered then spoke again more strongly. "My father was falsely accused, could not pay the fine and was banished. I myself was set upon twice while in the service of Prince Aethelwold by this man. I saw him at Winchester, just before you were attacked lord. He bears me ill-will, but not being content with owning my father's land, he sought to end my life and that of my son; to say nothing of causing my father's mind-sickness." Udda added bitterly.

Udda had risen to his feet with emotion. Now he reddened with embarrassment as he stood while the King still sat. Fumbling for his stool he continued without waiting for the king to speak.

"I beg you, look into his claim, and more, why was he at court that night?"

"Let me check I have understood you correctly. You say that this man claimed to be kin of your father but did not stand for your father at his trial. In addition, he was given your father's land by King Edward and has attacked you twice…"

He was interrupted by Udric almost unable to speak coherently so great was his concern.

'Yes my lord, but he is also one of the men who attacked me in the mews. He left before my father came to our aid. He wears a very dark cloak with no colours or brooch."

The king had gone pale, his eyes now wide with apprehension. His half-brother's death played on his conscience even though he had ordered masses and prayers to be said for his soul. The attack in the mews, instigated by Prince Edwin, had been the first indication that there were those in the royal household who preferred another to be their king. All disloyalty, regardless of rank had been dealt with severely. His shoulders sagged at the memories which came back unbidden to his mind.

"I never benefited from the death of my brother, you know. He admitted being behind the attack and I gave his lands to the church. Two of his men I know of, the one dead and the other wishing he was dead! Perhaps my own clerk should find the charter and bring it to me secretly. It can then be examined for legality. You say you are quite sure your father did not commit the murder for which he was punished?"

Udda nodded, unable to speak. His throat was tight with emotion, tears pricking behind his eyes. He wiped them on his sleeve ashamed of his lack of control. Udric put his arm round his father aware of his distress after all these years.

"Yes my lord,' replied Udda formally, getting a grip of himself. "I was not allowed to support my father, being a few days short of my twelfth summer. Oath takers must be of age," he reminded the king gently, "and I had not taken my place in the fyrd so my words were not heard by the Sheriff your father sent to hear the case.

My father hit the king's messenger who raped my sister. She was simple my lord, from birth. The neighbour accused my father; yet if he saw my father hit out, then he probably saw why. Surely no man condones behaviour like that!"

Aethelstan confirmed that he would look into the matter the following day. He was clearly in pain and asked Udric to sleep close by in case he was needed during the night.

"Edith will have arrived safely at your hall now. She grows into a beautiful woman. And you have two sons? I declare I could be jealous of you." If the king had not been smiling rather enigmatically, perhaps with unbidden thoughts crowding his mind, Udric might indeed have come to the conclusion that his wife interested his friend more than was proper.

Turning then to his father, Aethelstan seemed restored, as if his momentary dreams had suddenly ceased.

"Udda I have not thanked you for Thor. He has proved a sound and courageous mount. You did well with him. No don't blush; there is no need for modesty between us. I also thank you for bringing a half-brother to him. My stableman reports that he has settled well. I may give him away as a gift but am loathe to part with him. Maybe a new sword would suffice!" Again the King became thoughtful, hardly noticing when Udda and his son moved towards the door.

Backing out of the room Udric asked for two pallets to be placed outside the curtain to the king's bedroom. Wrapped in cloaks and fur rugs the two men whispered in the darkness which was only broken by the flickering of a wall mounted torch. Impassive faced guards stood several paces away but ignored them as the hours of darkness passed.

Two days later Udda and Udric were summoned to the royal quarters. A clerk stood behind the king looking extremely nervous as the deed was stretched out.

"I have examined this, and it appears to be in order, but I have instructed a sergeant at arms to make discreet enquiries as to the family of this man, 'Garth'."

The clerk, dressed in the black robes of a cleric visibly relaxed, stepping forward to collect the document from the king's table. Waving him away the king said he would keep it for a while. "Are any of the witnesses in my household?"

The clerk, his Adams apple bobbing up and down nervously, looked puzzled but examined the names carefully. "Ah, this one, he is old now but writes tallies for your monies in Winchester my Lord. I do not know any of the other names there."

Udric turned the document so that he could read it but his concentration was interrupted by the king rising to his feet.

"There is nothing to be done until the enquiry is complete. I leave for the North tomorrow to gather all the forces I can muster. The Scots have allied themselves with that wretch Anlaff from Ireland. I have called on the Mercians this time so you can go back to that pretty wife of yours Udric. Let me know when the child is born, a little girl would make a handsome addition to your family, mmmm?"

Udda and Udric stayed long enough to watch Aethelstan leave the city riding 'Thor'. Magnificently harnessed, Udda's heart swelled with pride as he watched the high-stepping horse leading the procession through the gates. Edmund, the king's favourite half-brother followed closely behind, the soldiers marching in ranks with pennants flying. A few knights were to accompany the King as he made his way north to meet up with the Mercian army. Swords glinted in watery sunshine, the storm having blown itself out during the night. In the distance the leafless trees showed as black tracery in the morning light.

"God grant him a safe return Udric. Meanwhile we must go home and wait for news, both of the King's victory and from the sergeant at arms. The man's name has never sounded right to tell you the truth, unless there is Danish blood in him."

Edith was waiting for them at Uddings, her eyes red-rimmed, with dark smudges of fatigue. She poured a welcome cup of ale before leading the way into the hall. There, when greetings had been exchanged she had to tell them the sad news that Galena had died in her sleep.

With a gasp of shock, Udda seemed to shrink, hugging his arms around his body, rocking backwards and forwards on the stool. "I wondered why she was not here to welcome me. She was not ill! A few aches, especially in cold weather. She looked so well. I would never have taken that dammed horse to the King myself if I thought she was ill. Oh, my love, my love!" He could hardly speak for the breath had caught in his throat and he could feel tears in his eyes.

A dog crept up to comfort him. He stroked its smooth head absent-mindedly. It pushed against his legs and sighed deeply. Udda turned away automatically hiding tears from a woman. Edith hugged him until he had regain control, and then grasped her husband's hand as if she too needed to hold on tight to a warm, living person.

Udda mourned his childhood sweetheart deeply, fighting back his tears when she was laid to rest in the town graveyard.

Despite the period of mourning both men were anxious for news from the king's enquiry, but it was not until shortly after they had returned to their own homestead that Udric was summoned to attend court. The messenger, accepting Udric's hospitality, was eager to tell his audience of the King's narrow escape from assassination while camped at Brunanburh.

"Had the King not moved his tent in the middle of the night he would have been slain. As it was, the royal pennants still flew outside the bishop's tent and he was badly injured, perhaps by mistake. The battle itself was extremely savage. We were giving no quarter you see. The King had told his battle commanders that they were to take no prisoners, no hostages. The young aetheling, lord Edmund led his West Saxon and Mercian forces so well that they killed hundreds of Irish sailors, the Danish princes, and the Scots King's son. The plunder was piled high in the treasury when I left."

Everyone in the hall had fallen silent listening to the young soldier enthuse about the victory. Youngsters, eyes round with wonder, listened to tales of heroism. It was late when Edith reluctantly left the hall. She suspected her labour had begun but was unwilling to interrupt everyone's enjoyment. Later, she would hear anything she missed as the deeds at the battle of Brunanburh were told and retold for many years to come.

Unlike previous pregnancies her pains were long and arduous. It was not until Alana, the most experienced of the womenfolk, thrust a bunch of strong herbs under her nose forcing a violent sneeze that the girl child was finally born. "There my lady, a dainty little maid! She is a bit small; you had better take her now. I hear lord Udric coming this way." Ever conscious that her master was now a thegn, Alana bobbed a curtsey as he passed her, beaming at her and everyone who had been attending to Edith.

Odda's tutor had kept the boy at his studies all day so that he only saw the new baby when she had been washed, fed and swaddled.

Now he stood with his father in the freshened room. A young woman whose husband worked at the mill held Alfred's hand firmly. She had been chosen to care for the young boy and was glad to move from the town where her parents had both died of the sweating sickness. Here at Didlington, as it was at Uddings, the water was clean, the air fragrant, neither being the case in the town where the sewage had polluted the river.

The matter would be raised again at the moot, still held as it was traditional on the cold and draughty slopes of Badberie. No one ever owned up to having allowed their midden to overflow into the river Wym and since no one in the town had slaves; the task of cleaning the river got left to nature and the spring floods.

Udric left for court reluctant to leave Edith but eager to hear the king's news. Entering the huge gates set in the walls of the capital city the sense of excitement was almost palpable. Those who had marched out behind the King bragged of their brave deeds and prowess in battle while those who had stayed on guard rolled their eyes heavenwards having heard the stories time and time again. The gossip in the market street and in the stables was all of the great battle.

"I grieve for the dead, Udric, so many good thegns, ealdormen and soldiers too. I left much of the fighting to Edmund, my belly ached so that it was hard to stand let alone ride to battle."

Trying not to reveal how shocked he was at the visible change in the king's appearance after just a few weeks. He had become thin to the point of frailty, with a deathly pale face. Trying not to stare, Udric asked if a peace treaty had now been signed.

"Uh …." the king hesitated, avoiding the subject. "We took no hostages. I ordered the prisoners to be slaughtered. Oh, some wanted to take them as slaves, but they were killed, every man of them. It's not something I'm proud of now and I have bad dreams. Only a few made it back to their ships."

"Your messenger did mention something about that. Also an attack on your tent, or was it that of the bishop. It was a bit muddled."

They went to the hall for dinner but Udric, seated a few places away noticed that the king was hardly able to eat anything. He did not see him leave because the sergeant at arms had sent a message asking him to come to the clerk's room. Hastily finishing his meal, Udric bowed in the King's direction, and then left the hall wiping his knife on the cloth by the door.

Passing through a dark corridor on his way to the King's chancery Udric could not help glancing over his shoulder. Once again he had been the target of rakish, sardonic grins and penetrating black eyes attempting to penetrate the very core of his being. “I shall have it out with you and your son before too much longer,” he muttered, referring to the proud Chester earl and his son, as he emerged into the gloomy office where so much of the behind the scenes work of ruling a nation was carried out.

The promised information on Garth's ancestry was disappointingly inconclusive, the sergeant reported. “His story, that as a younger son he had made his own way in the world living in Normandy for many years was born out by the fact that he did indeed speak French. His copy of the lease is also signed by King Edward and witnessed by the same people so no irregularities to be found there.

My man also said that the rent was paid, albeit grudgingly. The tenant was apparently unpopular among the villagers as not only were his own fields full of weeds but he disliked helping others in harvest-time.

I am only sorry that we could find out no more, but that only deepens the mystery. Most people reel off their father's father, mother's mother. Indeed sometimes we have to stop them relating their entire life story!”

Udric thanked the sergeant for his efforts even though there appeared to be no proof one way or the other as all witnesses who might have known the family history were dead.

He was surprised some time later when the King ordered him to attend the Sexpenna Hanlega moot to assist the Bishop of Salisbury, where Garth, as an independent land-owner would be obliged to attend.

“But, don't you see Udric,” enthused the King. “You are not known to them. You will be the Bishop's assistant, time to look around. If this man bears a grudge, whether it is against your family or in league with Edwin's erstwhile friends, then you may hear about it. I cannot order his arrest without good reason! Go in the Bishop's retinue, make yourself useful. Tell me what you discover when the churchman has finished his tour of the northern part of Dorsetshire.”

A chill wind was blowing across the small mound on which the Bishop's chair had been placed. Between the two small hamlets of Sexpenna and Hanlega, convenient for the landowners, the treeless rise was neatly mown by villager's sheep. It was too cold to sit down. Most huddled in their cloaks wishing that the Bishop would be brief so they could return to work or to their hearths. If the owner of Woodcutts farm had recognized Udric he gave no sign. He had only the haziest memory of seeing the dark browed face of Garth beyond the perches occupied by the King's hunting hawks. A fleeting glimpse before being knifed was not conducive to being certain that Garth was the man in the mews.

The man's neighbour Richard, son of Guthrum, complained of the weed seeds blowing onto his land. This gave Udric the opportunity to ask if there had been a feud between the two land-owners in the past which was emphatically denied. Various other small complaints were quickly settled and the meeting broke up after a blessing from the Bishop. Under the guise of being part of the escort for the Bishop, who was anxious to return to Cranburne, Udric rode past the Woodcutts Farm, the home of his father and his father before him. It did indeed look unkempt. There was no sign of life in the little house, no fowl pecking round outside. Sunshine brightened the landscape; fields were full of growing crops, the barley turning from green to dull gold as the season progressed. A light wind blew the seed heads in waves, stopping abruptly at the raised path between fields.

Disappointed that he had learnt so little, Udric rode thoughtfully to Uddings to report the sergeant's efforts and the scanty information gleaned at the quarterly moot. In the shelter of the small hill his father's hall was relatively warm, a fire burning brightly in the central hearth. They sat companionably but both were conscious of the empty stool and the neglected loom in the far corner.

"There is no point in pursuing the matter, Udric. According to the sermon last Sunday it is not for me to look for vengeance. I am filled with mistrust of the man but not on my own account. You think he attacked you at court and I saw him there. Presumably there have been no further attacks and we are both mistaken. We should let the matter drop or I will be the one accused of starting a feud!"

Together they walked out to a small fenced paddock where Owenson was teaching a small boy to ride. Neither of them called out to attract attention. "I watched you once, riding at the King's Tun, with a hawk on your wrist. Lord Algar and I stood and admired the way you sat on the pony. How one uses the reins with only one hand is still a mystery to me!"

Odda was now a proficient rider, fearless of even partly trained horses. He had been first to sit on the colt's back and although the roan mare had watched the child warily, she had stood quietly as her offspring walked slowly round the field with a rider in control for the first time.

Despite missing Galena sorely, Udda took great comfort in the love shown to him by his grandsons who frequently came to Uddings accompanied by a trusted house-servant. He relied on the kitchen women to help young Alfred with his meal while Odda hardly noticed what he ate in his eagerness to get back out to his beloved horses. Like children the world over, he had questions, some of which could not be answered. Udda had lost count of the number of times he had replied "You'll have to ask your father!"

At night in the darkness, when he was so alone, then he truly knew that the light had gone out from his life. From the moment he had met Galena, from the first stirrings of adolescent longings, he had loved her with all his being. Now she was gone, irreplaceable in his remaining years.

CHAPTER SIXTEEN

For two years the kingdom was at peace, during which the King had done penance at the shrine of St. Dunstan to salve his conscience over the slaughter of prisoners which he had authorized. Udric only went to court briefly but each time he saw the king he had greater concern for his health. His hair was receding until only a few fair wisps covered his scalp. Now the King wore a hood most of the time to hide his sallow complexion and sunken cheeks. Normally a cheerful ruler, the King's temper was becoming uncertain so that servants feared his wrath over the smallest misdemeanour or clumsiness. He was tall, lean and stooped; the hooded eyes seeming to watch everyone, any glimmer of kindness had been exchanged for cold flint-like hardness.

It was on his last visit that he had argued with Aethelstan over the trial of a minter from Winchester who had debased the silver used in coins. The king had ordered amputation of both hands. Appalled at the severity of the punishment Udric had attempted to persuade the king to only cut off the man's right hand. Dismissed curtly from Aethelstan's room Udric later told his father of the rift in their friendship.

"He is in pain from his stomach and can hardly swallow a morsel now. Without a hood you would never believe how like a skull his head has become, without hair, without eye-brows. I'm still shocked that he spoke to me so cuttingly. "'What did I know of ruling, of appropriate punishments?' Thank the Lord that the Earl of Chester was not present. That sort of dismissal would have been exaggerated into banishment at the very least!"

"I believe you did the right thing. When a similar punishment was carried out when I was watching from the stockade, the man died of his injury. Mind you I think it might be better to die quickly rather than have to rely on others for the rest of his life....

Talking of coins, would you check my coins? I have many that differ but they have not been exchanged for many years.. "

Udda brought out the chest buried beneath his bed. The deed of Uddings lay in its clay pipe beside the small leather bags of silver pennies. Udric checked them all carefully and promised to exchange them next time the coinage was re-minted, the king's own measure to discourage fraud.

Every time coinage was re-minted the King would send a heavily guarded patrol round to each town. Wymburne townsfolk were always suspicious of these events for the clerk would record the number of old coins received from each man or woman and return perhaps a month later with the new coins. During the interim period there was a great deal of anxiety, often expressed at the meeting of freemen, about the safety of their life savings. The fee charged for the exchange was always held to be unfair because people had no option if they wished their coins to be legal tender. Udda had obviously not taken his little hoard to Wymburne. As with every other activity, there was little thought to privacy. One's affairs could quickly become common knowledge if there was anything which attracted the attention of gossips.

For weeks Udric fretted that his long friendship with the King had ended. While regretting his interference in the king's justice, he had no doubts that Aethelstan's ill health was affecting his judgment. It was this possibility which he put to the king as tactfully as possible when he was eventually recalled.

"You must rest, let Edmund gallop round the country on your behalf. He is your heir, you trust him, let him earn that trust," suggested Udric as he lay the King's sword beside his bed.

"For one last time I must lead the armies my friend, the Danes have fired the lands on my border and the Scots attack Tamworth. I will have peace in my realm so that people can sleep easy at night. The levy I have raised is not popular so they must see that it has paid for soldiers who will force the submission of Olaf once and for all. He may now be king of the Scots but he must learn that my boundaries are not to be crossed."

Even this brief conversation exhausted Aethelstan. His white face shone with beads of moisture. Irritably his untied the leather thongs which tied the collar of his tunic and mopped the wetness which gathered below the neck-line. When Udric passed him a glass of ale the King gulped it greedily and held it out for more.

After a brief battle the king left the Bishop to oversee the peace treaty. The return journey had mostly been made in companionable silence, some overnight stops being made at the manors of loyal nobles. The King's return to his capital was low key; Aethelstan appeared pre-occupied, tired and uncomfortable. Udric was with him in the King's private chamber waiting for the Bishop's report when he suddenly clutched his belly.

"God, it is killing me! Hold me tight Udric." Stools tumbled over; an ale jar was knocked from the table as Udric rushed to comfort his friend of twenty years. Clutching Udric's arm the king doubled up spewing blood violently over those who had jumped to their feet and were now attempting to restore order.

"Fetch the physicians!" shouted Udric as he almost carried the king to his bed. He was shocked by the lightness of the King's frame, feeling every rib, the shoulder blades and the knobs of his spine under his hands, a body wasted away under the many layers of fine wool. The other companions seemed to be rooted to the spot with shock. Some dropped their drinking cups on the ground spilling ale on the blood spattered rushes.

Servants rushed in with basins but were quickly dismissed by the doctor who could do nothing to help and stood beside the King's bed wringing his long, well manicured fingers.

"Could you send for the King's own priest," Udric gently suggested to a man who seemed to have recovered from the shock. "Our Lord King needs spiritual comfort. I am not sure how aware he is. Best be safe and send for the priest."

The room was rapidly becoming crowded as more servants and even some counsellors pushed their way in having heard rumours of the King's violent illness.

The priests were performing the last rites as the king died in a huge spasm, his back arched in agony, before falling back into the arms of his most loyal friend. Udric held the body of the king while hot tears ran unashamedly down his cheeks. There was a shocked silence. No-one had thought to summon Prince Edmund; no one denied Udric his right to embrace his old friend as the ravaged face relaxed in death, the wide, fearful eyes glazing over as the last focus dimmed. Gently laying the body down he signalled for one of the bodyguard to fetch a clean cloth.

"I must clean the King's face before others see him in this bloody state." Gently wiping away the blood and closing the king's terror struck eyes, Udric gave up the body to the monks who had been summoned from the monastery. He was on the point of following them when the bodyguard pointed out that his own clothes were soiled.

"I have a spare tunic in my saddle bag. First let us open the shutters. The King's father always believed that the spirit needed to be set free."

They struggled to open the shutters, Udric still fighting back tears which threatened to un-man him. He had been a close friend of the King since he was a young boy. They had got into scrapes together, learned Latin by rote and ridden against each other while being taught military skills. They had argued, fought and wrestled; sided with each other against common enemies, distrusted the same people and admired elders like Lord Algar. Udric felt utterly bereft, a novel emotion. He had been sad when his grandfather had died, very upset when his mother Galena had passed away, but the death of a relative from whom one has already partially separated by marrying and living under another roof was different to this wrenching loss.

The ritual laying out of the king in his robes was done by the monks before the body was laid on a trestle table in the King's hall. Torches were set at each corner, the flickering light insufficient for those who came to pay their respects to see the detail of Aethelstan's emaciated frame.

It gave time for Udric to adjust, to change his soiled tunic and pull himself together as far as the outward world was concerned. Inwardly Udric grieved deeply for Aethelstan, his friend since long before he became king over fourteen years ago.

Reluctantly he attended the council of magnates and thegns which met immediately to record the date of the King's death on 27th day of October in the year of our Lord nine hundred and forty-one, and authorize the continued use of Aethelstan's army. Many of them, like him, had changed into more sober coloured clothes. Few for the same reason, thought Udric bitterly giving no thought to whether the King's blood could ever be washed out.

"The council was at pains to point out that the great King Alfred died in this month forty years ago, almost to the day," muttered a thegn who had hoped to get Lord King Aethelstan's permission to marry.

"Well there are not too many around who remember that, although

I was there when his coffin was re-interred in the new Minster when it was completed. It will be the same again, a young King, a new council no doubt, and more taxes to pay," replied a cynical voice. "Don't worry about your young lady, the young prince will be giving favours to all and sundry for the next few months."

Udric ignored most of the conversations, eating automatically, sleeping poorly. His eyes had taken on the colour of flint, hiding his inner turmoil yet noticing everything. For his own safety, now that Aethelstan was gone, he made sure that he stayed in crowded places. His instincts were to hide away and grieve in isolation but having seen the Earl of Chester strut up to the late King's bier, nod his head briefly then greet friends the other side of the room in tones of hearty bonhomie, Udric had been reluctantly forced to admit to himself that he no longer had royal protection.

The burial and Mass took place at Malmesbury, the king's favourite monastery where prayers would be said for his soul. Hardly able to follow the service and making automatic responses, Udric struggled through the ritual of burying a King. Immediately afterwards the witan, the council of thegns, barons and knights gathered at Chichester. There was only the one candidate. Edmund was duly elected as King followed by lengthy oath-taking and rather subdued feasting.

"It was so sudden. How did he die?" queried one man who had only just returned from negotiation the peace treaty at Tamworth. The gory details of the bloody stream which had emanated from the royal mouth were being exaggerated but no-one who had been there corrected the stories.

Udric took his oath, assuring the eighteen year old of his continued loyalty before obtaining permission to return to his estate. He rode back absorbed in his own thoughts, not feeling the keen wind which blew across the land, nor seeing the fields of growing crops and grazing beasts. He waved to no-one, never gave his safety a thought. He was so sunk in the gloom of depression and loss that he was almost unseated when his horse shied at the leaves whirling and dancing in the wind.

The outcome of the peace treaty with the Scots would have made King Aethelstan turn in his grave had he known of it. The land north of Watling Street, the ancient Roman road, now belonged to them.

"I went to Wymburne to see to one of the late King's horses. The palace servants had heard the news from one of the new lord's messengers. Edmund his name is it? I find their names confusing now. Anyway, the young man has married. He was betrothed before lord Aethelstan died; she is a young girl called Aelgifu. No details of her family were mentioned. Anyway, their marriage bed was blessed, and the usual prayers for fruitfulness intoned. He's not wasting any time is he!

I have received no word about the horses so I presume they are to stay here until the King decides. Now that is something that your lord Aethelstan was trying to deal with. Is the matter to be brought to the Bishop's attention?"

Udda and Udric were sat companionably outside the latter's house in the lea of the autumn breeze. A few clouds scudded across the horizon but they were too white to threaten rain.

After some debate they decided that for the time being the horses would stay at Uddings. They were no doubt on someone's list at the Chancery and would be dealt with in due course.

"I wonder if Aethelstan's sword and purple robe have been inherited by lord Edmund? They were very fine you know, the scabbard alone held so many jewels, more than a knight's ransom you could say. He is young and had his own friends. We met on many occasions but I had few dealings with him so may not be asked to court so much. One family in particular will think that is no sad loss. The Earl of Chester's son hates me for winning the hand of Edith, even though he is now married to a really wealthy girl. Time away from the back-biting and cloying toadiness of petitioners will be good. We have much to catch up on!"

Udric, now the father of three children, spent his time on his estate or at Uddings apparently content with the routine. He was careful not to make too many decisions without referring to Owen who had uncomplainingly looked after Didlington during his long absences. There was now a deputy who would take over much of the farming work while his son, Owenson, had already become skilled with the horses.

Owen often spent time at Uddings, especially if Udda was also away. There were occasions when he was glad to leave Didlington for a few days. Alana's moodiness had deteriorated to bad temper. He had tried soothing words and affection but had been rebuffed time and again. The pain in her chest sometimes became unbearable and could not be dimmed with common herbs. Udric had once brought back ground poppy seeds which had been used to help his friend, King Aethelstan dull the pains in his stomach. No-one knew what dosage was correct so Alana used it sparingly before apologizing to everyone for her temper and rudeness. She determined to find a regular supply, possibly from a pedlar who frequented Hamtun where it was known that spices and exotic fruits from Eastern countries were imported.

A thegn travelling to the royal palace at Wymburne detoured from the Cranburne road specifically to visit Udric.

"I crave a night's rest friend. They said I would find you at home."

Edith had hastily filled one of her precious glasses with best quality ale and presented it to the visitor.

"Is King Edmund coming to Wymburne then?" she asked as they walked into the hall with its welcoming fire burning brightly in the centre. Stools were placed around it with small tables to hold sweetmeats or drink. Fortunately new straw had only recently been laid, not that anyone was allowed to foul the floor in her house.

Servants slipped quietly in with cinnamon biscuits, honey cakes and small pieces of local cheese with plain squares of unleavened bread. Their guest's cloak was hung on a peg before the three of them sat down.

"Tell us the news then. We heard that the lady Aelgifu gave birth to Prince Edwy nine months to the day after the marriage. The child thrives?"

"Yes as far as I know, the prince is in the nursery. At court the king's companions are now mainly churchmen. They supervise the exchequer, trade and when they can, the King's policies. Many of Aethelstan's companions, like you Udric, are not invited to court. It is as if the King is emphasising that he is different to his elder brother. At least the succession is assured, something lord Aethelstan never did.

Everyone thought that when the Scots invaded Northumbria and stole cattle and sheep before killing the inhabitants, there would be a general call to arms."

"Yes I heard about the slaughter. Actually it crossed my mind that you were bringing a message. It is not just awaited by me but probably all able-bodied men in Dorsetshire. The men-folk of Wymburne were reminded to practice with their bows and spears only recently. They grow lax, then eager and when there is no call for them, the weapons get put aside once more. Surely the Scots need to be put in their place once and for all. It was fretting about the peace treaty which upset my late lord." Udric spoke bitterly then spat in the straw. His face had become hard, the skin stretched tightly over the cheekbones. He hastily muttered an apology for soiling the floor, rising briskly from his stool and pacing the floor.

Edith frowned, even though she understood his anxiety. Excusing herself, she left the hall to supervise a guest bed and the evening meal. Despite having had three children her figure remained striking. It was with difficulty that their guest returned his attention to Udric and a less emotional subject.

"The King has asked the Abbot of Glastonbury abbey to join his court. Dunstan was related to Aethelstan but I'm not sure how closely. He's certainly an odd character! He's so thin, emaciated almost but he has those piercing eyes that see into a man's soul. There are stories that years ago after he gave up his lady-love, he had a fatal fever. Apparently at its worst he was raving but got up from his bed, climbed up onto the church rafters and threw himself down. Most men would have been killed outright but he claimed to have been supported by angels or some such thing and was unhurt. He lived in some sort of hut outside the church after that, fasting and working on a forge. It's said that the cell was not big enough for him to lie down and that he fasted until he saw visions. Anyway, his work is thought to be very special and it is clear he is no fool for the Council questioned him closely on many matters and his answers must have satisfied them.

Personally, the man unnerves me – makes me feel like a callow youth. He has quite a lot of influence and is definitely against war and fighting. Maybe that is why the King is so slow to call men to arms."

"I have sent messages offering my small force," Udric told his father as he fretted at the delay. "No order to join the king's army has come. The only contribution I have made is the delivery of corn and flour for the soldiers." He lunged his spear at a target once again, venting his frustration on the stuffed sack until it split, kicking the dirty wool furiously. "What is our King doing to guard his boundaries? My lord exhausted himself to build strongholds, leave garrisons of soldiers and ensure the loyalty of nobles with gifts of land and horses. God is not going to lift a finger unless he helps himself. All this talk of turning the other cheek is soft. My lord's battle commanders must be fretting at the delay just as we are down here in Wymburne. I know of twenty men who could leave tomorrow to fight." He gave the broken sack a final disgusted kick and stormed off to vent his anger somewhere else.

Udda struggled to fill his days so that he was tired when it grew dark. There was still an enormous gap in his life. The steward seldom had queries which needed much time to sort out. He held meetings of all the fieldworkers, the two craftsmen and the household servants at regular intervals, agreed to the cull of surplus animals and sold wool to the merchant. There were no outstanding problems for Udda to address. Owenson now looked after the horses, overseeing a younger boy who was delighted to clean stalls, clean tack in the shelter of the stables and have a bed to himself. Udda forced himself to follow the developments of training, schooling and breeding. He now had no confidante with whom he could discuss the day's events, and no soul-mate to embrace him and share the rare private moments in the dark of the night. Sometimes he thought that time passed with excruciating slowness.

Edith was secretly pleased that her husband remained in Dorset, advising him to be patient. She provided hospitality for travellers whenever the opportunity arose so that Udric could learn the news from around the area. Her main concern was that the children received basic education so that they should have some of the advantages which he had received.

"I can look to our lass, but even she enjoys her lessons. You should take the boys out with you more often. You're like a bear with a sore head. Can you not be content without fighting in a battle? Think of the children; give them time to grow up in peace. If the King does not want Dorset thegns or men he must be relying on soldiers from another shire."

They hugged as Udric apologised for being brusque and pre-occupied. He playfully slapped her bottom when she pulled away saying that the cream would have risen and must be collected for butter and the cheeses which she now made herself.

He trained the two boys in arms, allowing the children of the cottagers to join the lessons. Treasured beyond any other possession Odda, the eldest son, practiced with his miniature sword and shield given to him by his father. Others used blunted pieces of wood made by one of the cottagers. He tended to pour scorn on Alfred's skill at reading and writing, his own untidy efforts falling a long way short of his younger brother's. In riding however, the two were almost equal, frequently directing their rough coated ponies in the direction of Uddings in the hope of being allowed a ride on the bigger horses.

Udda's own roan mare had given him a colt each year. Both boys dreamed of owning one of these animals, their glossy coats so different to the rougher texture of the native horses.

"Not for a few summers yet," retorted Udda warning them to ride home before dusk fell. "I am getting too old to train them; it needs a younger backside to stay on when they buck!"

The boys, dressed alike in brown wool tunics, would hastily ask him for his blessing before arguing fiercely as to who might own one of grandfather's colts first.

It was not until King Edmund had retaken the Mercian lands with the help of Odo, the Danish Archbishop of Canterbury and the Northumbrian borders were once more safeguarded that he came to Wymburne to hunt. Despite not being allowed to shed blood in a battle, churchmen often wielded a huge knobbed weapon with great effect. All day carts trundled down the road to Wymburne, the heavy wheels churning up the surface.

At last Udric received orders to go with the Bishop of Salisbury, the shire-reeve of both Somerset and Dorsetshire. As he dressed in his best tunic, watched by his sons, he told them of the justice that would be meted out by the King. "Some cases are too serious for the Sheriff to deal with. The kin and oath-takers are held responsible for the accused being present on the day of the trial."

"What happens if the man runs away?" interrupted Alfred thoughtfully, following Udric outside tilting his small face upwards to look his father in the eyes.

"Then the kin have to pay the fine for him. That's why they are so worried!" laughed Udric, steadying the horse as he kissed Edith heartily. "Behave well while I am gone. Your mother will tell me of any misdeeds on my return!" Laughing, Udric urged the stallion into a trot and left Didlington for the short ride to Wymburne.

At the palace he renewed his acquaintance with other thegns who had been invited to hunt with the king. Stories of Edmund's prowess in battle circulated during the nightly feasting giving Udric a chance to study the new female companion seated at the high table. He had not heard that Aelgifu had died and had initially been surprised to see the blond, heavy featured woman hanging onto Edmund's arm.

She carried the young aetheling Edwy before passing the three year old to a nurse. He had his uncle Aethelstan's blond hair and was obviously adored, even spoilt by his indulgent father.

Udda and Owenson went to the palace early one morning to ask the King to appoint the latter as his horse healer now that Udda had reluctantly admitted that he was too old to train the young animals. He already ached in most of his joints from falls over the years. Introducing the young man to the palace stable staff was a pleasant way of passing a day for Udda. He shared so many memories of the late King's horses and their prowess in battle with the older stable-hands. Owenson listened, nodding occasionally when he too remembered 'Thor', the cross-bred stallion who had carried King Aethelstan into battle. As the afternoon sun waned, the braziers were lit while they waited for the hunters to return. Not far away the butcher sharpened his knives on a whetstone, the rhythm of the strokes like the motion of a scythe in the corn field.

Having had a good day out hunting the King was relaxed. His hair was more mid brown than his uncle's but he had inherited the same long nose and stubborn chin. He had not bothered to change, the aroma of sweat from both man and beast pervading the stuffy atmosphere. Udda was admitted privately, his name still meaning something to some of the elderly retainers who worked at the palace.

My lord King, for many years I have healed the royal horses when I could and supervised the breeding of some Norman horses on behalf of er…. Kings," he finished lamely forgetting the names. "May the young man I have trained since he was a small boy take the task from me? The horses will have the same care as before."

King Edmund readily agreed, thanking Udda for his services to his half-brother and his father before him. As he rose, signifying the end of the audience, the King gave him a ring and promised a purse of silver as reward for his long years of hard work. Owenson knelt, offering his oath and service to the King. Udda smiled at this young man, not much older than he was when he had first healed Thegn Algar's horse all those years ago.

"Have you been ordered to collect a headband showing the lord King's colours?"

The young man's eyes were shining in a face radiant with happiness. "I have met the King!" he exclaimed. "I work for the King!"

Udda left Owenson to collect his royal insignia and hurried to the royal stables to see the stallion 'Thor'. He could not prevent himself grinning at the boy's obvious delight and pride in his new appointment.

The magnificent stallion, now in his prime, had been trained for King Aethelstan, a man who was known from childhood to be scared of horses. "God knows it is many years since I pulled him from under the bellies of the horses here! Then the marriage to my beloved: Oh Galena, I miss you with every fibre." Sniffing and wiping the moisture below his eyes with his sleeve, Udda found the stall and paused to listen to the regular chewing of hay. The healthy smell of sweat still overlay the gloom inside.

King Edmund, had insisted that the late King's horse should pass to him and was frequently seen visiting him with titbits. Udda stroked it affectionately as it nosed his jerkin, proud of his achievement in preparing a horse fit for a king.

Owenson stood at the doorway listening to Udda talking to the beast. He admired the understanding between them and vowed to develop the same empathy. His new diadem was still stiff as he passed it from hand to hand before tying it proudly round his brow as he joined Udda.

They spoke a few words together before Udda introduced the young man to the grooms who had brought the tired horses home.

"It is important to treat them all with respect. Many of them are in the King's household, going round the country with him. Now ask if you can see the horses which hunted yesterday. Check their...."

"Yes I know, their legs, for swellings sometimes come out hours after the injury. You have taught me well lord. Ever since that night when I watched over them; you were away; I was alone with the mares. They knew of my fears but not one harmed me. Anyway, I will go and check their legs. My thanks lord." Owenson bowed his head respectfully before turning back to the horse-lines.

Udda sighed for the end of an era. He left for Uddings, the purse of silver weighing heavily on a cord inside his tunic. He was about to count it but was interrupted when Owen arrived, anxious to hear if his son had been promoted.

"He will wear the king's colours then, as you have done all these years?"

'Indeed, Owenson will be home soon and show you himself. I left him to inspect the horses which went on the hunt.'

Owen thanked him, his voice thick with emotion. "I know that my son's rise in status is due solely to you, lord. He is my pride and joy, a child I never thought to raise." Straightening his bowed back and adjusting his jerkin, the one-time slave turned from Udda with a grin and went to tell his wife the news.

Udda often expressed hopes that his grandson, Odda, would rise high in the King's favour. He was even now with his father at court having learnt the ways of Bishop Wulfric's rich and learned household.

"Udric has made me proud,' he announced to Owen. 'Hearth companion to a King, and already a thegn! Odda is young yet but there is many a man who would envy his riding skill."

Owen nodded in agreement as they enjoyed the sunshine beside the herb garden which Galena had planted. They sipped ale side by side companionably. Neither of them had any dark hair left. For years they had both had a measure of silver mixed with the youthful darker hair. Now, two old white haired men were able to take their ease while the younger generation carried on the work in the fields, woods and pasture.

"He is indeed a well mannered child; they both are, though with different skills. Edith has taught them well."

"He is well liked by my lord Wulfric and will inherit Uddings and Didlington in due course. Alfred is better at writing and reading. He will have to make his way in the church or perhaps in the Kings' exchequer."

"I cannot see him in the church. His father already leaves him in charge of the mill. Perhaps he should have his father's land and Odda should have Uddings. It would be fairer," prompted Owen hoping that his long association and loyalty to Udda allowed him to be so forthright in giving advice on such a personal subject.

They continued discussing the matter as the light gradually faded and they went into the hall to warm themselves by the fire.

To a very large extent it had been decided to farm the two estates as one larger farm. There seemed little point in each of them sowing barley, wheat, beans, and peas. First class hay was cut from fields left un-grazed for nine months while those which lay fallow to help with the fertility of the ground were cut for lower grade forage. Edith had cows for milk, cream and cheese. Uddens now had more fowl laying eggs for everyone. They too were penned on fallow ground before the pigs dug the worst of the weeds and pests from the soil. There was salted pork, smoked pork, brawn and chitterlings to share out. All the women spent time spinning and weaving when they were not working in the kitchens or fields. Little was wasted, hides being cured, skins stretched and fire wood collected by the children who enjoyed the adventure. There were many breaks in the routine. In the late summer and autumn everyone went out to collect the beech-mast and acorns, the small black whynberry fruits which grew close to the ground on the heath and later the blackberries. Eaten with bread and honey, as a sauce or used for dying the home-woven cloth, the latter was a most sought after crop. Collecting nettles for dyeing was not such a popular task. Gauntlets had been stitched but could not prevent all the stings. Many an ankle had to be soothed with balms to relieve the angry welts.

So the days passed with little to disturb the cycle of the year. Sundays, the Mass in church then a day of rest or for games; Archery practice at the butt in Wymburne, a bit of flirting for the younger girls, catching up on the local gossip after the service when only the church news or barest details of new laws would be relayed by the priest to the congregation.

"By my oath, the man was drunk!" exclaimed Owen who still insisted that his family attended the Church of St Mary in Wymburne. Occasionally the nuns from the monastery could be seen returning to their enclosed life behind stone walls. Apparently they were learned ladies who copied out gospels with beautiful illustrations. "Not that I've ever seen their work," he muttered into the jug of ale he had just purchased. "They say daughters of Kings and nobles live in luxury there, but again, no-one really knows."

Owenson returned from the butts rubbing the inside of his wrist where the cord had grazed the skin. "Why we have to do it every week," he grumbled, "I'll go straight back, there's a mare almost due, you know." He straightened his headband self-consciously then set off at a brisk, jaunty walk, the soreness of his wrist apparently forgotten. Owen smiled proudly at his departing back.

Royal messengers on sweating mounts suddenly disturbed the daily routine when they galloped through the towns and villages, horns blaring. Pulling their horses savagely to a stop they announced that King Edmund called for armed men to march north to fight the Danes. "The fyrd is called to arms," announced the leader unnecessarily. Word had already spread to the furthest cottage where young men hastily retrieved weapons; brushed the worst of the rust off, grabbed bread and cheese and ran to join their companions for some badly needed excitement in their lives. Within an hour there was a steady tramp of boots and the sound of chattering young voices leaving the ford on the north of the town.

Secretly pleased to break the monotony of his yeoman lifestyle, Udric rolled his thickest cloak around hastily packed food, sharpened his battle axe and saddled a horse. The sword in its scabbard swung with every step. With his hair hastily neatened, Odda joined him similarly prepared except that he carried a spear, the blade glinting as he secured the butt in the carrier beside his right foot. They joined other men from Wymburne, leaving Alfred staring after them wistfully. The field hands watched as the two soldiers walked their horses briskly up the road. Once again they would guard their lord's manor in his absence. Horns would be used to signal others if aid was required.

Progress of the King's army through Nottingham and Derby was rapid, the enemy forces being caught unprepared. Leicester too was retaken after a short skirmish but Stamford held out, the Danes having stockpiled arms and food inside the fortress.

Udric was wounded by a glancing spear thrown from the stronghold while guarding the King's flank just as they entered the gates. The polished head had gone right through the muscle so that both wounds bled heavily when the weapon was drawn out. Holding his arm to his chest he had been forced to withdraw from the front row of soldiers.

"God's blood!" swore the eighteen year old king scowling at the thegns who gathered round him. "I give them peace so that the traders prosper. They reward me with deceit. Hang one rebel as a warning to others who would oppose my right to enter."

Udric was resting on a straw paillasse when the King visited his soldiers, a practice which made him popular. No fancy plate or domestic servants followed him into battle; neither did he shirk from leading the force himself. Pulling aside the flap of Udric's tent Edmund came in, his clothes unlaced and head bare. Totally without ceremony the king crouched down beside his wounded thegn.

"T'is but a scratch lord, I'll lead both Wulfric's and my own men tomorrow. Did we lose many today?" They talked in low voices of the dead and injured soldiers before the King moved on to the next tent, his bodyguard keeping pace to keep watch.

Not for anything would Udric have admitted the pain his wound was causing. Not daring to chew a pain relieving seed in case it made him less alert the following day, he spent a restless night, shivering despite being wrapped in the fur-lined cloak. He was glad that Odda had joined other youngsters and so far was unscathed.

In addition to supplying food and fodder, the sullen townspeople of Stamford were forced to provide hostages to ensure their future loyalty. To add to their burden, soldiers would be garrisoned on the reluctant traders for the foreseeable future. The king was anxious to push on to the border before the rebel Danish and Northumbrian armies had time to regroup.

"I know you are sweating and tired, but think of the rewards which will be yours when the battle is won." encouraged Udric leading his horse beside the marching men. His arm was bandaged but throbbed in unison with his heartbeat. "We are always in the front with the king because we can live off the land. The London men and Oxfordshire forces are slower than us so the king relies on us to be with him, even if the baggage horses are well behind."

It was on the second day of this headlong march over tracks and roads that were frozen hard with winter frost that a peasant, objecting to the slaughter of his ox, had thrown a scythe. No doubt it was the frustration of the moment but the blade severed Udric's arm above the elbow as he shielded the king's head from the weapon's curving flight.

Udric fainted with the pain and shock of his horrific injury, his sword falling from slack fingers. Blood spurted, spattering his horse and those who had crowded around him. Odda saw his father fall from the saddle but by the time he had reached him it was clear that Udric had little time to live.

Ignoring the dirt and the soldiers crowding round, Odda knelt beside his father. Blood pumped rhythmically from the stump soaking into the mud. Painfully raising his remaining arm Udric blessed him. "Serve the king well and keep our family's honour. Do not mourn my death, it's been a good life, more than I deserved."

His breath now came in gasps as he fought to remain conscious, His body cooled rapidly so that Udric appeared to shrink before his son's brimming eyes. "Honour my father for he is a good man. Bid him God's blessing for me." Udric's last words faded to a whisper as his life seeped away, his hand slowly falling to the ground.

A thickset man, protected by a hard leather breastplate was the first to recover from the shock of seeing his lord die in such gruesome circumstances. Nodding at Udric's son, he respectfully removed his make-shift helmet before bending down and gently closing Udric's eyes. Many of the soldiers were crossing themselves for no priest had performed the last rites. Some openly wept for Udric had been a fair and popular leader.

For a moment Odda was stunned by his loss. He rose to his feet unsteadily to find the king beside him.

"I know you want vengeance, a life for a life, but punishment has already been carried out. The man is already dead, slain by one of your father's soldiers. His family's lives are also forfeit…."

At this point the Bishop came up and gently pointed out that such retribution was God's prerogative.

"Take them as slaves, sell them quickly and bond them to another. I want no kin of my father's killer on my land. There was no time to call for a priest. He has died unshriven!" declared Odda, waiting only long enough for the king's hastily summoned clerk to note the details before excusing himself. His heart was still beating wildly; he needed to be alone to come to terms with the events of the last hour. The sun shone weakly but that did not lift the young man's spirits. He had absent-mindedly picked up his father's weapons and studied the blooded blade of the sword. He wiped it slowly on the frosted grass, the blood joining with the sparkling ice on each tuft.

The body was buried rapidly, the severed arm wrapped carefully so that it could be rejoined in heaven as the Bishop reminded Odda when he stood beside the hastily dug grave, twisting Udric's ring on his own finger.

"He may have died unshriven in men's eyes but his sacrifice has been noticed in heaven as well as earth. Prayers will be said to ensure a place for your father so have no fears on that account."

Stony faced, his brown eyes now deepened to blackness with grief, Odda now rode his father's horse behind the king's bodyguard. Udric's sword now hung from his own belt. He was even more eager to prove himself in battle. Whether it was his grief or the thought of vengeance which made him less alert will never be known. The Danish forces were already beaten, the English soldiers set on plunder. As Odda ducked under a low doorway of a hall he was surprised by an axe-wielding Norse warrior in full armour. His companions saw him killed outright and reported his death to the King on the triumphant homeward journey.

Saddened by the loss of two good men from one family he ordered that a portion of the plunder be sent to Edith at Didlington. "News of her double bereavement will have reached her fast enough, let their share be sent with a Dorset man. The horses will be sent to my stables for to send them back straight away will be hurtful. I believe there is a second son. When he is ready to join me in battle, then he will have a suitable mount."

Edith bore her grief with dignity, thanking the soldier from Wymburne who brought the sad news. Pouring him ale politely she encouraged him to tell her how each of them had fallen. Some details she later shared with Udda who mourned for his only son, and for the loss of his beloved grandson. Too old now to bother turning his face so that he would not be unmanned by others witnessing his tears, Udda had wept openly. Great sobbing gulps resulted in his throat becoming inflamed so that when at last he could speak the tones alternated between deep, husky words and tight, high pitched squeaks. In their joint grief Udda and Edith stood together, alternately wiping streaming eyes with the edge of her linen apron.

Alfred, matured suddenly by circumstances, wrapped his father's sword carefully, secretly hoping that he would never be called to use it in anger.

'I am glad Odda did not take vengeance on the man's family. To kill a man's beast, when that might be his only livelihood would have turned his brain for a few moments. God knows our men might have reacted in exactly the same way. It is little comfort mother, and we do not even have a grave here.'

At Uddings it became obvious that the death of Udric had aged Udda overnight. "It is not natural for the son to die before the father, let alone the grandson too." He grumbled to the Bishop when he called offering words of comfort. The churchman left with his armed escort for Didlington to offer similar condolences to Udric's widow, and arrange protection in the years to come until the young boy was full grown. It was always possible that a widow would re-marry but Didlington could in no way be described as a wealthy estate. Edith might be left in peace unless the King demanded that she take a man of his choice.

"Somehow, I don't think that King Edmund would force another on the widow of Udric. If he were to ask my advice about the matter, which he probably won't, then it would have to be the kindest of men to take on Lord Algar's granddaughter," mused the Bishop when Edith was absent for a few moments. He smoothed the embroidery on his gown absentmindedly, the raised stitching catching on rough skin.

The Bishop left Edith's hall to travel to Gloucestershire, the King's money in his charge well protected from vagabonds and thieves. Even the recently introduced death penalty for the eldest member of any gang caught robbing travellers had not removed the danger of long distance travel completely. He was pensive as he rode, the handle of his mace rubbing comfortingly against his leg. A young widow with two underage children on a relatively isolated holding would be deemed a prize by the unscrupulous. He had liked Udric's honest, open face and his sensible fair judgments. "Protection of his young family and widow is not only my duty but will be a pleasure. That young Odda, now he was bright, learnt quickly. He could have commanded men. What a loss!" the Bishop rode on, his bright alert grey eyes noting how well farmed the widow's land appeared to be.

Shortly after the cleric's visit Alfred was called to attend the King. Despite being only seven summers old, he was mature for his age and knew that only by serving the king could he gain favours and advancement. Being heir to two small holdings in Dorsetshire had not excited him as much as the thought of going to court. Dressed in a new tunic of wool dyed the colour of autumn beech leaves and a sheepskin jacket under his father's old cloak which had been shortened to suit his diminutive height, the young boy could not prevent a slight trembling of his lower lip.

"Honour the memory of your father and of Odda too, for they were both good men. Obey the king in all things for he is your liege lord. Give your word to him, even though you are young." Edith blessed her son as he knelt before her in the courtyard. Many of the workers had taken time to see the young master leave with the two armed soldiers who would escort him to the King.

To a man they had promised to defend his mother and the estate in his absence while Owen watched the proceedings paternally from the comfort of a high backed chair. He still advised when necessary but was happy to leave most of the work to the younger stewards. Edith was grateful for his presence, representing as he did, part of her late husband's childhood. Even more valuable than this, he was still capable with weapons having fought in the army on two occasions. Now white haired and stooped on wet days, Owen's creased face smiled as he watched the young boy ride away with a straight back, the adult sword, far to big for him, in a scabbard at his waist. Alfred had insisted that he wanted to take it with him. Indeed he had rarely been parted from it since his mother had been so dramatically widowed and he left fatherless. Many times he had drawn it slowly out of the greased leather which kept it bright, the sharp blade catching the light. If no one was around he had made practice moves with it until his narrow wrist ached with the weight of a grown man's weapon.

Arriving at court the fatherless boy found himself assigned to quarters adjoining those of Eadred, the king's younger brother. As the son of a thegn, the King had responsibility for educating, training and even the marriage of an orphan. Edith could not have overseen the military training required and if she re-married there was no certainty that her new husband would have any affection or responsibility towards the child of her former marriage, especially if he had sons of his own. Girl orphans too would join a queen's household, and eventually be found a suitable husband.

At first Alfred was awestruck by the magnificent hangings, the size of the hall and fascinated by the glass which had been set in some of the windows. Prisms of light spilled into the hall like darts, forming a row of bright squares of rainbow colours on the dull rushes. Dust motes rose and fell unseen into the shadows.

Shown into a chamber with several truckle beds he chose one in the middle of the row. Owen had told him that he might be sharing a room with several other boys and to avoid being in the corner which would make it difficult to be part of any night time chatter. "I was given so much advice that my head span but he may be right about this," he muttered to the empty room placing his saddle bag carefully on the bed covers. There was only one window, far above his own reach and no wall coverings; obviously a room intended for practical purposes only.

From their first meeting the boy and young man became companions, Alfred serving Prince Eadred as page. He had already made his vow of allegiance, learned by heart on the insistence of a burly man at arms, to the king in the presence of Bishop Wulfric, who in his capacity of shire-reeve of Dorset had been instrumental in bringing the boy to court. A memory stirred but was difficult to form. Something his grandfather Udda had mentioned about his father having been a companion to an older prince. The name escaped him, but he was sure his father had also come to court in similar circumstances.

"It is important that the king knows you are a loyal subject," stated the Bishop when they had left the hall. "The king has been talking of your mother. There is no kind way to say this - I have been charged with selecting a new husband for your mother."

"But mother would not wish to re-marry, I'm sure..., well she has not mentioned it. Would the king force her to marry against her will?"

Finding a convenient window seat the Bishop sat down carefully arranging his robes comfortably to accommodate his considerable girth. Patting the cushion beside him he waved his podgy, be-ringed fingers indicating that Alfred should sit beside him.

"It is considered a valuable estate my son, it is the King's to dispose of as he wishes. It may be small but the mill flourishes, the land is now fertile and the beasts grow fat. Your mother is a fairly wealthy widow because your lord father's share of the plunder amounted to er.., many pounds." The bishop faltered not knowing if Alfred was aware of the value that had been apportioned to his mother. "The king can reward a man with a ready made estate and a rich wife to go with it! King Edmund needs to ensure the treasury receives the monies from the mill but he is not insensitive. I doubt if he would force the Lady

Edith to marry against her wishes. We'll talk again later; I have to go to the church now."

Alfred hastily bowed to receive his sponsor's blessing, and then watched the cleric stride off, his robes blowing in the draught.

"Well I shall pray that the King does not find my mother a new husband! She loves my father's hall and everyone loves her. Besides what would happen to the horses? Owenson is the King's man in charge of them." Pressing his lips firmly together Alfred began to wish that his mother was not so attractive. The thought of losing her as well as his father and older brother brought a pricking sensation behind his eyes. He blinked fiercely several times and sniffed loudly hoping that no-one would witness this soft and caring side of his nature.

The feast of St. Augustine on twenty-sixth day of May was celebrated firstly with a special mass led by the newly appointed Abbot of Glastonbury, Bishop Dunstan, followed by displays of armed combat. All over the country this saint's day was a public holiday. At court the kitchen staff sweated for hours, starting long before the sun had risen, to produce meats of all kind. Both doors were open allowing the delicious savoury smells to waft into the courtyard. The cobbled surface had been swept clean of all the detritus which usually collected when soldiers, horses, dogs and ox carts used the same space.

When at last the gong was beaten signalling everyone who would attend the first of the two sittings for the feast to hurry to their places, the trestles were creaking from the weight of the dishes displayed. Everyone was dressed in their best clothes so that all colours of an artist's palette were represented. Ladies accompanied their husbands, squeezed onto the benches on either side of the tables which were arranged at an angle to the high table where the King and the most noble of his thegns were to sit. Bishops mingled with lay people; each person allocated a place according to their importance. The steward directed a constant stream to their seats, his knowledge of their rank one of the most essential attributes of his position. Even the guards, who would attend the second sitting, paid much attention to the gorgeous array of food which continued to be carried in by the cook's staff and pages.

Seated some distance from the high table, Alfred only noticed the sudden movement near the high table out of the corner of his eye. Prince Eadred however suddenly leapt to his feet calling the guard and pointing to another guest. All heads were now turned towards the young man whose face was now red and distorted with anger.

"Remove this man. Take him away. Leofa was banished by my father. He has returned unlawfully to the King's land and has the nerve, the impudence to eat at his table."

Momentarily there was complete silence before people craned to see who the young prince was pointing at. Men fumbled for their swords, forgetting that all weapons had been left at the guardhouse.

As the soldiers moved to arrest the outlaw he swiftly pulled out a double edged dagger. Even as spears were poised for a deadly thrust, Leofa leaned over the high table and plunged the weapon into King Edmund's heart.

Women screamed in horror and panic. The King's lady fainted and fell slowly from her chair. Men attended the stricken King, ignoring the lady's plight.

Stunned by the suddenness of the attack most of the diners remained rooted to the spot, their indrawn breath exhaled in unison. Vaulting the table, scattering dishes and drinking cups, Prince Eadred snatched a guard's longsword and drove it through the assassin's body, skewering him like a fowl on the cooking spit. Alfred rushed forward guiltily to the Prince's side, aware that his attention, in common with the majority of other diners, had been wandering.

The hall was in uproar as men called for their weapons. Dogs barked as food laden tables were upturned and benches toppled sideways. Still impaled but alive, the robber was dragged screaming from the hall by grim faced guards. Men of all ranks followed, some hastily wiping greasy fingers on their braes or tunics.

Pausing only to snatch up the prince's jewelled eating knife from the table, Alfred followed him outside. Gathered in groups, many exclaiming in horror, Leofa was tied to the whipping post in the courtyard. The women were ushered away by Queen Ethelfleda, the King's third wife, who crossed herself repeatedly as the ladies reluctantly moved away. She had quickly recovered and took charge of the situation. At a nod from Eadred, the Captain beheaded the dying man as the shocked court watched.

"So die all traitors." The call was repeated time and time again, long after the drama was over. The feast was abandoned except by the dogs which had taken advantage of the chaos to steal whole fowls and other choice morsels from the overturned tables.

The fully robed body of the King was taken in a richly canopied cart to be buried at the monastery at Glastonbury. Alfred, his eyes round with amazement stood behind his young lord during the ceremony watching the richly dressed priests carry out their duties. King Aethelstan's half brother and successor was laid to rest during a long burial mass amid the perfume of incense and beeswax candles.

The court was in a state of confusion, the king's chair empty at the noon meals. Magnates who had celebrated the Saint's Day at their own hearths continued to arrive at the Gloucester court. Messengers had been sent to alert them to the state of affairs after the murder of their King. During the days following the King's death Eadred explained that there was no king. "My brother died without making a will. He had only ruled for six years, indeed, I think he was only twenty-four summers old. Until a new king is elected and hallowed, the council acts for the general good of the realm. Then the new King can make any orders he chooses. I am quite happy as an Aetheling, I don't want to sit and make laws all day. Besides Edmund has a son, young Edwy.'

"But that's the point. He's a child, only five years old I think. Surely it needs someone who is mature. You've already seen a battle!" retorted Alfred completely without guile. He rarely stopped to consider his words, something he would learn to do in the royal household. His frankness and obvious admiration of a man who had actually witnessed fighting made the Prince smile. They retreated to the stables, the Aetheling because he foresaw problems arising over the succession and wanted little part in it and Alfred because the prince was rapidly becoming his hero.

"I almost wish that I too had given thought to my words," muttered Eadred, "if I had not recognised that man, Leofa was it, as the thief my late father had banished from these shores, then he would have had no cause to kill like that. Not much use having regrets now. God's blood! What a mess."

Alfred kept silent not knowing how to comfort a man suffering a fit of conscience however misplaced. The presence of the horses was calming. Some looked for treats. 'Thor', whose size totally fitted the name Udda had given him, looked disdainfully down his nose when no titbits were offered.

Chapter Seventeen

In Wymburne the lack of a King affected few people. Only the man in charge of the royal estates at the King's Tun wondered whose orders he would be following in the future.

Courts were suspended as officers were fearful that their positions had little legal standing without the royal backing. "How many others have returned to these shores without permission? Mind you it was insane to eat at the King's table! Surely the man must have intended harm to someone to take the risk of being recognised?" pondered the King's reeve after church the following Sunday. An interested crowd of townspeople had gathered round him in case he could enlarge on the rumours they had heard. Many had attended the special mass for Saint Augustine and enjoyed the holiday designated for that day. Now the market was in full swing in the early summer sunshine, children for once without fleece jackets and woollen shawls.

"What happens now? Surely the King's brother is the choice of most people because he is of age. Hasn't he already fought in battle?"

The King's reeve plucked at his small beard, his face a picture of concentration. Having a pale, freckled face with a slightly receding chin the representative of the crown had endeavoured to make up for natures failings and grew his red gold beard so that it disguised the symptom seen by many as that of indecision or lacking firmness.

"I have not yet been summoned to attend the Council," he said importantly, "they are in charge for the time being so no-one should think that crimes will go unpunished. There will be no poaching in the King's forests or taking of wood." He glared at two men in the crowd who had already been punished for such crimes in the past. They had both been whipped soundly but from the sly looks on their faces they had obviously thought of getting up to similar mischief in the very near future. The two felons had the grace to lower their eyes and retreat to the back of the crowd.

There were already factions of thegns and churchmen who were in favour of making the late king's son ruler in name only while a council ruled for him until he was of age.

Bishop Wulfric, Dorsetshire reeve, representing the King's rule in both that county and its neighbour, Somerset, hoped he might be elected to the ruling Council should the young boy be chosen.

"Surely if a King has a son, regardless of age, he would have left the kingdom to Edwy in his will. We can train the boy to King-ship and teach him the God fearing ways that a ruler should obey." Turning his rings round on his short fingers the Bishop tried to look humble as he tried to persuade senior thegns to adopt his stance on the succession.

Lord Brihtric, brother of Edith, having taken his father's seat on the council, sighed dramatically. Unlike his father and grandfather he had little time for debate being rather self-important and opinionated. His eyes were hard; hooded so that it was difficult to learn his real feelings. Having been appointed to the Council he expected the weight of his opinion to carry any argument. When others sought to differ the whole of his face became hard, the cheek bones became even more prominent than usual, the chin became more pugnacious.

He had supported the Bishop's application for his grandson to come to court. His own tentative offer to house the young boy himself had quickly been withdrawn when the order from King Aethelstan, before his agonized death, allowed Alfred to undertake his training at court. This would give Edith's son much greater chances than his own household could offer and being of a less generous nature than his father and grandfather, be cheaper. Now, sure that he had everyone's attention he launched into his defence of his choice of candidacy for the throne.

"The child is still in the nursery. Surely Eadred, now almost twenty-two years old, is the obvious choice. He is already a proven leader of soldiers in the battles against the Scots and Northumbrians. He is no greensick youth but still young enough to accept advice."

Several others were of the same opinion, voicing their concerns that the news of the sudden death of King Edmund might encourage the enemies of Wessex and Northumbria to take advantage and attempt to annexe territory.

As the summons to attend the Witan in London was sent out, Alfred received news that his grandfather was dying. Udda had been part of his entire life, a loving and affectionate character to whom he had always been able to turn for advice. Torn between supporting Prince Eadred and the love he had for his grandfather, the Bishop urged him to return home promising to assure the Prince that Alfred would return in a few days.

Before the sun had even warmed the early morning air, Alfred hastily rode back to Dorsetshire with the Bishop's guards. He arrived, exhausted from the long journey to find his mother and his sister Aethelflaed already at the old man's bedside. His mother's face showed her deep concern. Beneath her eyes dark smudges told their own tale of sleepless nights. There were creases in her robe from sitting on the low stool.

The wool-filled paillasse had been placed beside the fire in the hall, screens sheltering the old man from any draught. He seemed shrunken, the bones of his face already looking skeletal. Women servants lingered between tasks to fetch a drink or tempt him with morsels of minced meat. Udda had long since lost most of his teeth, now his eyes were also dimming. At times he dreamed; the name Galena often on his lips. Between them the tiny house at Uddings had evolved into a comfortable homestead with fertile fields long since cut from the heathland. The two dogs lay quietly watching their master, heads resting on outstretched paws, unblinking and unmoving, their canine devotion so obvious that no-one shooed them outside.

Udda blessed them all, raising his thin arm shakily to touch each of them. He signalled to Alfred that he had something to tell him but fell asleep after a few mumbled words. Leaving Aethelflaed to sit with him, Edith and Alfred crept out to talk softly beside the fire in the hall.

"Many times your grandfather has talked to Galena as if she was still here. He imagines that she replies to him. I do not think he will last much longer. Hopefully you were given leave to come home. Bishop Wulfric told me to send a message to him if ever there was great need so I took him at his word.

With the king dead there will be no more talk of re-marrying for the time being but I need to get your father's deed extended. My own father is dead now and my brother inherited his estates. The last thing I want to do is return to my family home and be dependant on my brother. It is hardly time to sound so mercenary. I should be ashamed of myself but Udric often mentioned the deed and what could happen."

Edith wiped her eyes on her bleached apron. "Maybe I am crying for my father in law, possibly for myself."

Alfred hugged his mother until she had recovered. She adjusted her wimple and smoothed the folds of her creased kirtle.

"I shall ask the Bishop to help us get the land grant extended. He says that the estate is mine at the moment, in name of course, but he acts for me until I am twelve. If Eadred is made king, he will do this for me." replied Alfred confidently.

"Why should he be king?" queried Edith puzzled by her son's statement. "Perhaps I am getting forgetful in my old age. You only went to court a few months ago. Udric served King Edmund. What has happened? I did not go to Wymburne last week as your grandfather has been so poorly."

Alfred gently explained the dramatic events on Saint Augustine's Day. He missed out the brutality of Lioba's death, telling her instead of the pageantry of the funeral at Glastonbury Abbey.

A servant brought the priest from Wymburne into the hall to warm himself by the fire. He had hurried up the hill but the wind was so piercing that his hands were blue. Already thunderclouds were gathering, the wind blowing them over the landscape. Beneath the clouds the sky was dark but where the sun managed to squint through gaps the fields were dramatically lit with bright gold. Edith drew aside the curtain and gently touched Udda's shoulder. His eyes opened briefly but failed to recognize her. Hastily the priest gave him the last rites. A servant brought hot potage in a bowl for the cleric who pulled a stool up by the fire to eat it. The family gathered closely round the dying man's bedside, each person alone with their thoughts and memories. Once or twice he attempted to speak, pointing at Alfred with his bony finger. Each time the boy knelt beside his grandfather, his ear to the old man's mouth to catch isolated words which were quickly choked by spittle. Gently Edith wiped his face as the light faded from the once sharp grey eyes. Udda died with Galena's name on his lips. He never had the opportunity or the strength to speak again to Alfred. He died in God's grace, taking so much knowledge and so many secrets to the grave with him.

The dogs sat up in unison and bayed their sorrow to the heavens before licking their dead master's face in a final salute. Standing silently, Alfred and Edith watched as the dogs pushed the leather curtain aside and left the hall to mourn in their own way.

Buried in the churchyard of St Mary's church in Wymburne, Udda's body was wrapped in the faded red cloak which he had clutched in his dying moments. Later a stone was erected to mark the resting place of the horsemaster to Kings and princes. His diadem was buried with him, its royal colours still recognizable though the cloth had become worn and threadbare.

"You will have to care for mother in my absence. I promised to return to Prince Eadred, although God knows, he may be King by now," added Alfred, talking quietly to his sister. "Send for me if there is danger; send your message to Bishop Wulfric. I will come with soldiers if necessary." Not entirely sure that the Bishop would actually react in this way Alfred fell silent, chewing his bottom lip. Once again he realized, he had spoken without thought.

Aethelflaed nodded obediently despite the fact that she could not imagine any circumstances when soldiers would be needed to defend her home. She felt the loss of her older brother more than she mourned her father. Udric had been absent for so much of her childhood when she had been too young to be of real interest to him beyond admiring her growth and childish achievements. Odda too had been much older and already learning the skills he would need to fight when she had been old enough to be conscious of his presence in the household. She missed his breaking voice which had been a source of amusement but from an early age Edith had kept her busy with household matters.

"Who will I marry?" she asked innocently after a pause. "Fathers find husbands for their daughters." Her un-braided hair hung loosely down her back as befitted a young maiden. Innocently she gathered up the long tresses and twisted them on top of her head feeling the unaccustomed coolness at the back of her neck.

Alfred frowned as he thought about his answer, her blunt statement catching him unawares. "I will ask the Bishop, but it will not be for many years yet." He took her hand reassuringly as they returned to their hall.

He could not sleep for thinking that it was not only King's sons who might be too young for the responsibility thrust upon them. He would try to get his father's manor granted to him, but also there was Uddings. If that grant was also only for two lives then the king could give it to anyone. Who was to be king?

His anxiety over the possible loss of his home and that of his grandfather was manifest in his inability to sleep. It could also have been due to the comparative silence of the countryside as opposed to the King's palace where someone was always awake. Guards in heavy boots patrolled both inside and outside the King's residence, servants fetched late night food and drink for restless sleepers and those whose work was done at night always made a noise, perhaps in retaliation for having to clean middens or start the days baking.

As soon as he could decently leave, Alfred returned to court, anxious to get advice from the Bishop. He found that the Aetheling Eadred had indeed been accepted as King. Whatever doubts he had expressed about becoming king he had confidently ordered the court to York so that his northern subjects could pay homage to him. Indeed, the baggage trains were already being prepared, the king's clerks loading their writing chests and materials into a covered wagon.

Anxious to assert his own authority on Wessex and its tributary kingdoms Eadred had designed a new diadem. The yellow and red cords were thickly plaited so that the colours formed lozenges on a man's brow. Alfred's long hair was hastily and painfully cut short and the diadem firmly tied around his forehead by the king's bodyservant before mounting his father's horse which had been given back to him. He looked down at the ground, so much further away than from the back of his native pony. He also wore Udric's sword as he was rapidly growing to a size when such a weapon could be wielded in safety.

Shortly after crossing the river further north, Archbishop Wulfstan of York and all the local magnates swore fealty to the King, many of them being forced to leave a son with King Eadred as guarantee of good behaviour. Alfred found himself busy finding space for these youngsters in the tents of the King's Wessex thegns. Some had never left home before but were comforted when he told them how content he was in the service of their new lord.

Alone in the king's tent Alfred hesitantly spoke of his concerns. "My lord, the Archbishop looked less than happy to have to kneel before you. He had one excuse after another. His legs hurt, he was a churchman and his oath should be sufficient…."

"He is influential in the North," interrupted the King, "it was essential that he was seen to do homage like all the others. However, if his reluctance was that obvious he will have to be watched like a hawk when we leave this place. He once arranged a peace treaty, between my brother Edmund and the king of Scots I believe. Perhaps I will leave a clerk with him. Ostensibly he can work for the Bishop but also be my eyes and ears."

When the King left York a few days later he did indeed leave a clerk attached to the Bishop's household just as he left conrois of tough soldiers in some of the towns on the welsh borders as he made his way back to Wessex.

While the King was with his counsel Alfred approached Bishop Wulfric on the subject of the grants for the two estates, Uddings and Didlington.

"My mother, the Lady Edith, is worrying that her lands might be taken from her. She thinks she might be sent to live with her brother who has taken his father's place on the King's council. He inherited their father's estates. Mother would be no more than a companion to his wife or something like that....," he tailed off uncertain how to make his case.

The Bishop already knew that they were both for two lives and then in the gift of the king. "I know both estates are productive, purely due to hard work by your family. As soon as the king rests for a day or two I will speak to him on your behalf."

Alfred fretted over the delay, especially when a boar hunt was organized. "If the court was back at Winchester, or even Dorchester, the records would be available."

Fortunately King Eadred chose to hold the Christmas festivities at Winchester, stopping briefly at Glastonbury with only his personal bodyguards in attendance. He talked to Abbot Dunstan, the cleric's drab monkish robes contrasting with the King's richly embroidered tunic and the emblazoned surcoats of the guards.

Alfred worried that in an absent minded moment the king might gift the two estates to another as a reward for services. He was deliberately kept busy by the bishop and on the king's return to his capital Alfred was further frustrated by many others who pressed for favours. It was well known that the young king was under the considerable influence of Abbot Dunstan and had already been persuaded to grant land to the clergy in addition to the tithes which normally supported them.

When Bishop Wulfric at last approached the king, he was very conscious that others listened to his audience. Abbot Dunstan busied himself clearing papers from the table while the Bishop told Eadred of affairs in his Salisbury diocese, assuring him that training in arms had been practiced regularly by the men of both Dorset and Wiltshire.

"My lord king, there is one other matter which I must raise with you."

"Must!" interrupted the Abbot testily. "No-one speaks of any matter without the king's leave." Full of righteous indignation the churchman had drawn himself up to his full height. His face was so mottled with redness that it looked as if he might have an apoplectic fit at any moment.

Bishop Wulfric controlled his annoyance and began his plea again with as much dignity as he could. "Forgive my rudeness Lord. Have I your permission to ask about two small Dorset estates which have recently suffered the loss of their loyal tenants. I speak of Didlington by Chalbury, and Uddings, north east of Wymburne. The former is of five hides, Uddings one hide in size. They were granted for two lives. King Edward, God rest his soul, granted Uddings to one Udda, healer of the king's horses, and your brother Aethelstan, also in God's care, granted Didlington to thegn Udric, son of Udda.

Both have died, the father of age and grief. The honourable thegn, and his eldest son, died in battle in the service of King Edmund."

After some further queries the king sent for both the charters. While they waited a servant poured wine for them. Silence fell heavily in the screened area of the hall where the king had heard pleas from his subjects all morning. The clerk sat at the table apparently studying the documents, uncomfortably aware that Abbot Dunstan's eyes bored into the back of his head.

"Tell me Bishop, what is your interest in these lands?" said the king waving his hand towards a stool. Bishop Wulfric drew a deep breath and related the events by which Alfred had been appointed his page. 'Father, son and grandson died within a few months of each other," he pointed out. "Udric's widow, the Lady Edith, daughter of Lord Brihtric, son of Lord Algar, is the mother of the remaining boy, Alfred. She lives at her husband's manor and stewards, very capable men, manage the two estates. I would hold the lands until he is of age."

The last phrase was so obviously an afterthought that the king smiled. With the merest glance at Abbot Dunstan he pronounced that both estates would be granted to the Bishop. "Grant them under one deed, clerk. I presume you can put in one of your own men to oversee the mill, bishop? It is important that the revenues of the crown are maintained."

Wulfric hastily agreed to provide a man to take charge of the mill and was on the point of leaving when Abbot Dunstan raised his hand.

"My Lord King, there is the matter of thegn Udric's widow to consider. The two grants are now to be combined under Lord Wulfric without any thought being given to the exchequer apart from mill rents."

The clerk stopped scratching with his pen hoping that he would not have to re-write all that he had already completed.

"The lady is still grieving my lord. She has a young daughter in addition to the boy Alfred who attends you." Wulfric was unable to prevent an involuntary scowl which he directed towards the Abbot. Where was the man's compassion? Three deaths in one family were enough for a man to cope with let alone one of the fairer sex.

King Eadred nodded sympathetically assuring the bishop that there was no need for unseemly haste.

Wulfric left the hall before more near disasters could befall him followed by the clerk who had also been dismissed.

Safely returned to his own quarters Wulfric called for Alfred. In the few minutes before the boy arrived the bishop chastised himself for his unchristian thoughts towards the Abbot.

"You will soon be of age and then we can approach the King again to put the lands in your own name," comforted the Bishop when he had explained the terms of the grant. "At least there will be less threat to your mother's widowhood if I own the estate."

Alfred frowned, not quite understanding the Bishop's last comment.

"Ah lad, you obviously do not know the practice of selling off rich widows, part and parcel with their land to the highest bidder. Your mother is comely, the estates well managed and productive. It has happened before when the king needed money and Abbot Dunstan has already put the idea into his head! Now you should go home. My old clerk will go with you. He knows nothing about milling but he can keep the figures. Lord King Eadred was only concerned that the mill continues to contribute to his exchequer."

Alfred bent his knee to the Bishop, thanking him for his efforts. The cleric smiled encouragingly at the boy who was quickly growing into a pleasant faced young man. "Go with God Alfred and take my good wishes to your mother. Her courage is an example to us all."

He was on the point of returning to his quarters on the other side of the courtyard when a stocky young man with a thin, earnest face barged into him. "Out of my way whelp!" spat the young lordling viciously. "Still got peasants serving him then?"

Alfred knew that the man was referring to him and took instant dislike to the derogatory tone of voice. His anger immediately flared into violent hatred of this haughty noble.

"My lord, your sarcasm is ill-deserved. I serve our King in any way that he dictates. My father and brother were killed in his late brother's service, fighting against the Danes. Lord Eadred took me into his care with other boys who had been orphaned. With God's grace I shall serve him as well as thegn Udric, my father."

"Pah! That boor, a peasant with no manners. Had to marry the lady Edith and show her off to all and sundry."

At the mention of his mother, the last shred of self control was blown away like a leaf before the wind. Alfred's voice became venomous, highly charged with the most poisonous words he could dredge up. "You are not fit to walk on the same earth as she does. She is loved by all who know her and would give their lives for her; but you, for all your airs and graces, your haughty manner and prideful speech should not even mentioned her name. Now I must be about my lord's business. Let me pass!"

Young Chester was so astonished that a page should outline his character in such a rude manner that for a moment he was shocked into immobility.

When he did react it was with lightening speed. With one swipe he wrenched Alfred's new diadem from his head, pulling several hairs with it, threw it onto the paved floor of the corridor and stamped on it. He was concentrating so hard on grinding the red and yellow strips into the dirt that he was not aware that King Eadred had entered the corridor from the far end.

Taking in the situation with one glance, Eadred strode angrily towards the pair. Alfred was endeavouring to push Chester away from his now filthy insignia of royal service, pummelling the lordling's hips and stomach when he could reach inside the older man's flailing arm.

"Guards! Ho Guards! Arrest this man." The king pointed at the heir to the earldom of Chester who had suddenly come to his senses. As the guards, with naked blades approached him from both sides he blustered, his words coming so fast that spittle sprayed the King. Stepping back rapidly Eadred indicated that the guards should hold their prisoner for a moment. He picked up Alfred's diadem and held the filthy fabric at full stretch while appearing to examine the damage.

"You have despoiled my colours. I believe that is treason! This young man here, Alfred, son of thegn Udric, is in my service. How dare you insult him when he wears my emblem?"

For several seconds there was silence as the full enormity of his deeds were realized. Young Chester had the good sense to bow his head in submission. Alfred gently took the soiled diadem from King Eadred and stepped back as Abbot Dunstan approached. He may have observed the King from a discreet distance and was now intent on becoming peace-maker.

"Lord, are you arresting the Earl of Chester's son? He is ready to submit and apologise for his actions if they have offended you."

"Abbot Dunstan, forgive me for ignoring your pacifist ideology but on this occasion there is the matter of treason to consider. I was made King of Wessex, Northumbria, of the pagans and Christians alike of both lands. My colours are worn by those who have sworn their oath of love and loyalty to me, in the presence of Bishops and other churchmen. For any man to despoil my insignia is to insult my person and the sacred charge of Kingship."

The guards still held their captive firmly between them waiting for the command to commit him to the King's prison. They watched the verbal sparring between their King and the Abbot, heads turning this way and that. Alfred was not sure if he should absent himself inconspicuously, without asking permission to withdraw. Now that the altercation was over, the sweat was drying cold upon his body, the stale smell around him becoming unpleasant.

"My lord, if it pleases you may I withdraw? The Bishop's man is ready to ride for Didlington as you commanded and I would go with him until you need me."

With a wave of his hand and a brief smile, King Eadred dismissed Alfred who bowed in the general direction of his King and the Abbot who obviously had not finished his argument to effect the release of the well-born prisoner.

It was with relief that Alfred reached his shared chamber and was able to wash the sweat from his body. He washed the diadem praying that the colours were fast, that the lozenges of red and yellow would still remain clearly visible. He rubbed his scalp where hair had been wrenched from his head in the unprovoked attack then tied the sodden diadem carefully.

He collected his spare tunic, stuffed it into his saddlebag and was on his way to the stables when the elderly clerk introduced himself. With skin like a nut the old man spoke quietly so that Alfred had to bend close to hear him.

"My lord has the grant. He promises it will come to you in good time and that he has already made the provision in his will to protect you."

In the courtyard Alfred's horse was stamping impatiently. The altercation with the errant noble had cost over an hour, a sore head and a wet diadem. He stroked his father's horse affectionately, giving it the crust of bread left over from his breakfast.

With the Bishop's blessing and two guards, Alfred and the clerk rode for Didlington in bright sunshine and clear blue sky. Butterflies rose lazily from roadside bushes to flutter to another flower where they competed with bees laden with yellow pollen. A dragonfly motored past in jerky spasms, its iridescent wings sparkling blue and green. Alfred led the way confidently. Talking was difficult because of the deafness of his companion but having stopped to rest the beasts and eat a hasty meal on the hills above Cranburne the riders announced their arrival at Didlington with horn blasts.

Edith, her hair now prematurely silvered and still wearing her widow's sombre dress, hugged her son impulsively as soon as he had dismounted. Her once smooth cheeks had lost their plumpness, sculpting the cheekbones into relief. It took a moment to realize that a guest was with him, and that two guards from the Bishop's private army had escorted them. She blushed with embarrassment but quickly recovered her composure.

The old man was hastily introduced and helped indoors to the fire. His docile beast appeared to be almost as old as himself so that the soldiers had become slightly impatient at the speed of the journey. Alfred had almost laughed aloud when he saw the stick like legs of the clerk below his robes when mounted on his mule. Being amused by such a sight broke into his thoughts on the recent altercation with the Earl of Chester's son. The naked hatred and condescension involved had affected his self confidence. It had never occurred to him that anyone thought the less of him for his comparatively humble birth. "I wonder what punishment Eadred thought appropriate? No doubt Abbot Dunstan persuaded him to turn the other cheek. The dust will have settled by the time I return, God willing!" Crossing himself fervently and hoping that the Bishop's clerk had not noticed, Alfred returned his attention to his sister.

Aethelflaed, quickly growing to womanhood, brought a welcome cup to her brother while the soldiers were shown their quarters. The meal would be livelier with company and Edith hastily went to the kitchens to order special dishes to celebrate her son's return. In the space of a few minutes she had regained control of her emotions, tucked stray tendrils of hair beneath her head covering and taken a few deep breaths to renew her energy.

After the initial exchange of news after which the soldiers tactfully retired, the terms of the new charter were discussed. The clerk was obviously in the Bishop's confidence and answered Edith's queries without hesitation.

He in turn was charmed by his new lady. "Lady, I shall serve you in any way I can. The bishop was obliged to send someone and I can figure or write for you. He already knew that the mill was well kept. There is not long 'til the boy becomes of age but my lord was concerned for you."

"He called here in person after my lord Udric was killed. I know they had worked together on a few court cases and such like but to come and say how sorry he was that both my husband and my first born son had been killed in battle was very kind. I miss Alfred but the Bishop felt he should take his father's place in due course and there would be more chance of that if he was at court."

"The monastery at Wymburne has a reputation for learning and for making decorated gospels. My lord Bishop has a copy; it is one of his most treasured possessions so he thinks fondly of the town. I look forward to visiting if your people go there."

Assuring the wizened little man that many of the field hands and cottagers went to St Mary's church in Wymburne on Sundays and that he was welcome to accompany them, Edith showed the clerk where he could sleep.

Alfred's proposal to the fyrd several months later was almost a formality. Without a father, the usual sponsor, Owen took it upon himself to formally introduce his late master's grandson at the court held after the harvest festival service. He would now practice arms with the men-folk of Wymburne after church and could be called to serve in the army. Not being a landowner himself once the task of introducing Alfred had been formally carried out, Owen was required to stand well back from the circle of wealthier men. Other servants waited in a small group, many carrying arms for some had to come some distance to attend the moot.

Udda had never insisted that his workers wearing a particular colour. Many manor lords issued coloured tunics so that in public the uniform appearance of their employees boasted to all and sundry that this or that person worked for him. In forest green serge and a stout leather belt, Owen was quickly made aware how work-a-day he appeared. Although now completely white haired and a little stooped, he stood as upright as possible, half a head taller than many of the other men and still bright eyed whereas other servants seemed to be lethargic and bored by the proceedings.

Even in a small town like Wymburne there were minor crimes to be considered. Someone's oxen had strayed into a farmer's barley field; the steward of the King's Tun again warned against poaching and taking wood without permission; a slave had been raised to villeinage in accordance with the late King Aethelstan's decree; and a wolf had been seen in Holt Wood.

"Vermin can be killed at any time. Lord King Eadred will pay twelve silver pennies to anyone who removes this danger. The head must be brought to me at the King's palace, but you may keep the pelt."

"Who'd want the nasty stinking thing? I would not mind the reward though!" called out one man who was starting to get cold.

"Bring me the pelt," interrupted the shoe maker who advertised his wares by wearing the shiniest boots. He had the habit of rubbing the toes against the back of his leg to ensure they remained free of even a speck of dust. His neighbours often suffered when he overbalanced and laughed at his pride even though he did make the best shoes in

Wymburne.

When the owner of the ox had apologised and paid his penny fine for allowing the beast to stray, the meeting began to break up. Most were anxious to return to the town and the nearest ale house while others had stood stroking the smooth surface of their bows prior to going to the butts on the slopes of Pamphill.

"Now if they introduced a twelve penny prize for archery, we would go their voluntarily. As it is, I only want to go because my cord broke last week. The youths all burst out laughing so this week we intend to show them how it should be done." The farmer spat in his hands and continued to stroke the yew heartwood. The new gut cord was in his scrip and would be fitted shortly before taking up the arrows.

Owen started off down the hill, slipping on the wet chalk where it was exposed. "I'll get myself a damn stick one of these days! Why they can't meet somewhere more sheltered – its enough to chill my old bones to the core. Young Alfred should have had his turn at the butts by now and be ready to come back to the town. A mug of beer would be welcome if the lady Edith is not finished in the market."

The evenings, when the sun had gone down, were often spent in story telling. Despite the slight hoarseness of his aging voice Owen was everybody's favourite, his lilting accent making him popular in both halls. He told how Alfred's grandfather had rescued the young Prince Aethelstan at the king's palace nearby, and how Udric had defended king Edmund from almost certain death. Stories were passed on from one generation to another, sometimes exaggerated; sometimes aspects of cruelty or baseness were brushed over according to the audience at the time. Ale or weak beer circulated so that it was fully dark and starlit by the time people made their way to bed.

News was frequently circulated by pilgrims or traders making their way to Wymburne or Twynham, many travellers mentioning the young king's illness, passed down from his forefathers. They spoke of how he was frequently struck down by griping stomach pains or bloody fluxes.

Alfred had seen these attacks for himself and offered a prayer for the king's recovery. "If Abbot Dunstan did not insist on so much fasting, Eadred might be stronger," he commented after they had eaten one particularly tasty meal.

"The nunnery has recently diverted part of the Wym to provide clean water for themselves. They cut a channel to feed their fishpond, after all they have to eat fish for the whole of lent," commented one trader who had accepted accommodation for the night.

"Now that the clergy have more land, Dunstan has ordered that they keep the Lenten observances more closely. They are getting fat on the labour of others. God knows where places far from the coast will get fish for Fridays; every river being the slop pool for the town above it."

Edith sympathized with those who could not always observe the fish days. Fortunately the cottagers' children loved trying to catch eels in the little stream which formed the boundary of Uddings. These dried or smoked well, adding a distinct piquancy to pottage. Making their own hard cheese helped to vary the diet, everyone eating it with bread and occasionally a pickle made from the wizened apples which grew wild on the heathland cooked with the blue berries from the whyn bushes.

"Thank God that my larder is well stocked most of the time. It is all very well having a planned visitor but an invasion of guards and a clerk stretches things a bit."

"Mother, you know that you welcome guests so stop worrying. Do you think Alfred is happy at court? I saw him walking towards the old oak tree with the dogs not long ago. He seemed, well, thoughtful as if he had something worrying him. It cannot be the charter for the clerk assures us that the Bishop had got that on his behalf. Has he mentioned anything?" Aethelflaed had always been close to Alfred but now he preferred to walk by himself. She had noticed the unfamiliar frown lines on his normally round and open face. Even his eyes were slightly hooded, defying anyone to read his innermost thoughts.

With the homesteads running smoothly without his direct involvement Alfred soon found himself missing court even though Abbot Dunstan's obvious dislike of jollity had influenced the king. Even living in relative obscurity, Alfred heard the King had already ordered men to rebuild Dunstan's abbey at Glastonbury.

"What I am not looking forward to is seeing that obnoxious lordling. I cannot keep running away when the atmosphere gets heated." Alfred was muttering to the dog who cocked its head on one side, listening to every word. He stroked its rough fur finding comfort from the motion and warmth of the dog beneath.

The peace of the kingdom was only disturbed by the Archbishop of York inciting rebellion after the Danes, under their self proclaimed king Eric had once more invaded the Eastern shores. Secretly he would like to have been among the forces that went with the king, in open opposition to Abbot Dunstan, to punish the rebels. Despite his physical weakness the King led his army on a forced march, plundering houses and fields without mercy.

"I doubt it was the king's orders to sack the church at Ripon. He would never permit defilement of a place of worship. That's the sort of thing the Danish pagans do, and the northern men too."

Edith attempting to calm Alfred's indignation commented gently, "It is only what is reported. Perhaps we will hear the truth of it soon." She was secretly proud of his grasp of affairs but her thoughts were interrupted as he continued.

"The king thinks much of the church. He even used to insist the Abbot was served before himself on feast days. A sort of penance I think," he added remembering the occasions when he had seen this. When he heard that Eadred was now king of Northumbria in fact as well as in name, Alfred was proud for his friend. Archbishop Wulfstan of York had finally fallen foul of the ascetic cleric and was demoted to Oxfordshire so that he could be closely watched. "The man who rid the country of King Eric has been created Earl and appointed to govern the area. His future loyalty to King Eadred will not be in doubt because of his gratitude to my lord."

The lands of the rebels were granted to others who had sent forces to the north. "Bishop Wulfric told me that land is often given as a reward. Perhaps it is time to approach the king for I am now of age and no longer need a proxy. Not that I am not grateful to him," he added hastily seeing the clerk look up.

"Can I talk to you in private? There is something on my mind and it is not for my mother's ears. It would distress her."

"I am not a priest Alfred. If you have done something, er… bad, then it is for a priest at a church to tell you what to do not a man of letters, a clerk, like me."

"Oh no! it is nothing like that. Come by the fire and we will be undisturbed until the meal is ready."

Reluctantly, fearing that Alfred should really be speaking to the Bishop about his troubles, the clerk used his stick to help him to a stool by the hearth. Massaging his arthritic hands, he sat carefully with the deliberate movements of an aged person.

"Very well, tell me what concerns you that you cannot discuss with kin or Owen, for I know how close you have been to him."

Alfred started nervously but gained courage when the old man nodded from time to time.

"You see, this man, for he is my mother's age, wanted to marry her but she preferred my father. He has never forgiven her and called her all sorts of names that made me lose my temper. Father had some trouble when they were both at court but Lord Algar was my father's sponsor and he wanted the match with his grand-daughter."

"Mmmm, I understand what you are worrying about. If land is given as a reward you think the lordling might persuade Abbot Dunstan that he should have the lady Edith and Didlington!"

"Yes, although I heard he was married to a rich heiress, if she has died, then there is nothing to stop him seeking out my mother. He would not treat her well for he vows vengeance on me and mine. His father was called 'Wolf' with good reason and the son will soon earn the name.

The bitterness inside him when he recognised me caused an almighty row in the corridor outside the King's chamber. He snatched my diadem, the new one, and ground it into the dirt with his foot. This was all witnessed by the King. I was only able to withdraw because Bishop Wulfric had arranged for you to travel here with me. My lord Eadred was white with rage and accused him of treason for despoiling his colours. Beyond that, well, what punishment was meted out I do not know."

"Go to court yourself my son, it will be at the palace at Frome at this time of year." advised the Bishop's man as he stretched his thin legs in front of the fire. "If my lord Bishop is there, tell him of your concern. He intends to transfer Uddings and Didlington to you now you are of age. The sooner it is done the better by the sounds of things. If he asks me about the lady Edith I shall say that she is still grieving and should not be married against her will, not that my opinion counts for much!

Take these records with you, they show that you have kept the land in good heart, the mill is flourishing. The peasants work well, not surprising when they share the profits with you! While you are there, keep an eye out for a likely maiden to take to wife!"

"I had not thought of my own marriage, but Aethelflaed constantly reminds me that she is not getting any younger. She's the one who needs to go to court to find a suitable husband. It seems she is not content to take a husband from Wymburne. She had plenty of admirers but would like a bit of excitement in her life." He laughed as he took the rolled parchment. He would speak to the Bishop for his sister when the matter of the ownership of the two estates had been settled.

He found the King's western court in a sombre mood. It matched the weather which had been grey, with low cloud preventing even a glimpse of the sun on the journey. Even the thickest cloak became damp and heavy in such conditions.

Built in the lee of moorland, the single storey wooden building blended in with the surrounding countryside. As in Wymburne there were many small buildings to accommodate the king's hunting dogs and falcons, simple stalls for forty horses and store rooms close to the kitchen.

In the hall many men were speaking in hushed voices about the king's grave illness which had worsened since he had returned from the north. Abbot Dunstan insisted that the King be taken to his own monastery for nursing by the infirmarians but the lay members of the Council were firmly against the idea.

"Surely the monks could care for him here. There would at least be comfort here and safety too," commented Alfred dryly as he joined the Bishop in his room.

"Ah yes, but the king is much influenced by the Abbott. Eadred is sick, probably close to death. Unfortunately the time is not right to ask for favours even though the king promised to amend the grant when you were of age. Be patient and make yourself useful, especially to King Edmund's sons. T'is a shame that Lord Eadred never took a wife."

Alfred looked sharply at the grizzled tonsure of the cleric not at first understanding his sponsor's advice. He left thoughtfully mulling over the relationship between the king and the two young aethelings. Groups of men were talking around the central hearth rubbing their hands in the heat. Outside there was now a sharp drop in temperature and Alfred too was glad to warm his back at a brazier.

The men, many of them in long woollen gowns, took little notice of him so that he was able to overhear snatches of conversation. Many favoured a counsel to rule for either of the young men, neither of whom had any experience of rulership, or on the battlefield. They were the children of King Edmund's third wife, the eldest at least ten years younger than Eadred. Returning later to the Bishop's chamber to discuss the debated issues he had overheard Alfred hoped for clarification on the succession. King Eadred had shown no inclination to share his royal duties being only a young man himself. Alfred knew Eadwig or Edwy as he preferred to be called, the elder prince.

"Surely as the older son of King Edmund he will be the new King?"

The bishop did not reply immediately being engrossed in the locking of his treasure chest. He drew the hasps together before shooting the bolt through.

"Why men talk of such matters while the King lives is beyond my understanding but since you have already heard much from others telling you my own thoughts, and they are just thoughts, will not do any harm.

Not everyone favours Edwy, for all he is the oldest. He spends a great deal of time with women and girls. Have you ever seen him with arms? No! Many think him a handsome boy but that is his sole attribute. His younger brother Edgar; now he is different, serious and studious too. He has long been allowed to listen to counsel. He sits still and does not interrupt the deliberations. He takes an interest in his uncle's affairs. Lord Eadred thinks quite highly of him. But I tell you this in confidence Alfred; I trust you will not let your tongue wag loosely."

Assuring the churchman that he would keep his own counsel, the Bishop gave him the amethyst ring on his thumb to kiss.

"Eadred lies dying while the good Dunstan kneels in prayer at his bedside. God knows it may not be an easy death but I must be there. Your father was present when lord Aethelstan, resting in peace in the kingdom of heaven, died rather violently. I pray that Eadred is shriven then given the pain-killing essence of poppy. The physicians from Winchester have been sent for. Remain in the hall so that I can call you." Assured that his treasure chest was firmly locked, the Bishop swept out of his chamber. The crowd in the hall parted silently as he strode towards the King's chamber, the black robes flapping like the wings of a crow about to take flight.

Alfred was sure that the entire court was crammed in the hall. Most were picking at the food laid out on a few trestles. No pages attended with washing bowls and towels. Servants renewed dishes as they were emptied. Occasionally a noble demanded that someone attend to his empty cup, but most talked in undertones. When the Princes were called to the King's deathbed everyone jostled for position to watch their lord's last moments. Through the doorway they watched King Eadred blessing his nephews before witnesses, requesting that they looked after his Kingdom. Those who had the best view related a running commentary for those less well positioned.

After the final shudder of breath left the King's body, Abbot Dunstan closed the dimmed eyes before kneeling again. His tonsured head reflected the flickering candles in the wall sconces. They were the sole comfort in the King's chamber which more closely resembled a monk's cell than a royal bed-chamber. There were no bright tapestries on the wall, no glowing brazier on which herbs could be scattered. It was not just the atmosphere which was chilly, a total lack of heating at this time of year meant that a bone chilling wintry cold affected all who had witnessed the King's final agonised breaths. Those who had been present in the sick room left quietly absorbed in thought, those crowded around the doorway silently drawing back to allow them to pass. Abbot Dunstan seemed impervious to the temperature, remaining at the bedside to pray for the soul of the dead King. His low voice could be heard when there was a lull in the conversation.

That evening's meal in the hall was plain fare. Few noticed the quality or variety of food being conscious once again of the empty chair at the high table. No rich sauces accompanied the meats. Desserts were served without decoration, the flavour often suffering from a want of sweetness.

Alfred served the Bishop quietly, noticing that all his jewels except the ring had been removed. Most of those seated nearby had also hastily changed and were dressed soberly as a mark of respect. The Abbot had already excused himself from attending, piously announcing that he would fast and watch over the King's body. It would be prepared for burial by monks from the Abbot's own monastery at Glastonbury. The two princes looked apprehensive, sitting either side of the vacant seat. Both wore royal robes of rich blue with gold embroidered trim which looked out of place among the more muted tunics of the other diners. Alfred pitied these young boys whose childhood would be abruptly cut short. Not for them the races in the woods or snow; they would not be allowed to splash in the river or couple with serving girls in the hay-barn, not if Abbot Dunstan had their training in his hands.

The funeral was held with due ceremony, snow falling outside as the King's body was laid to rest beside the altar at Glastonbury. Alfred carried a lighted taper inside the chapel while the thegns stood in order of seniority round the bier. The Princes looked nervous as they were ushered to the graveside to pay their last respects to their uncle. The stones from the floor which had been raised were stacked discreetly to one side with the earth dug from the gaping hole. The very blackness seemed threatening, the light from the few candles not penetrating into the depths. There was no incense to perfume the air. The chill of the small church affected everyone. Throughout the long burial mass nobles, thegns and churchmen alike shifted their feet and tried to disguise their shivering.

As the body was lowered Edwy was ashen and looked as if he would have fainted had not Abbot Dunstan gripped his arm firmly, diverting the Prince's attention from the entombment.

As the company filed out, Alfred found himself alongside the older Prince, "Shall I get a cup of wine my lord? It would restore you quickly before the Council meets."

Edwy nodded silently, still visibly upset. Only hours before he had been a relatively carefree Prince of the royal blood enjoying the company of his betrothed, the lovely Algifu. He had not believed that his uncle was so sick; after all he had still been a young man, only twenty five years old, who could have taken a wife and had children of his own to become his heirs. He, as a royal prince and Algifu, his soul-mate and betrothed, would have had their own manors and land; paid annual homage to the King and lived a life of relative luxury with servants and few responsibilities. His thoughts were interrupted when Alfred thrust the cup into his hand.

"Who do you serve?" asked the Prince when he had drained it.

"I serve the Bishop of Salisbury, Lord Wulfstan, my lord. I am Alfred, son of Udric of Didlington, grandson of Udda of Uddings, in Dorset. My father and brother died in battle at Stamford. Grandfather Udda was horse-healer to your father and his royal brothers before him. The King's horses are bred and trained at Uddings," he added proudly. Relating his immediate forefathers Alfred gave Edwy time to recover. Throwing his cloak around his shoulders, his colour now restored, he nodded his thanks and hurried off to the hall. There the Council, composed of the late King's senior magnates and most likely Abbot Dunstan, would make a decision as to his future.

Following at a respectful distance, still holding the cup, Alfred found a space at the outer edge of the assembled company, from where he could watch the proceedings. He was fascinated by the ceremonial robes and the formal way the thegns addressed the leader of the court, Archbishop Odo, before voicing their opinions. The two Princes stood stiffly, in the centre of the crowded hall, only their eyes turning towards each speaker. Once again guards were positioned at all the doors, their spears inverted, faces schooled into granite sternness.

Despite his good looks Edwy looked younger than his years. As yet his frame had not filled out despite being of age, nor had his voice broken to such an extent that a treble squeak would not occasionally and embarrassingly interrupt the more manly tones.

His younger brother looked the more mature of the two, less in awe of the occasion. He stood quietly, not fidgeting but watchful as men sought to debate the future of the Kingdom.

Alfred caught Prince Edwy's eye during a brief pause in the proceedings and smiled reassuringly. Bishop Wulfric noted the exchange between the two young men before turning his attention quickly back to the matter in hand. Someone stepped on a dog's paw causing it to squeal in pain. It was quickly cursed causing Abbot Dunstan to frown at the un-godly interruption.

It was late in the evening before the meeting finally ended with the decision that Edwy would rule Wessex, while his younger brother, Prince Edgar, was to have his court in Mercia. The torches had been lit, the initial burst of foul smelling smoke adding to the over-riding odour of unwashed and sweaty humanity crowded into the hall. Unable to leave the hall until the business had been finished many had been forced to urinate where they stood. Alfred was glad when the doors were finally pulled open and fresh air entered with a cleansing draught. In the courtyard servants scurried to and fro fetching cloaks, refreshments and charters for signature. The meal in the hastily rearranged hall was hardly fit for a King, let alone a king and his brother, now a sub-regulus having immediately paid homage to his elder brother.

Some meats were hard and over-cooked while others were almost raw. The whole meal was lacking in refinement but conversation varied from deafening to so quiet that it was little more than the hum of honey bees. Many had changed into richly embroidered tunics with jewelled brooches or pins. The two brothers sat side by side, Edwy in the late King's chair and Edgar in the next chair which had been hastily covered in purple fabric.

The Earl of Chester, now more than sixty summers old with sparse white hair swept over his bald head sat at the high table. His hands shook so that food and drink spilled onto his expensive gown. A length of spittle hung from his wattled jaw which a servant discreetly wiped away. He turned his red, rheumy eyes on Alfred but could not focus through pale, filmed eyes.

'What happened to his son?' wondered Alfred during a lull in conversation with his neighbour. 'No-one mentions the incident and I daren't ask for fear of stirring up a hornets nest!' He wiped his mouth with a small linen cloth, returning it carefully to his scrip.

Chapter Eighteen

Within hours Alfred witnessed the two brothers embrace before taking their leave of each other. Obviously Edgar was going to get to grips with his territory. He left surrounded by a small contingent of the late King's hearth knights, their tabards still showing lord King Eadred's colours. He knelt to receive a blessing from Archbishop Odo before mounting his destrier, a horse far too big for the diminutive size of the new sub-king. Clerks and an ox cart followed the colourful cavalcade as it went through the stone gate of the capital, trumpets sounding joyful notes in the crisp dawn air.

King Edwy had already announced his intention to marry his beloved Algifu, a childhood sweetheart. She had sat on his left at the high table the previous evening, her eyes smouldering with naked passion and sexuality. Edwy gave her a long, lascivious look as if he was seeing beneath the close-fitting robe then let his eyelashes drop insolently in a blink that was nearly a wink which was seen by any man whose attention was riveted on the only young woman at the King's table.

A voluptuous young lady she was waiting to greet him on his return from the gate where he had watched his brother's procession ride away northwards. He publicly embraced her unaware that many thegns thought that sort of affection was for the privacy of the solar not in the middle of the courtyard for every hot-blooded male to witness. Soldiers and stablemen sniggered, some less discreetly than others.

"Disgusting behaviour," the Bishop muttered as Alfred helped him with richly embroidered robes. "God knows, the boy has no dignity and we've just made him King. Has he no sense of honour, of what is proper?"

Alfred hesitated to reply sure that the Bishop's diatribe was about to continue in the same vein.

"You have already come to his notice, boy. For heavens sake try your best to clean him up. I noticed the soiling of his robes. If he must fornicate with sluts he should do it away from God fearing men." The bishop's face reflected his disapproval, his normally jovial face etched with frown lines, the derisive description of the new King's habits causing his eyes to narrow to slits.

Alfred had never heard the Bishop speak so disparagingly of anyone, let alone the boy who had just been appointed King. He was glad that he had only recently assured the Bishop that he could keep his own counsel for surely what he had just heard was nothing short of treachery!

'God's blood', thought Alfred as once again the Bishop checked that his coffer was securely locked. 'Chester's son is obviously absent from court as punishment for treason, what happens to a Bishop for the same crime?'

The two entered the hall, the Bishop taking his place on the high table indicated by the Seneschal. Alfred hastily picked up a basin and towel from the row set on a sideboard. He offered it to the Bishop who hesitated to use the facilities pointing out that no page had yet attended the King.

"Me, my lord, but surely he has his own ...."

"Get on and take the bowl to the King before me. I cannot be responsible for the laziness of the King's servants but never let it be said that I pushed myself forward.... but you can. Go!"

Alfred nervously offered the bowl to his new King. Recognition flashed across his face so that he smiled broadly.

"My thanks... Alfred isn't it. Actually I am not very hungry and the speeches bore me. It seems that not only do I inherit my uncle's counsellors but also that crow of a churchman, Dunstan. He gives the impression that he has personal access to God and wanted me to pray with him for hours on end."

The King turned back to the table. Alfred withdrew gracefully, dodging other pages that had suddenly appeared. He attended to the Bishop who smiled approvingly at him. "What was the King saying?"

"Only that he inherits the former council and churchmen from his uncle. I think he wants to select his own advisors in time. We shall see!"

The feast for King Edwy's crowning was a lengthy affair with wine and ale flowing freely. Minstrels related stories of the glorious battles and conquests of the new King's ancestors while some sang of love and brave deeds. Smoke from the fires filled the hall, quickly increasing the heat and the stale odour of dogs and sweat.

Edwy left the table quietly and went out through the curtained doorway, the guards standing aside to let him pass. Seated far from the King's high table, Alfred saw him go but as no one else had risen to their feet the feast continued regardless of his absence. Few diners were still sober enough to notice the Abbot rise slowly to his feet and leave the hall by the same door. Bishop Wulfric too, hastily wiped his fingers and rose, signalling to Alfred to accompany him. They followed Abbot Dunstan, past the food laden trestles.

The night was starlit, the air crisply cold. Both men took deep refreshing breaths to clear their heads of the smoky ale fumes of the hall. Alfred shivered briefly at the change of temperature, glad that he had not discarded his woollen cloak.

"You need me to fetch something for you lord?" queried Alfred as the Bishop paused uncertainly.

"My lord Abbot looks to mould the King into a pious ruler like his uncle," muttered the elderly Bishop as he tugged his cloak firmly round his shoulders against the cold. "Stay behind me in case you are needed, but be discreet and say nothing of what you see tonight. I think Dunstan may have over-stepped his authority but someone has to coach the boy to behave like a King."

In an adjoining anteroom entered by an outside door, the Abbot was upbraiding the young King for his lack of dignity. Both Algifu and her mother, dressed in low necked kirtles were in the room, clearly upset.

"I am the King," shouted Edwy angrily. "If I wish to meet my lady, in the company of her mother you note, then I will do so. The feasting has gone on too long, and anyway it was boring," he added petulantly. He was lounging insolently on a settle, a nasty little sneer on his handsome face beneath a gold circlet.

The pious cleric, frowning, was clearly not impressed by this excuse. "Return to the celebration my Lord Edwy; it is your coronation feast," he ordered, gripping the King's shoulder. "Your presence will be missed. It is undignified for the King to absent himself, especially in order to amuse himself with womenfolk. They should be in their own quarters."

Bishop Wulfric and Alfred stood aside quickly to let the women pass. Neither of them spoke but their irritation and embarrassment was obvious from their haughty but reddened faces. They pushed past, roughly wrenching the folds of their cloaks to cover the low neckline of their clothing.

The King was clearly furious at the interference into his private life and ordered the Abbot to leave him immediately. Satisfied that the women had already gone, Dunstan turned abruptly towards the door and came face to face with Wulfric and Alfred.

"Not a word of this to anyone my lord Bishop. And this is your man? Can he keep his own counsel; keep his mouth shut?"

"Indeed my lord; neither of us are gossip-mongers. The King is young yet. He will learn to behave with dignity with the right guidance, but I think the young lady means no harm."

Dunstan frowned as he considered whether Wulfric was in some way criticising his stern dismissal of Algifu and her mother. Deciding to let the matter drop, he bade them return to the feast as if nothing had happened and strode off to the hall. Alfred returned unobtrusively to his humble bench in the shadows, all eyes now watching the King retake his seat, glowering darkly at the Abbot.

It took Edwy several weeks to accept the homage of those who had not attended his coronation. During this time his young face reflected his boredom, his eyes frequently glazing over and straying from the formality of the occasion. He had to grasp the reins of government, taking advice from the council that he had inherited.

"Since I never thought to become King there was little opportunity to learn the workings of governing. Nor do I know much about the ancient crones who do much of the work for me. For God's sake, they are in their dotage, all of them should be quietly by a hearth toasting their toes not debating where the army should go and which fyrd should be called out next."

"It must be hard for you lord, learning so many new skills and being responsible for everyone. As you say the men are old but they also have experience which they put at your disposal."

Alfred congratulated himself on the tactful way he had coached the young King to accept the counsellors' advice, remembering how Owen, probably toasting his feet before the Didlington hearth, had gently explained how older people could guide youngsters.

'My thanks Owen – No doubt if father had not died so young he would have taught me the same valuable lesson.' He sent the silent message of appreciation to his mother's loyal steward, hoping he would remember to say it to his face when he returned home.

There were many problems in the various communities within King Edwy's territory to be discussed although the fact that Edgar now held Mercia would hopefully reduce border incursions from that area.

"There is always a threat to the border defences of Wessex. But there is grumbling among the lay councillors over the continued influence of the church on state affairs. Not that any were bold enough to voice their thoughts in the hearing of Dunstan's sharp ears. He is quick and can untangle the knottiest problem within seconds but his voice annoys the rest of us. Somehow he manages to have an edge of sarcasm which does not go down well with men of an age to be his father! The King makes his dislike of the man very obvious. The hostile looks shoot across the room. If they were darts the Abbot would look like a hedgehog!"

Edwy appeared to enjoy the company of someone near his own age, frequently asking Alfred to accompany him on hunting expeditions or to the falconry mews. His belongings had been moved into the late King's chamber but he had refused to leave it so comfortless, insisting on wall hangings, floor coverings and a brazier.

"I'm not a bloody monk" he swore vehemently. "I have heard gossip from servants that if Abbot Dunstan had not encouraged so much fasting and denial of comforts to the lord Eadred, of blessed memory, he might have been in better health." The King crossed himself casually and wiped his nose on the sleeve of his short cloak. Alfred frowned, the grimace completely automatic. Edwy looked down at the smear of mucus that now stained his garment and shrugged.

Pleased to be in the king's confidence, but anxious to make amends for his implied criticism, Alfred told him of the attack on his father which had taken place there. "My father, lord Udric, probably saved the life of King Aethelstan, when he was knifed here," he boasted one day as Edwy admired the birds. The gerfalcon preened herself on a low perch. They knew that some captive birds live for years. "I don't know how long falcons live but there is a possibility that this is the same bird that took out the eye of one of the assassins." Edwy stepped back quickly, regarding her with cautious respect, lowering his hand poised to stroke the tawny feathers.

They talked of the incident walking slowly round the perches until the pungent smell drove them back into the fresh air. Both men wiped their eyes and breathed deeply.

Servants scurried purposefully across the courtyard. Guards lounged by doorways but hastily corrected their posture when they saw the King emerge from the mews. A slave swept dirt into the gutters, the broom wielded from side to side as rhythmically and monotonously as a pendulum.

"I am to be married tomorrow," confided the King suddenly, gripping Alfred's shoulder impulsively. "Dunstan leaves within the hour to visit his beloved monastery while Archbishop Odo has already left. I sent him away to inspect the churches in the west. He will be gone for days." He was grinning broadly, partly no doubt in anticipation the celebration of his nuptials with his beloved Aelgifu and partly at the thought of outwitting two clerics that he disliked intensely.

"Will the Abbot not marry you? I mean who will bless you?"

The King shrugged his shoulders. "Come to my room tomorrow, when you have eaten. Say nothing to anyone. For once I will have my own way. Ever since the Council meeting there has been a never-ending stream of people asking for favours, chivvying me to do this or that because it is expected of me, their King. Now I am going to marry my beloved and no one, I repeat no one is going to stop me!"

Edwy's voice had risen as he emphasised his determination. Colour had spread unhealthily up his neck to colour his normally pale face. In the ensuing silence Alfred could hear Edwy's stomach churning. The King turned quickly, striding off to his quarters. Realising that his question had been naive, Alfred stayed away from Bishop Wulfric's room lest he betray the King's secret. He slept restlessly in the hall that night, rising early to wait near the King's private room where the other hearth-companions among whom he was now numbered were already gathered.

Outside there was a coating of snow which had fallen silently during the night. Guards stamped their feet to keep warm. Servants had already lit braziers but their warmth did little to heat rooms when doors and curtains were drawn aside so frequently. Alfred was glad of his thick cloak even though its plainness marked him out as a person of lesser birth than some of the young men lounging casually in the outer room of the King's apartment.

In the church the ceremony was held quickly, without the usual pomp and ceremony which should have accompanied such an event. There were few candles, no gold or silver ornaments on the altar. Even the floor had not been swept since the Sunday Mass. No-one was dressed in their finest clothes or bejewelled. No singing boys chanted sacred songs, no bells rang in celebration. The service was conducted nervously by a comparatively minor cleric who was overawed by the task, stumbling over the final blessing of the young couple. Dressed in his simple black robes, with stains and worn patches, the priest's anxiety infected everyone present. Alfred could feel a pricking at the back of his neck and frequently turned, expecting to find a furious Counsellor at best or the outraged face of the Bishop at worst. The hearth-companions put on brave faces but some of them were aware that the mother of the bride, smiling smugly at the rear of the group, had been the young King's mistress before his attentions had been drawn to her daughter.

With ill-concealed glee, King Edwy swung his lady round, their eyes conveying such sexual messages to each other that the audience was embarrassed and moved apart to allow the newly weds to reach the privacy of the King's chamber in the shortest possible time.

It may have been the slight to his position, imagined or otherwise, which finally made Abbot Dunstan denounce the marriage between King Edwy and the lady Algifu as illegal. Archbishop Odo, for once in concord with the Abbot, emphasised the fact that the marriage was uncanonical. Algifu was regarded as closely related to the King, her mother having been his mistress for several years. Few thought the deeply religious man would dare to take revenge.

Standing uncomfortably in bishop Wulfric's chamber while that churchman berated him for not giving warning that the marriage was to be held, Alfred could hardly contain his irritation.

"The King himself demanded my silence! At the time I felt my loyalty was split. It is unfair of the Archbishop to blame you for not preventing the union. The King was determined to marry her. It was witnessed; surely there is little he can do about it now?"

"Don't fool yourself Alfred. I feel let down beyond measure by your behaviour. I advised that you befriend the King not encourage him into foolhardy escapades like this. Get me a drink, my head aches with all the matters that need attending to. Soothing the temper of my superior, to whom I owe obedience, is the least of my worries."

Out hunting in pale wintry sunshine with his friends one day shortly after the ceremony, the cares of the court forgotten for a short time, the King galloped wildly after one beast after another. Lymer dogs careered across the frozen ground dragging their handlers ever faster. Terriers yapped excitedly darting between horses adding to the pandemonium. Servants followed his progress as best they could, bearers removing the carcases to the butchers yard some distance from the palace.

The days approaching Christmas are short, the purple hues of dusk quickly chasing the pearly whiteness of daylight over the horizon.

Edwy returned, sweaty and flushed, to find his wife gone. When questioned by the King, the nervous soldiers admitted that she had been taken unwillingly from his court. All their apologies and excuses were brushed aside brusquely. Furious at the Abbot's obvious interference, screaming with rage and frustration, the King's colour rose alarmingly. "God's blood, he calls himself a man of God! He will die for this," he swore in front of the astonished huntsmen.

"I don't care if the horse is tired. Guards! To me! We ride to the Archbishop's quarters. Hell's spawn! That he dares to take my wife; T'is no less than treason. Ride!"

Edwy's wrath was obvious as he stood in his stirrups laying about him with the flat of his sword when the Archbishop's guards tried to prevent his entry. His young face was suffused with blood, his eyes flashing across the faces of those who denied him. One soldier, obviously more loyal to the King than the churchman, or frightened by the royal wrath, hastily withdrew the bars from a stout door. Algifu ran out, blinking at the sudden light, her dress soiled with blood. Appalled at her condition, Alfred gasped with horror. Her forehead had been branded with the letter H. That letter, announcing to all and sundry that she was little more than a whore, stood proudly on the previously smooth brow, the edges of the burn still livid and puckered. The viciousness of the Archbishop's attack on the woman, regardless of her recent marriage to the elected King angered the men crowding round the pair who were embracing in their midst. Alfred looked round noticing the looks of frozen astonishment on the faces of the men who had ridden out with the King. “There is little honour among this lot but not one of them would mark a woman like that. Edwy’s rage is understandable,” remarked one dour humoured man.

“Whether the marriage is legal or not, there is no need for such cruelty. He has forsworn carnal knowledge but the rest of us have lady-loves at home or close-by in the …”

The last speaker was rudely interrupted by a loud, red faced man in a thick and cumbersome jacket above leather boots which came up to his knees. “Your lady love is not at home, man, your woman is any one of the serving girls who will pleasure you for a silver coin.” He laughed crudely before falling silent abruptly, suddenly finding great interest in the leather palms of his gloves which had almost been shredded by the leash of the hounds.

“I will kill him,” vowed the King, almost beyond reason with rage. “He has branded my wife a harlot. Traitorous viper, full of wise counsel he may be, but I will see no more of him. Hush my sweeting, we will have our revenge. Your mother has salves and cure-alls. She will care for you.” He took his wife up before him on the horse, holding her in a close embrace on the slow return journey.

The court as a whole, seethed with indignation at the cruel, inhuman treatment meted out to Algifu. There were few who dared to point out the truth of the Abbot's claim that the newlyweds were in fact closely related and that her past behaviour, like that of her mother, had been somewhat promiscuous.

“I was torn between my loyalty to my superior in the church and my affection for Edwy, only a young man, and to my mind, raised to Kingship prematurely.” Bishop Wulfric admitted later to Alfred in the privacy of his chamber. “Archbishop Odo and Lord Dunstan have gone too far in this matter. They may wish to control a young King but no-one wins the trust of a dog by beating him!”

Alfred had had no such doubts. “I witnessed the marriage and also the love between my lord King and the lady Algifu. Almost literally, for I was present at their bedding! It may not have been their first time together, I am not so naïve as to believe that, but we gave them a rousing cheer nevertheless.”

King Edwy signed the order banishing Dunstan from Glastonbury Abbey, moving his court rapidly to Cheddar so that his forces could oversee the disbandment of the famous monastery. The Abbot's fall from favour was made public when messengers were sent to all parts of the Kingdom and to his brother Edgar in Mercia to proclaim the edict. Secretly many were glad that the Abbot had at last been discomforted and embarrassed, his scrutiny of their behaviour casting an aura of gloom over the court.

"No doubt he will deal with the Archbishop in his own time. Abbot Dunstan would not have acted on his own; he dislikes violence after all. Odo has left for the north, probably until the dust settles. As for the Abbot, he would undoubtedly be dead had he not fled when the soldiers arrived at Glastonbury. There were many riches in the Abbey, some of which reached the King's coffers." stated one of the older hearth companions bravely. Grandsons of councillors and senior nobles made up the small crowd of well bred young men who hunted, practiced with arms and amused the King on wet days. There were times when Alfred longed to return to the comparative peace and tranquillity of Uddings where there were fewer intrigues, jealousies and above all, clean air. If the King relaxed enough to sign charters and other decrees which awaited his attention, Alfred would have the ownership of Uddings and Didlington transferred to his own name. Bishop Wulfric assured him that it was in the pile awaiting signature and sealing.

The King's behaviour in general however, still caused anxiety. Some ministers favoured asking his brother Edgar to rule over Wessex in addition to Mercia which enjoyed peace and prosperity without scandal. "How can this be done when we will be accused of treason. Damn the man, why did Dunstan have to flaunt his power?" pronounced the earl. Bishop Wulfric had wisely absented himself from the latest meeting fearing that the very fact that he was a cleric would lead to arguments. He had already admitted to Alfred that he wanted no more of the rumours and counter-rumours so prevalent in court. There were always factions fighting for control and of course the King trying to establish his independence.

Algifu's wound eventually healed under the ministrations of her mother's poultices and ointments. She then introduced a new hairstyle with a fringe of hair falling across her brow to hide the imperfection in the otherwise flawless complexion. Many ladies, married to loyal thegns or servants of the King, hastily adopted similar styles, proclaiming it to be very feminine and flattering.

Occasionally in the privacy of his own room, the King talked frankly, aware that Alfred's friendship was sincere and loyal.

"Archbishop Odo has taken Dunstan's part. He says the church is appalled at the sacking of Glastonbury Abbey and the banishment of a senior cleric. He too now denounces my marriage." His face, normally so pallid now showed angry red flushes below his cheekbones, his lips pursed in disapproval.

Alfred offered no judgement on the matter, concentrating on calming the King's temper when the matter was raised. The King's palace at Cheddar was high on the chalk hills, exposed to wind and rain. Shutters could rarely be opened so that the atmosphere became imbued with household smells, the odour of unwashed men and smoke from the fires which had to be kept burning night and day.

"If your child was born whole and of a good temperament, maybe the Archbishop would relent," advised Alfred carefully after some thought. "Some children of close kin are born ailing right from their birth, and if they live, are idiots or witless."

"There is no child," admitted the King. "My lady has not yet conceived. It is my opinion that her mother interferes too much and may have a hand in this. She constantly calls for revenge on Dunstan. How can I do this when he has fled the country? Maybe she should be married and have her own household to run! I will give this some thought, though who would willingly take her off my hands is a mystery at the moment!"

Now into his sixtieth year, and feeling increasingly frail, Bishop Wulfric withdrew from court. He gave Alfred his blessing, promising to pray for him in the monastery to which he would retire. Never one for the over-decorated tunics or cloaks of some churchmen, Alfred was sad to see the old man leave court on a humble donkey, no sword hanging from his belt, no retinue of guards keeping a respectful pace behind.

The old grants for Uddings and Didlington had at last been given freely to Alfred. The boundaries of the two estates were copied out faithfully onto one scroll, the writing becoming smaller and smaller as the scribe wrote all the details carefully.

'In the Year of our Lord nine hundred and forty six ....' read Alfred over the clerk's shoulder.

"I suppose you will want to go to Uddings now?" stated Edwy in a matter of fact voice when the clerk had gone. "Come back after the Christmas celebrations. I shall miss you. You do not keep asking for favours. Shouldn't really say this but family pressure makes many of the other young men angle for my attention, grants of land, or gifts of gold or silver. You mentioned you had an unwed sister a long time ago and even then did not push for a place for her. Bring her if she wishes to come. There is a place in my lady's household.

Dunstan mentioned many times that widows should be married off for the benefit of the treasury but that is one thing he never persuaded me to do. A woman knows when her grieving is done and until then I say that they should be left in peace."

Alfred nodded his understanding. Edith would be pleased, not only for the offer of a place at court for Aethelflaed, the manor now secure for the time being, but also that there would be no pressure for her to re-marry. He longed to return home to reassure everyone, to the people he had known all his life and to see the horses in their paddocks. He missed the dogs who offered companionship and undivided loyalty. At court the curs which scavenged in the hall belonged to no particular man. Their mangy coats advertised their lack of care. He got no pleasure from mistreating them when they got underfoot and went out of his way to avoid the cruel games which often involved the death of one of these poor creatures.

They went together to the hall for the main meal of the day, Alfred carefully taking a place at a lower table. Afterwards the gift was announced and the copies of the deed duly signed and witnessed. Alfred bowed, accepting his copy graciously. His face was split by a huge grin, evidence of his happiness and relief that he finally had his own grant.

Such occasions were not uncommon as the King often used such occasions to emphasise his generosity. Many of the seated diners continued to eat if they were not involved in the ceremony. One never knew when the King would leap to his feet demanding that all present ride out immediately and a good meal had often been wasted in the past when the lord King had been unable to each much. It was not until Edwy called again for silence that people turned to stare, conversation stilled, cups lowered.

"As further evidence of our friendship, I raise you to your father's position of thegn," announced the King, momentarily astonishing his companions, many of whom had longed for such status if they were not automatically entitled to inherit their father's title. "Alfred of Uddings shall assist the sheriff of Dorset, to oversee the territory of East Dorset on my behalf, collecting dues to the crown. He shall attend the moot courts to deal with local issues. He will act on my behalf and wear my colours henceforth."

In the stunned silence which followed the announcement the King passed Alfred a broad diadem to wear on his forehead, demonstrating to all that he was the King's man.

"This baton will serve to give you rights of food, board, a horse and feed for the beast, when on my business," continued the King smiling broadly, enjoying the attention his munificence had caused. Realising that the requirement to give his oath of loyalty again had all been part of the king's plan when he insisted that he attended dinner in the hall, Alfred took the staff, stroking the carved surface polished smooth by many hands. Responding to the latest gift he thanked the King formally for his favours before resuming his seat modestly.

Throughout the meal he ignored the whispering, being stunned by his good fortune. The baton, held tightly against his chest was proof enough that he really had been promoted, his hunger momentarily forgotten.

He left the court and its array of temporary tents some days later. Lord Alward was anxious to make the acquaintance of his new assistant. He was a stocky, bluff man with a weathered face and a booming voice. His black hair had been left uncut and was held back from his face by a diadem in the King's colours. Equally untamed was the huge black beard falling well down his huge barrelled chest. The same black hair grew in profusion on his strong hands, covering the joints of his fingers so that he appeared to be wearing gloves.

"Now then young man, tell me of yourself. Are you Dorset bred?"

"Yes lord, my father and grandfather's lands lie to the North East of Wymburne. We or rather I, now have six hides although some of it is still heathland. There is clean water, a mill at Didlington and we breed horses for the King from Norman stock as well as heal those who are sick or have been misused."

"I know that your father and brother were both killed in battle. Their deaths bring great honour to your family but also grief and hardship. Your mother still lives and also a sister I understand. Is she of marriageable age?"

Alfred's expression lightened as he described his sister, reminding his new lord that she had been invited to court after the Christmas festivities.

"I will take her to the Queen's rooms and then be ready to join you wherever you need me lord. I believe my road turns southwards from here. If you have orders for the King's steward at Wymburne I could take them. He keeps order at our meetings and checks who has provided a man for the fyrd. As usual the most unpopular time is when the harvest is due and men also grumble if their hands are ruined by road building or other rough work when their trade requires nimble fingers! A man who sews cloth or leather cannot work until his palms have softened again, a common complaint in every town surely. Wymburne is well served for trades and the nunnery on the King's land there means that we get most of the news fairly quickly."

The two men parted in friendship, Alfred careful to bow his head respectfully when the new Sheriff of Dorset turned his horse back on the road to Wareham, the base from which he was expected to work. His guards marched smartly behind the horse, the iron studs on their boots clattering loudly on the flinty surface.

In the bright morning sunshine the few clouds resembled fluffy balls of newly teased wool. A sparrowhawk suddenly plummeted from the sky to take a pigeon, the feathers floating lazily to earth. Alfred watched fascinated as the raptor took its still living prey to a nearby tree stump.

With his charter safely in his saddle bag, and his baton slotted into the leather spear holder affixed to his saddle, Alfred returned to Uddings stopping occasionally to rest. He had no intention of changing mounts and risk losing his father's horse at a hostelry. He used the old roman road across the ridge north of his own lands, enjoying the softly rolling hills with wooded valleys where pure streams ran. He spoke out loud frequently to his horse which seemed to understand his mood, standing quietly each time Alfred reined up to admire his surroundings.

The breeze was no more than a whisper across the heath where a few turf cutters temporary homes, in various states of repair, showed that the cycle of life continued at a slower pace in Dorset.

The manor was thrown into uproar by the return of Udric's son. He now exhibited the lean wiry strength of stamina rather than breadth of muscle. He sat on his father's horse as his late father had done, his legs hugging the beast's flanks closely. It had whinnied loudly on scenting the other horses in the paddocks as if it too, knew that it had come home. Edith had aged a little while Aethelflaed had grown almost beyond recognition in the one and a half years he had been away. While she may not have been classically beautiful, her pink and white complexion glowed with health, her unbound hair showing hints of red and autumn colours in the sunlight.

Two dogs rushed towards him mouths gaping, tongues lolling so that it looked as if they were grinning. One now showed the grizzled greyness of age around its muzzle and insisted on being petted first, wriggling in ecstasy when Alfred scratched behind its floppy ears.

"We have missed you so much," sighed Edith as she led her son inside for refreshments. "There has been news of you through the Bishop's clerk, bless him, but now we shall hear it from you." Edith's face was thinner than he remembered, the dimpled cheeks having lost much of their roundness. Small lines around her eyes reflecting the laughter of her youth now made her look more careworn and matronly.

Aethelflaed could hardly wait to ask her brother if he had found her a husband. She drew her long brown hair over her shoulder, running her fingers through the soft tresses. She longed to wear a housewife's wimple like her mother.

"I have to admit to failure on that count but I have some news which will please you. The King has restored father's estates to me. I have the charter here. It is ours again!" He took the valuable charter out of his jerkin and waved it in front of them triumphantly.

Edith expressed her joy unreservedly while his sister's gladness was tempered by her disappointment. Her face showed happiness but her eyes did not reflect the same joy. She was however impressed when he mentioned that he had been granted the status of thegn, like his father, as this improved her chances of a good marriage. Torn between happiness that he had come home she still needed to persuade her brother to put his mind to the matter. She itched to accept the king's suggestion that she join his wife's household even though that would leave her mother alone.

"Surely I will need a new dress! At court the ladies must wear brighter colours, finer fabric than this." She plucked disdainfully at the bright tan dress she was wearing. Fastened at her slim waist with a narrow decorated leather belt, the folds gathered gracefully as they fell just above neat leather shoes of the same hue.

"Indeed, the King's lady wears reds of various shades but gossips condemn her past. She cut her hair to cover a scar and many copy this style."

"Cut her hair!" Aethelflaed cried out in astonishment, "I could not do that. Surely she plaits it and wears it round her head like mother does?"

Alfred explained why Lady Algifu had been forced to adopt a new hair style, the women's faces reflecting their horror and abhorrence of the cruelty involved.

"Even if a man steals he is only whipped to teach him a lesson. A woman in Wymburne would hardly get a chance to become a harlot. Many men died in the pestilence and others have died in battle. If a woman has a good man she does not give him the opportunity to stray." Edith reflected on her own lost love, and the loss of her first-born son. At Mass she was drawn to the other widows sharing their grief while trying to cope bravely with running the two manors.

Before he was called to attend to the business of the shire Alfred spent his time inspecting both estates. Run by two competent stewards he spent hours admiring the horses at Uddings, descendants of his grandfather's roan mare and the Norman war stallions.

Owenson was now a mature young man, in charge of the horses which were grazing peacefully. "It is good to have you back lord. Three times there have been summonses to look after the King's horses from Wymburne. The messengers ride them to exhaustion and scar their flanks with spurs. The last one who rode in here stayed overnight. My boy took his spurs and blunted them on a whetstone! He'll not be damaging a horse's hide with them anymore. Even the head man at the palace agreed that there is no need for blood and welts to make a horse go faster. They think they can ride – well my boy could show them a thing or two!"

Alfred nodded approvingly watching youngsters riding a stallion which had recently completed its basic training. "Has King Edwy ordered a new horse then? At the moment he uses his father's mount but he could well do with another for he tires a beast with all the hunting and racing he likes to do."

"It is ready but has no battle schooling. Everyone joins in the training when noise and sudden movements are needed to ensure he will not be startled. My father told me that this was how it used to be done – men and children rushing round banging pots, shouting and waving cloths. It makes a break from weeding or gathering bracken for the floors so everyone is happy to help."

The pigs were turned out safely in the nearby woods, now cleared of wolves, while the in-fields, lying fallow after the harvest, grew good crops of grain. Much of the barley was crushed to make ale, the corn being made into flour at his mill. Even the lowliest bondsman was proud that his lord was now a thegn in his own right, greeting him with exaggerated bows whenever he passed until he laughingly asked them to treat him as they had before.

Stories of the King's wild lifestyle were circulated by pedlars and other travellers, as was the news that Archbishop Odo had finally separated Lady Algifu from the King. She had been taken to Ireland, apparently as a slave. Most gossip did not unduly disturb Alfred and he refused to comment on this latest rumour which privately appalled him.

Within days however, he received confirmation that the King's wife had indeed been taken by the Archbishop's forces. He had gone to the King's palace at Wymburne to see the steward. During his absence Owenson had tried to attend the moot each month on behalf of both his manors. Being a freeman he was entitled to a place but had been told in no uncertain terms that he was not a land owner or even a property owner and therefore could not stand with the other men of Wymburne to hear the news or orders from the King.

"My man had to stand so far away that he could not hear what was being said and therefore came home each time. Surely he is entitled to a place in his own right for my grandfather made Owen a free-man many years ago. It was done before the congregation in church just like you did when lord Aethelstan allowed one slave to be freed each year. Owenson is therefore free and should take his place. I really do not care whether the miller, the butcher and the harness maker do not like me but Owenson has done nothing. My father and elder brother were killed fighting for the King. Owen served in the fyrd for Uddings twice. We were ready to serve again but Lord Dunstan was against it. Anyway I digress … do I tell Owenson to attend in his own right? How many others are not joining in because they too have been bullied?"

"You are right Thegn Udric, all freemen should attend. Those are the rules from King Alfred's time I believe. Perhaps an announcement in church that all freemen should attend will make it plain. Mentioning Owenson or any man in particular is perhaps not a good idea but if emphasis is put on all, more may feel they should be there." The steward smiled, toasting Alfred with his raised mug. The two men were sitting on a bench in the lee of the wooden hall. Not far away the wind blew the leaves lifting them up and whirling them a few feet before letting them settle once more on the courtyard. There were subdued noises from the kitchens but as the King was not in residence, nor expected, it was only the garrison and the few permanent staff who needed feeding. A servant had brought a jug of ale and two mugs. The froth spilling down the side until it pooled on the bench between them.

"The town is a-buzz with my lord's affairs once again," stated the steward in his usual practical manner, eye brows raised in expectation of a response from his companion.

"There are no children of their marriage," commented Alfred, "so I am surprised that Odo has continued to persecute the poor woman. As for the tale that she has been hamstrung, I really cannot believe that is true. King Edwy is apparently ignoring the pleas of his clerks that writs should be signed, and finances checked. There is no doubt he is fretting for his wife."

The King's steward lowered his head to study his boots. "My lord is still young and had little training for the weight of responsibility suddenly thrust upon him. Perhaps in time he will be persuaded to attend to the business. That is one thing Abbot Dunstan insisted on from what I heard but of course he has been banished. The King took a dislike to him immediately I'm told. Mind you he had no time for women at all. Apparently before he went to Glastonbury he was to be married but was forced to become a churchman. Ever since he has hardened his heart against women in particular and any sort of feeling that would indicate softness. It is as if he does not understand love, grief or even affection. A strange man indeed!"

"Your loyalty is to be commended and I agree with much you have said. My lord is indeed still very young. He has no trouble with love and now he knows grief. The Archbishop has made an enemy of Edwy. He will never forgive him, not just for taking his legal wife from him but for the injuries we hear she suffered. I cannot comment but you hear news straight from court. My sister was supposed to be going to the lady's household. She is very disappointed to lose the opportunity of seeing the court, the dresses and finery of the ladies but her biggest hope was to find a rich husband!"

The matter was discussed frequently, but in public, wearing the royal diadem, Alfred maintained a stoic attitude, settling minor disputes and travelling widely within the East Dorset area, being much admired for his modesty and fairness. Once or twice he attended hearings with lord Alward, the Sheriff of Dorset, learning from the older man.

When a man was found dead in the mill stream of the River Wim, now called the Allen, in Wymburne, the widow was convinced that foul play was involved. Messages were sent to Wareham asking the Sheriff to come and examine the circumstances and the body. Until he had seen the battered corpse the man could not be given a decent burial.

"The monks have already wrapped him for burial but the Sheriff will demand to see for himself. I will ask them to keep the body cold. It is unpleasant for everyone when suspicions are raised. I do not have authority to allow a burial. You and any witnesses must appear before him when he calls an inquest."

Seeing the widow's crestfallen expression Alfred tried to soften his words but she was wild-eyed, her hair hanging in a disordered tangle round her shoulders.

Several days later the Sheriff arrived with trumpets and his guards. The crowd stood back respectfully allowing his party to reach the church unhindered. Silently thanking God for the continued cold weather, Alfred approached and bowed to Lord Alward. His greeting was acknowledged with a stony stare before he was recognised.

"My apologies Lord Alfred! I did not recognise you in that fustian tunic. What have we here then?"

Ignoring the older man's slight regarding his countrified appearance, Alfred related the details of the case as far as he knew them.

"Have the body brought here then. Presumably it is on a bier of some sort? The widow makes these accusations but does she have a son or other male relative standing for her?"

When Alfred shook his head, not aware of any relatives who lived in Wymburne, the sheriff sighed dramatically.

The body was brought into the gloomy interior of the church by two monks, neatly tonsured and rosy cheeked. Already a faint smell of decay rose from the corpse which had swelled so that the neat shrouding was already stained with fluids. The crowd backed off, several averting their faces from what was to come.

Women accompanied the widow, her sobs clearly audible in the silence. "I want justice," she screamed, her strident voice echoing in the vaulted ceiling. "Edwin was murdered. He would not just fall into the river, he was pushed, he was forcibly held, I know he was."

For moments there was shocked silence, men looking at their neighbours with renewed suspicion. The Sheriff called for silence, ordering the woman to speak only when called to do so. "Unwrap him them, don't just stand there gawping!"

The two monks hastened to unfasten the binding. No one smiled as the stench suddenly issued forth from the swollen flesh. The widow fainted with shock seeing the discoloured chest of her late husband finally exposed.

"Bring her a stool," ordered Alfred when none of the townsmen reacted to the woman's weakness. Many were now openly holding their noses or obviously breathing through their mouths to avoid inhaling the noxious airs released into the atmosphere.

"Who found the body?" demanded the Sheriff whose normally tanned face had become a pasty hue resembling uncooked dough. He too was breathing hoarsely through his mouth. He regarded the two men who stepped forward with a concentrated stare from lizard eyes as if he were seeking the truth before they had said a word.

The harness maker and his brother reddened, the involuntary flush causing sweat to break out and they shuffled uncomfortably before the hooded gaze of authority. Alfred felt some compassion for the two men. They may well have been 'first finders' and innocently pulled the man from the river. This involvement was often enough to cast suspicion on their motives. The Wymburne men watched impassively as the Sheriff demanded the details of where, when and how they had found the body of the man now lying exposed and rotting on the bier.

The tension was broken when an apprentice suddenly rushed out. He could be heard vomiting against the outer wall. He did not reappear for some time and when he shuffled unsteadily back to the rear of the crowd there was an unhealthy green tinge to his sweating face. Few heads turned to watch as to do so would have broken their concentration on the unpleasant matter in hand.

Questions and answers flowed between the judge and the judged. The Sheriff winkled out the indebtedness of some men, the unrequited love of others. Accusing eyes were now turning to a weaver, known to flirt with the dead man's wife. His long face with its overfull red lips gave him an effeminate appearance. His nails were always manicured, his long fingers stroking a fabric in nothing short of a sensual manner. He had always found one excuse or another to avoid serving in the fyrd, subjected to teasing alternating with disdain among the others of his trade. Now all heads turned to watch as he was pushed forward into the space in front of the sheriff. Alfred moved to stand just behind his shoulder, one hand resting on the hilt of his father's sword.

Flies were now being attracted by the nauseating smell, settling on the lips of the bloated corpse. When one of his arms suddenly dropped down from the bier they rose in an angry crowd. Only the strongest stomach could now bear to witness the seeping fluids. Even Lord Alward who had checked for injuries which might not be compatible with those caused by a mill wheel stepped back in alarm.

"Cover the man decently. There is no need for women to see the body of a man exposed to public gaze."

The two monks who had fussed around the candles and ornaments on the cloth covered altar came forward reluctantly. Their previously healthy complexions now looked waxy as they re-wrapped the corpse, flicking away the persistent attentions of the feasting flies which now descended to the pools of stained fluids seeping into the floor.

The accused tried to turn away but was held securely between Alfred and a guard whose unsheathed weapon promised quick punishment for anyone who quailed before the steadfast gaze of the Sheriff.

"You owe this woman's dead husband money?" he demanded, his

booming voice silencing any muttering in the crowd.

In his terror the man nodded mutely. Alfred and the guard were now forced to help the weaver stay upright. Another smell now pervaded the shadowy interior of the church. Some sniffed in disgust and then regretted their actions when the full import of the weaver's fright became apparent. A pool of urine lay at his feet, seeking the lowest point at which it could settle. The once pristine leggings were now soiled, the dark stain spoiling his once immaculate appearance. Even the bright tan shoes had suffered from nature's failings.

"Does anyone else own the dead man money, labour or goods?" demanded the Sheriff who had difficulty dragging his eyes away from the poor specimen of manhood held before him. He seemed to look at each man in turn, unsurprised when two men stepped forward to admit that they owed money in return for goods bought but not yet paid for. A hum of chatter immediately broke out among the jurors and voyeurs.

"Silence! Shame on you then, that you have not paid his widow what is owed to him. She has not only lost her man, her support, but has no recourse to justice because she is a woman."

The miller and one of the three Wymburne butchers admitted that they had not yet paid their debts, contrary to custom. "Presumably the deceased was attempting to rectify the situation and collect his money when he called at the mill. What happened then?"

"Nothing Lord," stammered the miller whose normal attitude of bonhomie and cheerfulness had just evaporated. "We had words, that's all. Edwin wanted immediate settlement but payment from the King's steward is not until next week. I have no funds to pay until then."

"And you, a butcher you say! What is your excuse? Did Edwin of Wymburne approach you too?"

Appearing to be unmoved by officialdom the butcher stood firmly, arms akimbo, his great hands resting on his substantial hips. "Yes lord. He came to me wanting interest on the debt. I told him to go away and come back and ask more politely for his money. Edwin rarely gave credit but I'm not going anywhere. My father and his before him ..."

His attempt at providing his pedigree was rudely interrupted by the Sheriff. He had been standing or leaning on a settle for a long time and was getting impatient with the speed of the enquiry. Not having discovered any bruises of hands or ligature marks on the corpse he was satisfied that Edwin of Wymburne had died accidentally. In order to ensure that the townsfolk remained in awe of his position he had deliberately withheld his verdict.

"Fetch a Bible! You do have a Bible in the church?" In unison the crowd turned towards the altar where a priest knelt at his prayers. "Lord Alfred, I beg you to find out if there is a Bible in this place. Time passes and my patience is at an end. God willing this mess can be sorted out before we all die of thirst."

Passing the amateur paintings on the whitewashed surface of the aisle wall Alfred was glad to stride towards the kneeling man. A poor candle guttered in the draught as he passed. The priest looked up, his eyes momentarily glazed and unfocused.

"The sheriff would like to borrow the Bible for a moment. Could you bring it to him?"

"Bible? We don't have a Bible – no money for one. Ask the Abbess, she has a Bible. She may govern the nunnery with great piety and competence but she never lends us her precious books. I don't envy you asking to borrow her Bible." He sniggered at the vision of Alfred begging the loan of her book.

The priest was on the point of returning to his devotions when Alfred gathered the hood of his cloak with one hand and frog-marched him down the aisle to the Sheriff. By the time he reached the august presence of the King's man the priest's eyes were almost popping from his head.

"We have no Bible lord," he stuttered when Alfred suddenly released his grip. "The Abbess might lend her copy to you," he suggested, some courage now returning, "but she would not let me look at it."

The Sheriff's normal good humour was quickly snuffed out and replaced by simmering anger. "Lord Alfred, request the Abbess to bring her Bible to the church. Take my token so that all will know that my demand is not to be taken lightly."

Alfred gripped the gold topped cane and left the church, blinking in the sudden brightness. The walls of the nunnery were only a few steps away, towering over the other buildings with their roughly thatched roofs. The bolt studded oak door was firmly closed, the smaller barred window set at shoulder height also securely shuttered. He used the Sheriff's baton to knock smartly, the thuds echoing hollowly on the wood.

Several minutes appeared to pass; he was on the point of raising the staff to demand entry when the window was opened. A diminutive figure peeped through, her soft voice demanding to know why he was disturbing the peace of their prayers.

"Forgive me, er… lady. The Sheriff, Lord Alward is conducting an inquest in the church. He wants, er… demands the loan of a Bible." Alfred found himself nervous before the bright blue-eyed gaze of the little nun. She did not blink but appeared to be studying him.

"Wait there!" announced the voice in clipped tones. The window was slammed shut in his face.

"What did she think I was going to do? There are enough bars on the door to make the stoutest suitor fear to enter. God's truth, is it a nunnery or a prison?"

He was still debating with himself when the whole door swung slowly inward. A tall nun in an immaculate white wimple and dark robes stepped out. The silver cross at her throat displayed considerable craftsmanship, the carved scene of the crucifixion and other figures standing out in relief. Alfred hastily closed his mouth and held out his hands to take the Bible from her long, white, be-ringed fingers.

"Oh no young man! You shall not touch the Holy Book. Where is this sheriff who demands our Bible?"

There was not a trace of artifice used on the Abbess's face yet her arched eyebrows and wide forehead displayed nobility and learning at a single glance. Alfred led the way to the church noticing that the woman glided, silently and smoothly after him. The crowd parted quickly, many crossing themselves hastily when they noticed the huge jewelled volume she was carrying.

Lord Alward jerked upright when the Abbess unhurriedly came and stood before him. He bowed with all the grace such a large man could muster, the gold chain of office around his neck swinging free like a pendulum.

"This man tells me that you command a copy of the Bible to be brought." She could not use a hand to indicate that she meant Alfred so jerked her head in his direction. Her tones were sarcastic, at odds with the placid, imperturbable expression on her face.

"My deputy Lord Alfred was sent by me Madam. I am surprised that there is no Bible in this church. It serves a town of considerable size. Since yours is the only copy we have need of it for a few moment. Lord Alfred will return it to you shortly." With these words most women would have retreated gracefully. The Abbess drew herself up to her full height, eyes blazing. A lesser man might have quailed before such penetrating darts of anger which showered like meteors upon unprepared earth.

The townspeople watched in fascination and amusement as these two strong willed titans matched up to each other. The Abbess refused to be parted from her precious volume, the Sheriff was unwilling to allow her to be part of what he saw as his duty in this unpleasant affair. The body might well have been wrapped again but flies still swarmed through the open windows to feast on the stinking fluids which had leaked from the corpse.

"Madam, you have no part in the judicial process. The Bible will come to no harm. Put it down on the settle and step away, preferably outside for a moment."

"Lord Sheriff, if aught happens to our Bible, as God is the witness here, His retribution will fall on all of you." The Abbess stalked to the doorway without a sign of the previous calm, gliding movement which had reminded Alfred of a sleek swan on the river. With each step her wimple bobbed, its weight no match for the irritation and displeasure which was evident in every step.

"I find no suspicious injuries on Edwin, no bleeding from wounds to his skull, no ligature or throttle marks. It is safe then to assume that having been refused payment by Master Miller here that he was clumsy, angered and missed his footing. However …" the Sheriff paused dramatically, aware that many of the men were holding their breath. "I find it un-Christian that debts owed to Edwin have not yet been paid and that his widow has endured her grief and suspicion without one of you lifting a finger to help her. The debts will be repaid to her in full on, or by, the last Sunday of this month. You will swear to do this now, on the Holy Bible, in front of witnesses."

The men who owed money gabbled their thanks moving towards the settle to make their oaths. The widow was gently pushed to the front so that she, as the offended party could witness the men swearing that they would repay what they owed. Even in the dim light the gemstones set in the cover glowed richly. Alfred marvelled at the workmanship. A leather strap and gold clasp kept the pages firmly closed against prying eyes.

"You have sworn a sacred oath in my presence and in front of these witnesses on the Holy Book. Should you default then you will be damned for all eternity." The sheriff's loud voice reached to the door and beyond where a curious crowd of townspeople had gathered. People crossed themselves rapidly before the last echoes of his words had died away. He gathered up his cloak and marched out of the church, children and dogs scattering as the guards fell into step behind him.

Alfred muttered a few words of comfort to the knife-makers widow, telling her that her late husband could now be buried in peace before following Lord Alward outside. The Abbess rushed to reclaim her precious volume before more curious hands could stroke the valuable cover.

The Abbess, restored to her previous calm demeanour passed the Sheriff, her Bible held before her like a talisman. The door to the nunnery opened on cue as she reached it and slammed closed behind her. The atmosphere visibly relaxed, the Sheriff once more smiling as Alfred thanked him for coming.

"Are you staying at the palace tonight? If not you are more than welcome at my home. My horse is at the ale-house and it would not take a moment to be ready."

"My thanks Alfred, but we ride for Dorchester. God knows that was an unpleasant business but not a murder. Keep an eye on the widow for she will find it hard to manage, even when the debts are paid. You have several moot courts to attend, you have the list. Let me have your reports in due course."

With a barked command the Sheriff and his guards set off for the ford at a brisk trot, bridles jingling, sheathed weapons secured over the rider's backs.

The townspeople of Wymburne breathed a collective sigh of relief. Normally peaceable, traders, artisans and housewives returned to their daily tasks and routine. A few followed the bier to the cemetery to watch the delayed internment of Edwin, the town's knife maker. A swarm of flies hovered over them, angry to be cheated of their host.

As instructed, Alfred satisfied himself that all the debts were paid to the widow. He was pleased that she would continue to receive an income from the workshop at the rear of her house. The matter could now be set aside; the knife maker's widow could grieve but still have the basic comforts she was used to.

He was already on the slope beside the rows of vines owned by the nunnery watching the lay workers trimming the knobbly bushes when he heard a commotion behind him. Although he was too far away to make out the words, he had no difficulty in recognising their angry nature.

Briefly experiencing a feeling of exasperation, Alfred retraced his steps and crossed the ford.

There was a fight going on, two traders arguing over an unpaid debt, accusations and angry words interspersed by blows. Already a crowd had gathered round in a circle, some encouraging the combatants with hearty cries. In vain the Town Reeve was attempting to restore order, demanding that the men bring their dispute to the next meeting of townsmen.

Alfred could see at a glance that their elected leader was being ignored. He was younger than both combatants but being a Sheriff's deputy might justify his interference in their affairs on this occasion.

Adjusting the King's colours on his head band he shouted out that both men should cease their brawling.

"The Reeve is right; all disputes should be settled at the moot unless you wish me to send for the Sheriff to mete out justice." He looked round at the red faces, aware that some already objected to their entertainment being brought to a halt. He could feel the hostile atmosphere and quickly checked that his long knife could be eased from its scabbard. This was not a time for nerves or uncertainty. He glared back until those who challenged his authority lowered their eyes.

The Reeve came to stand beside him straightening his tunic. Already a bruise was showing on one fore-arm and he rubbed it to ease the ache.

"Don't need a perishing Sheriff to sort this out. He says I owe him twelve shillings and I say that the price agreed was ten and that's all I'm going to pay him." The carter flexed his muscles threateningly aware that by comparison his were puny; his eyes narrow with hate as he stared at his opponent.

Alfred recognised the sawyer but would have known him anywhere because his clothes were always sprinkled with wood shavings and saw dust. Although a slighter man, the strength in his arms was legendary, pulling the blade through unseasoned timber day after day at the saw pit.

Already his left eye was swollen, closing to display short dark eyelashes on his red cheek.

"No, we have already been through all that. You are not going to cheat me again." He took up a belligerent stance obviously prepared to back up his claim to payment in full. "If you are so certain that your memory is better than mine then I challenge you to prove it. Carry the hot iron or pay me in full."

There was a gasp of indrawn breath as the crowd realised the sawyer's intention. Such a thing had rarely been seen in living memory. The men of Wymburne sorted out their disputes with much less severe methods. A fight with staves or at worst trial by water when the innocent party would be dragged from the depths of the river, half drowned, coughing and spluttering.

The Town Reeve and Alfred's faces mirrored each other in masks of shock, both appalled at how the fight had degenerated into the possibility of a man having to prove that he was right by accepting the challenge.

In the silence, apart from the harsh breathing of the two men, a skein of geese flew overhead their honking cry dying away as they flew upriver.

"I say the matter should be heard at the moot," stated the Town Reeve stubbornly, privately aghast at the mere thought of a man's naked hand gripping a red hot bar of iron.

"Surely you two can agree to that; if either of you have witnesses they can be called and the money paid," said Alfred supportingly.

"What - and have him bribe men to take his part? No, I issued a challenge. Either he pays me in full, now, in front of witnesses or proves that he was right and only owes ten.

The crowd broke into two groups with whispered arguments and contentions from each man's supporters. Alfred and the Reeve had a hasty consultation turning their backs so that their words would not carry to either party.

"By all the saints! The only thing we can do is to delay the trial to Sunday after the town moot. That will give everyone a chance to calm down and for the sawyer to be satisfied with some sort of alternative settlement."

"I agree, but just in case you had better check that the right weight of bar is available and that the bandages and so forth are ready."

Alfred could not help feeling distaste even as he prepared for the worst. "The women should have left for their hearths by then. I am not unduly squeamish but this ordeal sounds barbaric."

"It will have to be done in the Church otherwise the whole town will treat it as a side show. I will announce our decision."

The market was packing up as men returned from their meeting. Most of the women had already left with their purchases and Alfred had insisted that Edith would take Aethelflaed home long before the men gathered in the church.

Already there was an atmosphere, the priest nervous, staring with abhorrence at the small bar of iron which lay on the altar. It looked harmless, a piece of dull metal not much longer than a man's hand. He would play no part in this ancient method of establishing the truth, indeed he was eager to leave this holy place, normally his place of peace and prayer.

The smith's lad had been blowing the brazier steadily until the charcoal glowed red. Alfred felt the sweat break out at the sight of it. Despite the coolness of the day when the warmth of a brazier might have been welcome, it sickened him to even think of the things he would witness.

The two men had been unable to come to any agreement and the challenge stood. Both parties had their supporters, men from their own tithing and others who professed an interest in seeing justice done.

"Ghouls! They just want to see something different. They are the same men who like to watch dog fights, badger baiting and such like." Alfred still hoped that the ordeal could be avoided.

The priest blessed the iron bar, prayed that the almighty would give justice to the innocent and scuttled out of the church. His haste would normally have been cause for amusement but not today. Candles wavered casting shadows on the wall paintings. Thin spirals of smoke drifted upwards towards the rafters and the audience of roosting pigeons.

The iron glowed, attracting all eyes towards the shimmering air around the smith's pincers which eased the bar from the heart of the fire and held it out to the carter's shaking hand.